Treacherous Moon

The Twelfth Carlisle & Holbrooke Naval Adventure

Chris Durbin

Chris Durbin

To Mark

Our son-in-law

Treacherous Moon

Copyright © 2022 by Chris Durbin. All Rights Reserved.

Chris Durbin has asserted his rights under the Copyright, Design and Patents Act, 1988, to be identified as the author of this work.

No part of this book may be reproduced in any form or by any electronic or mechanical means including information storage and retrieval systems, without permission in writing from the author. The only exception is by a reviewer, who may quote short excerpts in a review.

Editor: Lucia Durbin

Cover Artwork: Bob Payne

Cover Design: Book Beaver

This book is a work of historical fiction. Characters, places, and incidents either are products of the author's imagination or are used fictitiously. For further information on actual historical events, see the bibliography at the end of the book.

First Edition: June 2022

Chris Durbin

CONTENTS

	Nautical Terms	vii
	Principal Characters	viii
	Charts	x
	Introduction	1
Prologue	The Challenge	4
Chapter 1	Escape!	9
Chapter 2	A Shape in the Fog	19
Chapter 3	The Wager	28
Chapter 4	So Close	38
Chapter 5	A Game of Cricket	46
Chapter 6	Transit of Venus	57
Chapter 7	Domestic Bliss	66
Chapter 8	A Particular Duty	74
Chapter 9	A Moonless Night	85
Chapter 10	Extraction	93
Chapter 11	Betrayal	102
Chapter 12	Moonlit Flight	110
Chapter 13	A Spy's Tale	124
Chapter 14	The Chaplain's Snare	134
Chapter 15	Belle Isle	144
Chapter 16	High Command	155

Chapter 17	Reconnaissance	164
Chapter 18	Under Fire	177
Chapter 19	Brave Grenadiers	187
Chapter 20	An Urgent Need	197
Chapter 21	Dark of the Night	206
Chapter 22	Pursuit	216
Chapter 23	The Narrows	225
Chapter 24	A Sordid Business	234
Chapter 25	A Feint	242
Chapter 26	A Sprig of Gorse	252
Chapter 27	Reaction	264
Chapter 28	Freedom Dash	272
Chapter 29	At All Costs	282
Chapter 30	At Peace	292
	Historical Epilogue	299
	Fact Meets Fiction	301
	Other Books	305
	Bibliography	316
	The Author	318
	Feedback	320

LIST OF CHARTS

Bay of Biscay	x
Brittany Coast	xi
Quiberon Bay	xii
Belle Isle	xiii
Gulf of Morbihan	xiv

NAUTICAL TERMS

Throughout the centuries, sailors have created their own language to describe the highly technical equipment and processes that they use to live and work at sea. This still holds true in the twenty-first century.

While counting the number of nautical terms that I've used in this series of novels, it became evident that a printed book wasn't the best place for them. I've therefore created a glossary of nautical terms on my website:

https://chris-durbin.com/glossary/

My nautical glossary is limited to those terms that I've mentioned in this series of novels as they were used in the middle of the eighteenth century. It's intended as a work of reference to accompany the Carlisle & Holbrooke series of naval adventure novels.

Some of the usages of these terms have changed over the years, so this glossary should be used with caution when referring to periods before 1740 or after 1780.

The glossary isn't exhaustive; Falconer's Universal Dictionary of the Marine, first published in 1769, contains a more comprehensive list. I haven't counted the number of terms that Falconer has defined, but he fills 328 pages with English language terms, followed by an additional eighty-three pages of French translations. It's a monumental work.

There is an online version of the 1769 edition of The Universal Dictionary that includes all the excellent diagrams that are in the print version. You can view it at this website:

https://archive.org/details/universaldiction00will/

Chris Durbin

PRINCIPAL CHARACTERS

Fictional

Captain George Holbrooke: Commanding Officer, *Argonaut*

Lieutenant Carter Shorrock: First Lieutenant, *Argonaut*

Josiah Fairview: Sailing Master, *Argonaut*

David Chalmers: Chaplain, *Argonaut*

Jackson: Bosun, *Argonaut*

Abraham Sawtree: Admiralty Intelligence Officer

Benjamin Duval: Admiralty agent

Ann Holbrooke: Captain Holbrooke's Wife

***

Historical

William Pitt: Leader of the House of Commons

Lord George Anson: First Lord of the Admiralty

Admiral the Honourable John Forbes: Lord Commissioner of the Admiralty

Major General Studholme Hodgson: Commander of the Belle Isle Expedition Land Forces

Commodore Augustus Keppel: Commander-in-Chief of the Belle Isle Naval Forces

Treacherous Moon

Captain James Gambier: Commander of the Vilaine Guard Ships

Nicolas René Berryer, Comte de La Ferrière: French Minister of Marine

Lieutenant de Vaisseau Charles-Henri-Louis d'Arsac, Chevalier de Ternay: French Sea Officer

Lieutenant de Vaisseau Jean-Charles, Comte d'Hector: French Sea Officer

***

Chris Durbin

Bay of Biscay

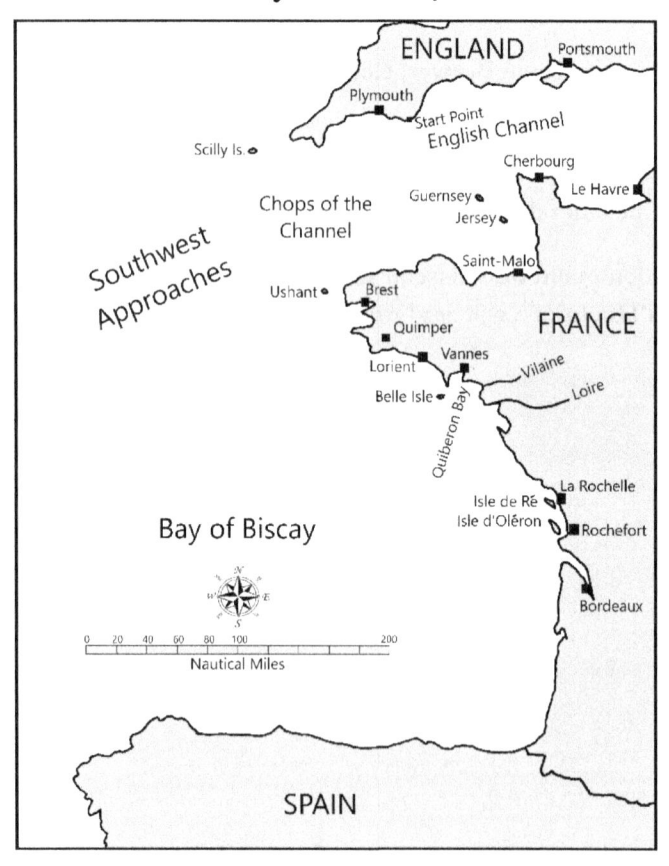

Brittany Coast

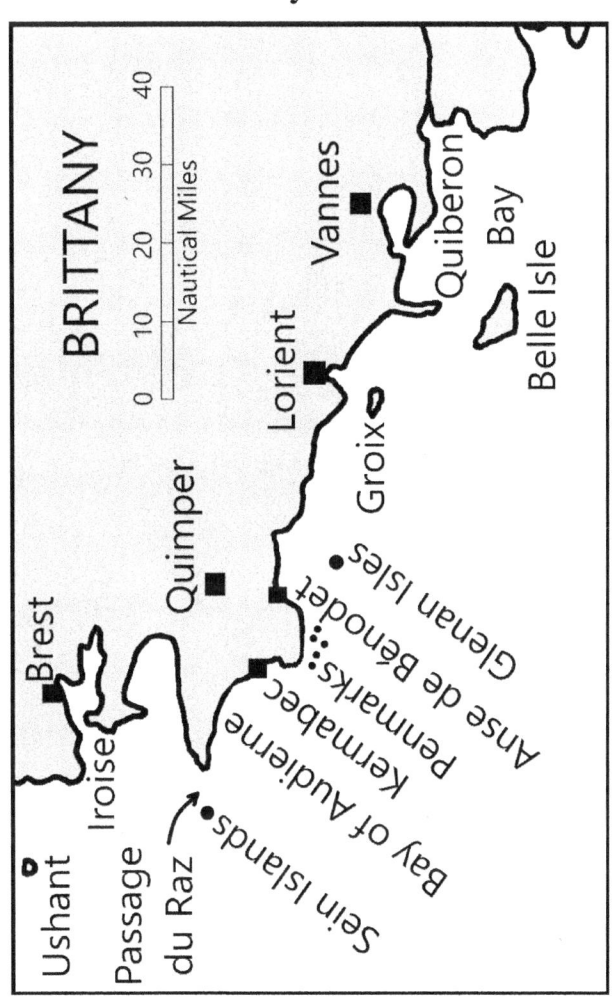

Chris Durbin

Quiberon Bay

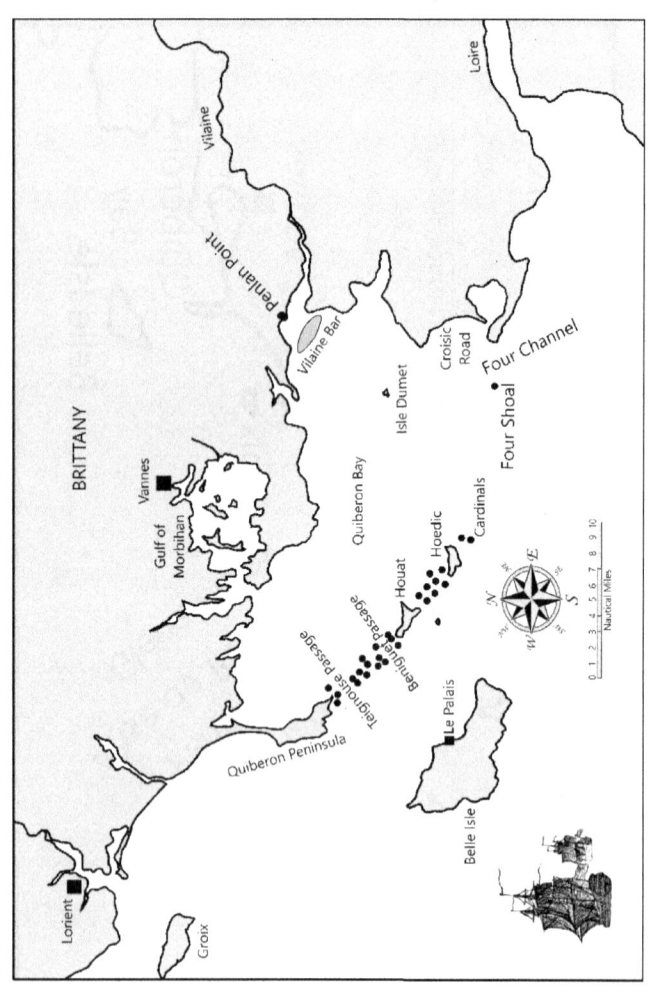

Treacherous Moon

Belle Isle

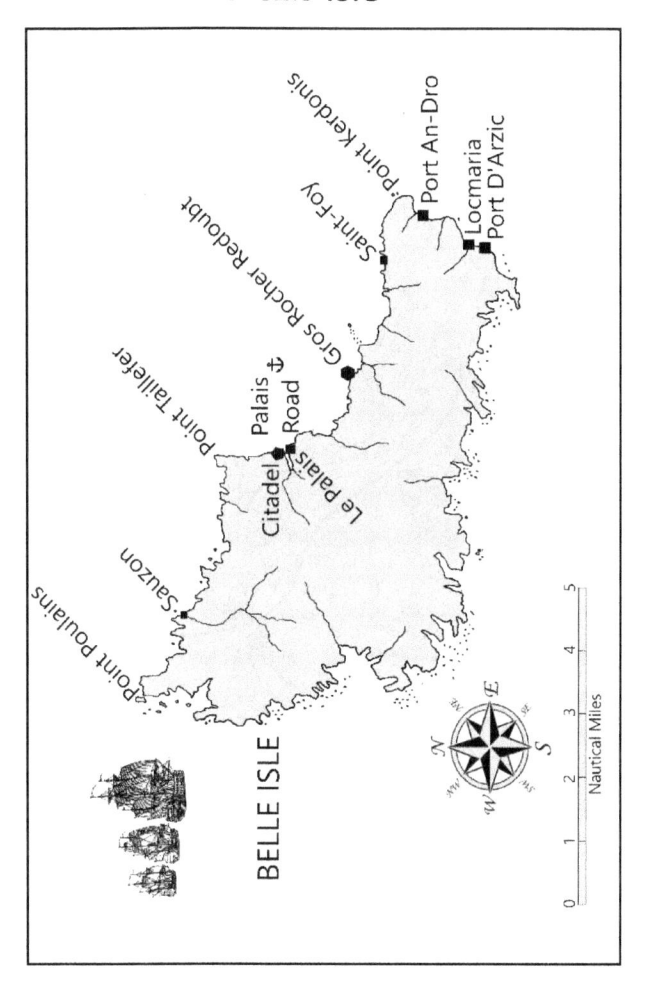

Chris Durbin

Gulf of Morbihan

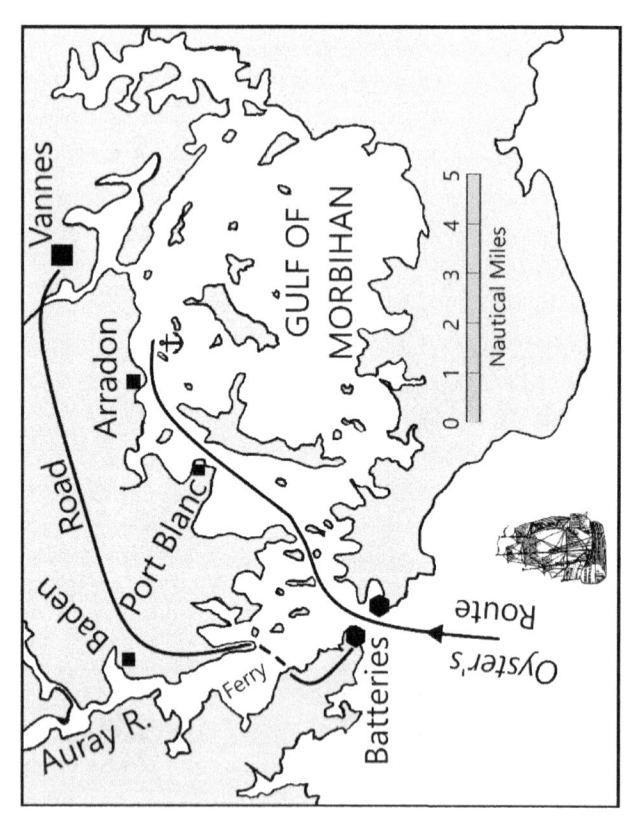

Let us be … gentlemen of the shade, minions of the moon … being governed, as the sea is, by our noble and chaste mistress … under whose countenance we steal.

Falstaff explaining his nocturnal behaviour
William Shakespeare, Henry IV Part I

Chris Durbin

INTRODUCTION

The Seven Years War at the end of 1760

The year 1760 saw something of a consolidation in the war, as Britain started to scent a victory and France sought a way out of the conflict. Without Spain, France could not see how to end the war with its colonies – and its honour – intact, yet Spain couldn't afford to enter the war. The squadron that Admiral Saunders took into the Mediterranean in 1760 was calculated not only to pin down the French in Toulon, but to make it clear to the King of Spain what awaited him should he join the war on France's side. However, there was a new King in Spain, and Carlos III was eager to renew the Bourbon family pact and embark upon a military alliance with his cousin Louis.

In North America, after a fearful winter in Quebec, the British army was defeated at the battle of Sainte-Foy in April 1760, just a short walk from where Wolfe had destroyed Montcalm's army in the previous year. However, the French commander at Sainte-Foy, the Chevalier de Lévis, was unable to follow up his success and when in May a British naval squadron sailed up the Saint Lawrence as the ice melted, it was all over for New France. The promised French squadron failed to materialise after the terrible defeats that the French suffered at Lagos Bay and Quiberon Bay, and the sinking of the supply ships on the Restigouche river. Lacking men, provisions and even a clear means of communicating with France, and with British armies closing in on three sides, Montreal surrendered in September. By the end of 1760 the long dream of New France was over, and the American colonists turned their attention to the great tracts of land to the west that the French had given up.

For France it was a year to rebuild, and to attempt to repair its navy after the devastating defeats of 1759. And, despite its financial difficulties, money was found for building ships. In all the great ports of France and in many of those of its friends and allies, the sound of adze and saw could be heard as a new navy started to take shape. Yet it takes more than a year to build a ship-of-the-line and France went into 1761 with its navy in a parlous state.

Carlisle and Holbrooke

Edward Carlisle spent most of the year 1760 in the Mediterranean in his fourth rate ship-of-the-line *Dartmouth* where he was sent on a diplomatic mission to the capital of the Kingdom of Sardinia. He became entangled in the affairs of his wife's family and was a witness to the inexorable decline of the house of Angelini. *Dartmouth* intercepted and disrupted the delivery of new ships for the French navy being built by the Republic of Genoa and in so doing engaged a French seventy-four gun ship and was narrowly saved from defeat by the appearance of a British third rate. In July of 1760 he was sent to Antigua to reinforce the Leeward Islands Squadron where a convoy for the Chesapeake gave him the opportunity to visit his own home at Williamsburg in the Virginia colony. The end of 1760 found him in the West Indies, where his story continues in *Carlisle's Duty*, the eleventh book in the series.

1760 was a good year for George Holbrooke. His promotion to post-captain had allowed him to marry his sweetheart and he had been given a new frigate – *Argonaut* – with orders to join the Downs Squadron under Commodore Boys. His ship was detached with two others to chase a French expedition that intended to make a diversionary landing in the north of Britain, in support of a full-scale invasion in the south. When the French squadron was cornered and defeated, Holbrooke shared in the vast amount of prize money, making him a more-than-moderately wealthy man. In *Nor'west by North*, the tenth book in the series, we found Holbrooke considering the purchase of a house in his hometown of Wickham while being courted for a position in his county's legislature. In December 1760, Holbrooke's frigate was sent to join Admiral Hawke's squadron off the French Atlantic coast, which is where this book starts.

***

PROLOGUE

The Challenge

Monday, First of December 1760.
The Palace of Versailles, France.

The two passengers sat in grim silence as the carriage swept across the cobblestones and out of the great golden gates of the Versailles estate. The weather matched their mood and the keen northerly wind and the low, leaden sky foretold snow before nightfall. The younger of the two was dressed in austere black and had a face that could have been carved with a chisel; he clutched a black leather and silk portfolio and his hand rested upon the engraved silver knob of his ebony cane. The older of the two was clearly the principal. He was dressed for a court appearance in a full-bottomed wig, and the gorgeous colours of his coat and waistcoat and the gilding of his sword hilt peeped out of the folds of his dark green cloak.

'I have never been spoken to in that manner, never. Who the devil does he think he is?'

Nicolas René Berryer, Comte de La Ferrière and minister of the marine to His Most Christian Majesty King Louis XV, swore a filthy oath and stared hard at his secretary, daring him to make the obvious, facetious rejoinder.

'His majesty is perhaps frustrated by the course that the war is taking, sir. His army in Westphalia continues to disappoint, despite the vast sums of money that it absorbs.'

The secretary forbore to mention the French navy's performance, which on this occasion was the reason for the King's vexation. The minister was not a man to be taken lightly and his reputation in his earlier appointment – as lieutenant-general of the Paris police – was daunting.

'Yet he knows – he's been told time and again – that Choiseul and Belleisle are handling all the operational aspects, at sea as well as on land. Heaven knows I wasn't appointed for my skills in strategy, nor yet in navigation or gunnery. I've done as I was directed, I've rooted out the corruption in the navy and the colonies. Even New France was coming into line until those fools threw it all away in the spring. They could have re-taken Quebec and given the English the whole task to do again. And I'm making headway on the officer corps, against centuries of deep-rooted self-defeating practice. Now he wants me to do something about those ships in the Vilaine.'

The secretary studied the clouds through the closed window. They'd be lucky to reach the minister's home in Paris before the snow was upon them. He leaned forward and snapped open the little hatch that communicated with the driver and the postillion.

'Can't you go any faster? Look at the weather, for God's sake.'

They heard the crack of the whip and felt the rapid vibration of the wheels as the carriage's speed increased. At least it was a good road between Versailles and the city, probably the best maintained in all of France, but it could still become impassable in bad weather.

'What does he want me to do about it? The whole world knows about those six of the line trapped in the Vilaine. It was Conflans' fault in the first place. Why on earth did he choose to flee into Quiberon Bay? Any landsman could have told him it was a death trap, it's a miracle that those ships escaped destruction. There are never less than two or three British ships blockading them, and any day now they'll make a landing in that area and that will be the end of them. This Admiral Hawke has been studying it for months, and it's quite clear what he intends. He'll land at Belle Isle or perhaps Vannes, Lorient even. In any case, when they have a base to supply their ships the blockade will get tighter and tighter, and those ships will rot where they lie. However, my admirals, who claim to know about these things, say that it is impossible to bring them out.'

They sat in silence for a moment as the carriage rattled along through the suburbs. Berryer was bitter about his appointment; he'd been a minister of a navy without a fleet for the past two years. The disasters at Lagos Bay and Quiberon Bay, and the steady attrition of his ships in the vain attempt to hold New France had seen to that. The King had a point, nevertheless, and those six of the line and the handful of frigates in the Vilaine would be of immeasurable value, if they could escape. Yet every day, whatever the weather, Hawke's ships kept watch from their anchorage off Dumet Island.

'Perhaps, sir, perhaps there is a way of solving two problems in one.'

The secretary knew his master well enough to leave that statement hanging and wait for him to take the bait.

'Two problems? I wasn't aware I had so many. Do proceed.'

'Well, sir. It's plain that your senior officers – your admirals and your captains – have no appetite for risk. They perhaps lack sufficient incentive being secure in their civil and naval ranks. Yet you have *lieutenants de vaisseau* who yearn for promotion, would do anything to advance their careers…'

'Yes, yes, this is an old story, and you know very well that I'll need to free up some promotions if I have any hope of reforming the corps, but as you well know my hands are tied. I cannot exceed the budget for salaries, nobody will retire while the war continues, and I therefore cannot make any promotions.'

'Indeed, sir. That was the situation yesterday. But today His Majesty himself has ordered you to find a way to save those ships. That changes the matter somewhat, I believe. Now, if you were to make a general order that any lieutenant that brings a ship out of the Vilaine to Brest or Rochefort will be instantly promoted to *capitaine de vaisseau* and given command of a ship, then I believe you will have sufficient volunteers. If none succeed then there are no promotions, you will not have exceeded the budget, and you will be demonstrably making your best efforts to obey the King's wishes. However, if one or two ships-of-the-line can be recovered, then the matter of an extra captain or two will hardly be noticed.'

The minister gazed out of the window at the threatening sky and shivered. His secretary made it sound so easy, but he knew the obstacles he would face. Any such general order would have to be made through the admirals at Brest and Rochefort, and as far as he was concerned, they were part of the problem, not the solution. They'd have objections, they'd propose their own protégés who wouldn't be the best candidates, they'd want to wait until the weather improved, until the British blockade was lifted, they'd delay until the second coming rather than commit to decisive action. All his sea officers hated each other, as far as he could tell, and not for a moment would they think of passing his general order on to their lieutenants, to allow those most eager for promotion to come forward. In his official capacity he was concerned with the officers of the pen more than the officers of the sword and he had no direct line of communication to the seagoing lieutenants.

He frowned in concentration, and then gradually a light dawned. There was perhaps a way, although not through a general order.

'Those ships have all been paid off; they have no officers, is that correct?'

'Yes sir. Their captains and lieutenants were assigned elsewhere, they are being watched by a few warrant officers.'

The secretary's face gave nothing away, but he was hopeful that the minister was groping towards the solution that had been dangled before him.

'How many lieutenants do we have?'

'Oh, about three hundred, sir. Two hundred of them are in the Mediterranean or the East or West Indies and perhaps a hundred within easy reach.'

'A hundred? And how many of those would you say are

candidates for this task?'

The secretary's brow furrowed as he recalled his lists, the columns of names with his own secret mark against each. Some of the lieutenants were old and worn out in the King's service, or too dissipated from high living, while some were too young and inexperienced. Fully half of them suffered from the same insidious apathy that afflicted their superiors, and they saw no need to exert themselves for their advancement.

'I could give you a dozen names, for a start, sir. You could expect enough volunteers among them to be able to select the best men. They all know that such an opportunity might not repeat itself in this war.'

'Then you and I will choose the right men and I'll write to each one individually. Then perhaps we can see some movement!'

***

CHAPTER ONE

Escape!

Wednesday, Seventh of January 1761.
Le Brillant, the Vilaine Estuary, Quiberon Bay.

The fog lay like a vast damp blanket, barely stirred by the easterly breeze, and so thick that the men on the quarterdeck could see no further than the mainmast. In the world beyond it was noon, and the winter sun was shining over Brittany, but there was no sign of it in the Vilaine estuary.

'Two hours to high water, sir. You can see the flood is almost at a stand.'

Charles-Henri-Louis d'Arsac, Chevalier de Ternay, glanced over the side where he could just see the river's debris moving sluggishly upstream, surrounded by the dirty foam that invariably attended a muddy tidal estuary. He'd studied the rise and fall, the ebb and flow for the past few days and knew that the constant outflow of the river Vilaine overcame the force of the incoming current an hour and a half before the tide was at its highest. Although its height continued to rise, the inflow paused, and an hour before high water it reversed. That gave him a window of perhaps two hours when the tide was at its highest, and the current was in his favour.

The bosun waited patiently for the captain's decision. He'd stood by the ship since it had been chased into the river over a year ago. He'd watched the tides come and go and he'd studied the weather patterns in the hope that this day would come. His beautiful ship had rested in the mud for most of its time in the river. It had been stripped of its guns and its stores, the commissioned officers had been sent to other ships in Brest and Rochefort and the crew had been reduced to the bare minimum to keep the standing rigging in order and to pump out the bilges. Then, a month ago, this lieutenant had arrived and had read aloud the orders that placed him in command, signed by Monsieur Berryer himself. He had stated his determination to sail *Brillant* and *Dragon* and two of the frigates to Brest as soon as the conditions allowed. The bosun had been sceptical at first but then the miracles started to happen. Drafts of men arrived. Guns – about half the normal allocation – were delivered, and stores for a month. Perhaps this lieutenant, this strange monk-like man, could work a further miracle and bring his ship out. Perhaps de Ternay's vows of celibacy, made before the Knights of Malta, or so it was said, would find favour with their patron, the blessed Saint Jean. The bosun crossed himself and muttered a prayer; his own name was Jean and he'd always sought the protection of his name-saint. He knew it was a sin to believe in omens and portents, but nevertheless…

'Are the boats ready, Bosun, and the men at the capstan?'

'They are, sir, waiting for your order.'

'And the weather, what do you say to that?'

The bosun held a wetted finger up to the slight breeze and gazed at the enclosing wall of whiteness.

'It's set in for the day, sir. It'll be like this all over the bay as far as the Morbihan and out to Belle Isle. There'll be nothing moving this day or this night, and when we're out it will be a fair wind for Brest. We could wait a year and not find another day like this.'

De Ternay nodded and slapped the bosun on the shoulder. He picked up the speaking trumpet and pointed it over the larboard quarter.

'*Dragon*. Are you ready?'

He heard a muffled reply from his friend Jean-Charles, Comte d'Hector. They had known each other for a long time, and they had both received a most astonishing letter from Berryer himself. The offer was almost too good to be believed. If they brought a ship-of-the-line out of the Vilaine and safely into a French naval port, they would be promoted to captain! In the normal course of events, they could wait ten more years before the list of names above them was thinned by death and elevation to flag rank, and the way the war was going, with so few ships left in commission, it could be a good deal longer. They had eagerly grasped the opportunity, and this day was the culmination of a month of frenetic effort to get the ships ready for sea.

'*Vestale*? *Aigrette*?'

'Ready, sir.'

The twin replies came from close on the beam where the two frigates lay to their anchors with the shortest of cables, ready for a quick departure. They were already fully manned and armed as their shallower draught would allow them to cross the bar at their maximum loading. Their captains knew their role and knew that their fate counted for little against that of the ships-of-the-line. France had frigates aplenty; her desperate need was for ships that could lie in the line of battle, great floating batteries that could take on a British battle squadron.

'Weigh anchor!'

De Ternay nodded to the drummer who beat the advance, the signal to the other ships in case they had not heard his shouted command.

***

In this desperately shallow estuary, *Brillant* was riding to barely half a cable and it took only a few minutes to haul the anchor clear and bring it up to the cathead. The boats had already taken down the slack in the towing hawsers and as soon as the anchor was clear of the sticky Vilaine mud they started pulling the two-decked ship slowly out of the river. De Ternay could hear the rhythmic sound from forward and he fancied that he could hear similar sounds from *Dragon* and the frigates, astern and on his quarter. These were boats from the other ships locked in the river, and from the towns and villages along the banks. He was determined on that point; with his reduced crew he would barely have enough men to set the sails in an emergency, and he could afford none at all to man two or three large boats.

'By the deep, four.'

The starboard leadsman reported four *toise*, fractionally less than four English fathoms. They hadn't reached the shallowest point yet where he knew that two and three-quarters was the most that he could expect. That was one of the key difficulties in getting out of the Vilaine, the depth of water over the bar. *Brillant* drew nineteen and a half feet fully loaded and *Dragon* drew barely less. They had needed to reduce that by five feet, and for that reason they had only embarked a handful of guns, and stores for that day only. Just enough to give the ship sufficient stability for the bay, no more. That in its turn determined that they would have to take on more stores, a few more guns, powder, shot and provisions before they could be on their way. A huge flotilla of boats had been covertly gathered in the Vilaine, and as soon as the ships were over the bar they would be alongside. It was that requirement for stores, more than anything, that constrained his escape plan. He needed six hours to take on the bare minimum, and if the British guard ships anchored only four miles away under Dumet Island saw them, it would be all over before it had truly begun. Today was the day he had waited for. A spring tide at midday to give his ships enough water to cross the bar with time to take on stores before dark, then a light wind that would carry them offshore and, above all, thick weather to conceal their movements from the blockading squadron.

'And a half, three.'

The leadsman's voice sounded loud through the fog.

'Approaching Penlan, sir.'

De Ternay nodded at the master's mate who was conning the ship. He should have had a pilot, but none had been prepared to accept such a great risk to their reputation. They all thought the ships would stick fast on the bar, and even if they didn't, the British would have them.

The mate had been out in a boat every day for the past month, sounding the estuary at all states of the tide, and he would know it like he knew the veins in the back of his hand.

Treacherous Moon

It was just past Penlan that the bar was at its highest. And yet, they could plan all they liked and make the most detailed calculations of tidal height, and still the variables were too great for absolute accuracy. An onshore wind could pile the water into the bay, raising its height, and an offshore wind could do the opposite. Some said that the air pressure – a concept reserved for scientists and of no practical application at sea – affected the height of the tide, but by how much they couldn't say. His calculations could certainly be out by a foot or more, and that could be disastrous. He'd emptied the ship all he dared and *Brillant* was on the very edge of its safe stability range. If they should be spotted before they brought in the stores, they would have to commit themselves to the Bay of Biscay in January with an unstable ship. It didn't bear thinking about, but he'd do it nevertheless; the prize of promotion and his own honour wouldn't allow him to tamely surrender.

Ah, he could feel the wind now. A little north of east perhaps. Perfect, if only it would stay in that direction.

'By the deep, three.'

Brillant had only a few feet under her keel, and they hadn't yet reached the shallowest point.

'The tide is at its highest now, sir and we should have a knot of current behind us.'

The mate's voice betrayed his nervousness.

'A quarter less three.'

The leadsman reported the soundings in a sing-song voice. It was very soothing and absolutely correct but de Ternay found himself lulled into accepting the numbers without thinking of their consequence. Two-and-three quarter *toise*. They were inches from disaster. If they should take the ground here, then the falling tide would leave them exposed and vulnerable. The first gap in the fog would bring the British down upon them and then all they could do would be to abandon the ship and save themselves, while the enemy put *Brillant* to the torch. If that should happen, he could at least warn those following him. If they were smartly handled the boats could drag the ships' heads around and even in this ebbing tide, they should be able to make it to safety. He'd thought of that already and had prepared a signal.

'Make ready, drummer.'

He didn't even turn to look at the marine, he was so intent on feeling the first touch of the bottom.

'A quarter less three.'

The seaman's voice had an edge to it now, he knew the draught of the ship as well as anyone. The bosun was at the fore chains, supervising the casting of the lead in this most crucial task.

'That sounding was just a few inches shallower than the last, sir. Muddy bottom.'

'Thank you, Bosun.'

Then it was still getting shallower, but only slowly. The whole Vilaine estuary was mud until it issued into the bay, when it gave way to sand. They must be almost at the top of the bar now.

'A quarter less three.'

'Depth is steady, sir. Still mud. The ship is moving forward.'

The bosun could see the lead line dragging astern as soon as it reached the bottom; that was evidence that *Brillant* was making way towards freedom.

Was that a scrape? No, it was only his heightened imagination, he needed to control himself. He could sense the mud under their keel, in fact he thought he could detect the slight retardation that came with only a few inches of clearance, as though invisible hands were clutching at his ship. And *Brillant* was starting to feel dead, as though it no longer had the power of independent movement. He heard the splash of the lead, the disembodied steady sounds of the boats somewhere in the fog ahead and the nervous shuffling of the drummer beside the binnacle.

Treacherous Moon

Now he felt it, a definite slowing of the ship's movement, and he swayed forward involuntarily. The master's mate stared at him, an unspoken question on his lips. The drummer, unbidden, raised his sticks.

'Silence! Lower those sticks drummer. Absolute silence, keep still.'

De Ternay's every sense was straining to understand what was happening below him. He picked up a chip – a foot long offcut of timber – from the basket beside the binnacle and threw it over the side, watching it carefully. It was moving forward, but very slowly, perhaps half a knot. So with a whole knot of tide behind them they must still be moving across the bar. The ship's keel must be ploughing through the top layer of soft, almost liquid, mud leaving a deep rut behind it. *Dragon* drew six inches less than *Brillant*, that was the crucial thing. Even if the tide dropped an inch or two in the next ten minutes, Jean-Charles' ship would still make it over the bar, if *Brillant* did. In any case, he was committed now. If he wanted to turn back, he should have done so the instant that he felt the mud's cloying embrace. Now it was too late. All he could hope was that his ship was at the shallowest point of the bar, that there was no greater pinnacle ahead.

'A quarter less three.'

He could feel the fog's dew on his upper lip, or was it perspiration? His body was rigid, willing his ship to keep moving.

'A quarter less three.'

Both leadsmen were showing the same depth. He threw another chip over the side. Ah, it was almost stationary, then *Brillant* was moving over the bar at around a knot. The whole body of water, with his ship in its bosom – *his* ship, hold on to that thought – was flowing towards the bay.

'By the mark, three!'

Were they over? It was almost too much for him, after this month of urgent preparation. And so much of his future hung on this. His legs felt weak, and he clutched at the quarterdeck rail.

'And a quarter, three.'

He could feel the ship springing forward under the impetus of the oarsmen. The deck moved again, the minute pitch and roll of a living ship, faint but discernible. They were free!

'By the deep, four!'

'Mud and sand, sir!'

De Ternay could feel his emotions threatening to overwhelm him. He pulled himself together with an almost physical effort.

'Three points to larboard. Standby to anchor.'

Every yard that he took his ship into the bay was a yard nearer the blockading squadron and a yard further for his supplies to be rowed to him. The tidal range today was fourteen feet and when he'd embarked his stores his ship could be as deep as eighteen feet. On this falling tide he needed a sounding of at least six *toise* before he could anchor.

'By the mark, five.'

'Bosun. Warn the boats we are about to anchor.'

'Aye-aye sir. Anchor's ready.'

'By the deep, six.'

Just a little further.

'By the mark, seven.'

'Let go!'

He heard the orders from forward and the whole ship vibrated as the cable ran out through the hawse. It didn't last for long; the wind was slight and the water shallow, half a cable would do it.

'The first boats are approaching, sir. The slings are rigged.'

***

Four hours of superhuman effort and by six o'clock it was all done, and *Brillant* had settled three feet deeper into the water. The additional guns on the lower deck had been placed by their ports and lashed temporarily to their rings

Treacherous Moon

and the stores had been struck as far down in the hold as was possible. She was still light, but safe enough for the short passage to Brest, as long as the weather didn't deteriorate and as long as he didn't have to fight an action against a British ship-of-the-line. He felt that he could handle a frigate, just, but even a fourth rate would have a greater weight of broadside than *Brillant*.

De Ternay rowed hastily across to each of the ships to reiterate his orders. He'd considered taking the Teignouse Passage between the Quiberon Peninsula and Houat Island. It would have been a bold move, but in this fog and without pilots it was a risk too far, and the blockading squadron could be anchored inside Belle Isle. That put it out of the question. Instead, the two ships-of-the-line and the frigates would give Dumet Island a wide berth and pass between the Cardinals and the Four shoal, keeping over to the east side. Then they would separate. *Brillant* and *Dragon* would sail in company, passing close to seaward of Belle Isle, trusting to the fog to hide them from the British squadron, if it was there. From Belle Isle it was a straight run to the Penmarks, and they could hope to make the Passage du Raz at first light on the ninth.

Meanwhile, the two frigates were to part company and stand offshore, trailing their coats to lure away any attackers or to warn the larger ships of enemy sightings. The frigates were expendable, the ships-of-the-line were not.

There was no signal this time; it was just possible that the British had a cutter patrolling close to the estuary and the sound of a drum carried well through fog. At eight o'clock in the evening with the winter darkness adding to the persistent murk, the four ships weighed anchor and ran down to the southwest under courses alone, in case the topsails should be visible above the fog. Silent as wraiths they slipped past the ever-present guardships off Dumet, past the treacherous Four shoal where so many ships had ended their days in the great battle of 'fifty-nine, and by the forenoon watch Belle Isle was on their quarter and they were spreading every sail to run up the coast towards freedom.

***

CHAPTER TWO

A Shape in the Fog

Wednesday, Seventh of January 1761.
Argonaut, off Dumet Island, Quiberon Bay.

The muffled bell tolled the passing half hours of the night watches. Four bells in the first watch, ten o'clock in the evening, and the sleepy seamen of the watch on deck stirred themselves for the well-worn rituals. The anchor watch and the lookouts were relieved, the marine sentries at the door of the great cabin and the magazine stamped their way through the drill of changing the guard. The bilge was dipped, and the anchor and binnacle lights were trimmed.

Charles Petersen was the officer of the watch. It didn't require a commissioned or warrant officer to keep the deck at night with the ship at anchor, not even here, just a couple of miles off enemy territory, and the mate of the watch could easily manage affairs while his betters caught up on their sleep or played cards in the wardroom.

'All quiet, Mister Petersen?'

Captain George Holbrooke was having one last turn on the deck before he also sought his cot for a few hours of sleep. It wasn't too cold, and the wind was light enough to be turned away by gregos and oilskins. If it wasn't for the fog it would be positively pleasant, but the damp air seeped into his bones, and he was glad to see that Petersen had allowed most of the watch on deck to seek shelter and warmth in the lee of the gunwales.

'Yes, sir. All quiet.'

Petersen removed his hat to reply to his captain but hastily replaced it as the lazy wind combed through his natural hair – few men of his age and station wore wigs – leaving a residue of moisture even in that brief exposure.

'How's the masthead lookout faring?'

'Very well, sir. As you ordered they're being relieved

every half glass and they go straight down to the galley range for another fifteen minutes. It's quite a popular duty, sir.'

Holbrooke nodded and continued walking fore and aft along the quarterdeck. He knew from long experience that he'd sleep well if he took exercise after his supper, before he turned in, and it gave him a chance to think.

Argonaut had been detached from the Downs squadron to assist with the blockade of the French Atlantic ports. He hadn't been out of Quiberon Bay for a month, and in that time he'd hardly strayed out of sight of the Vilaine estuary; he felt like he knew it as well as any other stretch of water that he'd ever sailed. And it was quiet, desperately dull. The seven French ships-of-the-line and four frigates that Admiral Hawke had chased into the river back in November of 'fifty-nine hadn't moved more than a few yards. How could they? Hawke had anchored three of his own ships off Dumet Island to watch them, and those seven, necessarily lightly armed if they were ever to cross the bar, would be no match for three of the superbly trained ships of the Western Squadron.

Captain James Gambier commanded the Vilaine guard in the seventy-gun *Burford* with the sixty-fours *Prince Frederick* and *Modeste* in support. Holbrooke had rowed across to *Burford* a few times over the past month, at Gambier's insistence, and he knew the man quite well. Yet still he couldn't get out of his mind the infamous court case where Gambier had been convicted of criminal conversation with Admiral Knowles' lady. A thousand guineas it had cost him. A thousand guineas! Holbrooke had to resist the urge to smile knowingly when they met.

For the most part the guardships anchored under the lee of Dumet Island overnight or in poor weather. *Argonaut*, with her shallower draught and greater agility, spent more time underway but this thick fog had brought her to anchor two miles to the nor'west of the island, in seven fathoms of water.

He had a feeling about tonight. When he had looked into

the Vilaine yesterday, before the fog brought everything to a halt, he found that the French ships had moved their berths; they were no longer in the positions that they had occupied for the past month. Five of the larger ships were well upstream, apparently aground, but two of them had shifted closer to the bar and as far as he could see they were swinging to their anchors at high water. The frigates were all afloat although one of them looked more like a sloop, similar in size to his own first command *Kestrel*. Gambier had given as his opinion that if they were to move it would be soon. The French must have seen the increased British activity in the bay, and a ship slowly moving along, backing its tops'ls to keep to a steady speed, was most likely to be running a line of soundings, a reliable sign that some action was contemplated. In Versailles they must suspect a descent upon this area, to raid the Morbihan with its swarms of small craft, to sack Vannes perhaps, to burn the ships in the Vilaine or to take and hold Belle Isle. Any of those actions was a possibility and they all threatened the security of those seven precious ships-of-the-line.

Would they use this fog to escape? Holbrooke had to admit that it was unlike the French navy to take such a risk. A French ship could be lost in the fog as easily as a British ship, and those seven hadn't been to sea for over a year. They would be unsure of themselves and navigating in this weather was a stern test of seamanship. It seemed unlikely but nevertheless Holbrooke had taken his precautions and stationing a lookout at the very peak of the main t'gallant mast was just one of them. It was uncomfortable – cold, wet, windy and lonely without sight of another human and nothing to see but the endless grey fog – but it was the best chance of spotting anything coming out of the Vilaine.

Holbrooke walked and walked through the strange claustrophobic world. From the taffrail he could see no further forward than the mainmast, and from the quarterdeck rail he could just perceive the jib boom losing itself in the murk. As for the lookout at the masthead, he might as well be on the moon, except for the monotonous five-minute calls. He heard one now, the voice curiously distorted by the swirling moisture-laden air.

'All's well, nothing in sight from the masthead.'

'Very well,' Petersen shouted back, 'keep a good watch.'

Holbrooke glanced at the steering compass. East-nor'east. Even though the ship was at anchor, the lamp in the binnacle was kept burning and a quartermaster was on watch, ready to bring *Argonaut* back to life at a moment's notice. The ebb had started, and the wind and the stream combined to keep the frigate's head towards the Vilaine. He stared again, as though by his sheer willpower he could see into the estuary seven miles away. The French might not take the risk, but he was damned certain that he would, if his ship had been imprisoned for over a year.

'I'll turn in now, Mister Petersen. Call me immediately you see or hear anything. Immediately, you understand. I don't want you calling the first lieutenant or the master to ask whether I can be disturbed.'

'Aye-aye sir.'

***

Holbrooke didn't turn in, or at least not in his cot. Instead, he stretched out on the cushioned bench that ran athwartships under the stern windows. It wasn't as warm as his wooden sided and sheepskin lined cot and the windows were never proof against draughts no matter how the carpenter tried, but he could be out of the cabin door a clear twenty seconds faster than if he had to struggle out of his hanging bed. And he knew that his servant would look askance if he didn't change into a nightshirt for the cot.

He'd been here a month now and it was starting to become tedious. Although Quiberon Bay was almost landlocked and was flanked at no great distance by Brest and Rochefort, two of France's three principal naval arsenals, it was quite clear that British sea power ruled supreme. There was certainly still a lot of local traffic, but it scurried from port to port, always seeking the security of shore batteries whenever a British cruiser came in sight. While Hawke's battle squadron patrolled the whole of the French Atlantic coast, Gambier's three of the line were more than enough to assert sovereignty over this patch of water. Holbrooke searched for an analogy; it was like the French navy dominating the Solent, although that was unthinkable, or Weymouth Bay or Torbay. Each of them lay between the great naval ports of Portsmouth and Plymouth and each had its own thriving commercial harbours. The British fleet should be forced to fight every day to retain this toehold on the enemy coast, rather than swinging complacently at anchor within sight of the shore.

He thought of his home in Wickham where Ann waited for him. Their baby boy, Edward, had been born in September and he knew that he had been lucky to be at home for the birth, although it still wasn't clear to him why his presence was needed. He'd spent the momentous day being pushed from place to place, apparently always in the wrong, and it hadn't got much better in the following weeks. He had felt utterly useless, yet Ann insisted that his presence was a comfort and even used the word *duty* in relation to his attendance at home for the important event. It was almost a week before he was trusted to be alone with the little fellow and even then Ann or the nurse or Ann's stepmother would crack open the door to confirm that all was well, that he hadn't dropped the baby or was found holding him upside down. He'd had two months at home while his ship was repaired and its bottom scraped, and then a month back in the Downs Squadron before their Lordships had decided to send him to join the Western Squadron. That had entailed another docking to clean his hull – an ominous clue to the length of time he was likely to be away – and he had sailed from Portsmouth in early December. Holbrooke had tried many times to analyse his feelings at that parting from his family. He knew he should have felt desperately sad, but deep inside – locked away from his wife's gaze – he felt nothing but elation at being free from the slavery of domestic life. The women may protest that he was needed at home, but the evidence said otherwise, and he was as certain that they would do very well without him as he was certain that his place was not – absolutely not – in a home with a squalling infant. It wasn't how he'd imagined fatherhood, but perhaps he was no different from fathers of this and other ages long past. With that thought his eyes closed and his breathing became regular and shallow.

***

The sound of movement on the deck overhead stirred him. An urgent knock at the door completed his awakening and by the time the midshipman had pushed open the door he was fully conscious.

'Mister Petersen's compliments, sir, and the lookout has seen something on the larboard bow…'

Holbrooke was out of the door in a flash and took the steps to the quarterdeck three-at-a-time, leaving the midshipman in his wake.

The fog was still thick on the deck and Petersen was a blurred, indistinct shape as he waited to make his report.

'A mast he thinks, sir, three points on the larboard bow.'

Petersen was evidently controlling himself with an effort. He knew what this could mean. The next hail from the lookout sounded like a call from some remote, unseen heavenly region. The voice was distorted by the fog, but it had a familiar lyrical accent.

'Deck ho! I can still see the very tip of a pole mast above the fog sir. It's moving left, and I think I saw another nearer the bow.'

'Who's up there, Mister Petersen?'

'Lewis, sir.'

Ah, the Welshman who knew all about Lundy Island. A dependable man.

'You have a gun cleared away?'

'Yes, sir. The linstocks are under the binnacle'

Petersen motioned towards the quarterdeck six-pounders; one on each side was ready for immediate use.

Treacherous Moon

The crews had emerged from their shelter under the gunwale and were fussing around, wiping the moisture from the touch hole and preparing the guns to be fired.

Holbrooke considered running up to the t'gallant masthead himself, but he knew that Lewis was a better lookout than he could ever be. And if he went to the masthead Lewis would have to come down to the topmast head, losing the continuity of the sighting; there wasn't space for two grown men at the t'gallant head.

Here was the first lieutenant hurrying to see what was afoot.

'Beat to quarters, Mister Shorrock. There's no need for silence. A gun to starboard then another in ten minutes.'

Shorrock rubbed his hands.

'The French are out then, sir?'

'They may be, Mister Shorrock, they may be. Ah, Mister Fairview, we'll weigh anchor immediately. Cast her head to the sou'-sou'west, if you please.'

The sailing master looked at the dog-vane on the hammock netting then at the compass, calculating the combination of sails that would be required to bring *Argonaut* cleanly away from her anchorage without a moment's waste of time.

All around was the bustle and hurry of clearing for action and weighing anchor. With that part of his mind not engaged in the matter at hand, Holbrooke heard the partitions of his cabin being knocked away, but mostly he was working through his immediate actions.

He was certain that Lewis had indeed seen what he reported. In which case it was ten-to-one that at least some of the French ships from the Vilaine had taken this opportunity to escape. The two guns that he had ordered were the night signal to the guard ships. He should show a light at the ensign staff as well, but in this visibility it would be futile. Gambier would certainly hear the guns and he'd know their meaning. He could be sure that within the hour the three guardships would be underway and looking for the foe. The problem was in knowing what the Frenchmen would do, most particularly where they would be heading. They would need the services of a proper dockyard after a year in the mud, and a naval one at that. Even if they were in perfect condition the French navy must be desperate for them to join their existing squadrons without delay. So Brest or Rochefort for sure. But Rochefort was itself blockaded and unlike Brest, it could be sealed shut by a few ships of the line cruising between Isle de Ré and Isle d'Oléron. Brest, however, was no longer under a close blockade. It must be Brest and certainly they'd want to escape from Quiberon Bay as quickly as possible, but which route would they choose? Rounding the Cardinals and the southern point of Belle Isle offered the quickest way out to the open sea, but it was also the obvious path. Would the French commander be bold and run to the east of the island, or even take the dangerous Teignouse Passage? But of course, there was no real question. Gambier with his three big third rates would certainly go outside Belle Isle when they weighed anchor, so he must go inside.

Holbrooke picked up the speaking trumpet and aimed it up into the fog.

'Lewis!'

'Yes sir.'

'Can you still see them?'

'I can see one of them now, sir. Just the pole mast, maybe half a mile away, way back on the larboard quarter now.'

Bang!

The first gun fired. It was a strangely flat sound as the reverberations were swallowed by the fog.

'Which way is it heading, Lewis?'

There was a pause.

'Hard to say, sir, but maybe dead opposite to our heading.'

Then the French were already well on their way to escaping the bay.

Fairview stole a quick look at the compass.

'Ship's head's nor'east-by-north, sir. They're steering sou'west-by-south to round the Cardinals.'

Not the Teignouse Passage then. He was sure that he'd lose sight of the enemy before he could weigh his anchor, even if he cut the cable, and by the time his sails were set they'd be gone. There was no hope of consulting Gambier, not in this thick weather. He'd round the Cardinals himself and sail inside Belle Isle. That was the best he could do.

'Anchor's coming home, sir. I'll cast our bows to larboard and set the tops'ls with your permission.'

Holbrooke felt the wind. It was faltering, if anything, which was to be expected at this time of night in a fog.

'Very well, Mister Fairview. Tops'ls and set a course to round the Cardinals. Two lead lines if you please, and unless we can keep them in sight we'll pass east of the island.'

'Aye, aye sir.'

'Deck ho! I've lost them now, sir, but just before they went I saw there were two of them and I think they were setting tops'ls.'

The timing was about right. They must have heard the first gun and guessed that they had been seen.

'Very well, Lewis. I'll send up a relief for you now.'

The lookout must be frozen by now, but it was right to keep him up there as long as possible. He knew exactly what he was looking for, and a new lookout would take a few minutes to settle in, minutes in which a fleeting glimpse of the enemy could be missed.

Bang!

The second gun. Gambier would be in no doubt now, and the French would certainly know that their escape had been detected.

'Anchor's aweigh, sir.'

Holbrooke looked aloft to where eighty men were letting fall the tops'ls. He felt *Argonaut* moving through the water and he could sense that she was turning onto her new course. The chase was on!

***

CHAPTER THREE

The Wager

Friday, Ninth of January 1761.
Argonaut, off the Glenan Isles, Brittany.

Fairview hadn't left the deck since *Argonaut* weighed anchor. He'd haunted the officer of the watch, obsessively supervising the half-hourly streaming of the log and watching for every change in the wind. Neither activity tended to help his humour. The wind was light and fickle although always from the east and the log never showed more than four knots and often only two or three. But that wasn't the worst of it. The fog hadn't let up for a moment and the sailing master was beginning to consider whether he should recommend that the ship make an offing to give it more sea room. He knew this coast of old, and the Glenan Isles made his flesh creep. He was conscious of their dreadful presence somewhere to starboard, and beyond them the Penmarks where many a good ship had ended its days. In this weather they would have no warning; they could see nothing, and the waves were so slight that they wouldn't hear them moving against the rocks until it was too late.

Five bells rang out – half past six in the morning – and the master's mate took up the log line again and beckoned to the boy who was trying to keep his eyes open under the break of the quarterdeck. He'd been on watch since four o'clock after less than four hours of sleep and his young body found that hard to sustain. Under the baleful eye of the master the boy streamed the line while the mate watched the thirty-second glass.

'Three knots and a fathom, sir.'

Fairview glanced at the line where the boy held it nipped between his fingers. He nodded grudgingly. The ship's speed was of the greatest importance and any inaccuracy would have a huge and possibly devastating effect on his calculations.

He'd been navigating by dead reckoning. That is to say he knew where he had started – he'd taken a departure, in the language of the sea – and the traverse board recorded the course and speed that the ship had made every half hour, according to the compass and log. He'd recorded the time when they passed out of coastal soundings on the twenty-fathom line to the nor'west of Belle Isle. That much he knew, and he could estimate his leeway and make a guess at the influence of the tidal stream. Armed with that mixture of hard data and suppositions, he could come up with a theoretical position at any moment. But it was just that, a theoretical position, and every hour underway without a fix from the land rendered that position less accurate. And the errors accumulated leading to an exponentially inaccurate knowledge of the ship's location. Realistically, he could be anywhere within a five mile circle of his estimated position, and when he looked at the chart the Glenan Isles showed stark and deadly just five miles on the beam. And to make matters worse, the tidal stream off the Penmarks, on both the flood and the ebb, was beyond any forecasting. Perhaps the local fishermen knew it, and the more diligent of the French pilots, but Fairview had always given them a wide berth and could only make an educated guess.

He touched his hat to Holbrooke.

'Five miles off the Glenan Isles sir, by dead reckoning. Our course is west nor'west to round the Penmarks, but I recommend we steer two points further to seaward, sir.'

Holbrooke knew the limitations of dead reckoning as well as his sailing master, and he guessed that the French ships would be as nervous as he was with the Glenan Isles so close and the fog so thick. He had privately determined to stand off but was waiting for Fairview's report.

'Very well, Mister Fairview. Make our course westerly.'

***

Yesterday had been one of the most anxious that Holbrooke could remember. He'd left his station without informing his superior officer and had struck off on a course of his own choosing, based on a fleeting glimpse of something that could have been the mast of a French ship-of-the line. It would be twilight in a few minutes and at this moment Gambier could be looking for his frigate, cursing its junior commander for a fool who cast aside his orders for a will-o'-the-wisp. Only Lewis had seen the masts, and he might have been mistaken. The fog played tricks with the eyesight, and it could have been a little *chasse-marée*, taking advantage of the weather to run past the British ships, out of the bay and down the coast. Or if the French had come out, Gambier could at this moment be off Belle Isle, damning his absent frigate while he tried to guess where the enemy had gone.

Yet in his heart he knew that he had made the correct choice. The worst case – and the most likely – was that the French had slipped over the bar and out to sea and were running for Brest, hoping to elude both the Vilaine guardships and Hawke's blockading squadron. Whatever they did, they had to round the Penmarks and there, if anywhere, they could be brought to action. *Argonaut's* task was clear; Holbrooke had to perform the classic role of a frigate captain, to find the enemy and bring the line-of-battle ships into action.

But that didn't help with Holbrooke's present dilemma. The fog hadn't lifted, and while it persisted no amount of daylight would help him find the French ships. If they were careful and their navigation was accurate, they could be past the Penmarks already, but if they were cautious or slow, then they could still be struggling towards the Glenan Isles. Well, there was no point agonising over it. Having done everything he could, Holbrook paced the deck, forward and aft past the guns that had been cleared for action for thirty hours now and past the single man at each one who was there to wipe the touch hole dry and keep the linstock alight.

Treacherous Moon

'Beg pardon, sir, but I do believe the wind's veered a touch.'

Fairview was holding his wetted finger up to the breeze. Holbrooke stopped dead and turned his face to the stern. Yes, there was a definite change. Ah, now it was coming from even further south.

'Wind off the sea, sir. It could carry away the fog.'

Indeed it could, Holbrooke thought, and it could intensify it. It all depended upon the relative temperatures of the land and the sea, and as no man could tell him what they were, only time would tell. He waited breathlessly. Nothing. No change, and there was no sign of the dawn through the smooth white veil of the fog. Yet the wind had definitely veered and that certainly heralded something.

The officers on the quarterdeck waited in silence, holding their collective breath. Then slowly, almost imperceptibly, the fog started to lose its substance. One minute it was a pure undifferentiated wall of grey, and the next it started to fragment. It whirled in shreds like a diaphanous bridal garment, now revealing the end of the jib boom and then concealing it again. And yet at every swirl of the air the visibility improved a little. Now it was obvious that the night and the fog were in retreat. The sun hadn't yet risen, but the light of a new day was starting to show through, refracted by the thick atmosphere so that there was no telling where the sun would appear. Holbrooke looked around in wonder at this first sight of the whole of his deck for two full days.

'Deck ho! Sails! Sails fine on the larboard quarter. Maybe three miles.'

Holbrooke reached for his telescope then thought better of it. If he couldn't see the horizon with the naked eye, then no arrangement of lenses within a brass tube would help. The lookout would have a better view from his lofty perch; the fog would be thickest at the water's surface, and he would be able to see over the worst of it.

'Two of the line, sir, under t'gallants on the same course

as us.'

'Is that Mister Carew there? Up with you and tell me what you see. Take the deck telescope.'

Two of the line! If that was true, then there was a good chance that they were the two French ships that he'd seen at anchor in the estuary. Of course they could be Gambier's ships, but in any case he needed to know who they were before making his next move. He could afford to wait for the midshipman's report.

'I've called the hands on deck, sir. The ship's already cleared for action, and I'll be able to report quarters in five minutes.'

Shorrock always relished the thought of action. He loved it for its own sake, not just as a means of fulfilling an end. Holbrooke had always wondered at that. For himself he would as soon do without the crash of the guns, the howl of the shot and the screams of the wounded.

'Very well…'

'Captain, sir. They're ships of the line for sure and they don't look like *Burford* or *Prince Frederick* or *Modeste*. They look like Frenchmen to me.'

Carew's voice carried easily to the deck, and it conveyed all his excitement.

'There! I can see them now.'

Shorrock was pointing urgently over the quarter. Holbrooke grabbed his telescope and levelled it in the direction that the first lieutenant's outstretched arm indicated. The ghostly images leaped into his view, but he could make nothing of them other than that they looked like ships of the line. Then a gust of wind – a definitely southerly blast – swept away the fog as though it had never been.

'They're not British ships, sir.'

'No, Mister Shorrock, I do believe those are our two Frenchmen.'

Holbrooke lowered his telescope and wiped the lenses.

'Masthead! Do you see anything else? Take a good sweep of the horizon astern and to larboard.'

Treacherous Moon

There was a pause before Carew called again.

'I think I see something out on the larboard beam, sir. It comes and goes, but it could be a sail.'

Fairview leaned across to Shorrock and spoke behind his hand.

'The Western Squadron. A guinea on it!'

'I'll take your guinea, Mister Fairview. Those are Gambier's ships; you mark my words.'

'Impossible. He'll be far astern of us!'

'Not if he slipped when he heard our guns. He would likely have come out to seaward of the island. There would have been more breeze out there and he could be making for the Passage du Raz to cut them off.'

Fairview grunted and turned away. He was starting to think he'd been a little hasty and he ruefully rubbed the golden guinea in his coat pocket.

Holbrooke grinned privately. His two senior officers were inveterate gamblers; they would stake a guinea on two raindrops running off an oilskin coat, or two weevils in the bread box. However, he felt that Shorrock's guess was the closer. If he were to hazard a guinea it would be on Gambier rather than Hawke.

It was still conjecture, but in all probability he was looking at the two French ships steering to round the Penmarks and make for Brest while Gambier's ships were running in from seaward in the hope of intercepting them. He glanced at the chart that Fairview was studying. He could see that Gambier would be too late. The Frenchmen would be through the passage before they could be brought to action, and with no close blockade of Brest it was likely that they would be safe. In which case, his task was no longer to report the position of the enemy, but to do whatever he could to slow their progress. It was a dangerous idea. A frigate against two third rates was a desperate venture, even if – as seemed likely – they hadn't embarked all their guns. Desperate, but still it had to be done. In the clash of titans, a frigate was a mere pawn to be sacrificed for a tactical advantage.

'The ship's cleared for action and the hands are at their quarters, sir.'

Shorrock had placed himself in front of Holbrooke and removed his hat, sweeping it in a great arc towards his stomach, for this most formal and momentous report. The first lieutenant had no doubt as to their duty and he clearly didn't wish it otherwise.

Holbrooke took a look up at the masthead. The last wisps of fog were streaming away to the north and the sun was just starting to show behind the French ships, for he was now certain of their identity.

Carew's next hail completed the picture.

'Three of the line out to larboard, sir, I can see their t'gallants.'

'Mister Shorrock. I do believe you will be able to claim your guinea.'

Shorrock smiled and winked at the sailing master.

'Mister Fairview, you may put the ship onto the starboard tack, full and by. Where's the wind? Sou'-sou'westerly? You should just be able to steer for the enemy.'

***

'Mister Shorrock. Draw all the round shot from the guns and load with chain and bar. Grape shot for the quarterdeck guns. You have fifteen minutes.'

Holbrooke shielded his eyes as he stared at the advancing French ships. Even from here he could see that they were riding high in the water. They were lucky that they had a good broad reach up the coast; they would have found it very hard to make way close hauled. They'd be light on stores, certainly, but they were so high that it was probable that they had shipped only one deck of guns. Most likely they had hastily embarked their lower deck twenty-four pounders after they crossed the bar, but the upper deck twelves would have been omitted as they contributed nothing to their stability and would have delayed the ships' departure. They were in line abreast with half a cable between them. Their intent was clear; they were running for the safety of Brest, and they had no intention of fighting, if they could help it. They would know the inevitable consequence of accepting battle with three British third rates in their present situation; it would only end with King George's navy strengthened by two new ships-of-the-line and King Louis' navy being that much weaker.

Fairview was studying the advancing ships through his telescope.

'That one on the larboard wing has a look of an Indiaman to me, sir.'

Holbrooke looked more closely. Yes, it was broader in the beam than most French third rates and it looked more massive overall than its consort, but its shape was all wrong for one of the big seventy-fours. And perhaps its mainmast was a little too short for a ship built as a man-o'-war. Fairview was right.

'That'll be *Brillant*, I expect. She was built in Lorient for the East India trade but bought into the navy after one trip to Quebec. I knew she was in the Vilaine, but I'm surprised she's one of the first to come out.'

Was that the French weakness? *Brillant* was certainly bigger than the other unnamed third rate, but would her bulk make her less handy? Well, that was the ship he would set his teeth into.

'Mister Shorrock! On the quarterdeck, if you please. And Mister Fairview, and Lieutenant Murray.'

Shorrock came hurrying back from his guns while the sailing master and the marine officer were already at their stations on the quarterdeck.

'Well, gentlemen. I find we must delay at least one of these two to allow Captain Gambier to come up. If we can grapple that larger one,' he pointed to *Brillant* on the starboard wing of the formation, 'then perhaps the other will come to his aid. That would be ideal, then we have a chance of detaining them both.'

Privately, Holbrooke thought it more likely that the smaller ship would leave the larger to fend for itself. They were perhaps fifteen minutes ahead of the ships closing in on them from the south, and they couldn't afford a moment's delay.

'Mister Fairview. Steer to cross *Brillant's* bows if you please. We'll give him one broadside from the larboard battery at long range and try to cut up his sails and rigging, then come off the wind and cross his hawse. A broadside from the starboard guns then we'll grapple him on our starboard bow, if we can.'

Holbrooke paused to look at his officers. He knew what he was asking of them.

'We'll be boarding then, sir?'

Murray looked pleased at the prospect.

'Well, if we can just hold onto her long enough for *Burford*, *Prince Frederick* and *Modeste* to come up, we'll have done our duty. I believe it will be sufficient if we can stop him cutting himself free…'

He saw the disappointment in the marine's face.

'…but I'll board if it's necessary. Your men must be principally employed in keeping the enemy gunwales clear. As soon as we have grappled, bring all the gun crews up to repel boarders, Mister Shorrock. Make sure they are armed.'

Holbrooke could see that his fighting officers, the first lieutenant and the marine, saw nothing at all absurd in a sixth rate frigate taking on a third rate ship-of-the line. Fairview was more sceptical, but then his role in the ship was to keep it safe, and this plan would decidedly not help.

'Then to your stations, Gentlemen.'

He shook each man by the hand, holding their faces in his memory. This was probably his most dangerous engagement yet, and he had no illusions about his own personal safety. There was no protection on the quarterdeck of a frigate. No comforting poop deck at his back and only low gunwales with flimsy rolled hammocks stacked into the cradles on top. He would be an easy target from the high poop deck of a French third rate.

***

He had ten minutes before he'd be in action. The British ships were hull-up now, and he could plainly see that they were Gambier's three of the line that had become so familiar over the past month. With the strengthening southerly wind they were coming down fast. If he could pin one of the Frenchmen he would only have to hang on for fifteen minutes or so. It could be done, if his men remained resolute, and a quick glance at the gun crews in the waist told him that he shouldn't worry on that score. He tried to imagine how the action would unfold. A broadside of chain shot at the enemy's bow; if he were lucky it would bring down a topmast or shatter a yard, making the Frenchman temporarily unable to manoeuvre. Then with the helm hard to windward the bows would pay off quickly and he should be able to deliver another broadside before smashing into *Brillant's* bows. That was Fairview's responsibility, and he knew he could leave it to him. Then a dozen grapnels and a hail of musketry from the gunwales and grenades from the tops to keep the French crew back. But how long could that be sustained? It was always an error to assume that the enemy would fall in with his designs and a sixty-four's crew – if they were all embarked – was nearly three times the size of a frigate's. In the end that sort of superior weight of numbers would overwhelm his own. It would be a long fifteen minutes, if he lived to see it through. He banished the image of his infant son from his head.

***

CHAPTER FOUR

So Close

Friday, Ninth of January 1761.
Argonaut, off the Glenan Isles, Brittany.

'Hard on the wind now, Mister Fairview.'

'Aye-aye sir.'

Argonaut's bows nudged closer to the southerly breeze. The wind had dispersed the fog. It had blown away so that not a trace remained and had strengthened as it veered into the south so that *Argonaut* heeled enough for the windward guns to be straining at their tackles. Holbrooke braced himself against the binnacle.

Fairview watched the sails and the wheel as *Argonaut's* bow came up.

'If this wind had come twelve hours earlier the French would have been at the Passage du Raz by now, and safe, sir.'

'That's so, Mister Fairview, and they'd have been unlucky if they found anything to oppose them. Admiral Hawke keeps a loose blockade of Brest, there's generally nothing more than a frigate or sloop in the Iroise, just enough to give warning if the French should come out. The Western Squadron is far out to sea, if it isn't at anchor at Torbay.'

Shorrock rubbed his hands and said nothing. He'd have preferred that the French found a pair of stout British seventy-fours between them and safety, but he was perfectly happy for *Argonaut* have a go at them alone. He could see the three British ships-of-the-line coming up fast from the sou'east and it was quite plain to him that the French must be blocked until Gambier's ships could reach them. He knew what he would do, if he commanded *Argonaut*. He'd put the frigate alongside the larger of the two and damn the consequences, but he also knew that his captain was no death-or-glory man.

Fairview took some rapid bearings of points on the newly revealed shore then consulted his chart.

'Just two miles off the Glenan Isles, sir. That's a little closer than I had intended, the tidal stream must have set us to the north.'

Holbrooke looked at the chart. The French were squeezed between the hazards of what was now a leeward shore and the menace of the approaching enemy squadron. They couldn't turn back or step aside; they must run for Brest through the Passage du Raz and only a flimsy British frigate stood in the way of their escape.

Holbrooke would rather not have been so close to the dangerous Glenan Isles, particularly with a rising onshore wind, but tactically it could hardly have been better. The French couldn't make any more offing without committing to an engagement that they couldn't hope to win, and they couldn't go much further to leeward for fear of the Glenan Isles and the Penmarks beyond them. They were in a bottleneck. Now all he had to do was to place a stopper in the bottle and keep it there as long as possible.

'Don't give an inch to leeward, Mister Fairview.'

The quartermaster was concentrating on his luffs, directing the steersman with hand motions so that the ship sailed as close to the wind as it could while keeping the sails full and not shivering. It was a fine piece of work, the fruits of the years and years at sea that had honed their skills. Holbrooke knew that he would have been hopeless in either of those positions. He could decide that the ship needed to sail close to the wind and he could determine the balance of the benefits and risks in doing so. He could give the orders that set the scheme in motion, but he could no more execute those orders than the steersman could command the ship in action. He hadn't taken the ship's wheel since his early days as a master and commander, when he felt that he should do so to set an example. When he was promoted to post-captain, it became rapidly clear that he imperilled the dignity of command by displaying his ineptitude. At times like these he realised how much he relied on the competence of his people.

'Full and by, sir.'

He watched as Fairview looked up at the luffs of the tops'ls and courses, moving from side to side to get a good view. The master seemed satisfied and nodded as he glanced at the dog vane.

The skills of his people for sure. He couldn't even supervise the quartermaster as thoroughly as his sailing master did. He was three steps removed from the actual steering of the ship, yet it was his commands that activated the whole, that exploited all that skill and experience and brought it to bear at the point where it best served his country.

'Train the guns right forward, Mister Shorrock and aim high. Let me know when they bear.'

Holbrooke had to shout against the rising breeze that was tending to carry his words away from the first lieutenant. He spared a glance for the gun crews who were hauling the guns around with the big hand spikes and knocking out the quoins to give them enough elevation to reach the Frenchmen's rigging. A glance, that was all he could afford, and then he had to leave the management of the guns to Shorrock.

The first lieutenant gave his orders to the midshipmen in charge of the divisions of guns, who gave specific orders to the gun captains who pushed and cajoled the powerful men who heaved on the hand spikes. Four layers of command separated him from the handling of the gun, and yet they unfailingly played their part in his plan. Furthermore, if any part of that chain was broken, if a gun captain was killed, for example, there was another man ready to take his place. Indeed, if *Argonaut's* captain should fall the first lieutenant would assume command with no more than a second or two's delay. And if Shorrock should be carried away by a blast of grapeshot, there was a master's mate ready and eager to take over the direction of the guns. It was a strong chain, but a flexible one; a system of command suited for the uncertainties of battle.

Holbrooke snapped himself out of his introspection. There was an action to be fought.

The French were clearly visible past the leeward bow at about a mile. That was too far to expect any hits, particularly with chain and bar shot that chose their own trajectories when they left the gun barrel, spinning and tumbling in flight in an entirely unpredictable manner.

Now he could see that *Brillant* had opened her gunports, but only the lower ones, the upper tier remained steadfastly closed. Were he commanding the French sixty-four, he would have opened them just to dishearten this insolent frigate, to suggest that perhaps he could fire a full broadside. It indicated that the Frenchman had only enough people to man the lower deck twenty-fours, and none to spare for opening redundant ports. That was a point worth noting. Perhaps the disparity in numbers wouldn't be as great as he feared; perhaps he could board after all.

The French ships looked bold enough with the wind on their quarters and a bone in their teeth. If it weren't for the expanse of planking that they showed and the closed upper tier of gunports, he could have believed that they were fully armed and eager for battle. They flew the Bourbon white from their ensign staffs, but they weren't the massive flags that were normally to be seen on French men-o'-war. These were modest affairs without even the distinction of the usual pattern of embroidered gold *fleur-de-lis*. Holbrooke guessed that the vastly expensive royal ensigns would only be supplied to them once they were safely in the arsenal at Brest. In the meantime, for this hazardous passage with an uncertain outcome, plain white would have to suffice. He noticed that neither ship flew a commodore's pennant. Was that important? Did it suggest that the two captains might have their own independent ideas on how to deal with the situation?

Fairview was watching the approaching enemy as keenly as he watched the steering of his ship.

'They're bearing away, sir.'

Holbrooke could see that for himself. The two ships were altering course to starboard in perfect unity, as though joined by an invisible hawser. Of course, they weren't going to tamely accept a broadside without fighting back. They could spare the few seconds to let their heads pay off to open the arcs for *Brillant's* broadside. Yet *Brillant* couldn't come too far off the wind without squeezing the other ship towards the Glenan Isles and the Penmarks. For a moment Holbrooke hoped that they'd make a mistake and founder on the wicked rocks under their lee. But they were in French waters and any French sea officer would know about the dangers here. Yet that caution – that natural desire to keep away from the unseen reefs – made it inevitable that *Argonaut* would strike the first blows before the French ship's broadside would bear.

'Mister Shorrock. The starboard guns are ready? You'll need to send the men across sharply.'

Shorrock waved his hat.

'Then stand by the larboard battery.'

Holbrooke watched the range carefully. Too soon and he'd reduce the chance of a crippling blow, too late and he wouldn't have time to bear away and bring his starboard battery into action. If waited too long the Frenchman would pass him by before he could bring *Argonaut* alongside.

'Stand by…'

Holbrooke brought the whistle to his lips and blew a single blast. With an almighty crash the larboard battery opened fire and *Argonaut* staggered against the recoil. He was aware of the gun crews hastily securing the larboard guns, hauling on the train tackles so that they were brought hard up against the ports. Then they rushed over to the starboard battery.

A quick look told him that *Brillant's* own guns must open fire very soon.

Treacherous Moon

'Bear away, Mister Fairview.'

Holbrooke felt the deck buck under his feet and was thrown back as something hard and sharp ripped through his coat and slammed into his chest. There was no pain, not yet, but he knew he'd been hit by a splinter, and he knew exactly what had happened. The French ship hadn't waited for its whole battery to bear but had fired as soon as the forward division of its guns could point at the British frigate. Perhaps only six gins had fired but at least a few of the twenty-four pound shot had found their target. Holbrooke hauled himself off the deck. Well, at least he could move and there wasn't very much blood at all. As he levered himself back onto his feet he had a momentary glimpse of Shorrock starting towards the quarterdeck, but he checked in his stride when he saw his captain standing.

Holbrooke was confronted with a scene of devastation. One of the quarterdeck six-pounders was on its side with a man trapped beneath and his mates scattered far and wide. He could see that the sails had great holes in them and realised that the Frenchman had fired chain and bar shot, just as *Argonaut* had. He could hear Fairview ordering the ship to pay off, as he had directed, and as though nothing had happened. Then it was still possible, he could still interpose himself between the French sixty-four and her safe haven at Brest. A brief glance confirmed that the main deck guns were all undamaged, it looked like the quarterdeck had taken the worst of the Frenchman's broadside.

One more broadside, then he'd throw his ship alongside the enemy and damn the consequences.

'Starboard battery! Stand by.'

It hurt to shout, and he could feel someone pulling off his coat and wrapping a bandage around his chest. It was his friend, the chaplain, who helped the surgeon in battle. He'd soon be needed below where at least one of his crew was being carried, moaning softly and leaving a bloody trail on the ladder.

'Can you stand unaided? Here, hold onto the quarterdeck rail until you have your balance.'

'Thank you, David.'

The rail felt solid under his grip and when he didn't have to think about standing upright he could devote his whole attention to the battle.

Chalmers tucked the end of the bandage and flicked Holbrooke's coat back into place over his chest, then without a word turned towards the man still trapped under the six-pounder.

Argonaut's bows were paying off fast and the quartermaster was gesturing to the helmsman to meet her. He needed to be steering straight across the Frenchman's bows to cut her course at a right angle. Then, after the broadside, he could bring the helm hard over and throw the ship alongside the enemy.

Holbrooke had a moment to wonder how badly his ship had been damaged in her masts and spars. Certainly there was a lot of cordage weighing down the splinter nets and he had an impression of tattered canvas. He could hear Jackson the bosun shouting at his crew as they hurried to repair the damage. Then he cast the speculation aside. Jackson could be relied upon to do whatever was possible, and everything else could be left to an increasingly uncertain future. All that mattered now was to grapple the enemy and hold him until Gambier could arrive. He looked quickly to windward to see the three British ships running fast towards the scene of the action.

One more glance at the French ships and down at the main deck guns. Shorrock was standing on the longboat's cradle, looking fierce and competent. He waved to Holbrooke to indicate that the guns were ready.

Holbrooke raised the whistle again and took a breath.

Then he felt rather than heard the dreadful rending of timber from forward. He watched, appalled, as the fore topmast sagged away to leeward. It hung for just a moment with the t'gallant mast still attached, then the whole arrangement of masts, yards, sails and rigging, parted company from the foremast and fell with a crash over the lee gunwale. He had a momentary impression of Jackson and a few men clinging to the shrouds of the main topmast. If they'd been on the foremast instead there would have been no hope for them, they'd have been catapulted over the side and in the heat of an action there would have been no chance of recovering them. Repairing damage aloft while a battle still raged was a perilous business; Holbrooke was glad that it wasn't he who had to do it.

The steersman fought hard, spinning the wheel as fast as he could, but with the reduced leverage in the forward part of the ship the frigate's bows swung inexorably into the wind. Fairview was shouting for the mizzen to be furled as Holbrooke released his breath and blew his whistle, but it was a forlorn hope. Half of the guns were masked by the wreckage of the fore topmast and the other half couldn't shift their aim fast enough to keep pace as the ship swung into the wind. Holbrooke saw in horror that *Argonaut* would present her vulnerable stern to the passing enemy.

'Down. Lie down on the deck!' he shouted, his voice almost a scream.

He felt the impact as the French ship's guns fired again. One, two, the frigate reeled to the mighty blows of twenty-four pound round shot, then nothing. He'd been lucky. It had all happened so quickly that his enemy had not been able to reload all the guns of his battery; he was short-handed for sure.

Holbrooke looked up at the huge French ship as it rushed past his crippled frigate beyond the range of either swivel guns or muskets. High on her poop deck, beside the plain, unadorned white ensign, a solitary uniformed figure raised his hat in salute to his defeated foe.

***

CHAPTER FIVE

A Game of Cricket

Friday, Ninth of January 1761.
Burford, Sein Islands East-North-East Four Leagues.

Captain Gambier had never been very welcoming, and every time that Holbrooke had been summoned on board *Burford* he'd left with the impression that he'd in some way offended this senior captain. Today was worse and Gambier was clearly furious at his own failure to prevent the two French ship-of-the-line escaping. Furious, and inclined to blame others, and for a whole hour he directed his acerbic comments at this most junior of the captains serving under him.

'What the devil did you think you were doing, sir? You weren't playing a game of cricket you know. All you had to do was put your damned frigate across that Frenchman's hawse and I would have had her, perhaps *Dragon* as well. It was an opportunity lost. Well, sir? What do you have to say?'

Holbrooke had guessed that Gambier would go straight into the attack. His clerk was sitting to one side but not taking any notes, which Holbrooke regretted, because he knew of Gambier's temper by repute, and he knew that a transcript of their meeting wouldn't show the senior captain in a good light in any inquiry. Gambier must know that himself, which was perhaps the reason for the lack of a written record.

He'd prepared himself mentally. He was the same rank as Gambier, albeit some twelve years below him on the post-captains list and fifteen years younger. It was that seniority, along with Gambier's parliamentary and social influence, that had persuaded Hawke to give him command of the Vilaine guard ships. Holbrooke's orders from Hawke were quite specific in putting him under Gambier's command, and he would have to tread carefully.

Treacherous Moon

Standing up for himself in front of domineering personalities did not come easily to Holbrooke. He was the son of a sailing master, one of the middling sort in Georgian society that inhabited the uncertain territory between leisured gentlemen and those who laboured to keep body and soul together. He found it difficult to assert the dignity of his rank when confronted by those of his peers who had been brought up in gentility. He'd spent the ten minutes that it took for the longboat to row him across to *Burford* in preparing to answer this very question and, more importantly, to meet what he knew would be a hostile senior captain.

'If I had merely thrown myself across his hawse, sir, I could not have had a decent shot at his rigging. It was only by chance that I didn't injure him enough to slow his progress. And as I hope you observed, as soon as I had fired my first broadside I steered towards his bow, with the intention of grappling him. Again, it was only by fortune that he shot away my fore topmast so that I couldn't keep my head off the wind.'

Gambier sneered and looked at a point over Holbrooke's shoulder.

'Fortune, oh yes, indeed. We may attribute all kinds of conduct to a lack of *fortune*.'

Holbrooke felt his hackles rising. This was more than a slur on his professional ability. Gambier had used the word *conduct*, and that had a particular meaning in this context. He didn't have to feign his rising anger and he hardly needed to consider how to express his outrage.

'I trust, sir, that you are not suggesting that I wanted conduct in this action…'

'I am suggesting, sir, that you could have acted differently, in a way that would have detained at least one of those ships until I could have run down and engaged them. What the hell do you think a frigate is for if not to bring ships-of-the-line into action?'

Gambier had shouted the last few words and slammed

his palm down upon the table. The two men glared at each other for the space of half a dozen heartbeats. Holbrooke could see that Gambier was not in control of his temper and that at any moment he was likely to make an accusation that cut to the heart of Holbrooke's personal honour, and that simply could not be ignored. He felt his heart racing. Was this how duels came about? A few words spoken in the heat of the moment that could neither be withdrawn nor adequately explained, and a meeting at dawn some days, weeks or months hence. No, he wouldn't be drawn into a rash response. If it came to it, he'd demand a court martial to clear his name. He'd had done his utmost to engage the enemy; he was blameless, wasn't he? Nevertheless, courts martial were always uncertain affairs and their outcomes were driven by factors beyond the accused officer's control, but it would be better than a duel with a senior officer. What he wouldn't do was back down.

Gambier opened his mouth to speak then caught his clerk's eye. Holbrooke couldn't see what intelligence passed between them, what unspoken warning was delivered, but he saw Gambier's mouth close, the teeth snapping shut behind thin, bloodless lips.

'Well, Captain Holbrooke. I see that it's best if I reserve judgement until you have had a chance to make a written report. I'll expect it by sunset and then I suppose you must be away to Plymouth to get a new fore topmast. God knows what the admiral will say to losing a frigate so be sure that you don't linger in port.'

***

Holbrooke returned to find a ship that was well on the way to restoring some sort of order. The fore topmast and t'gallant, along with their yards and what were left of the sails, had been hoisted inboard and secured between the pinnace and the yawl. With no immediate likelihood of meeting an enemy and with an easy run up channel to Plymouth – how he wished he were bound for Portsmouth! – it was better to preserve the wreckage to be re-made into smaller spars for other vessels. Timber for masts and yards was always in short supply and replacements had to be brought over from New England or the Baltic in specially adapted ships. Anything that could be salvaged would be gratefully received in the yard at Plymouth. The other scars of the short battle were being temporarily repaired and he was lucky that there was no damage below the waterline. The Frenchman had conducted himself to perfection, only engaging *Argonaut* to the extent necessary to allow the two ships an uninterrupted passage to the safety of Brest. From the moment that they swept past Holbrooke, there was no doubt of their escape.

Collins looked tired as he made his report, fresh from the sick bay.

'Three dead and six wounded, sir, not counting yourself.'

Holbrooke had actually forgotten about his own injury. He touched his fingers to the bandage wrapped tightly around his chest and felt the stiffness of dried blood below. Gambier must have noticed the bulk under his waistcoat but chose not to ask about Holbrooke's health. It was an ordinary splinter wound that had been prevented by his ribs from doing any real damage. In a week he'd have forgotten about it, but he could imagine Ann's distress when she saw the scar. Still, he was bound for Plymouth and would certainly not be given leave to visit his home near Portsmouth, and Ann would not come down to meet him, not with a new baby to consider.

'Yes, I know about our three losses, Doctor.'

Two men had died on the quarterdeck, one crushed by a six-pounder gun and the other having his femoral artery severed by a splinter. Another had been slow in leaving the foretop when it started to sway and he fell to the fo'c'sle, landing across one of the timber heads and breaking his back. They had been sewn into their hammocks; three forlorn packages to be laid atop the water barrels in the hold. David Chalmers wouldn't hear of them being buried at sea, not with Plymouth only two days away, if the wind held.

The cold weather of January would prevent their bodies becoming noxious for at least that long, and they could be taken ashore for a decent burial.

'One broken forearm, sir, the radius and the ulna have both severed. I re-set the bones and the arm has been secured in a leather splint. I expect he'll be in sick bay for a few days then perhaps he can be employed as a mess cook until it's healed. The other five have lacerations that will all do very well, I expect. A remarkable result for an engagement with a ship-of-the-line, if I may say so, sir.'

'Well, we should all give thanks for that. I hope that we'll be at anchor in the Hamoaze in a few days, and you can discharge them to that new hospital up Stonehouse Creek, if it's ready to receive.'

'Oh, I doubt whether that will be necessary, sir. They'll do just as well if they remain aboard, and they won't be tempted to wander as soon as they're mobile.'

Holbrooke nodded. Naval hospitals were notorious for their wastage of sailors, and they lost far more to straggling than ever succumbed to disease or wounds. The six injured men had been made easy in the screened area at the forward end of the berth deck where they could speak to their messmates and receive their ration of beer and victuals, so most likely they'd prefer to remain with the ship. He turned to the sailing master.

'How does she steer, Mister Fairview?'

Holbrooke hoped that the memory of that unpleasant interview with Gambier didn't show in his face. He had to write his report within the next two hours, and he had no real idea how he would approach it. The temptation to immerse himself in the handling of his crippled ship was overwhelming, but he knew that procrastination wouldn't help.

'Well enough, sir. She'll lie eight points off the wind, just about, and as long as we keep the main t'gallant on deck and the mizzen brailed, she'll run before the wind without ripping the steersmen's arms out of their sockets. If this wind holds we'll weather Ushant and run up the channel to Plymouth Sound without any difficulty.'

Holbrooke studied the sails. He'd been lucky, really lucky. The forestay hadn't been damaged and although he'd lost the main t'gallant stay, the main topmast stay had held. The shot that had undone them had ripped through the fore topmast shrouds and into the topmast itself a yard or so above the planking of the top. What they had left was perfectly secure, but they had lost the prime advantage of a frigate, its speed and manoeuvrability. They needed the services of a yard with competent carpenters and riggers before they could be of use to the blockading squadron.

'Stay to windward of *Burford*, Mister Fairview. I expect Mister Gambier will be wanting to make an offing with this sou'westerly, but he won't want to be set to the north. I'll be in my cabin. Pass the word for Mister Chalmers, I would be happy if he could join me.'

***

David Chalmers had sailed with Holbrooke since the long-ago days of 'fifty-six in the Mediterranean. He was entered on the ship's books as a chaplain, which was something of a stretch for a mere frigate, but the navy board clerks who scrutinised the books had little appetite for querying the status of a man of the cloth, not in a navy that demanded that church be rigged every Sunday in its ships at sea. Chalmers did in fact carry out his religious duties, but he had two other tasks: first he was a companion to Holbrooke, the only man on board that the captain could confide in without imperilling his position, and second he was a voluntary assistant to the surgeon and his mate. None of his tasks were particularly onerous, in normal circumstances, and Chalmers had leisure to indulge his principal interest which was the study of mankind. He was engaged in that discipline now, watching his captain over the rim of his coffee cup.

'… so you see I must write this report most carefully. I'm as certain as I can be that Gambier will make a complaint against me if he sees any chance of it being upheld.'

'Then I can only suggest that you keep it short and state the facts as plainly as possible. Perhaps it would help if you described the meeting, George.'

Chalmers sipped his coffee. He messed in the wardroom with the first lieutenant, the marine lieutenant, the master, the surgeon and the purser; all excellent fellows, but to a man they preferred tea or strong spirits, and consequently the wardroom servants had no notion at all of the preparation of coffee. He'd tried buying the most expensive beans and providing a stone mortar and pestle, but the results were barely drinkable, and he'd become used to indulging his coffee habit only when he was invited into the cabin. Holbrooke's servant knew that and could be relied upon to keep his cup replenished, hot and fresh.

'It was so unpleasant that I hardly like to recall it. You remember that interview I had with Captain Chester after we parted company south of the Faeroes? Well this was far, far worse. Chester is essentially a reasonable man who was frustrated that he had to face the French frigates alone. When he heard all the reasons for *Argonaut* and *Fortune* being unable to join him, he had the grace to apologise for his hasty words. I was in no doubt that he was satisfied with the explanation. Gambier is a different man altogether. No amount of reasoning will persuade him that his subordinates are anything other than poltroons and blackguards, and he seems to believe that any blame that can be directed elsewhere will unfailingly leave his reputation unscathed. If he spots anything in my report which will allow him to complain to Admiral Hawke, he'll fix upon it, I'm sure.'

Chalmers considered for a moment, gazing absently out of the great stern windows. Sometimes he wished that his friend would invite him to share the great cabin, rather than be an occasional guest, but that, he knew, would irrevocably change his relationship with the officers. To his wardroom friends he'd be one of *them*, not one of *us*. They'd be guarded in their conversation and with the best intentions would freeze him out of their company.

'I wonder what it is that he fears most. You know his reputation of course.'

'I do. His trial and the uncommon scale of his fine have been common knowledge throughout the fleet.'

'Then what, I wonder, keeps him in employment? He has no particular ability as a sea officer, I understand. He's just averagely competent and he seems to have a talent for making enemies.'

'Political and family connections, I suppose,' Holbrooke replied. 'I know that he's related through a sister to Admiral Cornish, and through another to Captain Barham, who is a rising star in the fleet, but that's surely trumped by Admiral Knowles' enmity. I'm sure I'd bear a grudge if a fellow officer had absconded with Ann. But of course Knowles is effectively retired from the sea and hasn't been employed for some years, and his influence is waning.'

'Indeed. But Gambier must feel his position is fragile, at the least. He'll need a solid case to make a complaint against you. You stood up to him, I gather?'

'I did, in fact he backed down when I challenged him to repeat his words when he questioned my conduct.'

Chalmers looked doubtful; he knew his friend's weaknesses very well, and he knew Gambier by reputation. But then, he had noticed that Holbrooke had become more assertive of late. It could be said that he was growing into his rank, and not a moment too soon.

'Well, in that case he'll know that you'll challenge any adverse comments, let alone an outright complaint to the admiral. I understand that it's not unusual to ask your officers to sign a copy of your report, warranting its truth. Could you ask Shorrock and Fairview and Murray to do that?'

Holbrooke paused before answering.

'I could, if you think it would help. But doesn't it seem that the very existence of such signatures suggests that I'm not confident of my own innocence?'

'My dear George,' David explained, smiling broadly, 'I'm surprised after all your years in the navy that you still accept the place of guilt or innocence in matters of naval discipline. What a romantic notion! No, no, this is a straightforward exercise in the application of personal power and influence. We've discussed Gambier's situation; he would need far more interest than he has to overcome a simple statement of the facts. In my opinion you have nothing to fear, and your officers, I know, will gladly support you, even to the extent of adding their signatures to a reserve copy of your report. You don't have to send that copy to Gambier, just keep it in case of future need. Now, it's a simple matter of declaring the facts without appearing defensive. Shall we look at your first draft?'

***

It was a relief when it was done, and Holbrooke was pleased to see the longboat casting off with the vital document, bound for *Burford*. His officers had signed his own copy without the slightest demur. None of them had thought it odd in the least, but then Shorrock and Fairview had served much longer than Holbrooke, and Murray came from a naval family.

A relief indeed and the cold January air seemed like the blessed zephyrs of spring to Holbrooke as he paced the deck, waiting for the boat to return. Then, unless Gambier had anything else to say on the matter, they'd be away to Plymouth.

'Deck Ho! Sail on the larboard bow, two sails, sir. No, three. They could be frigates, sir, on a broad reach on the larboard tack.'

So much information in one report! The lookout must have missed their first appearance over the horizon, and now he was trying to cover his lack of attention by reporting everything at once. Holbrooke could see that Shorrock thought the same and was looking upwards to ensure that he knew the lookout's name.

'Probably Admiral Hawke's inshore squadron,' Shorrock commented.

Holbrooke nodded. It was hardly likely that they were French, but it was better to be safe.

'Red flag at the main, Mister Petersen, and a gun to leeward.'

That would alert the three ships of the line who were still to the east of *Argonaut*. With their taller masts they would see the sails any moment now, but it was as well to demonstrate *Argonaut's* zeal.

They came on slowly, and as they became visible from the deck, the reason became clear. One of them was undamaged, a British frigate for sure, while the other two were knocked about at least as badly as *Argonaut*.

'I do believe that's *Seahorse* with the damage aloft, and *Unicorn*, sir, she's taken a battering too. The third one is French. I'm not sure, but it could be one of those that were in the Vilaine.'

Shorrock had a keen eye for identifying ships and he was rarely deceived.

'What on earth have they been doing? *Seahorse* was fitting for the East Indies the last I heard, taking an astronomical expedition for the transit of Venus, or some such thing. *Unicorn* is with Hawke, and she'd have been cruising off Ushant, I expect. Yet they all seem to have been in a fight. Anyhow, the longboat's returning and we'll be on our way, I expect.'

Holbrooke stared across the water at *Burford*. He doubted whether they'd be away so soon. It looked likely that both of those frigates and the French prize would have to return to Plymouth. *Seahorse* was certainly in no state to continue to the East Indies, and *Unicorn* couldn't survive a winter gale any more than *Argonaut* could, and the prize looked in no better state. It would be a sorry looking flotilla of four frigates that rounded Ushant and steered up-channel. Gambier would have to take the responsibility for diminishing Hawke's squadron by three frigates, as well as the prize, and he wouldn't do that lightly. He'd want each ship to be surveyed by his own officers.

'I wouldn't be so sure, Mister Shorrock, I wouldn't be sure.'

***

CHAPTER SIX

Transit of Venus

Saturday, Tenth of January 1761.
Seahorse, the Chops of the Channel.

The sou'westerly tops'l breeze couldn't last long, not in January, and Holbrooke was relieved that Gambier's carpenter had taken only a few minutes on each ship to declare that every one of them – the three British frigates and the French prize – needed the attentions of a King's yard before they could be of any further service. By sunset they were underway and even in their shattered condition they rounded Ushant before eight bells in the middle watch and put up their helms for the run into Plymouth Sound. They'd heave to for a few hours, but they'd have the light of the new Smeaton's Tower on the Eddystone off Plymouth Sound as a point of reference in what was likely to be a dark night. If the weather stayed fair they'd be in the Hamoaze by Sunday morning, awaiting a berth alongside or a place in the dry dock.

'Well, our only consolation is that it's Captain Gambier who'll have to explain to the admiral why he's lost half of his frigates in one day. I wouldn't like to do it.'

James Smith had hung out the flags for an invitation to dinner, knowing that they had an easy run down to Plymouth. Four frigates, but only two captains dining, for Hunt of *Unicorn* had succumbed to his injuries and the French captain of *Vestale* had also died in the engagement. Smith was senior to Holbrooke by a good year and older by at least a dozen; he'd been commissioned a lieutenant towards the end of the last war but had languished on half pay through the peace. It reminded Holbrooke of how lucky he'd been to be commissioned so early in this war when the navy was expanding rapidly and needed to bring talented officers quickly through the ranks. Only by the very earliest of promotions to post-captain could an officer have any chance of living long enough to make the highest ranks. Smith would likely hoist his flag as a rear admiral in the fullness of time, but the body's ageing couldn't be denied, and the grim reaper would inevitably catch up with him before he moved further up the flag ranks.

'You had no luck in stopping those French third-rates, I understand. It's a difficult question for us frigate captains, whether it's worth the sacrifice of our ships and our men to bring the fleet into action.'

Holbrooke felt at ease with Smith. He was a straightforward sea officer who could comment on a colleague's actions without sounding as though he was making a judgement. And that was his concern, that his actions of the day before could be construed as a reluctance to engage the enemy closely. Smith had hit the nail on the head. If he'd put *Argonaut* across *Brillant's* bows without any manoeuvering, he'd probably have detained the Frenchman for that crucial fifteen minutes, but it would have meant the loss of his ship and most of his people. He'd opted for a more prudent approach and now all he could hope was that the navy in general would see the sense in his decision.

'I came so close. If my foretopmast had held for another minute I'd have grappled her.'

Smith nodded. Would he have done the same? Probably, but he was glad that he hadn't had to explain to Gambier why the two French ships-of-the-line had escaped into Brest. Still, in the end it was Gambier's responsibility. He'd been placed in command of the guard over the Vilaine, and it was he who had allowed them to escape out of the river in the first place. One thing was for certain, he'd be looking for a way to shift the blame, and junior post-captains were fair game.

'Well, we're both in a better place than poor old Hunt. It was a famous fight, and his widow will still claim his share of the prize money. He lived to see them strike you know, and whatever his condition at that point he was still in command, which is more than can be said for his opponent.'

Holbrooke nodded. That was the crucial point. If Hunt had expired before the Frenchman struck, his widow couldn't claim his share. Then it would only be by the charity of the whole ship's company that she would receive a discretionary sum. He had no idea whether Hunt was loved or loathed by his people, but if they chose not to include their late captain in the distribution, his widow would get nothing.

'His first lieutenant did well. When he saw us engaged with that other frigate he came down like a good 'un, even though his ship was barely fit to keep the sea, and the Frenchman ran for Brest, which I imagine was in accordance with his orders. It could have gone badly for me if he hadn't come to my aid, what with half of my guns struck below to make room for the scientific fellows. You know that I was bound for the East Indies, don't you?'

'I'd heard something about the transit of Venus. It's expected in June, isn't it?'

'Yes. The sixth of June. It hardly seems right to send a frigate away in the middle of a war, particularly as I'm told there will be another opportunity in eight years or so, but there it is. I'll ship a new main topmast and hope that I won't have lost too much time. It was already a tight schedule to reach Sumatra in time.'

'You have a survey party on board, I gather.'

'A Mister Mason and a Mister Dixon and their assistants and servants. So much equipment! And it all needs to be consulted on the passage, apparently, so it has to be readily on hand. That's why I had to strike my guns down into the hold. What with Hawke stalking the entire Atlantic coast, and Keppel at Belle Isle, there was a good chance of making a passage undisturbed by our French friends, so you can imagine my surprise at meeting them only two days out of Plymouth! When they offered battle, I could hardly refuse, and in any case they were to windward and I had no escape. As I said, it could have been a bad day for me if *Unicorn* hadn't arrived. Would you like to meet them? Mason and Dixon, that is.'

'I would, very much. It's a grand undertaking, for sure, to determine the size of our solar system. It will set the mark for all future measurements and who knows what benefits it will bring?'

'Yes, and I understand the French are also sending out expeditions. Really, we should come to an agreement to leave each other alone, after all this is for the good of all mankind, and the Royal Society and the Académie Française have already agreed to share the findings. However, if I stay in command of *Seahorse*, I expect I'll be taken up by whoever commands in the East Indies and it'll be years before I see England again. Mason and Dixon will have to find a John Company ship to bring them home.'

Holbrooke looked at him quizzically.

'Oh, I thought you may have heard. I had been promised a fifty-gun ship, *Guernsey*, and Charles Grant was being posted to take *Seahorse* east, but he had a fever and hadn't recovered in time. That's why we were so late in sailing. I sincerely hope that their Lordships haven't yet given her to anyone else, and I pray that Grant has recovered enough to take *Seahorse* off my hands.'

'You would prefer a ship-of-the-line?'

'At this stage of the war? Certainly. Unless the Spanish declare for France, there'll be no more glory nor prize money for frigates. It's all very well for you young fellows, but I feel the cold hand of time on my shoulder and a fifty will suit admirably. I'll have far more chance of being employed when peace breaks out, and in the meantime I'll have my feet on the quarterdeck of a small ship-of-the-line that doesn't cost a King's ransom to keep up, unlike those fat seventy-fours. Their Lordships will find that I won't be easily dislodged.'

Smith smiled broadly at the thought of the fourth rate that may or may not be waiting for him in Plymouth. Fourth rates were popular ships in peacetime because they were cheap to maintain and man and were thus often kept in commission for foreign stations. He was still haunted by the memory of those inter-war years on a lieutenant's half pay.

'And as for our arrival at Plymouth, if you'd be so kind as to bring up the rear, we'll anchor off St. Nicholas Island – Drake's Island, as some call it – and await the port admiral's pleasure. Before I left the Hamoaze the master attendant was wringing his hands in despair at his mastpond's poverty. He swore that he had not a spare topmast in the whole yard. He was swinging the lead, of course, but I wouldn't be surprised if we are invited to send one of our number to Portsmouth. I imagine you'd volunteer for that singular honour, Holbrooke. I know you have family in those parts, and a new wife and youngster, I hear. In fact, now that I think of it, I believe I once met your father. Was he a sailing master in the last war, by any chance?'

Holbrooke was always wary when anyone mentioned his father. Most meant it well, but a few were delighted to point out the superiority of their own breeding, and the son of a sailing master was always a good target for social sharpshooting. That wasn't the case with Smith, though, and his evident pleasure at meeting the son of an old shipmate was genuine enough.

'He was in *Wolf* in the Caribbean for a while and...'

'Ah, that's it,' Smith exclaimed. 'I was sent to *Wolf* as a youngster when my own ship was laid up in Port Royal. I'm sure my lack of hair dates from your father's cuffing me when I couldn't make the noon sight place us in the right ocean! Do give him my warmest regards when you see him. I imagine he's still with us, isn't he?'

'Hale and hearty, and still terrorising the trout in the Meon. I'll be sure to remember you to him.'

'But of course, you came up under Edward Carlisle, didn't you? I shared a watch with him in *Wolf*. He would never have survived without your father's protection, always in one scrape or another, but weren't we all, eh? I saw Carlisle at Quebec; it was a pleasure to see how he handled

Medina in the Saint Lawrence.'

'Indeed, so I've heard. But one good deed deserves another, and I owe a lot to Captain Carlisle's feeling of indebtedness to my father. *One last chance*, he said as we sailed from Mahon, *one last chance for your father's sake, and after that I'll put you ashore wherever we happen to touch at…*'

It was a pleasant dinner and both men needed it after difficult and unfruitful actions in which they had both lost members of their crew. Smith was clearly still distracted having suffered far worse than Holbrooke. *Seahorse* had lost eleven dead and thirty-seven wounded in just an hour, and although he didn't admit to it, Smith must have been considering striking his colours before *Unicorn* appeared on the scene. It was good to be able to speak on terms of equality, to discuss the matters of war that so consumed the captains of men-of-war as peace started to show its golden rays on the horizon.

***

Holbrooke was deep in thought as he was rowed back to *Argonaut*. He was giddy with the glorious prospect of heading up-channel to refit in Portsmouth and was surprised at how much he wanted to see his wife and son. Plymouth held no interest for him, and it was a certainty that even if his refit lasted a month he wouldn't be given leave to go home. Not with the roads all but impassable in their winter state and the imminence of winter storms at sea. He was still thinking about it as he went up the side and gave the order for his ship to get underway and fall into line at the rear of the flotilla.

An hour later he was sharing a bottle of sherry with Chalmers in the great cabin, recounting his visit to *Seahorse*. When he described the frigate's mission to Sumatra and its passengers, it brought an amused twinkle to the chaplain's eye.

'Forgive me, but this *Transit of Venus* sounds somewhat disreputable, like a salacious sideshow at Vauxhall Gardens. I trust that in this case you are referring strictly to the astronomical phenomenon.'

Holbrooke smiled at the mild teasing and took a sip from his glass.

'And did you meet Charles Mason and Jeremiah Dixon?' Chalmers asked.

'I did. Captain Smith was kind enough to ask them to join us for coffee. Very learned gentlemen, I would say, and thoroughly knowledgeable in their professions. One of them is an astronomer and the other a surveyor, but I forget which. They showed me some of the great piles of equipment that they need for their observations. I've never seen so many octants and telescopes in one place, as well as instruments that I can't even name. If Fairview had been there I could never have persuaded him to leave.'

'I had always understood that the transit of Venus occurred every hundred years or so, yet you mentioned a second transit in 1769.'

'Yes, every hundred-and-thirteen years or thereabouts, but they come in pairs with about eight years between them. The next pair starts in 1874. That's why it's so important to grasp these opportunities, and the more observations with the greater angular distance between them, the more accurate will be the result.'

'And are these two gentlemen aware that they may not reach Sumatra in time?'

'Oh, they are aware, very much so. Smith has – or had – discretion to land them at any suitable place along the way if it became obvious that they wouldn't reach Sumatra with time to set up the equipment before the sixth of June. They were talking freely of landing on the Dutch Cape, and they carried letters requesting co-operation from half a dozen authorities between Gibraltar and the East Indies, just in case. Of course, the transit only lasts a matter of a few hours on that one specified day, and then only if Mister Halley's calculations are correct. If they miss it the whole expedition will have been wasted.'

'Well, I wish them good luck and a cloud-free sky. It's a

worthy cause for sure.'

Chalmers looked thoughtful for a moment.

'Do you remember the Christmas that we spent at Williamsburg, when we saw Mister Halley's comet? I resolved then to pay more attention to astronomy. Some say that it tends to deny the very existence of God, showing us, as it does, a window into the infinite without the faintest hint of a biblical heaven in sight. Yet I take a contrary view, that God is not to be found in such a gross physical form, but his wonders are to be explored to bring us to a greater understanding of Him.'

***

Argonaut had hardly stretched her anchor cable in the lee of St. Nicholas Island when the port commissioner's barge came alongside *Seahorse*. Holbrooke paced the deck nervously, waiting. He thought he could imagine the conversation. The three British frigates needed at least four new topmasts between them, as well as reels and reels of cordage, and timber and iron fastenings. The navy yard would almost certainly have them available, but it would be rash indeed to expend all their reserves on a few frigates when at any time Hawke's battle squadron could appear, demanding huge quantities of all of those sorts of items. It would be tempting fate indeed to send *Seahorse* away in the depths of winter in her reduced state. *Unicorn* was not in a much better case, while the prize crew in *Vestale* would be weary of guarding their charges. *Argonaut* was not badly damaged by comparison with the others, nor was she greatly depleted in her complement.

'Commissioner's barge is putting off, sir.'

Shorrock could guess what was putting his captain on edge.

'It's setting sail, sir, heading to round the Island.'

Holbrooke sighed and turned away for the quarterdeck ladder and his cabin. If he was to be sent to Portsmouth the barge would undoubtedly have delivered his orders after it left *Seahorse*. Then it was Plymouth. It could be months before he saw Ann and his baby son.

'There's a yawl putting off from *Seahorse*, sir. It's rowing towards us.'

Holbrooke stopped and watched the approaching boat from the top of the ladder as it made its laborious way against the wind. It didn't stop at *Unicorn* or *Vestale*; whatever the news it was evidently intended for *Argonaut*. A midshipman stood in the stern sheets, his hand on the coxswain's shoulder for balance.

The quartermaster made a trumpet of his hands.

'Boat ahoy!'

The midshipman swept his arm in a horizontal motion and shook his head, he wasn't coming alongside.

'May I speak to Captain Holbrooke?'

'The boat's lying off, sir. A midshipman wishes to speak to you.'

The quartermaster smiled, he thought he knew the message already. Holbrooke walked to the gunwale and raised his hat to the boat.

'Captain Holbrooke sir! Captain Smith's compliments. I'm bound for the Cattewater and can't wait upon you, but he thought you would want to know immediately. Your orders will arrive from the port commissioner before noon. You're to sail for Portsmouth and there to refit before rejoining the squadron. He wishes you a pleasant voyage and a happy homecoming, sir.'

***

CHAPTER SEVEN

Domestic Bliss

Monday, Nineteenth of January 1761.
Mulberry House, Wickham.

The hard sleet had swept all day across the square in vicious waves from the north but now it had paused, and the wind had dropped. The afternoon sun, long past its trivial zenith, was just touching the front of Mulberry house and flooding the parlour with light. This was Ann's favourite place to sit on these cold winter afternoons. If she drew her chair close to the window she could see the square with its busy people all coming and going. Wednesdays were best, when the market stalls brought a new energy and purpose to the town. On market days Ann always walked out onto the square, regardless of the weather.

Today, Ann had a particular objective in sitting beside the window. Her husband had left for the navy yard at Portsmouth in the first grey light of the day, and if all was well he should return before dark, and that was only two hours away. Little Edward was asleep in the nursery and was unlikely to wake for another hour or so and in any case the nurse could deal with him when he made his presence known after the manner of babies. For now, Ann could just sit and wait for George.

She heard the rumble of the coach's iron wheel rims, then the sharp sounds of the horses' hooves on the cobble stones, followed by the coachman's gruff shout that brought them to a halt. She could see the children running towards the house, eager as always to be part of the glory of a two-horse carriage delivering a real naval captain to his home.

'Captain Holbrooke's carriage has arrived Ma'am,' said Polly with a hasty curtsey.

'Thank you, Polly.'

Ann was always amused at Polly's changed behaviour

when the master of the house was coming home. She and Ann had more-or-less grown up together; Polly had been Ann's father's servant, and she had followed Ann when she married George Holbrooke. When Holbrooke was away they were more like friends than mistress and servant, but with every mile and every hour that heralded the master's return, her demeanour grew more and more correct, culminating in what she imagined was the behaviour of the perfect servant as he stepped across the threshold.

Holbrooke was frozen to the bone; he could hardly imagine how cold Billy Stiles was, having been exposed to the harsh north wind in his face for the past two hours. But Billy wasn't too concerned with elegance of dress; he had not had to visit the officers of the navy yard, nor be piped aboard his ship in the basin. Billy had layers and layers of good South Downs wool below a waxed canvas coat with doubled cloth at the shoulders and collar. He wore a woollen cap comforter below his only real badge of office, his crowning glory, an enormous tricorn hat that had to be tied down against the wind. Billy Stiles was a part-owner of the coach and when Holbrooke was at home it was reserved – at a substantial retainer – for the captain's own use. Billy settled the horses, then with the reins still grasped in his hand, he jumped down to open the carriage door.

'You look frozen, dear, Polly will bring some tea. Was it a harrowing day?'

Holbrooke stood before the fire, letting the heat sink into his bones. He knew what Ann meant when she asked about his day. What she really wanted to ask, but shied away from for want of appearing dependent, was how long *Argonaut* would be in the yard, and consequently how long she would have her husband at home before he had to sail away again. She had not mastered the fine art of asking that question in a straightforward manner without either sounding accusing or pathetic.

'Oh, not so bad. Shorrock has the ship under control and the master attendant has already given his estimate of the work.'

He looked sideways at Ann, wondering how he could soften the blow. For some reason she had convinced herself that he would have at least a month at home, and nothing he had been able to say had shifted that optimistic view.

'I'm sorry, but it will be only two weeks. They have a stock of topmasts for my class of ship and the shipwrights believe they can patch up the shot holes in a week. Of course the decks and gunwales must be made good before the topmast is shipped and the rigging set up, so a week in the basin and a week alongside the sheer hulk and then we'll have to be away.'

Ann nodded slowly. She hadn't told George that his father had visited that morning, along with David Chalmers who was lodging with him while the ship was in the yard, and between them they had given her a more realistic estimate of the repair time. So Holbrooke was wrong in his estimate of his wife's expectations; Ann had been expecting to hear two weeks, had been prepared for a bare week, but all along had still hoped for a month.

'Two weeks. Well, we'll have to make the best of it. I just wish it was spring, rather than this interminable winter.'

Holbrooke could see that Ann was starting to descend into morbidity. He knew that it wasn't unusual after a first child was born, and he grasped at something to cheer her.

'How is Edward? He looked full of energy before I left.'

'Oh, he'll be due to awake any moment…'

As if on cue, the sound of a baby's wail drifted down from the nursery on the first floor, closely followed by the sound of hurrying footsteps as the nurse rushed to sooth the little fellow. Ann gave him an apologetic smile then walked swiftly towards the stairs.

It was impossible not to notice how involved Ann was in looking after their son. Even with a full-time nurse, she reacted to every sound from the nursery, and he knew that she would be gone until whatever the baby needed – food, a change of underclothes, comforting, or just company –

had been satisfied and he was once more asleep. Not for the first time he felt redundant. Ann would bring Edward to see his father when whatever ailed him had been squared away, and for half an hour they would be happy, until the next crisis in the baby's life. He stretched out in the chair that Ann had vacated, and idly watched the people in the Square. He'd brought *Argonaut* into Portsmouth on Friday, after a trying passage up-channel. They'd barely lost sight of Smeaton's Tower and hadn't even raised Start Point before a hard squall brought a dramatic change in the wind. Six days it had taken them to reach Spithead, six days of perpetually foul winds, and it was only Fairview's skill in working the tides that had allowed *Argonaut* to weather Bembridge Ledge at last and run down to her anchorage on the Friday evening. After a brief meeting with the master attendant they were in the basin on the Saturday afternoon tide, just in time for all work in the yard to cease for the Sunday. Still, news of his arrival would have reached the Admiralty secretary on Saturday, along with a report of *Unicorn* and *Seahorse* and the French prize. If their Lordships felt it necessary to send out another frigate or two to reinforce Hawke, then those unknown ships would be getting the bad news about now. All this passed through his mind as his fatigue and the heat of the fire, and Polly's tea had its inevitable effect and his chin started to nod towards his chest.

'Captain Holbrooke, sir.'

Polly's voice startled him into wakefulness.

'There's a letter come by courier, sir, and the man is asking for your receipt, otherwise I wouldn't have disturbed you.'

Holbrooke shook away the sleep and glanced out of the window to where a light carriage stood in front of the door, with the ominous, looming figure of an Admiralty courier peering back at him.

'Oh, bring him inside, Polly. When we've finished you can offer him a cup of tea and a bite in the kitchen and take something out to the coachman too. They've come all the way from London in this weather.'

Holbrooke straightened himself as he tried desperately to imagine what communication from their Lordships to the captain of a mere sixth rate frigate was so urgent.

This courier was as inscrutable as all the rest. Holbrooke knew a few of them by sight, but his was a new face.

'From the secretary, sir. If you would sign here.'

The courier held out a receipt, evidently expecting it to be signed immediately, before Holbrooke had read the letter.

Holbrooke busied himself with pen and ink, all the while wondering what was inside the letter. It was evidently something important, or sensitive, otherwise it would have come by a regular express, or even by the usual postal service. An Admiralty courier was a different level of expense, and even assuming the man had business in Portsmouth, the cost and inconvenience of a side trip to Wickham was not inconsiderable.

The business done, Polly took the courier away into the kitchen, leaving Holbrooke to open the letter in peace. He turned it over, trying to guess its contents. His reason told him that it was nothing to be concerned about, but there was still that niggling doubt about his action against the two French ships-of-the-line, and the horrible possibility that he'd be sent to Sumatra in lieu of *Seahorse*. And he was already regretting offering refreshment to the courier. Polly was hardly the right sort of servant for a house like this, nor did she have the manner to support a post-captain's dignity. He knew that she would be flirting outrageously by now, and the courier would return to Whitehall with tales of Holbrooke's disorderly establishment. He needed something along the lines of a butler. A man of some substance at least, who would know how to deal with Admiralty officials. His life was nothing if not complicated.

With a sigh he took a paper knife and broke through the hard wax seal. The letter wasn't even in an envelope, it had just been folded and sealed, so its contents couldn't be very confidential after all. He smoothed out the creases and held it up to the light from the window. It was in the secretary's own hand, not one of his clerks. There were the usual brief salutations, then the body of the letter.

Admiral the Honourable John Forbes has directed me to request that you wait upon him at the Admiralty on Wednesday next at two o'clock in the afternoon. Your receipt of this letter will be sufficient acknowledgement.

That was all. No explanation, and then there was that assumption that he would agree to travel to London for the meeting. He felt that he'd been trapped by the demand for a receipt before he'd even opened the letter. He would never in this world have been summoned like this if he was not such a junior captain, or if he came from an established family. Was he being treated with disrespect? It was possible, but then there was no remedy for it. A command from an admiral of the blue and a commissioner of the Admiralty to boot couldn't be ignored. He would just have to compose himself and obey the peremptory order. He could take the express coach tomorrow and spend the night in London. A visit to his prize agent and his bank would be worthwhile, and he could catch up on the latest naval gossip in one of the coffee houses.

Nevertheless, he couldn't help wondering why he had been summoned. Was it a censure? Probably not, unless Gambier had made a particular point about the action off the Penmarks. In any case it wasn't likely that a letter penned off Ushant could have reached the Admiralty and been considered, and action taken, in such a short space of time. Most probably it was some particular duty that required a personal briefing.

His heart beat faster as he considered the possibilities. He had already tired of watching the Vilaine estuary, and if he didn't have to come under Gambier's command again, it would be all to the good. But what could it be?

***

Ann was true to Holbrooke's expectation and shortly after the courier left, she arrived bearing Edward in her arms, with the nurse close behind, fussing with the vast number of garments and sheets that entombed him. Holbrooke had to admit to himself – privately of course – that his son wasn't a very exceptional nor even interesting specimen of humanity. He was at his best now: cleaned, fed, warm and reasonably alert and he was offered to Holbrooke to hold.

'Do sit down first, George, support his head now. No! not like that.'

Ann looked alarmed and nudged her husband's arms into the approved shape.

'Keep him wrapped against the draught.'

There was no point in resisting these instructions. In all probability they were meant well, although they had that whiff of a wife putting her husband in his place, an assertion of dominance. He held the little fellow close against his chest and watched the wide blue eyes staring at him with what looked like a deep, unfathomable intelligence. They seemed to say that although he was physically helpless, he was perfectly conscious of what was being done to nurture him, and one day, in his own good time, he'd show the world what a man could do.

Yet all good things come to an end. The light of intelligence faded from his eyes and soon Edward's soft snores told Holbrooke that he'd slipped back into that blessed state of sleep. The nurse gently took the babe from his father, and with a perilously balanced curtsey, left to take him back to his cradle.

'What was in the letter from the courier, George?'

Ann would never quiz her husband in front of the nurse, even though she had been casting covert glances at the folded letter ever since she'd come back into the room.

'I have to go up to town tomorrow, dear. A meeting with Admiral Forbes. I really don't know what he has to say to me.'

Ann's shoulders slumped and her mouth fell, but she recovered quickly. She was well aware that she looked unattractive when she sulked.

'I've heard you speak of him. You've met him before, I remember.'

'I have. In fact I believe it is he who gave me the push I needed to be made post.'

'Then he's a friend, is that so?'

'Well, as much as anyone in that position can be my friend, yes. However his friendship is conditional, I believe, on my success as a captain. None of the commissioners will tolerate failure, not in a great war like this, and as you know I have no family interest at all.'

'But is this normal, for a captain to be summoned to the Admiralty?'

'Not captains of frigates that are already allocated to a squadron, not at all. Normally all dealings would be through Admiral Hawke and whatever commodore or senior captain is immediately above me. Their Lordships would be far too busy if they had to individually instruct the captains of every one of the three hundred odd ships in the navy. No, I really don't know what it's about, but I fear I'll be away for three days and two nights, at least.'

'London…,'

Ann's eyes took on a secret intelligence.

'…there are a few things that you could pick up for me while you're there. I can give you the names of the shops and write a list so that there is no doubt.'

***

CHAPTER EIGHT

A Particular Duty

Wednesday, Twenty-First of January 1761.
The Admiralty, Whitehall.

The dark clouds had cleared with the dawn and London's overnight snow had turned to a thick, grey slush that clung to the horses' hooves so that they danced as they pulled the hackney coach, creating an uncomfortable skittish motion. The slush was so thick that it encased the wheels, releasing a disgusting spray of part-frozen water mixed with horse dung that covered the coach's windows. Holbrooke couldn't see anything of the world outside, and he didn't dare open a window for fear of covering himself in the filthy mess. The four wheels of a true coach meant that the spray from the front wheels was directed up to the windows, where in a cheaper but less comfortable two-wheeled hackney carriage the spray would mostly have been directed to the rear. He would be charged nearly double the fare for the dubious advantage of the extra wheels. It was like being entombed in a square box that rattled and vibrated to a beat all of its own. A stiff blow off Ushant was a delight compared to this stinking coffin.

The coach drew to a halt. It could have been anywhere for all Holbrooke knew.

'The Admiralty, sir,' shouted the coachman. 'That'll be two shillings, your honour.'

The coachman didn't deign to alight to open Holbrooke's door. He knew the routine at the Admiralty and the messengers who always waited by the entrance could expect tuppence for holding the door for a post-captain, and a whole sixpence for waiting on him until he was called by whomever he had come to see.

Tuppence it was, but it was money well-spent because the messenger kept the path clear and clean, briskly sweeping the odd puddles in his way, and Holbrooke was able to walk dry-shod from the coach to the door. He arrived twenty minutes early for his appointment with no more than a slight dampness to his coat. Even that was taken care off by the officious messenger who, sensing a promotion from copper to silver, had attached himself to Holbrooke like a limpet and had carefully spread his cloak in front of the fire.

There were only three other sea officers in the waiting room, two lieutenants and a midshipman or master's mate, and Holbrooke knew none of them. To a man they looked like supplicants with no fixed appointment, and they waited there as perhaps they had done for a number of days past in the hope that one of the commissioners would see them when they had a gap in their schedule. They had no love for Holbrooke, who was clearly a very young post-captain and evidently had a ship or was so wealthy with prize money that he could afford to shower sixpences among the messengers and clerks. Nevertheless, they stood when he entered, bowed politely, and shuffled along the seats to leave the best – the closest to the fire – for this god-like newcomer.

He settled himself to wait, trying not to look at his fellow officers, but acutely aware of their envious gaze.

It had been over a year since he had met Admiral Forbes, and on that occasion the admiral had been instrumental in Holbrooke's promotion to post-captain. Perhaps without that influence Holbrooke would still be a commander and wondering how long he would be employed before the pressure of newly promoted officers from below and the impenetrable promotion barrier above forced him sideways into an early retirement. He was indebted to Forbes, but he also knew that Forbes held the interests of the navy above all other concerns, and he would be ruthless if he felt that Holbrooke had not fulfilled his trust.

His performance as a post-captain, Holbrooke was well aware, was a mixed bag. His ship had been part of the squadron that had defeated the attempt to invade the north of the country, and that was a significant and very public success. On the other hand, he'd been sent to capture the single French frigate that had escaped the battle off the Isle of man, and he had let it slip through his fingers. And, of course, Gambier's report could have reached the Admiralty by now. It would have passed through Hawke's hands, and he could hope that the commander-in-chief would have drawn some of the vindictive sting from it, but nevertheless he was worried.

'Admiral Forbes will see you now, sir.'

Holbrooke was caught by surprise and knew that he must have jumped. That would have shattered the illusion for the other three officers; he was as nervous as they were.

***

Forbes hadn't changed. He was still the same bluff, forthright sea officer that Holbrooke remembered, and the admiral rose to greet his guest with evident pleasure. Holbrooke had a moment to notice another man, seated unobtrusively in a corner by the window. He was dressed all in black, even his buttons were covered in some dark material, and the tiny scrap of white stock at his throat gave him the look of a clergyman. A clerk? No, this was a man of substance. A secretary then? Perhaps, but that wasn't quite right, and Holbrooke could speculate no further as Forbes demanded his attention.

'You've been busy since we last met, Captain Holbrooke. Captain Chester's report of that affair with the French expedition was most complimentary. The Lord knows we needed that victory, what with it being so long since the navy had anything substantial to show for all these new ships.'

Holbrooke couldn't help grinning. His name had been in all the broadsheets as they trumpeted the defeat of King Louis' last throw of the dice. Of course, if their Lordships felt any exasperation at him missing the last ship of the French squadron, they wouldn't have let it show outside of the Admiralty boardroom. It would have been forgotten now in any case, and if Forbes even remembered he wasn't showing it.

'Did you suffer much in your scrape with those two French third rates?'

Ah, so that was how it was being portrayed.

'Well, sir. I threw *Argonaut* into their path hoping to grapple one of them at least and allow Captain Gambier's squadron to run down to us. However, they shot away my fore topmast and I couldn't hold my luff. I lost three dead and six wounded, sir.'

'That was a good decision to send you to Portsmouth. Hawke sent three ships in after you left Plymouth Sound, each needing topmasts. One of them would have been disappointed if you had already been served.'

Holmes studied Holbrooke critically.

'Admiral Hawke suggested that you may have been hurt yourself, but I see no sign… Ah, you have a bandage under your shirt, sir!'

Holbrooke had hoped that it didn't show. He'd reduced it to the minimum turns that would stop any seepage, but evidently even that modest bulk was noticeable.

'A splinter raked my chest, sir. I'll be good as new before *Argonaut* is ready for sea again.'

'Well, that's what your ribs are for, I'm told. They sacrifice themselves to protect the vital organs. Evidently they did their duty well. So there's nothing preventing you – I mean you personally – taking *Argonaut* to sea as soon as you have your topmast and gunwales?'

Was this an opportunity to beg some shore leave? He had spent little enough time with his son, and he was certain that Ann would be delighted if he had a month or so at home. There must be plenty of itinerate captains who would be delighted to take a nearly-new sixth rate to sea while its owner recuperated. It would be so easy; the door had been opened a crack and all he had to do was give it a push.

But he couldn't do it. His desire to please Ann pulled him one way while his duty and his urgent need to consolidate his position in the navy pulled him in the opposite direction. And then, he wasn't so sure that his presence in Wickham, hanging around his home for weeks on end with nothing to do but irritate the ladies, who were far more concerned with little Edward, would be so welcome, not after the first day or two. And then again, Forbes had sent for him for what looked like a particular employment, and the thought of disappointing the admiral cast all other considerations aside.

'Nothing at all, sir. I'm entirely at your disposal.'

Forbes studied the much younger man. He could guess at the conflicting loyalties that lay behind that simple statement. Forbes had married late, only three years ago, and his lady wife was in the last few days of her confinement. The doctor said that they were to expect twins. Already the house had been taken over by the paraphernalia of child rearing and he felt less and less comfortable at home. He could barely imagine the full horror of having an actual baby or two in the house. In his case he couldn't get away from it, as his home was only a twenty-minute walk or ten-minute ride from the Admiralty. Recently he'd found himself spending longer and longer at work…

'Very well. In that case, may I introduce my colleague?'

The man in black rose from his chair. He was of middling height, but he stooped, making him look shorter than he was. Holbrooke noticed a walking cane that he guessed was more a necessity than an ornament. It too was black from its tip to its toe. He bowed, and Holbrooke caught the brief pained look as his back bent, a tightening of the lips, no more, but a certain indication of a severe medical condition. He was suddenly glad that he had made light of his own wound.

'Mister Sawtree commands an office that concerns itself with matters in France. Intelligence you may call it, but the office has no real name, and is normally referred to merely as the discretionary funds department. Now, before we go any further, you must understand that whatever is said in this room, and hereafter on this subject, must be treated in the utmost confidence. You may not discuss it with your officers, your wife or your father; is that quite clear?'

Holbrooke gulped. Of all the possible reasons for being called to town, this one had not even reached the edges of his conscious thought. He had heard of the department of course, and he knew in a vague way that the navy gathered information on its enemies – and sometimes its friends – by clandestine means. It had never occurred to him that he might be involved.

Sawtree cleared his throat.

'It's a pleasure to meet you, Captain Holbrooke; you will understand if I sit. It may be convenient if you do also.'

Holbrooke sat abruptly. He realised that he had almost been guilty of a want of consideration, keeping Sawtree standing.

***

'You will readily understand, Captain, that His Majesty's navy has occasion to require information from within France that cannot be gathered by the conventional means: newspaper reports, letters from friendly embassies, and other more-or-less open sources. To gather that information, we need from time-to-time to covertly *insert* people into France, and to equally covertly *extract* them once their duty is done.'

So much Holbrooke guessed, but he had always understood that it was work for cutters and other small craft that could approach the wilder, less populated coasts unnoticed and be away before the dawn. A frigate was too big for that kind of work.

'I can see what you are thinking – it is my profession after all to divine people's thoughts…'

Sawtree smiled briefly, an austere smile that differed from his earlier grimace of pain only in the fractional change in the pull of the muscles around his lips.

'…and you are correct. If I had to place an agent in Normandy or Picardy, Admiral Forbes would provide a cutter which would be altogether more suitable. However, in this case my target destination is the Atlantic coast of Brittany, and without a larger ship in support, a cutter would be too vulnerable to the weather. I could of course place it under Admiral Hawke's wing, but then there would be too many men who knew of the operation. What I need is a frigate that can act independently, with a cutter assigned as a tender for the inshore work.'

Holbrooke was desperately trying to keep up with this flow of revelations, but his mind kept wandering off to consider the technical problems of wind and tide, of moonless nights and unfamiliar coasts.

'Your orders – Admiralty orders – will make it clear to any senior officers who are tempted to interfere, that you are to be left alone.'

Forbes hadn't taken his eyes off Holbrooke while Sawtree was speaking. Admiralty orders, that meant that he wasn't subject to the authority of any commander-in-chief, nor was he to be delayed or given any other tasks. Holbrooke noticed that he had not been asked whether he was happy to be involved in this kind of operation; it had been taken as read that he would do it. Whatever happened to the notion that an officer could decline to carry out clandestine operations? Lost to the exigencies of war, perhaps, along with so many other cherished prerogatives.

'The cutter will have a lieutenant in command, I imagine, sir.'

'Not in this case, Holbrooke. It will be a tender to your frigate and under your command, but I'll give you a good master's mate. Oh, you explain the rest, Sawtree.'

Sawtree stared at the window, marshalling his thoughts, then he leaned forward as though he was preparing to impart a confidence.

'If an operation is carried forward successfully, then there is no need for anyone other than the agent to set foot in France. The cutter lies off at a navigationally safe distance, allowing for wind and tide, but that's your business, Captain

Holbrooke. If it is an insertion then a small boat is sent in, the agent jumps ashore and the boat returns. If it is an extraction, a system of lantern signals will tell you when the agent has arrived at the appointed place, and a boat is sent in to bring him off. That is what happens nine times out of ten. However, if something goes wrong, and it's almost always during an extraction, there may be a need to send a small party ashore to help the agent to the boat. It's important that any party that lands is commanded by a commissioned officer, in case of capture by French forces, and that will be you, Captain Holbrooke. That part of your orders, which is to be read here and will not leave the building, must be committed to memory. However, it states very clearly that unless there are particular circumstances that keep you in your ship, you are to embark in the cutter, and you are to personally command any party from your ship that lands in France.'

Holbrooke felt the weight of both men's gaze and tried – unsuccessfully, he imagined – to look as though he was quite familiar with these arrangements. He grasped for something useful to say, but his invention failed him.

'You may wonder why you were selected for this, Holbrooke.'

Forbes didn't wait for a comment.

'We needed someone who has shown a certain flexibility in his approach to his duties. Now don't take that as a criticism, it's a quality that is not evident in all post-captains. Commodore Howe reported that you made a successful reconnaissance of Cancale Bay when you commanded that little Dutch sloop, and you performed well in that debacle at Saint-Cast, and the expedition to Niagara, of course. Very few captains have had such a varied experience of war.'

Holbrooke nodded. It was a compliment, of a sort, but he was privately dismayed at having the reputation of an *irregular* post-captain. Such men couldn't be trusted with command of a ship-of-the-line, where the principal duty was to hold a position in the line of battle and batter away at the enemy without any independent thought or action.

'May I ask what the agent's task will be, sir?'

Forbes and Sawtree exchanged glances, and Holbrooke noticed that it was Sawtree who nodded his assent and Forbes who spoke.

'What I am about to tell you is covered by my previous insistence that not a word of this leaves this room. I assume you are content with that restriction, sir?'

Holbrooke nodded. What on earth was he getting himself into? But of course none of this was of his choosing, and really he had no choice at all.

'It can't have passed your notice that Admiral Hawke has been sounding and surveying Quiberon Bay and Belle Isle. The conclusion is obvious, that an action is contemplated in that area. Whether it is against the mainland or an island, and where and when the attack will be launched, is not a subject for today, and frankly it hasn't yet been decided. But in any case there is an urgent need to know what French forces are in the area and more particularly what movements are afoot. Our agent – he uses the name Benjamin Duval, and that will suffice for now – is the descendent of a French family that left the country after the Huguenots were suppressed, and he has returned often. Mister Duval can move around relatively freely and meet his contacts to gather the information that we need. He will spend no more than a week ashore, probably less.'

Forbes continued the narrative.

'You can perhaps imagine how critical this information is to the force that is being brought together for the expedition. You'll have seen them at Spithead and St. Helen's, no doubt.'

He had seen them, a strong squadron of ships-of-the-line and a few assorted bomb ketches, frigates and sloops. They were mostly anchored at Spithead within easy reach of the dockyard at Portsmouth. There was nothing unusual in a gathering of men-of-war off Portsmouth, but it was the scores of transports and storeships at St. Helen's, off the northeast tip of the Isle of Wight, that had really caught his eye.

'The army has no appetite for a full-scale landing on the French coast unless they can expect at least a week ashore before a French field army arrives, and I can't say that I blame them. An island is a different matter, and we can seal that off from reinforcement without too much difficulty. So a certain knowledge of the movements of the French regiments is of the first importance.'

There was a silence interrupted only by Sawtree shifting in his chair. Evidently whatever his injury was it caused discomfort both in standing and sitting.

'So now you know, Captain Holbrooke, and I hope you don't mind if I stand and take a few steps.'

Holbrooke looked away as Sawtree walked backwards and forwards, his steps becoming firmer with each turn at the door and the window.

'Well, Holbrooke, there you have it. You can use the clerk's office next door to read the orders and Mister Sawtree will brief you on a few more details. I'll send your covering orders – not the secret ones – down to you when Lord Anson has signed them. I regret that you won't meet Mister Duval until he arrives at Portsmouth, and Mister Sawtree will communicate with you to arrange his embarkation. Your cutter is *Oyster*. She's at Portsmouth being made ready, and John Finch is her master. He's been on that coast for about a year with Hawke, and he knows it well. Oh, and I've informed Admiral Holburne that you are to be away by Friday the thirtieth, without fail. There's a new moon on the sixth of next month and every day that you delay after that will render the mission more hazardous. Now, will you be in town tonight?'

Holbrooke smiled. He had hoped to spend only one night on London, but Ann's commissions at the shops would require a whole day to fulfil, so he would do what he could this afternoon and the remainder in the morning before he caught the midday express for Portsmouth.

'Then would you join me at my club for supper? My home is no fit place for gentlemen, what with Lady Mary near her time and the place full of women who hustle me from place to place. I've half a mind to take a room at the club for the next few nights. What do you think, Holbrooke? You've been through this recently, I understand.'

'Oh, a room at the club, sir, no doubt about it, and I'm entirely at your disposal this evening.'

'Then White's at six o'clock, and I look forward to your company.'

***

CHAPTER NINE

A Moonless Night

Friday, Sixth of February 1761.
Armed Cutter Oyster, Anse de Bénodet, Brittany.

'Two fathoms, sir. I'll anchor here with your permission.'

Holbrooke was impressed. Finch had brought his cutter into the bay behind the Glenan Isles on the darkest of nights with not a glimmer of moon showing; the few stars that came and went behind the clouds shed no light at all. It was accomplished on dead reckoning – that most fallible of navigational methods – and the lead line. His knowledge of this area was truly astonishing, and it could not have been gained by merely cruising through. He must have run lines of soundings at every opportunity, and the obvious familiarity that his people had with the lead line confirmed it.

These little cutters could tack with their jib sheets hauled to windward and lie quite happily with their head four points off the wind, all in a few seconds. Holbrooke was aware of the helm orders and the almost instantaneous quiet that came over the deck, but his whole attention was taken up in imagining their position. The mouth of the River Odet that ran through Quimper must be somewhere to the north, and the beach that they had chosen should be to the nor'west.

'Heave to for a moment, Mister Finch. How far from the shore are we, do you think?'

'A little under a mile, sir, eight cables perhaps. The lead was bringing up sand and shells until we crossed the five fathom line about five minutes ago and now it's pure, white sand and two fathoms. You may have noticed that I stood to the west a little until we reached the two fathom line on that side, so I'm confident that this is the centre of the bay.'

Holbrooke didn't immediately reply.

'The tide is setting towards the river estuary, sir.'

Finch was smiling but he clearly wanted a quick decision before he would have to tack out of the bay to safety and make the approach again.

'Very well, Mister Finch, you can drop the anchor. Don't veer more than you need, I imagine six fathoms will suffice.'

'Aye-aye sir. I'll have a man keep his foot on the cable once the anchor's set.'

Finch busied himself anchoring the cutter. The short length of cable was necessary, even though it risked the anchor dragging, because Holbrooke was determined that they should be able to get underway quickly if they were discovered. There was a moderately strong spring tide sweeping them inshore, but a sensible seaman would be able to feel the vibrations in his foot if the anchor started to break loose from the sandy bottom.

***

Holbrooke stepped down into the yawl and took his seat in the stern. He stared into the darkness, but he could see nothing, only the steady beat of the surf on the sandy shore ahead gave him any idea of direction. He'd brought his own yawl for the landing. The longboat was too large, and *Oyster's* little jolly-boat was too small for his taste. The yawl had the added advantage that it was *Argonaut's* boat, and it was only natural that his own coxswain, Dawson, would take the tiller. There were six oarsmen, a leadsman, a coxswain, Holbrooke and Duval, who sat shrouded in his cloak, looking eagerly towards where he imagined the shore would be.

Holbrooke didn't envy the agent's task. He had contacts ashore, he assured Holbrooke, although of course he gave no details, but those contacts didn't know which day or where he would land. That was a naval decision based principally on the wind and how quickly they could make the passage from Portsmouth. In fact, the wind had come steadily from the east for a week and *Argonaut* had made a fast run down-channel and now she was standing off and on to the west of the Glenan Isles, sheltered from the easterly wind. It had been a week of wintery weather. The wind from the continent brought fine clear skies but with a bite that shivered even the most hardened mariner.

'One fathom less a foot.'

The leadsman's voice came in a hoarse whisper. Despite his title, he was armed with a twelve-foot sounding pole rather than a lead line. It was handier in a boat, and quieter, but it was limited to two fathoms, which should be enough for this night's work.

The wind was as near perfect as it could be, and this bay was sheltered against anything other than a strong southerly. If he had been forced to postpone the insertion for more than two or three days, it would be another four weeks before Duval could be put ashore. *Insertion*: he was becoming used to these terms that Sawtree used and had to admit that they aptly described the operation. *Insertion* and *extraction* called to mind a fine, surgical procedure, thoroughly planned and executed with cool precision. That was all very well in the comfort of *Argonaut's* great cabin, but as always, everything in the navy came down to seamen getting cold and wet.

Duval was to meet his contact – or was there more than one contact? – at a remote house to the south of Quimper, a regional centre about ten miles from the beach. He knew the road well and even on this dark night he was confident that he could reach the town before dawn. He had started to say something about this being his ancestral home and hoping to return one day but had stopped abruptly when he realised he was talking too much. Holbrooke knew nothing about agents and their contacts, but he could guess at their loneliness, their thirst for straightforward human contact without fear of betrayal. Perhaps it was normal for them to want to confide in relative strangers before they cast themselves, alone, on a hostile shore. If that was the case then Duval must have been aware of how close he had come to indiscretion. There was one particular incident that stuck in Holbrooke's mind. When he had mentioned that he had commanded *Kestrel* and that he had landed on French shores before, Duval looked startled and open his mouth to say something but closed it firmly before a word had been uttered.

'A fathom less two feet.'

Holbrooke could feel the swell as it was forced upwards into waves by the gently shelving seabed. He could feel Dawson tensing beside him, ready to keep the boat running straight at the beach. It would be a dismal end to the night if the yawl was to overturn before it reached the shore. Finch had assured him that he had been this way a few times before and had noted the surf on the beach. He was certain that today, with this wind, it would be safe.

'Easy starboard.'

Dawson's voice carried no further than the oarsmen. He had sensed a current pushing them to northeast. It was the flooding tide, almost certainly, but it would affect the stern as the water shallowed and would tend to swing the bows to larboard. He was using the power of the oars to compensate before it dragged the yawl off course.

'Half a fathom, sir.'

They could wade ashore now, if the boat capsized. That was no good to Duval, however. He needed to be dry-shod for his long walk and a person wet from the waist down could expire of cold during the night. Apart from those considerations, a man dressed as a gentleman with soaking breeches and sand-encrusted coat tails would arouse suspicion. Duval would be carried ashore by the stroke oar, a massive able seaman who would find his weight inconsiderable.

'Pull larboard.'

Dawson was keeping the boat perpendicular to the waves. Holbrooke could feel the stern rising as the sea ran under the keel to break on the beach. First he heard a deep bass rumble as the wave fell onto the shore, followed by a prolonged hiss as it receded, dragging the top layer of sand out to sea.

Treacherous Moon

'Stow the pole,' Dawson called quietly.

The water was too shallow for soundings to make any sense as the boat was lifted two feet on each wave.

There was a bump, clearly felt through the timbers, as the yawl's stern dropped behind a passing wave and struck the hard sand, but the boat was still moving forward. The shoreline was marked by a dim glow from the modest surf. Holbrooke fancied that he could see dunes at the back of the beach.

Another bump. Now the forefoot was grinding in the sand and the boat was almost stopped.

'Boat your oars. Over you go bowmen, drag the bows around to larboard.'

The water must be freezing but the two men at the bow oars had been forewarned for this task. They leaped over the side into water up to their thighs and hauled the bows around until they were pointing out to sea.

It was strangely calm now. The waves really were quite small, they had just seemed larger in the dark. Holbrooke looked around but could see nothing, not the faintest glimmer of light anywhere. That was as expected. The nearest houses were half a mile away in each direction and even if they were inhabited at this time of year the people would all be in bed with their candles and lanterns extinguished.

'Are you ready?'

Duval grasped Holbrooke's hand in the darkness, betraying the nervousness that he had tried so hard to hide, and in a moment he was taken up by the stroke oar.

Why he did it he couldn't tell, but Holbrooke grasped the seaman's shoulder to stop him wading off, then settled his pistols in his pockets, climbed over the gunwale and dropped onto the hard-packed sand of the beach. His trousers were soaked in an instant and he knew that his servant would have to spend days getting the salt out of his shoes, but he felt the need to see this anonymous man on his way at least as far as the dunes.

The water was cold, but the wind was far, far colder and Holbrooke had to fight to stop his teeth chattering, and it was a hard walk to the dunes. When covered by water the sand packed hard, but where it had not yet been touched by the flooding tide it had been dried by the keen wind to a powdery texture, making every step a struggle. The sand clung to his trousers and found its way into his shoes. It only took five minutes but by the time the dunes appeared, Holbrooke was exhausted, and he could feel that already his ankles were rubbed raw where the sand had ground away at his flesh. Just a few more steps, then they stopped. Holbrooke looked hard at Duval's face, expecting some sort of trepidation at starting out into enemy territory. But then, this man probably still thought of France as his own country, and a walk of eight miles in the dark as no more than a stroll in his own back yard.

'Two nights from now at nine o'clock to ten o'clock and every night after that for three nights. The boat will be here, on this beach. You have your lantern?'

Duval wordlessly parted his cloak to show the small lantern that could be fitted with screens to direct its glow.

'Show a light when you reach the beach. If I see no light, I won't send in the boat.'

Holbrooke was deliberately looking stern. He wanted there to be no doubt that he'd obey Sawtree's instructions to the letter. No lantern meant that the agent was not on the beach, or it was too dangerous to send a boat.

'Yes, sir. I fully intend to make the first appointment, but bear with me if I have to revert to a later day.'

'Yes, of course. But Wednesday will be the last night. After that the chances of our being seen increase with every night of the moon's waxing.'

Duval nodded and looked as though he was about to say something more, but if that was the case, he changed his mind and just shook Holbrooke's hand again before turning away and setting himself to climb the low dunes. Holbrooke saw his heels disappearing in the blackness and heard the soft sound of the dislodged sand running down the face of the dune, then he was gone.

He sat down and removed his shoes and cautiously touched the places where his skin had been rubbed away. He felt curiously safe here, enveloped by the pitch darkness. A few stars showed through the lazy clouds, but their illumination rather served to emphasise the blackness. There was no sign of the boat and of course Dawson wouldn't be able to see him at all. He thought about Duval, now presumably striking towards the road. It was a good plan. The rising tide would erase any signs of the boat landing, and this keen wind would blow away any trace of footsteps in the soft sand. There was almost no chance of a passing local, not on a cold February night with no moon, and only a betrayal could ruin the insertion. But of course, a betrayal was hardly possible. Holbrooke had chosen the landing site out of a selection of a dozen only the day before, so nobody ashore could possibly know when or where the viper was to be released into their bosom. Extraction was another matter altogether. In one sense it was less hazardous for Duval, who would be fleeing towards safety rather than stepping boldly towards danger. However, the chance of betrayal was hugely increased. These unknown contacts could guess at the day that the extraction would take place and they could follow Duval to the beach, alerting units of the French army or the militia. Well, he would make the rendezvous if it was humanly possible, but he would be on his guard.

With his shoes in his hand he waited a few more minutes and listened. Nothing. He didn't know what he expected or even feared. A pistol shot perhaps, or the sound of galloping hooves, but it was silent, save for the wind across the sand and the waves on the beach. He turned and walked quickly back to the boat. His feet were warmer without the shoes, and the raw patches hardly hurt at all.

He remembered other days on French beaches. At Cancale where he had found the hidden French batteries before the landings, and again at Saint-Cast where he had nearly lost his life to French bayonets as he struggled in the surf. His friend Major Hans Albach of the Austrian Artillery was there on both occasions, allied with England's enemy of course, but still and always his friend.

He'd ordered a tot of rum for each of the boat's crew when they returned to the cutter; perhaps he'd have one himself.

***

CHAPTER TEN

Extraction

Sunday, Eighth of February 1761.
Argonaut's Yawl, Anse de Bénodet, Brittany.

The two-day old moon made a shocking difference. Its right-handed sickle hung low over the flat, windswept land that sloped down to the sea where the land's underwater extension formed the deadly rocks of the Penmarks. It would set in only half an hour, but until then the cutter and the yawl could be seen from the shore, if anyone was about at this time on a cold February night. Holbrooke could see the outline of the shore ahead with the little waves shining in the moonlight, and he could just make out the dark shape of the dunes behind. He could guess how the low silvery light would pick out the masts and sails and hulls of the two vessels, and how the splashes of the oars would gleam against the dark sea. He just hoped that he'd be taken for a late-returning fishermen. He'd seen plenty of them leaving the shore with the first light of dawn and returning in the gathering dusk, taking advantage of every minute of the short days. None had stayed out after dark and certainly no fisherman would willingly be at sea at this late hour in this month of the year.

Dawson was steering by eye for the very centre of the bay, as close as he could to the exact place where Duval had been inserted two days before.

This was the earliest night that he was expected, and Holbrooke shuddered at the thought of returning for three more nights. The moon would grow in brilliance and linger in the sky for an extra hour each time, increasing the risks exponentially as each day passed. It wasn't just the isolated chance of being seen from the shore, that on its own was not to be feared because they would only wait an hour or so before they departed, and no military force could be summoned in that time. No, the real danger was in some intelligent person guessing the cutter's mission and, on the chance that it would return a second night, laying an ambush. And it wasn't only the cutter that was at stake. If their true mission was suspected, then Duval may well find himself walking into an ambush on land. As far as Holbrooke could see, the risks doubled every time they returned to this bay, and after a few more days the danger would become intolerable.

Murray had come in the boat with three marines, just in case of need, and he was scanning the shore as anxiously as Holbrooke.

'I see a light, sir, right down by the water, on the starboard bow.'

The marine lieutenant had good eyes and now that he'd reported the light, Holbrooke could see it. A weak glow, just such as might issue from a shielded lantern. It shone for about half a minute then disappeared.

'Steer for the light, Dawson, two points to starboard.'

Holbrooke stared through his telescope hoping to catch another glimpse of the lantern. He felt the yawl's head turn. Now the waves were on its beam and, with two hands for the telescope and none to spare to steady himself, the first roll nearly pitched him into the bottom of the boat.

'There it is again, sir, right on the head now.'

It took a few seconds to focus the telescope, and the light only stayed visible for a few seconds, but it was looking more and more like a lantern, and it was moving westwards along the beach, jerking up and down as though the person carrying it was running.

'You see that he's moving, Dawson? Steer a point to larboard and aim for the point that he'll reach when we arrive.'

The light had gone again, but now, by the faint glow of the moon, Holbrooke could see a dim, dark figure running along the strand. He stumbled and fell to his knees but got up and ran again. A quick sweep of the beach showed nothing untoward, no explanation for the man's haste, but something must be urging him on. He looked again, concentrating on the north-eastern end from where the man had come. Ah there, at the far end of the beach, moving figures, perhaps twenty of them, and two horsemen. Duval was pursued!

'Pull for all your worth, Dawson.'

There was the light again. It was bouncing up and down as its owner ran hard along the beach. It must have been seen by the pursuers and probably – no, certainly – they would have seen the yawl by now, in this treacherous moonlight. He saw the taller shapes of the two horsemen spur ahead of the running figures.

Then suddenly the bay was plunged into darkness. The little crescent of moon that was so close to dipping below the land to the west was extinguished by a bank of cloud. It was as though a curtain had come down. The approaching shore had quite disappeared and there was no sign of Duval's light either.

'Hold this heading, Dawson.'

It was the two horsemen that worried him. The men on foot, French soldiers he assumed, couldn't overtake an unencumbered running man, but the horses could.

He could feel the surf now, it was even slighter than two days before, and the current cutting across the bay had lost the full force of the spring tides. They must be almost there.

'One fathom, sir, or thereabouts.'

The leadsman was having trouble using his pole because the boat was moving too fast. He couldn't reach the bottom before the yawl's speed swept it astern.

'A mort less than a fathom, sir.'

Ah, the blackness on the starboard bow was punctured by pinpricks of red light. Musket fire! Then he heard the sound, a distant pop-popping, its sharpness dulled by the sound of the waves on the beach. The pursuers must be two hundred yards away from the running man and they couldn't possibly see him. Those who had fired were wasting powder and shot and they wouldn't be able to reload in time to influence the unfolding drama. Militia then, not French line infantry, who would never behave in that fashion. But where were the horsemen? They were lost in the darkness and hadn't revealed themselves by firing carbine or pistol.

'Half a fathom, sir.'

'I'll run her straight in now, sir,' said Dawson.

Still no sign of the runner. Had he fallen? Had he by some evil chance been hit by a musket ball? Had the two horsemen overtaken him?

A shout! Holbrooke stared hard at the pitch-black shore. Was that something, just a little on the larboard bow? He nudged Dawson and pointed and felt the boat's bow swing towards where the sound had been heard.

Yes, he was certain now. There was a figure wading out to meet them. No lantern. Was it a trap? Well, there was no time for the niceties and if he was being duped then they'd just have to fight it out.

'Lieutenant Murray. As soon as we have him onboard you may try your luck against those fellows.'

The marines were crouched between the oarsmen. They were some of his best men from *Argonaut's* detachment, marksmen who could be relied upon to aim and fire and reload independently.

Dawson could see the fugitive clearly now and he was concentrating on bringing the way off the yawl so that they would meet without bowling him over.

Holbrooke saw the two horsemen. They had been slowed by the soft sand, it appeared, not having the sense to stay close to the water where the wet sand provided better going, but they were coming on fast now. They were dragoons, those most deadly of horsemen for a fugitive.

They reined in and pulled their carbines from their leather holsters. Beyond them he saw the dark militia uniforms rushing forward.

Treacherous Moon

A bump. The leadsman had thrust his pole into the sand to halt the boat. There was a scuffle forward and someone was hoisted bodily over the gunwale. Holbrooke peered keenly for a second to confirm that it was Duval and then the marines fired, destroying his night vision with the flash.

'Backwater larboard, pull starboard.'

Dawson spun the yawl around without it ever touching ground. Holbrooke ducked so that a marine could get another shot over his head – he must have brought an extra musket – and then the yawl was pulling hard for the cutter. The oarsmen's breath came in great gasps as they bent the oars in their haste to clear the shore. Everyone knew what was coming next. Those militiamen would have reloaded and the officer or sergeant would be ordering them to take aim. Any moment now…

The muskets sounded fearfully close and the flash of their discharge was like a prolonged bolt of lightning. Holbrooke heard the shots hissing overhead and heard the sound as two or three lead balls embedded themselves in the gunwales. There was a soft cry from somewhere amidships. A quick look told him that all the oarsmen were still pulling hard. He could see the marines reloading and preparing to fire again. Then he saw a figure between the oarsmen, right down on the boards under the thwarts; it was Benjamin Duval!

Crash!

The marines fired again and one of the horsemen fell from his saddle.

'No more firing, Mister Murray, we'll only give away our position.'

Duval was lying in the bottom of the boat, gasping in pain, but he was still conscious. Holbrooke knelt and brought his face close.

'Are you hurt?'

'I…I don't know. I'm bleeding, I think.'

His voice was weak, and he clutched at Holbrooke's arm.

'Listen, we must…'

His mouth moved wordlessly and then his eyes glazed and he fell back. Holbrooke felt his heart. It was still beating, hard and strong, but the man was barely conscious, and the only movement was a feeble fluttering of his eyelids and nervous twitching of his fingers.

'To the cutter as quick as you can, Dawson.'

'It'll only be five minutes sir. I can see the masts ahead now and they're showing a light.'

***

Finch had seen and heard the musketry; he had weighed anchor and was hove to, holding the cutter neatly in position, balancing the wind against the tide. All Dawson had to do was bring the yawl alongside and pass a painter and the cutter could get underway.

Holbrooke thought fast. Clearly his man had been discovered. Whether it was treachery or bad luck he couldn't yet tell, and Duval was in no state to enlighten him. If it was a planned ambush, then the way out to the east of the islands may be watched, perhaps by a pair of those wicked gunboats that the French seemed to have in every little port along the coast. The cutter could have been seen coming from the east so he'd go west, and that would also save him having to beat out of the bay. He'd formed his plan before ever he reached the cutter's deck.

'Bring our man up carefully, Dawson. Mister Finch, douse that light. Can you bring us safely to the west of the islands?'

Finch paused before answering, glancing keenly to the west where the moon was nowhere to be seen.

'I can, sir. I've done it before, in daylight of course. I took bearings before the moon dipped, sir, and I can find my marks.'

'Then make it so. And you are to find *Argonaut* as soon as possible. She won't be showing a light, so you'll need your best lookout at the masthead.'

'He's bleeding a bit, sir,' said Dawson, looking dubiously at the crumpled figure of the agent as he lay him down on the cutter's deck.

'Surgeon's mate! Surgeon's mate! Lay aft, where is the damned fellow.'

Finch had a roar that could awaken the dead and it had the desired effect as a small, slight man ran back from where he'd been lending a hand with the stays'l sheet. In a small cutter every man was a seaman and even the surgeon's mate – a cutter's complement didn't run to a proper surgeon – lent a hand when the ship was being worked.

Holbrooke looked up from his examination of Duval.

'Surgeon's mate?'

'Aye, sir.'

'This man has been shot. I can't see where and he's swooned now, so he can't tell us. Get him below, find the wound and stop the bleeding. Do whatever else you can. Dawson, you and the yawl's crew can help him.'

***

They found *Argonaut* at two bells in the middle watch, or rather it could be said that *Argonaut* found the yawl. After fruitless searching to seaward of the Glenan Isles, Holbrooke had ordered a light shown and a gun fired. In ten minutes the tall spars of the frigate loomed out of the dark and Finch brought the cutter alongside to transfer the wounded agent. It was Chalmers who, after an anxious half an hour, came up to report progress.

'Well, he'll live.'

The relief showed clear on Holbrooke's face.

'What's his injury.'

'Ah, well, he was lucky. A musket ball entered at the lower left rib. It cracked that one and the two ribs above it, and it was deflected without reaching any vital organs. It lodged under his armpit, from where Mister Collins retrieved it.'

Chalmers held out his hand to show the flattened piece of lead. It was a dull grey colour except where it had been distorted allowing the bright clean metal to show. Holbrooke took it and weighed it in his own hand. So much energy and such a great store of treasure had been expended on this expedition, and this little piece of lead so nearly undid it all. Without Duval to tell what he learned there would be no intelligence from Brittany. Certainly there would be nothing written, that was far too dangerous, and the spoken word would have died with him if the unknown militiaman had just shifted his aim fractionally lower.

'Will he be able to speak soon?'

'Oh he looks like a man of fortitude. I expect he'll feel like talking in the morning. Now, I know nothing of this mission, but I gather that this man – or what he has to say – is of vital importance, is that so?'

'It is, David, and I must get that information to the Admiralty as fast as possible. If he's in any way fit to speak before the morning then I must hear him. But the nature of his retreat – he was pursued with determination all the way to the boat – makes me wonder whether there is something else. He tried to tell me something in the boat, before he swooned, something urgent.'

'Then I'll let you know the minute he is conscious.'

'You know, he was on the verge of revealing something a number of times before we put him ashore, but each time he thought better of it. I was intrigued and I still am.'

'As I understand it, he should be saying nothing at all, it's a matter of the secrecy of his mission. Even the smallest detail of his personal life could help the enemy if you or he are taken.'

'Indeed, and that's what makes me wonder what was so important or interesting that it almost caused him to betray his oath of silence. I had been led to believe that he was highly experienced and totally dedicated, but there was something significant that concerns me, I'm sure.'

'Well, whether you will learn anything useful, I cannot say, but I'll go now and discuss with Mister Collins whether we can safely withhold the second dose of laudanum. One thing is for certain in this strange world of unknowns, if he receives that dose you'll get nothing from him before tomorrow forenoon.'

***

CHAPTER ELEVEN

Betrayal

Monday, Ninth of February 1761.
Argonaut, off the Glenan Isles, Brittany.

'We were betrayed.'

Duval was still groggy from his first dose of laudanum and his voice was distorted as he lay flat on his back in a makeshift cot in a screened off portion of the great cabin. His skin was pale and waxy in the candlelight, and the sheet was soaked in his sweat. The bandage around his chest was stained with blood, and he didn't have enough strength to raise his head.

'It was the villagers' behaviour that alerted me,' he gasped weakly. 'They hurried past the house without looking at it and stayed indoors more than is normal. The whole atmosphere was wrong, so I trusted my instinct and fled. I saw columns of soldiers moving in from the north as I took to the fields, making my way south. I hid in hedges and ditches and moved only when I was sure there was nobody about.'

Holbrooke could imagine the sheer terror of being a fugitive with every man's hand raised against him. He glanced at Collins who carefully took Duval's pulse and nodded for him to continue.

'Did you get the information that you came for?'

The agent grimaced as he tried to shake his head.

'Some, not all. My contact was to meet a man today who would provide the last, vital intelligence; the information that I came for. He insisted that he could still make the meeting and he fled to the west as I came south. I have arranged to meet him at Kermabec tomorrow, or is it now today? And then we must bring him away from France, it is far too dangerous for him to stay there.'

Duval passed a hand across his eyes and looked

Treacherous Moon

confused.

'Yet I find that I may need assistance to travel, I feel a little weak.'

How on earth did this man believe that he could go ashore later today? He couldn't even rise from his bed! It was impossible, and yet Holbrooke knew that it was his responsibility to gather as much intelligence as he could. And there was the matter of this unknown agent, expecting to meet Duval tomorrow and perhaps be carried away to safety.

'Kermabec? I don't know it.'

'A small village half a mile inland, five miles north of the Penmarks. I promised him…'

Holbrooke could sense Duval's feeling of helplessness. He could imagine how he would feel responsible for his contacts in the country and would want to ensure their safety.

'What are the arrangements?'

'Ten o'clock tonight at a ruined cottage outside the village. There is a small church to the west of the village, closest to the sea. It has a short tower and a squat steeple, a typical church of the country. The whole is just twenty feet tall. The ruined cottage lies fifty yards north of the church on the other side of a path leading from the sea.'

'Nothing more? No signals, no passwords?'

Duval shook his head.

'He knows me well; no special words are necessary.'

'Mister Collins, if you please.'

He drew the surgeon aside, out of Duval's hearing.

'I assume there is no question of him undertaking this mission tomorrow.'

'Not the slightest hope, sir. He won't be able to stand for a few days and even then he won't move far. It's the laudanum, he doesn't realise the gravity of his condition. He truly believes that with a little help he can walk into France tomorrow. No art of mine can make that possible.'

Holbrooke looked thoughtful.

'Yet he is lucid enough about his contact and about the arrangements.'

'Yes, that's quite normal. He can remember perfectly well but he's incapable of rational thought, quite unable to relate his own condition to the task at hand. You can rely upon his information, perhaps, but not his judgement.'

Holbrooke flipped back the curtain to see that Chalmers was helping Duval to a drink. It looked like wine and water.

'Mister Duval, the surgeon tells me that you should be left to sleep, but I have a few more questions. First, this information, what is it and why is it so important?'

Duval painfully twisted his head right and left, as though to determine who was listening. Apparently satisfied with the presence of Collins and Chalmers, he dropped his head back into the cot. His voice was deep and liquid, coming from his recumbent position.

'I can't tell you where the information is coming from, that would compromise too many people. It is nothing less than the totality of the French army's planned movements to prevent a landing on the Atlantic side of Brittany, from Brest all the way down to the Gironde. It is the principal information that I was sent to collect, everything else is trivial by comparison. My mission is ruined if I return to London without it.'

'And this contact of yours. Do you trust him?'

'You fear a trap, Captain. I can't say I blame you, but it's my decision to meet him and yes, I trust him implicitly. There are particular reasons why his loyalty is not in doubt. I shall go ashore tomorrow with the greatest confidence. You'll forgive me if I don't reveal my contact's name or any personal details, in case there is any chance that we can use him again.'

Collins shook his head solemnly as Holbrooke tried to concentrate on learning as much as he could from Duval.

'You see, Mister Duval, there is no possible question of you being fit to go ashore tomorrow…'

Duval opened his mouth to protest, but only managed a

gurgling croak. He was starting to understand the gravity of his condition.

'…and as this information is of the first importance, I find that I must take your place. You will remember that Mister Sawtree made provision for this in my orders. Now, I need to know everything that's relevant.'

***

'Alone, sir?'

Shorrock looked distraught. He could guess at the necessity of his captain going ashore – no more than half a mile inland, or so he said – but if it were his decision he'd send the whole detachment of marines and a dozen of the best marksmen in the ship. He'd seal off the village before ever knocking on the door of some allegedly abandoned cottage and he'd be ready to meet anything less than a full company of infantry or a squadron of dragoons. Shorrock was not a man of great imagination and in his view the greater the numbers the better the chance of success.

'Alone, Mister Shorrock. This task was laid upon me and I cannot ask anyone to follow me, nor would it help to take anyone else. Now I'll hear no more on the subject.'

Shorrock closed his mouth, but he looked doggedly at Holbrooke, as much as to say that the matter was not yet closed.

Chalmers had been standing quietly beside the window listening to the plans being laid out. He had that uncanny ability to draw everyone's attention merely by a gesture, and now his barely perceptibly bow brought all eyes upon him. He was always correct in addressing Holbrooke when any other officers were in hearing, despite their being the best and closest of friends.

'I beg your pardon, sir, but may I offer an observation?'

Holbrook inclined his head cautiously. He really didn't want any more objections and he always found the chaplain's forensic analysis difficult to refute.

'Mister Duval was injured in escaping, and it's not beyond the realms of possibility that this unnamed contact will also be wounded, or at least exhausted, if he has travelled far over the country to gain this intelligence. It would be a poor end to the mission if you find yourself in a lonely cottage on the French coast with a man whom you must save but is incapable of moving.'

The problem was that Chalmers made sense, and Holbrooke wasn't fast enough to prevent Shorrock leaping into the opening that he had made.

'I could come with you, sir. Mister Fairview can look after the ship.'

'Certainly not. If I'm ashore, your place is on the quarterdeck, Mister Shorrock. You have perhaps forgotten that that we are cruising in enemy waters. You must remain here.'

Chalmers interrupted. Was that the hint of a smile of triumph?

'I wasn't suggesting any such thing, sir,' he said, nodding towards Shorrock, 'but I'm pleased that you agree that you need help.'

Holbrooke had no words. He didn't remember agreeing to any such thing, but he found Chalmers' rhetorical skills hard to counter without looking foolish.

'Now, Mister Jackson will volunteer, I'm sure, and he has all the physical strength that you could need, and you'll want another man who speaks French. I think that is a good compromise between landing *en masse* and a wholly covert operation. I of course speak the language, not quite like a native but close enough so that anybody in these remote parts will be able to believe I'm a Parisian, or from the south of the country…'

Holbrooke looked dubious while Shorrock at least looked less displeased than he had before.

'…and if that's agreed, then may I suggest we ask Mister Fairview to root through his charts to find this place Kermabec?'

***

Treacherous Moon

Duval looked a little better in the afternoon, but still far too weak to undertake the expedition and in any case, Holbrooke had entirely discounted his participation. Chalmers had won the point, and he, Jackson and Holbrooke were clustered around Duval's cot, teasing out the very last points that may prove useful.

'Kermabec is marked on our chart, but only as a tiny dot some way inland with no hint at its size or the surrounding land. Can you tell me anything more?'

Duval looked briefly at the chart as it was held before his face. It showed two lines of soundings, one at half a league from the coast with depths of eight, nine and ten fathoms, and another a league off with depths over twenty fathoms. It was a typical west-facing bay where the seabed shelved steeply from the sandy beach. A string of vague dots scattered across the land close to the coast presumably marked hamlets or villages. Most were incognito but a few were distinguished by outlandish Breton names, and there, looking innocent enough, was Kermabec, five miles north of Penmark, as Duval had said. There was no other information, just a hand-written warning about the force and unpredictability of the tidal stream on the Penmark rocks.

'I have been that way a few times, mostly before this war…'

Duval's eyes took on a faraway look, as though he was remembering things that meant a lot to him. He was one of those itinerate refugees, a Huguenot as Holbrooke had been told, but his family must have been in England for at least a few generations. Did he retain an ancestral memory of his family's lands, confiscated long ago in one of the wars of religion? Was the family's anticipated return discussed over supper every evening, like the European Jews spoke of the Holy Land?

'…the beach is white sand, just like Bénodet and it's backed by dunes covered in tussock-grass. The land behind is barely above the high-water mark and there is a fringe of marsh perhaps two hundred yards deep. Then the land rises slightly, and it is flat and dry until you come to the village. Half a mile in all, from the dunes.'

'You mentioned a path last night, Mister Duval.'

'Yes, there's a path. If you hit the beach at the right point you'll see a notch in the dunes and some timber beams let into the face, to help in climbing on the soft sand. There will be a shallow lake to your left and the marsh before you and stretching away to your right. There's a wooden walkway across the marsh, or at least there used to be, but the timbers don't last long in the water and if they haven't been replaced they'll be in a poor condition. You'll see the church as soon as you reach the top of the dunes, if there's any moonlight.'

'There'll be a moon and if this wind holds there won't be many clouds.'

Duval nodded painfully.

'Then follow the wooden path, if you can find it, but the marsh is passable in any case, with care. If you keep the church in sight you'll find your way. The cottage stands alone to the left of the church as you approach. Its roof has mostly collapsed but six months ago it still offered some shelter.'

'And are you confident that the person who betrayed you doesn't know of this place?'

Duval attempted a shrug, but the pain caused him to stop before it was half-formed.

'I have never mentioned it to anyone but this contact whom you are to meet. But then, I don't know the source of the betrayal, not with any certainty. On balance I would say that it's safe.'

'What should I say to reassure this man?'

Duval again looked as though he was about to say something important, but the moment passed.

'He speaks good English although he will sound foreign. If you say my name clearly without a French accent, he will be reassured. However, he is a cautious man – he has had to be to survive so long in this business – and you may expect him to be wary. You must forgive me, Captain, if I don't tell you any more about him, you will just have to take it on trust. You see, if he is not at the cottage, he may still be at large, and his life will be in danger if his identity is known. You may be taken, and in that case the less you know the better.'

***

CHAPTER TWELVE

Moonlit Flight

Monday, Ninth of February 1761.
Kermabec, Brittany.

'Well, here we are, sir. The Penmarks are sou'-sou'east five miles, as best I can tell.'

Fairview gazed suspiciously at the darkened land ahead. He'd done everything humanly possible to ensure that the longboat would be launched exactly in line with the path that – allegedly – ran from the dunes to Kermabec. In the forenoon he'd taken a good departure from the seamark that warned mariners of the dangerous Penmark rocks, and he'd personally checked the traverse board at every turn of the glass to ensure that he kept a good dead reckoning. It was the tide that was the great unknown. It swept past the Penmarks at a great rate, both flooding and ebbing, and if he miscalculated its rate by only a knot, then he'd be far out in his reckoning. As soon as Holbrooke had decided on the plan *Argonaut* had reached to the south, past the Penmarks, so that nothing would be suspected to the north. Then, when the sun had set and the tide had turned, Fairview had brought the frigate back to the north with topsails and t'gallants furled, past the Penmarks again and into the broad bay of Audierne.

Holbrooke looked east to where the beach was just visible in the moonlight and then southeast to where he knew that the Penmarks lay waiting for any unwary mariners. Fairview saw the turn of his captain's head.

'The tide's on the ebb now, sir, so it will be setting us away from the Penmarks. We are safe for two hours, but after that I can't tell when the flood will start.'

'The safety of the ship is of the utmost importance, Master. The longboat can join you wherever you are. If the wind backs or veers more than four points, or if you suspect

Treacherous Moon

the tide has turned early, you are to stand out of the bay; I'll find you.'

Fairview nodded. He and Shorrock had pleaded the case for *Argonaut* to carry the captain into the bay, rather than the little cutter. *Oyster* could safely lie off the Penmarks watching for any intrusion from the south. At five miles on a night like this even her small guns would be heard and seen.

'Well, bring the longboat alongside, Mister Shorrock. Let's get this over and done.'

The longboat was full to capacity. Although only Holbrooke, Chalmers and Jackson would go ashore, there was a fighting reserve in the boat: Murray, a sergeant and six marines, a quarter gunner with his swivel gun and a full crew of oarsmen. There was no question of sailing up to the beach because the wind – what there was of it – was dead foul, but it would be fair for the return journey, and the mast and spars and the sails were all stowed down the centreline. Holbrooke had agreed that Murray could throw out a screen around the boat, but only as far as each marine could see his neighbour. He knew how easy it was to become disorientated, even with the sea as a fixed point of reference, and it wouldn't help at all if they had to search for stray men before the longboat could leave the shore.

'Shove off, Dawson.'

***

The quarter moon shone dangerously upon the wide, white beach. The wind had dropped and the clear sky – not a cloud had crossed the broad expanse of stars since sunset – had sucked away what warmth there had been. The land breeze was bone-cold, and Holbrooke shivered in the stern of the longboat as it pulled steadily towards the Brittany coast. There was not the slightest point of reference on the shore, no sign of the notch in the dunes, and the silvery beach gave no clues as it spread out to the left and right, eventually losing itself in the blackness of the night. There was nothing to be said. In default of any useful marks, Dawson was steering a direct course from the ship to the shore.

It seemed like an eternity of time, but in only twenty minutes the boat's forefoot ground upon the sand and the sergeant leapt ashore, followed by the marines. Holbrooke waited until they had established their cordon. It was only fifty yards in radius with the boat at its centre, and when the marines found their positions and took up a kneeling posture, they almost disappeared into the night. The quarter gunner was fussing with the swivel gun, checking that it swung freely and keeping his linstock alight in a leather bucket part-covered by a tarpaulin to allow enough air to feed the glowing fuse.

Holbrooke checked his pistols and adjusted his sword. He exchanged a glance with Chalmers who spread his hands wide; he couldn't see any distinguishing feature on the dunes either. Jackson exchanged a word with Dawson then settled his cutlass into his waistband and grasped the short, wicked, brass-barrelled musketoon that he had chosen to take ashore.

'Straight for the dunes, then,' Holbrooke said with finality.

***

Just like the beach at Bénodet, the sand was firm underfoot where it was wet, but dry and powdery once they had pushed beyond the high-water mark. Nevertheless they made a good pace and when Holbrooke looked behind him the boat had been swallowed by the night. Two hundred yards at this state of the tide, that was Fairview's estimate of the distance from the sea to the dunes. It seemed more like three or four hundred but at last the little party came to the end of the flat sand. The dunes gleamed in the moonlight and appeared much higher than he had thought.

'Mister Jackson,' he hissed quietly. 'Go a hundred paces to the left and come straight back and tell me what you have found. Mister Chalmers remain here, if you please. I'll go to the right.'

Chalmers had a pistol but no sword, and he was only

carrying a weapon under the moral force of the opinion of all *Argonaut's* officers. Shorrock had checked the load and the priming, confirmed that the chaplain carried cartridges and ball and gave him last minute instructions for its use. Holbrooke knew that it was futile; his friend may go as far as to throw his weapon at a particularly aggressive enemy, but he'd recently said privately that he had sworn against his own personal use of a firearm. It was better to leave him in the centre rather than wandering away into danger.

Holbrooke watched Jackson go, then strode briskly away, keeping the steep dunes on his left. He was looking for the steps that Duval had spoken of. They weren't necessary for scaling the dunes, although it would certainly be easier, but they were supposed to lead to the path across the marsh. Striking that path would be a distinct advantage, rather than wading through an unknown morass, however passable Duval said it was. There was no particular need for stealth at present and in only a few minutes he had made his hundred paces, found nothing at all, and turned back.

'Not a sign of steps, sir,' Jackson whispered, 'not like the gentleman described, but just before I turned back I saw a sort of path to the top; easier than here in any case, sir.'

Holbrooke looked up again. Yes, they could scale the dunes here, but it would certainly create noise as they slipped on the dry sand between the tussocks. It would have been extraordinarily fortunate if the longboat had come ashore exactly opposite the made stairs. Duval's *about five miles from the Penmarks* was vague enough, but when their own navigational inaccuracies were added to the equation, they could easily be a mile away from their intended landing point.

'Any sort of path would be better than scrambling up there,' said Chalmers.

They were all speaking softly although the chance of meeting a stray Frenchman at this time of night was slim indeed.

'Very well, guide us to your path, Mister Jackson.'

It was certainly a track used by people, and the fact of its existence in this spot suggested that the stairs must be some distance away, otherwise there would have been no need for it. It wasn't difficult at all and in just a minute or so they were lying flat on the top of the dunes, their outlines merged into the mounds and tussocks that fringed the footpath. The moon was at their back and dipping fast towards the horizon, and their silhouette would have been easy to see from inland if they had stood up. Its light shone over the flat landscape ahead of them, offering a panoramic view of their objective.

Right ahead of them at somewhat less than a mile lay a cluster of houses and a low church with a squat spire.

'Kermabec,' Holbrooke whispered, 'and over to the left is the lake. The road should be right below us.'

It was easy to see the lake and the flat land between them and the village, because where the moonlight struck the standing water, it threw back a deeper blackness than the dry land. The village, low though it was, represented the only objects that stood above ground and the slanting rays of the moon outlined every building. However, of a path across the marsh, there was nothing to be seen.

'That looks a little wetter than we had expected.'

Holbrooke hardly heard Chalmers, he was deep in thought. As far as he could see they had struck the shore at the right place, within perhaps a quarter mile either way. One look at the land before them had persuaded him that it would be folly to attempt crossing it anywhere other than on a regular path. Now, the route they had taken to climb the dunes had been well-used by people, and it appeared unlikely that they would have built it if it was close to the made stairs. What would be likely? Perhaps three or four hundred yards separation? He could see that far towards the lake and there was nothing. And Duval had said that the lake was half a mile north of the path; they must be closer than that already. To the south, then. One last attempt to find the path before they embarked on a perilous crossing of the marsh.

He whispered his plan to the three men and motioned to drop back down to the beach. Jackson looked reluctant, and he hissed to get Holbrooke's attention.

'If we go down the other side, sir, we'll be shadowed by the dunes and we'll be able to see a path before we come to it.'

Holbrooke grimaced. He should have thought of that himself.

***

This side of the dunes was much less steep than the seaward face and they found they could easily walk down. There was a path at the base, not the one they were looking for, but a trail of beaten earth and sand that followed the line of the dunes. They turned right and walked stealthily south.

Jackson had been right, of course. They were in the moon's shadow here and invisible to anyone either from the top of the dunes or from across the cold, wet land on their left. Half a mile, Holbrooke told himself, ten minutes of fast walking. He couldn't see his watch, but he started counting his steps instead. A thousand steps, and if they found nothing they would have to strike off across the marsh.

They all knew that they should keep a little distance between them. Far enough so that they wouldn't make a great dark mass in the darkness, but close enough so that a low voice would carry. At five hundred steps Holbrooke judged that they were passing the furthest extent of his earlier patrol to the south. At six hundred steps he was stopped by a hiss from Jackson ahead of him. He came on cautiously to find his coxswain crouching low beside a wooden post. He looked to the left and there was the path! A trail of twelve-foot lengths of undressed timber, unevenly spaced, disappeared east towards where he guessed the village lay. They were old timbers and many of them were broken or had slid into the marsh on either side, but it was undeniably a path.

'The cottage will be on the left,' he said to remind them, 'and right across the path and a little way further on we'll see the church.'

He strained his eyes into the darkness. No, they were too low, and now the shadow of the dunes was lengthening. Three quarters of a mile. One thousand, four hundred steps, he had calculated after his last meeting with Duval. Dead reckoning on dry land was simple, without having to worry about the wind and tide. Put that way it sounded easy, all he had to do was mentally adjust his calculation when they found obstacles and again when the going was good.

They strode on, Jackson leading again. The cold was forgotten, banished by their stretched nerves in this night-time expedition and by the exertion of walking on soft sand, on dunes and now on an uneven roadway of rough tree trunks. Holbrooke concentrated on counting his steps, but a part of his mind was free to wonder at the beauty of the night. Here inland there was hardly a whisper of wind and their white exhalations hung around them as they walked through the frosty air. Overhead the minor stars were starting to show as the moon lost its brilliance and the patches of water to the left and right reflected the light in silvery points and pools.

Eight hundred steps and he sensed that Jackson had stopped and was again crouching. He slid stealthily alongside him and heard Chalmers' breathing as he also lowered himself to the ground.

'There, sir.'

Jackson pointed off to the left of the path, and then to the right.

'I saw the church and the cottage at the same time. Just as the gentleman said.'

It took a moment to see what Jackson was pointing at. The church, as described by Duval, and on the other side of the path, a one-storey cottage. They could be fifty yards apart although it appeared a greater distance in this uncertain light. They were perhaps half an hour early,

Holbrooke guessed, but he couldn't see his watch in the dark. This was it, then, he was about to make contact with an agent on foreign soil. He instinctively touched his breast pocket where he had stowed his commission; the safeguard for him and his followers against being taken up as spies. Now, he had to announce himself in a clearly English accent. He remembered the conversation on board *Argonaut*; he still thought it a little strange that Duval should think that this agent would readily accept that he was who he said he was.

'You go to the right, Mister Jackson, and stay between the church and the cottage, but close enough to hear a whistle. Run back and tell me if you see anything.'

'Aye-aye sir.'

'Mister Chalmers, come with me if you please. You may wish to half-cock your pistol.'

He saw the shake of Chalmers' head out of the corner of his eye but ignored it. Weapons would likely be of no use tonight and in any case if he had wanted a fighting man he wouldn't have chosen the chaplain, French speaker or no.

Keeping low, Holbrooke crept towards the cottage door, or at least to the space where a door should be. He felt a tap on his shoulder.

'Wood smoke,' Chalmers whispered, touching his nose.

Holbrooke stooped and studied the cottage afresh. Yes, he could distinctly smell wood smoke, but the village was to windward, and it was possible that they could smell some Frenchman's hearth that had been left burning through this cold night. But now he was expecting it, he could just see a faint trail of smoke from the cottage's chimney, or at least he could see the stars dancing and weaving as their light passed through the smoke. Then there was someone within.

His heart beat faster as he crept the last few yards. The door had long ago decayed, but there was enough left to rap against, and he chose that method of announcing himself.

Two raps on the old wood and the sound rang harshly through the night. He heard stealthy movement inside. He realised that he was afraid, scared of what might be waiting for him in the darkened ruins, and he felt his palms sweating even in the frigid air. There was no way of introducing himself that didn't sound either melodramatic or absurd.

'Good evening, sir. I am here as a friend of Duval.'

He noticed that his pistol was trembling, and he moved his finger away from the trigger, just in case. A bulky figure came into sight, with its lower half caught in the moonlight, while all else was hidden in shadow. Holbrooke's attention was on the man's hands, and the pistol that he held, pointing at the ground. The figure moved a step forward and now his face became visible. Holbrooke almost reeled with the shock of recognition, but it was Chalmers who reacted first.

'Why, Major Albach, how good it is to see you again, sir.'

***

Holbrooke stood rooted to the spot. When he had thought about it at all, he had expected that he'd be meeting a disaffected Frenchmen, perhaps a junior officer or some minor local functionary. What he had not anticipated was that Duval's mysterious contact would be none other than his old friend Hans Albach of the Austrian artillery. Duval's hesitation in identifying his contact now made sense. An agent lived by his anonymity, and the fewer who knew his identity the safer he would be. If Holbrooke and Albach had not met in the course of this business, then it was better that he remained anonymous, and it was by no means certain that this expedition would have resulted in a meeting.

Albach was even more surprised, but he strode forward and took first Holbrooke's hand in his own massive paw and then Chalmers'. He tried to speak but no words came.

'Duval is injured, and he sent us to bring you to my ship.'

Albach was recovering fast from the first shock of recognition, and he had the quickness of thought of a hunted man.

'Then there is no time to lose. You have a boat, I imagine.'

'Yes, on the beach, perhaps twenty or thirty minutes

from here if we hurry.'

'You come in the nick of time, Captain Holbrooke. Another five minutes and I would have been away. Pursuit is close behind me but they're plodding infantry and we'll hear them long before they are upon us. There's half a squadron of cavalry as well, but I fancy they've gone further south.'

Albach was dressed in a blue French artillery uniform. He shouldered a pack as he was speaking, and it appeared that he had nothing else. He started towards the fire and kicked away the unburnt wood and threw dirt onto the rest.

'They'll find it anyway and perhaps this will give them pause for thought. What's the ground like to the beach?'

'There's a good path over the marsh but it's very exposed, no shelter at all.'

'Then I am ready.'

Holbrooke turned towards the cottage door and gave a low whistle, but Jackson was already running back, crouched almost double.

'There's movement, sir, approaching from the other side of the village. It sounds like men marching, they're not trying to keep quiet.'

Jackson looked startled for a moment then he gave Albach a familiar nod. It had been nearly three years since they had last met, but time cannot erase the memory of nights such as they had spent on the dunes of Cancale Bay.

'Very well. Mister Jackson, you lead the way. We'll go straight for the dunes, down to the beach and keep going until we reach the sea. Then turn right and three hundred paces should bring us to the boat.'

***

They had only been in the cottage a matter of a few minutes, but in that time the moon had dipped below the top of the dunes, the world had been plunged into darkness, and the path was barely visible in the starlight.

They paused for a moment before setting off. In the silence they could hear the sounds of approaching men, and was that the jingle of horses' harnesses? They must be no more than a few hundred yards away now.

'Walk fast, Mister Jackson, but don't run. There's too much danger of losing our footing on these timbers.'

Jackson set off and they all followed, passing like shadows into the dark of the night. They were certain of pursuit. If the enemy knew enough to come to this village, then they would know that their quarry was not far ahead. The path to the sea was the obvious escape route and they'd be quick to follow.

The going was much more difficult without the help of the moon. A fast walk was optimistic in the extreme but at least a horse would make slow work of it. It was the infantry that Holbrooke feared; horses were not to be dreaded on poor ground in the dark. By the starlight, they could just pick out the next transverse timber, but placing a foot accurately was challenging, and after the first fifty yards they were each wet and muddy past their knees. And their progress wasn't silent. None of them uttered a word, but their boots thudded as they reached each timber and squelched every time they missed their footing.

The dunes appeared quicker than Holbrooke had hoped, and soon they were climbing up the path to the top. He had no need to tell everyone to slide over the summit without exposing themselves, and the moon that was now visible, just kissing the western horizon, emphasised their vulnerability. Holbrooke motioned for a stop and lay between two tussocks to look back along the path. The white uniforms of their pursuers were quite visible, perhaps two hundred yards behind. There were two horses and around twenty men, all struggling along the same path that the fugitives had taken. One look was enough.

'We run from here,' Holbrooke said softly. 'Speed before stealth. Lead on, Mister Jackson.'

They slid down the seaward face of the dune rather than take the steps and set off at a steady jog towards the dark sea ahead. Two hundred yards, Holbrooke remembered, but the tide had been ebbing so it would be perhaps another fifty yards. It was so dark that they felt the little waves lap over their boots before they realised they had reached the furthest limit of the sand. Without a word they turned right and hurried on.

'Up there!'

Albach pointed to the dunes and his words came in breathless gasps.

Holbrooke spared the dunes a quick glance then looked over his shoulder. The pursuers had split their force and although he couldn't see any details there was a group of men running along the path at the top of the dunes and another was angling across the beach from the foot of the steps. He couldn't see any horses; they were probably still struggling to reach the summit of the dunes. That damned moon! Only the upper half was now visible, and it was a quarter moon at that, but they must be clearly visible by its treacherous light.

'The boat, sir!'

Jackson didn't pause in his running. Holbrooke could see it now, only a hundred yards ahead; it was a three-sided race with the longboat as the goal. He could see that his own party would win, but the other two contestants wouldn't be far behind.

'Captain Holbrooke?'

Murray's voice was horribly loud and very close. They must be upon the marine pickets already.

'Bring your men in, Mister Murray, they're close behind.'

Holbrooke was gasping now as he neared the finish.

'I'll command the withdrawal, sir, if you please.'

Evidently Murray wasn't going to be rushed, and Holbrooke didn't argue. The marine lieutenant would have seen the converging enemy and he was better qualified to manage the situation.

Ah, the blessed feel of the boat's gunwale! They splashed through the shallow water and jumped in. Dawson looked calm and confident at the tiller. Holbrooke could see the glow of the gunner's linstock and saw that two seamen were holding the boat's stern out into deep water, with two more at the bow. The boat was rocking gently, and its shallow forefoot wasn't even touching the sand.

The measured tones of the sergeant broke the silence of the night as he formed up his marines either side of the bow. The heavy breathing and the solid sound of boots on wet sand heralded the approach of the French infantry. Holbrooke had time to note that they had not wasted powder and shot by firing on the run, they were a different class of soldier to the militia. In all probability they were coming on at the point of the bayonet.

Crash!

The sound of the marines' volley shattered the quiet and the flash of their discharge split the darkness of the night. More orders, and the marines came back in an ordered rush, vaulting over the gunwales amidships, leaving a clear shot for the swivel gun.

Holbrooke still had given no orders; he found that he was no longer in control. He felt the boat being pushed away from the beach as the sodden oarsmen hauled themselves in before they lost their footing in the sand.

The French were firing now, but at last the moon had dipped below the horizon, casting the beach into a profound blackness, lit only by the flash of muskets. The boat must be invisible to them.

The sharp crack from the swivel gun sounded much louder than the muskets, and the flash lit up the beach for twenty yards. Holbrooke had a momentary sight of twenty or so Frenchmen, some standing, some kneeling to fire and some lying where they had fallen under the marines' volley. Jackson's musketoon added to the mayhem, discharging its load of small shot into the night. The flashes lasted long enough to see the swivel gun's load of musket balls tear through the nearest pursuers, then all was dark again.

'Back water starboard, pull hard larboard.'

Dawson was turning the boat and Holbrooke had that

Treacherous Moon

old feeling of vulnerability as he sat exposed in the stern sheets, waiting for the musket balls to tear into his flesh. But only a few shots followed them, and none came near. The surviving Frenchmen must have entirely lost their night vision in the flash of the swivel gun and the musketoon, and in a few strokes of the oars the longboat was lost in the utter, profound darkness of the moonless night.

***

CHAPTER THIRTEEN

A Spy's Tale

Tuesday, Tenth of February 1761.
Argonaut, at Sea, Ushant East Three Leagues.

The wind had veered in the middle watch, and it had been a hard beat down to the Penmarks to find *Oyster*, but now they were both profiting from the sou'westerly as they bore away past Ushant and hastened up the Channel to Portsmouth.

'You have cleared your account with Mister Duval, I gather.'

Holbrooke was feeling refreshed after a few hours of sleep and the tension of the preceding night was slipping away with the sea-miles under *Argonaut's* keel. The change in wind had brought in a thick layer of low cloud and outside the great cabin's window the sea and sky merged into a grey sameness.

Before Albach could answer, Chalmers put his finger to his lips and stepped softly to the curtained partition that hid the agent's cot.

'He's sleeping with a good draught of laudanum. He'll hear nothing until past dinner.'

Holbrooke smiled. It appeared that his friend the chaplain had taken to this espionage business like a man born to it. Holbrooke's mind rebelled at the thought of having to whisper in his own ship, and having to wonder who was listening, but Chalmers had no such difficulty.

'Ah, Duval, so that's the name that he's been using,' Albach said with a sly look. 'I know him under a different guise but that's best not revealed.'

He studied his two old friends before he continued.

'Yes, I've told him what he needed to know. His mission has been a success and if he survives he'll be the toast of the Admiralty.'

'Oh, he'll survive,' Chalmers said. 'Mister Collins cleaned

the wound and let it bleed a few minutes before he bound it. The ball touched nothing important, and his ribs will soon heal.'

'I'm glad of that, he's a good man. Quite fearless, you know, and he returns again and again to France in the certain knowledge that he'll be hung, or at best shot, if he's discovered. He's completely exposed now, so I expect this will be his last expedition. He's the most discreet man I have ever known. He knew very well that you and I were acquainted, I told him all about Emden and Saint-Cast, of course, and yet he didn't say a word about you commanding this ship. If we hadn't been discovered I would have stayed in France and continued my work, and I would never have known that you were so close and that we were working to the same end. Although now I think of it, he appeared on the verge of telling me something on a few occasions, perhaps that was it.'

Holbrooke glanced again at the curtain as though to reassure himself that the man that he knew as Duval wouldn't suddenly appear.

'Aye, he told me nothing about you, but I also had the feeling that he was on the cusp of committing an indiscretion. How much easier it would have been to walk through that cottage door if I knew that you were inside!'

Chalmers smiled his confidential smile. He'd seen Holbrook's pistol shaking and he'd seen his hesitation, but that was his secret.

Holbrooke's servant brought a fresh pot of coffee and they carried on an idle conversation until he had left the cabin.

'Would it be indiscreet to ask what brought you to this service? I ask in mere inquisitiveness, never having been involved in these matters before.'

Chalmers was the perfect person to ask such a question. He had the ability to raise a subject that other men took as striking at their very honour, without sounding as though he was casting judgement.

'Ah, yes. If you had asked that question two days ago you would have got nothing out of me. However, I certainly can't return to Brittany now, and probably not France. I'm too notorious and the militia and the army now know what a viper they've been cradling in their bosom. Now let me see. We first met in the North Sea in 'fifty-eight, isn't that so? You took the ship – a little pink as I recall – that was carrying me and my field guns to Emden.'

'Yes, I remember it well, and on that occasion the last that I saw of you was leaving with your men to march away after Emden fell.'

'That's so, and I still owe you a debt of gratitude for that kindness. The French utterly abandoned us you know. And that is the last time I saw you Mister Chalmers, although Captain Holbrooke and I met again, rather later in that year.'

'We did indeed, and you handsomely repaid any slight debt that you may have imagined. I would certainly have perished on that beach at Saint-Cast if you had not saved me. And again, I believe I owe my early parole to you. It is I who owe you the debt, sir.'

Albach bowed and glanced again at the curtains.

'Well, so much for the history of our friendship, but I believe that's not the real question on your mind, Mister Chalmers. So, why did I choose to engage in espionage on behalf of King George, and why have I been prepared to make myself anathema in my own country? After all, Austria is allied with France for the war in Europe, even if we have no formal declaration of hostilities against Britain. There is no good reason now why I shouldn't tell you, and in truth it will be a relief to unburden myself.'

Holbrooke and Chalmers settled in their chairs.

'You'll remember, Captain Holbrooke, that because of the Emden disaster, I felt that I wouldn't be welcomed back in my own country; I was right! Every letter that I sent to my old regiment—if it elicited a response at all – was discouraging. I should stay in France, make myself useful to the militia, not attempt either a land or sea passage back to

Treacherous Moon

Austria. Well, I accepted that for a year, served the artillery of the Brittany militia faithfully, and hoped for a short war so that I could return home. That was very well for some time, but it must have been just after Saint-Cast that I started to doubt the objectives of the war. The fall of New France and the battle in Quiberon Bay…'

Albach stared abstractedly towards the windows, gathering his thoughts.

'…I was a witness to it, incidentally, from the shore at the mouth of the Vilaine. I even sent a few six-pound balls towards where I fancied the British ships were. In any case, it brought me to realise that France should seek peace immediately and at all costs. Her dogged pursuit of ever more unlikely victories only prolonged the agony and kept Austria fighting for land that most of my people didn't even want. The Prussian army on land and the British navy at sea are a fearsome combination. I met the man you know as Duval at a strangely anonymous gathering of foreigners in Quimper. When I look back on it, his approach was most ingenious. For three months he let me speak about how misguided the war was, always leading me to believe that he was one of the few remaining French Huguenots in Brittany. The conversations became deeper and more confidential, and when the opportunity arose, I gladly passed him little pieces of information on French troop movements. The small led to the large and I suppose by the end I was his chief informant in Brittany. I trust – I hope – that my actions have gone some way to shortening this war.'

Albach sunk back into his chair as though exhausted by his confession. Chalmers studied him carefully, recognising the face of a man who had unburdened himself after years of secrecy. The cabin's silence was broken only the by the normal sounds of a ship working at sea, and those passed the three men without being noticed.

'You'll be honoured in England, I expect,' Holbrooke said at last.

Albach jumped as though startled from a dream.

'I expect you're right, for what it's worth. Those papers that I brought are the culmination of my career in espionage, and if their Lordships plan a descent in Brittany, on the mainland or any of the islands, they will prove invaluable. The whole plan for reinforcing the coast is laid out, and the best thing is that they are copies, created by my anonymous colleague in secret, so the full extent of what is to be revealed to the Admiralty will be hidden from the French. And yes, it's very well that England will value me, but I'm more concerned at how I'll be received in my home country once this war is over. I fear it won't be with open arms.'

***

'Beg your pardon, sir, Mister Fairview sends his respects. Start Point's in sight two points on the larboard bow, and the wind's backing and strengthening.'

The midshipman looked fresh and eager, as well he might after a full four hours in his hammock.

'Thank you Mister Carew, I'll come on deck in a just a minute.'

Holbrooke was breakfasting with Chalmers, Albach and Duval, who was sitting up in his cot. He finished a piece of toast and drained his coffee then excused himself to walk up to the quarterdeck.

'Well, what do you think of it, Mister Fairview?'

The dawn had brought a definite change in the weather. The sky was almost clear of clouds to the south and east, and the damp sou'westerly had given way to this southerly wind that was backing even as they spoke. Prawle Point and Start Point were clearly visible to larboard and the beyond them the land that trended towards Dartmouth and Lyme Bay could be guessed at.

'I don't like the look of it, sir. We could be in for an easterly blow, but even if it doesn't back that far I'd like to make an offing and keep clear of the bay.'

Holbrooke leaned out over the starboard gunwale and studied the wind. Fairview was probably right, and at best they would be headed, at worst embayed between Portland

Bill and Start Point. Neither of those outcomes were attractive, and a prudent mariner would tack to the south before he was forced to do so. Duval had spoken of the need to get this information to the Admiralty as soon as possible. He could put into Torbay now and send it by express, but it was a long and uncertain road from Torquay to London, and if the wind stayed in the south he'd look foolish when he made Portsmouth tomorrow morning, with the vital documents stuck somewhere in the muddy miles from the west country, perhaps not even having reached Exeter. And then again, if he anchored in Torbay, any wind between sou'east and north could see him trapped for days on end, and Duval had stressed the need for both he and Albach to present themselves in person at the Admiralty as soon as possible. The express from Portsmouth to London was so regular, so certain and so comfortable that it was conceivable that Duval would be fit to undertake that journey in a day or two, but the coach from Torquay or Brixham was quite another matter and at this time of year it could take a week to reach London.

He had already considered sending in *Oyster* with a duplicate copy of the documents, but Duval had looked shocked at the thought of transcribing the precious and sensitive material and had flatly rejected the proposal. In any case, there were pages and pages of it and at the very least his clerk would have to help with the copying, and that would widen the pool of people who knew about it.

'Very well, Mister Fairview. Call the hands and put us on the larboard tack,' he looked up at the pennant and felt the strengthening breeze, 'and take a reef in the tops'ls, if you please. I'll rely upon you to make the best of the tides to bring us up the channel.'

***

Argonaut and *Oyster* thrashed up channel for three days with Fairview employing every trick of science, art and sheer intuition to work the tides and winds to their advantage. They even passed to the south of Alderney to catch the strong flood, braving the wicked Casquets upon which many a good ship had perished. The sailing master was by far the best channel pilot that Holbrooke had ever sailed with, the best he'd ever heard of in fact, and not for the first time he wondered what malign forces in the navy board or at Trinity House kept him from being promoted into a ship-of-the-line. Fairview could tell the frigate's position from a single cast of the lead and seemed to know the seabed between Dover and the Chops of the Channel as well as most people know their own back yard. Seasoned old seamen would stand in awe as he studied the sample brought up on the lead line, rolling it between his fingers, sniffing it and even tasting it before he declared his judgement.

'Black mud and a bit of green ooze with crushed scallop shells, sir. Nine or ten leagues north of Cap de la Hague, I reckon. The wind's veered a point or two and we'll catch the flood in mid-channel. You could come about now, sir, and we'll weather Bembridge.'

They sighted St. Catherine's Point in the forenoon of Friday the thirteenth – an inauspicious day if ever there was one – and shaved past Bembridge ledge with barely a mile to spare, and so at last to an anchorage in the soft sand and mud of Spithead. The eastern Solent was a stirring sight, with men-of-war and transports anchored in every available berth from St. Helen's to the Gilkicker. The great expedition was gathering, and Holbrooke felt a surge of pride that the information that he was bringing would materially assist in launching it against the enemy.

'Is the gentleman fit for a boat to shore and an express to London, Mister Collins?'

Holbrooke scrupulously avoided using Duval's name, even though he knew it to be an assumed identity, and even though all of his officers must have heard it slip out by now. He looked dubiously at the choppy waters of Spithead. Normally it was a safe and secure anchorage, but not in a wind that blew from a few points south of east. The water

Treacherous Moon

between *Argonaut's* anchor berth and the narrow entrance to Portsmouth harbour was a mass of short steep waves with their peaks blown away in white spume.

The surgeon shook his head.

'I will warrant his fitness for the express, sir, but not a boat, not in this weather. His wounds have healed well, and I'm not concerned about them, but his ribs still need to be treated tenderly.'

Colling knew better than to attempt to impose a course of action on his captain, and he'd gone as far as he dared in stating his concern at his patient being committed to a boat journey. However, the conclusion was inescapable, and *Argonaut* must get into Portsmouth.

'Very well. Mister Fairview, are you happy that the ship has found her anchor?'

'Yes, sir, she's lying back nicely without any hint of dragging.'

'In that case, I'll take the longboat ashore and plead for an alongside berth. Mister Shorrock, bring the boat up and pass the word for my coxswain and crew. I don't expect I'll be gone long, and you can bring the anchor to short stay when you see my boat put off from the shore.'

***

Holbrooke had found Admiral Holburne in his office, and it took only a few words to obtain his agreement, even though the conditions were marginal for movements through the harbour entrance. Messengers were sent scurrying to stir up the riggers to shift the sheer hulk that occupied the only available space alongside; all the rest were taken up by ships needing urgent repairs before the great expedition. Two of the largest type of longboats were readied to nudge the frigate through the entrance and into the safety of the harbour.

By the time that Holbrooke returned to his ship, the anchor was up-and-down, and the yards were manned. Fairview was nervously watching his bearings in anticipation that they would start dragging at any moment, while the bosun kept his foot on the cable, alert for the slightest vibration that hinted at the great anchor shifting uneasily through the mud.

'You may get underway immediately, Mister Fairview, I think this wind will serve.'

It took the utmost skill to bring *Argonaut* safely into Portsmouth Harbour with a following wind, even at the top of the tide. The tops'ls were backed as often as they drew and the frigate inched carefully between the Round Tower and Fort Blockhouse. As soon as she'd cleared Portsmouth Point, the two stout dockyard boats took lines from her bows while her own longboat and yawl took the stern. In a moment the sails were furled, and her management became a matter of directing the boats to bring her alongside. There was a carriage awaiting them and thirty minutes after the first line was passed to the shore, Holbrooke, Duval, Albach and Chalmers – who was to see to any medical needs on the journey – were on their way to the London Road.

***

With the Hilsea Lines and Portsea Island behind them, the coach set itself for the long climb up Portsdown Hill. Duval had been packed tight with blankets and coats and he seemed comfortable and cheerful, eager to bring his information to his masters in the Admiralty.

'Will Mrs Holbrooke know of your ship's arrival?'

Albach had heard all of Holbrooke's family news over the four days that he'd been on board. He'd congratulated his friend on his marriage and his son, and he knew just how close to Portsmouth he lived.

'Oh, rumour spreads fast in naval ports, and you'd be surprised how soon it reaches the closer towns. My father will know before he sits down to his dinner and Ann will know before the afternoon's over.'

'Won't she expect you in that case?'

'That's the worst of it. If *Argonaut* was at Spithead she wouldn't expect me, she knows very well that I would have to stay with my ship. In fact, I would need permission to sleep ashore in wartime. But no doubt she'll hear that *Argonaut's* alongside and in that case I would usually find the means to have a few hours at home. I've sent her a note, of course, and told her that I must go up to town, but rumour will outpace any note of mine, and I fear that her hopes will be dashed. I'm not sure that naval wives are ever truly reconciled to the ugly reality that their husbands are not masters of their own destiny.'

'Well, I hope you won't be detained long in London.'

'I can hope, but nothing I say will change anything. I expect I'll be back to join that great armada that you saw in the Solent.'

'Where are they bound, if I may ask?'

'You may ask indeed, and I suspect the intelligence that you bring will determine the answer.'

***

Chris Durbin

CHAPTER FOURTEEN

The Chaplain's Snare

Saturday, Fourteenth of February 1761.
The Admiralty, Whitehall.

The low morning sun slanted through the admiralty building's screen wall, casting stark shadows on the courtyard. Holbrooke couldn't shake off the idea that he should be keeping out of the light, moving from cover to cover to avoid being detected. It was absurd, of course, and if he felt like this after only a few hours ashore in France, what must Albach be feeling after two years of looking over his shoulder, waiting for the moment that he was betrayed, anticipating the dread hue and cry when his trail was discovered?

Holbrooke hadn't seen Duval and Albach since they arrived at London. They'd been whisked away to wherever Sawtree kept his agents almost before the wheels of the coach had come to a halt, while he and Chalmers had been left to their own devices to find a lodging for the night. He'd come to the Admiralty as early in the morning as he thought decent. It was Chalmers' first visit and for the first time that Holbrooke could remember, the chaplain appeared awed by his surroundings, looking furtively around and trying not to draw attention to himself.

Holbrooke feared looking ridiculous, not really knowing whether anyone would want to talk to him now that his mission was completed. After announcing themselves to the porter, he and Chalmers sat quietly, blending in with the half dozen other officers who were waiting to be called by the great men who dwelt within.

He was so lost in his thoughts that he positively jumped when the porter announced that Admiral Forbes would see him immediately. The expressions on the faces of their fellows said it all: these were chosen men, the privileged officers that were kept waiting only minutes, not the hours and days that they had to endure.

'This must be the Reverend Chalmers. It's a pleasure to meet Captain Holbrooke's companion of so many campaigns.'

Forbes was in his most avuncular mood, all smiles for the younger man and his friend. He offered seats and called for coffee. That had never happened in any of Holbrooke's previous visits.

'I've had a note from Sawtree. It appears that he spent all night poring over Major Albach's intelligence and the results, at first sight, answer most of the urgent questions. A most remarkable coup and I understand that you had to bring Albach out yourself, is that so?'

'Yes, sir. Mister Duval was too badly injured when we brought him off, and as Mister Sawtree predicted, I had to take his place the next day. Mister Chalmers accompanied me as he has better French than I, and my bosun came to keep us out of trouble. It was a close-run thing; we were only steps ahead of a company of French infantry, and we had to beat a hasty retreat to the beach.'

Forbes glanced at a single sheet of paper on his desk and looked up again, fixing Holbrooke with a steady gaze.

'Sawtree's note suggested there was a fair amount of fighting on the beach.'

'Well, sir, my marine lieutenant had to cover our withdrawal and then the swivel gun discouraged them from firing on us to any evil effect. I estimate that we left half a dozen fallen Frenchmen behind us. I've mentioned Mister Murray in my report, sir. It was a most creditable rearguard action and he brought all of his men back.'

Forbes continued to study Holbrooke, with the hint of a wry smile at the corners of his mouth. Holbrooke felt surprisingly comfortable under that gaze. He knew he'd done well, and he hadn't fallen into the sin of boastfulness, while still telling the bare bones of the story.

'I was never involved in this kind of escapade,

Holbrooke, and I regret it. You seem to have had a splendid adventure. You're getting quite a reputation, you know, you and Mister Chalmers.'

'May I ask, sir, what will become of Major Albach? As far as I can tell it's out of the question for him to return to France, and he's not wanted in his own country.'

'Oh, Sawtree has already petitioned for him to be brought into the secret funding, although that won't mean he has to reside in London, in fact he may have a more direct role.'

Forbes stopped and stared at his desk as though embarrassed to look Holbrooke in the eye.

'He'll be on a retainer, as it were. He'll be useful for his knowledge of Brittany for at least as long as this war persists, and he may be able to return to Austria after that. Now, that leads me on to the real significance of the information that he brought. I rely of course on your absolute discretion in these matters.'

Forbes looked at each man in turn, and they both answered with a nod, nothing more seemed to be needed.

'Very well. You'll have seen the armament gathering at Spithead and St. Helens, and you'll no doubt have noticed from the transports and storeships that a landing is contemplated. It's been waiting for better weather but also for a decision on where a landing would have the greatest effect on King Louis' determination to continue the war. There has been much rumour on the subject, and a great deal of ill-informed speculation, in fact I'd be interested to know what you have heard.'

Holbrooke had indeed heard the rumours. They were common gossip everywhere on the road between Portsmouth and London, and every inn-keeper and coach driver had an opinion.

'Mauritius, Martinique, Belle Isle, the other French Atlantic islands, Vannes; they're all being talked about, sir.'

'Yes, as I thought. Well, at one time or another all of those have been considered, as well as the Dutch Cape and

Louisiana. However, with the prospect of Spain entering the war – I won't go into the details – we must keep the bulk of our fleet close to home. Mister Anson is meeting the King and Mister Pitt as we speak, and he'll advocate that we take Belle Isle. That will give us a base to keep our blockading squadrons supplied, it'll deny Quiberon Bay and the Morbihan to the French, and it'll draw regiments away from Germany. Captain Keppel will command, with a commodore's pennant, and you'll join the squadron immediately.'

Holbrooke exchanged a glance with Chalmers. They'd discussed this at length; whether *Argonaut* would be sent back to the blockade of the Vilaine, or to some other duty. It was a day for revelations, and he wondered how many other captains knew that Keppel – a mere captain himself – had been selected to command this huge force. And how would Admiral Hawke take it? He'd already struck his flag once in protest at a junior officer being given an extensive independent command within his area of operations, would he do so again?

'Now, you may wonder why I'm telling you this.'

Holbrooke inclined his head cautiously. He certainly had wondered; it was not at all usual for a junior frigate captain to be brought into the councils of the great.

'Your orders will instruct you to join Keppel's squadron, nothing more, and for the most part he'll use you as he would any other frigate. However, Mister Keppel will have a supplementary letter which only he will see, that will instruct him to use you and *Argonaut* for any clandestine operations of the sort that you have just returned from.'

Forbes sat back, apparently waiting for comment.

So that was it! Holbrooke didn't know yet whether to be pleased or disturbed that he had been selected from among his peers. It was certainly dangerous to go poking about on an enemy's coast, but was it any more dangerous than the normal duties given to a frigate?

'I see, sir. It is contemplated that another agent will need to be inserted or extracted, then.'

'Not necessarily, Holbrooke. There's no specific plan, but it's best to be prepared. Now, you mentioned Major Albach earlier. He will also sail with the squadron, in an advisory capacity. However, the flagship will be far too public a place and at least initially he'll be embarked in *Argonaut*. You may enter him on your books as a supernumerary; I'm sure you'll make him comfortable. Mister Keppel may call on him, but he'll invariably return to *Argonaut*. And I warn you that he may be required to enter Brittany again, if the situation demands more up-to-date intelligence.'

'Excuse me, sir, but I thought it had been determined that Brittany is too dangerous for Major Albach, and yet now we are to contemplate landing him again.'

It was the first time that Chalmers had spoken, and he knew that he was treading on dangerous ground in coming so close to disagreeing with a decision that came directly from a lord commissioner of the Admiralty. Yet he was concerned about his friend Albach. Those French soldiers hadn't stumbled by accident upon that lonely cottage in Kermabec. They had been sent there with the expectation of finding their man, and that meant that Albach's identity was well known to the French. He wouldn't last a day in Brittany, and he'd surely hang if he was caught.

'No such thing is being planned, Mister Chalmers, it is merely a contingency, but I do understand your concern. His role will be to advise on conditions ashore in Brittany, nothing more, unless there is a dire need. It would be disingenuous to state firmly that he won't be sent ashore, one cannot tell how far necessity will drive us, but I do not expect it.'

Forbes thought for a moment.

'In fact, Mister Chalmers, I'll have something to that effect added to Mister Keppel's letter. And that brings me on to your part in this.'

It was Chalmers' turn to look discomforted. He'd been

reluctant to accompany Holbrooke to the Admiralty, it was no place for a frigate's chaplain, and he'd assumed the summons was merely because of the part he'd played in bringing Albach home.

'You are properly borne on *Argonaut's* books, I believe.'

Chalmers looked sideways at Holbrooke. It was a sensitive subject, and it wasn't entirely clear that a sixth rate's establishment included a chaplain. Nevertheless, it wasn't something that a man of Forbes position should be involved in, and he clearly wasn't concerned as to whether Chalmers' pay and victuals had been properly disbursed.

'Yes, sir. Mister Chalmers is borne as the chaplain.'

'Very well. In that case you will understand that you are as much under orders as Captain Holbrooke is. You will be the intermediary between Mister Keppel and Major Albach. This is to reduce as far as possible Albach's exposure to the curious gaze of the flagship's people. Unless there is some good reason otherwise, Mister Keppel will send for Captain Holbrooke or you rather than for Major Albach. That is the condition under which Mister Sawtree is prepared to allow his agent to sail with the squadron.'

Chalmers said nothing; he didn't make a sound or gesture to encourage Forbes.

'You will need to discover as much of Major Albach's business as you possibly can. To that end, when Sawtree has finished with him, he'll return to Portsmouth with you and I hope that you will make him welcome at your home, Captain Holbrooke.'

So Forbes knew that he had purchased a house near Portsmouth. Did he know exactly where it was? How much more did the admiral know about his circumstances? Holbrooke was starting to glimpse how the secret part of the navy operated, and he wasn't certain that he liked it.

'Major Albach and Mister Chalmers will need to be in each other's company daily. He'll be told not to wear his uniform, and in fact Sawtree was pleased that you had found a suit of plain clothes for him to come to London. It's of the greatest importance that he doesn't stand out in any way, that he doesn't attract attention to himself.'

Forbes looked again at Chalmers who was steadfastly refusing to give any hint of what he thought of the affair. He frowned.

'Does this meet with your approval, Mister Chalmers?'

There was a slight pause. Chalmers was no fool and he was well aware that not only was he subject to the orders of the Admiralty as well as any sea officer, but his somewhat anomalous position in *Argonaut* could easily be declared null and void, with implications for the pay and victuals that had been expended upon him for the past years, not to mention the prize money for which he could retrospectively be declared ineligible. How that weighed against the danger that he thought Albach was being exposed to wasn't evident to Holbrooke, and he waited for Chalmers to speak with as much impatience as Forbes.

'I'm honoured, sir,' he replied, 'but I'm sure you understand my caution with regard to Major Albach's personal safety.'

Forbes looked less than entirely pleased.

'Very well. *Argonaut* will no doubt have to join the squadron at Spithead in anticipation of Mister Keppel's commission. I know that your first lieutenant is competent, Captain Holbrooke, so I'll send a note to Admiral Holburne which will explain that you both have leave to be ashore until the squadron sails.'

***

'You're not happy to have come to the attention of the Admiralty, I gather, David.'

Holbrooke could see that Chalmers was distracted as they walked back towards Charing Cross and their lodgings. He wasn't looking at their surroundings as he normally did; his eyes were rooted firmly at the ground. They'd mutually decided to walk back on this fine day rather than take a Hackney coach, but this first day of sun after a cold winter wasn't moving them as it should.

'Not particularly. However, I do feel that the subject shouldn't be addressed in the street. Perhaps we can find somewhere less public to speak.'

'Admiral Forbes put my name forward for the Young Club last month, there being no vacancies at White's. I'm yet to be subjected to a vote but I have a letter,' he patted his breast pocket, 'inviting me to visit on two occasions in anticipation of becoming a member. We could go there.'

'Would we find a quiet spot, do you think?'

'Oh, I gather that at this time, well before dinner, the clubs are generally quiet. It's in St. James's, we can walk there in fifteen minutes. Perhaps we should reserve any further discussion until we are there.'

The Young Club was a sort of gilded purgatory where one waited for elevation to the heavenly altitudes of White's, but it shared much of its older brother's grandeur. After a few moments' examination of Holbrooke's letter, they were allowed in and shown to a quiet pair of deep leather chairs looking out onto the street. It was as confidential a place as they would find in London. They ordered the club sherry.

Chalmers looked around in frank admiration.

'I gather that the members have to unanimously agree to your induction, is that correct?'

'Well, not quite. It would be impossible, I gather, to question every member, so the matter is left to an election committee. If any single member of the committee objects, the application is rejected. I can't think that I know of anyone in either club who will object to my membership, except perhaps on the grounds of obscurity.'

'That fellow Deschamps who made an attempt on your life in *Kestrel*, he's not on the committee or a member is he?'

'Oh no. Forbes mentioned that particularly. He was nominated but was blackballed, largely because of rumours of that affair, and none of his family are inclined to remind people of it now.'

'Well, I wish you success. This is rather better than lodgings when you are in town, and I imagine you can afford the membership fee.'

Their sherries arrived in vast thick glasses, and they were left in peace.

'I'm not well pleased to be noticed, it's true.'

Chalmers' face displayed his disapproval and not even the excellent sherry could force a smile.

'I've been largely anonymous to their Lordships so far, which is just as I wish it. It leaves me free to pursue my own interests and to come and go as I please, within the constraints of my captain's needs, of course, and they have been remarkably light.'

Holbrooke nodded. He'd rarely had to do any more than suggest to Chalmers that he might like to be on board at such-and-such a time or attend to a particular duty. Theirs had been very much a relationship of equals.

'Now, I fear that I may be called upon at any time, even to the extent of tearing me away from your company. I have become a foot-soldier in the Admiralty's secret war.'

'I fear that you're correct, David, but I also fear that the die is cast.'

'Just so. However, that's the lesser of my two concerns. My greater objection is that for all Admiral Forbes' protestations, for all Sawtree's obvious concern for his agent, our friend Hans Albach is nothing more than a pawn in this game, and as expendable as any pawn in the front rank of the chess board. I can see it in Sawtree's eyes, he has the look of a fanatic. He will cast Albach to the devil with nothing more than a false tear if he believes that it will advance the cause. I have a great respect for Hans, and I fear that he doesn't understand how ruthless the people are who now control him.'

Holbrooke stared out of the window. He couldn't fault his friend's logical argument and deep inside he knew that it was true. A few years ago he would have wholeheartedly agreed with Chalmers, but he'd seen war for what it really was, and he had objectively observed his own attitudes hardening. The war must be ended on favourable terms for

Britain, that was his starting point. It had already consumed many of his friends and although he also had a great regard for Albach, his personal safety was no longer the most important point. He could see Chalmers studying him and could imagine what was going through his mind.

'Well then, we must do what we can to preserve Hans from the dangers of the war. I'm as certain as I can be that he doesn't count the perils, so let us be his protection.

***

CHAPTER FIFTEEN

Belle Isle

Wednesday, First of April 1761.
Argonaut, off Point Poulains, Belle Isle.

The warm spring sunshine was already doing its duty and a fine mist of water vapour lay over *Argonaut's* deck, carrying away the remains of the moisture from the morning scrub. Holbrooke stood at the quarterdeck rail and looked forward in satisfaction. The frustration of beating out of the channel against a sou'westerly was behind them and after the ship had weathered Ushant the previous evening, they had enjoyed a pleasant overnight reach to the sou'east. Holbrooke wanted to approach Belle Isle in the daylight, so the sailing master had set a leisurely course well to seaward of the Sein Islands, the Penmarks and the Glenan Islands, and now the frigate and its attendant cutter had a fair wind for Point Poulains at the north-west point of the island.

Albach was using Holbrooke's telescope to methodically quarter the horizon.

'Is that Belle Isle, Mister Fairview?'

'Yes, sir, you can see the north western part of it now. The lookout has a view of the mainland, but we won't see it for a while.'

Albach and Fairview were old friends from the sloop *Kestrel* and the Emden campaign, and they both found it hard to keep the social distance that was required between a sailing master and a secret supernumerary. Officially, Fairview couldn't know anything about Albach or his mission, but like the rest of the ship's company he could make an educated guess. Albach had been entered on the books under a false identity and indeed a false nationality, but his real name soon became known, and the mysterious assumed name only increased the thirst for information. The ears and eyes of every man were finely tuned to any hint of his purpose in being on board *Argonaut*. If ever Albach had thought that he could continue his secret career, the open speculation and curiosity of some two hundred men of half a dozen nations had persuaded him otherwise. No power on earth could stop them telling the tale as soon as they had shore leave and no vows of silence would be remembered after the first few drinks in the taverns of Portsmouth Point. His days as a confidential agent of the Admiralty were over, he was sure. All he could do now was advise at a safe distance from French territory.

'I've never seen it from this side although I've walked over most of the island. Surely there can be no question of landing here, on the seaward side.'

'Well, Commodore Keppel is unlikely to ask my opinion, but of course it's impossible. The wind blows from somewhere to the south of west for most of the year and with a fetch of some thousand leagues from America, it can build up quite a sea. Look, even in this fine weather you can see the waves breaking on the shore, and it's almost all rocks. No, we'll be looking at the north side, anywhere from Point Poulains in the west to Point Kerdonis in the east. Maybe a little further round on the east coast, Port Locmaria or somewhere like that, if the wind isn't too far south.'

Albach continued his study of the island. He'd been sent there a year ago to inspect the artillery positions and he'd made some very useful maps for the French Royal Artillery. Those maps had found their way to the Admiralty of course, because those were the early days of his spying career, long before he came under suspicion. Looking back, he realised that his French masters hadn't given him any tasks like that for some months, and the latest – and last – information that he had gleaned had been through a third party. Whether they suspected him or whether they were just tightening up their security, he couldn't tell, but they certainly knew all about his activities by now.

The defences on the northern side must have been significantly increased since his visit. Then, the only real fortifications had been at the citadel and at Gros Rocher where a redoubt commanded the eastern approaches to Le Palais and to a certain extent covered the area down towards Point Kerdonis. Between them they could have prevented an enemy anchoring in the Palais Road and could have made a landing between the two into a most dangerous enterprise. However he also knew that since Hawke started taking an interest in the island the French had sent across material and guns in a steady flow, and it was most important to understand where they had been deployed.

Holbrooke came on deck having finished his breakfast. He looked up at the tops'ls and over to the larboard quarter where the cutter obediently followed the frigate's movement. He nodded a friendly greeting to Albach.

'Mister Fairview, heave to if you please and hang out a signal for *Oyster's* captain. When he comes, I would like to see you and Mister Shorrock in my cabin.'

Holbrooke stood quietly as Fairview gave the orders to heave to.

'Would you also join me, sir?'

He could never remember his friend's assumed name and so chose the easy alternative of denying him a name at all. It was all so much nonsense of course. Three of the ship's officers knew Albach's real name, and each of them had used it inadvertently. It was well known throughout the ship, and Holbrooke had even heard it used openly by the seamen on deck. The problem was that everyone liked Albach. He had the same effect on the crew of *Argonaut* as he had on Holbrooke's first command, the sloop *Kestrel*, where his open, frank manner and evident good nature endeared him to everyone from the lowliest ship's boy to the captain.

***

'Will this wind hold, Mister Fairview?'

Holbrooke was studying the chart of Belle Isle while Fairview held his finger at the ship's position, four leagues to the sou'west of Point Poulains.

Treacherous Moon

'I believe so, sir. Sou'west-by-south but it's likely to back a little.'

'Then can we bear away and round the eastern end of the island?'

'Aye, sir, we can.'

'Good. I want a preliminary look at the northern side to see if there are any obvious new defensive works. We can do that before the end of the day, if we start in the east.'

They could all see the problem. If they started in the west and the wind did indeed back, they would have to tack along the northern coast and that made it difficult to carry out a systematic surveillance of the shore. By starting in the east they would have a fair wind right up to Point Poulains, taking in all the possible landing sites in one day.

'We have perhaps a week before Mister Keppel arrives, and we must make the best of that time.'

'Is Captain Gambier still blockading the Vilaine?'

'I believe so, Mister Shorrock, and we may well see him, although he's been ordered to keep a close watch, and to do that he'll need to be at anchor off Dumet Island most of the time.'

Neither said what they thought. The two best ships-of-the-line and the two best frigates had already escaped, and although there were at least four French ships still in the estuary, it was a bit like shutting the stable door after the horse had bolted.

'Well, that's nothing to do with us. You all know that our only task is to provide Mister Keppel the latest information on the island's defences. Mister Finch, you'll proceed inshore of *Argonaut*, running lines of soundings for all you're worth. You'll set the pace unless you see a blue flag at my foretopmast, in which case you'll match *Argonaut's* speed and take what soundings you can. If you see a red flag, you are to make an offing and join *Argonaut*. And of course you must give the citadel at Le Palais a wide berth, at least two miles. I want to be off Point Poulains before sunset so that you can give Mister Fairview your draft soundings before dark.'

Finch looked thoughtful. He knew these waters well and had already surveyed much of the expanse of water inshore of the island. Now, however, he would need to sail much closer to the shore, at the extreme range of any batteries, and he'd have to take soundings while his cutter was moving faster than would be ideal. Well, if he must, so be it.

Holbrooke turned towards Albach and caught himself before he uttered the Austrian's name in public.

'I would be grateful if you could station yourself on the quarterdeck with Mister Chalmers, being the only one of us who has set foot on the island.'

***

The sou'westerly wind wafted *Argonaut* slowly along the coast of Belle Isle. The narrow eastern side of the island had a bold coastline rising from five fathoms to a rocky shore. It had only two or three possible landing places, all around Port Locmaria and Port An-Dro. The problem with them was immediately apparent as they came into sight; even with the wind three points to the west of south, the swell ran right along the coast making the anchorages perilous, and if it should back any further and blow a little, they would be untenable. Nevertheless, they would be candidates for invasion sites if the wind came anywhere from the north of sou'west.

Albach studied the shore carefully.

'Is it as you remember?' Holbrooke asked.

Albach lowered the telescope and turned to him with a shocked expression.

'A year ago there was but one small battery with four nine-pound guns, and no real attempt to create any obstacles to landing. Look at it now.'

Holbrooke took the telescope and scanned the passing shore. At first he could see nothing of significance, then, as he became accustomed to the shape of the land, he started to see the ugly signs of defensive works. Here the land had been scraped away to make a cliff that was almost overhung, there a beach had been fortified with huge timbers embedded in the sand with whole trees entwined in them. At every vantage point he could see the scars in the earth where new batteries had been erected.

'Your General Hodgson will have to fight to gain a foothold and fight again when Monsieur Sainte-Croix counterattacks. It won't be a simple matter at all.'

Holbrooke kept his eyes on the shore as each new defensive work came into view.

'I had expected nothing less, and I doubt whether Commodore Keppel or the general imagined that the French would quietly await an attack without making any preparations. It must have been clear for at least a year that Belle Isle was under threat.'

'Aye, and there's a few things I learned from the French army: always to prepare for the worst possible situation and never, ever to underestimate an enemy. They are remarkably industrious you know, and they've been the experts at fortifying a coast ever since the great master Vauban turned his attention to it.'

***

They had to give Point Kerdonis a wide berth – Finch had warned them of some rocks lying offshore – and then they had a broad reach up the leeward side of the island. This side was naturally split into two by the island's principal town, Le Palais, that lay at the half-way point. The first part was not encouraging with a shallower approach frequently strewn with rocks, but good shelter, nevertheless. Two miles to the east of Le Palais, Vauban had built a redoubt on a rocky point of land called Gros Rocher. It looked formidable and if its guns were well served by determined crews – and the French Royal Artillery had an enviable reputation – it would render a landing anywhere along the coast from Le Palais to half a league short of Point Kerdonis all but impossible. The ships-of-the-line would have to lie quite far offshore, too far to cover the landings with their guns, and it would be a long pull for the flatboats that would take the infantry in. Holbrooke had commanded a division of flatboats in the landings on the north coast of Brittany, and he remembered how important it had been to launch the attack from close to shore. At least a landing on this part of the island would be close to Le Palais and its citadel, no more than five miles from the furthest point to the town, which would ease the army's task once it had been established ashore.

Like the eastern coast, every possible landing site that they observed had been fortified. Batteries, earthworks, abatis, gentle slopes turned into vertical cliffs, everything that art and science could imagine had been accomplished by the French engineers. It was an impressive example of what could be achieved by energy and organisation.

Argonaut approached Le Palais in the afternoon. Holbrooke hadn't left the quarterdeck all day and his legs were starting to protest, but there was no help for it and not for anything would he call for a chair.

'Remind me, Sir, what guns does the citadel mount?'

Albach took a moment to realise that he was being addressed.

'My information is a year old, sir. There were four thirty-two-pound naval guns, all at the seaward end, and thirty twenty-four pound guns on land carriages spread around the walls. The seaward approach is shallow and there's no room to manoeuvre, so they were more concerned about an attack from the land than the sea. I expect it hasn't changed.'

Holbrooke studied the citadel through his telescope. It lay on the north side of the inlet that formed the port of Le Palais, with its walls touching the sea and the waters of the inlet. There would be no attacking it by naval assault, the only hope was for a regular siege from the landward side. If an army could be landed anywhere on the island, and if it could hold off a counter-attack until it was reinforced, then it would be a mere matter of marching to occupy the whole island. At the first sign of a successful landing, all the villages would have to be abandoned, as well as the town of Le

Palais, and the defenders would have to concentrate in the citadel and hope that they could hold the walls long enough to be relieved. It would be a vain hope with Keppel's squadron blockading the defenders and supplying its own attacking force with food and ammunition and reinforcements. It would take the whole of the French naval force from Brest and Rochefort to clear a way for a relieving squadron. With only better weather to come, it was certain that the army could force a surrender before the onset of the usual problems that afflicted besieging forces: lack of food and munitions, disease and apathy. He wouldn't like to have the task of defending Le Palais.

***

The coast to the west of Le Palais was much the same as the east – rugged and rock-strewn and lined with defences until the port of Sauzon. Yet here the water was deeper as it approached the shore, offering the hope of covering fire for landings. Sauzon had potential: a good, sheltered anchorage and no impregnable citadel to defend it.

'Now there's a place that can be more easily taken.'

Argonaut had moved in close, almost as close as *Oyster*, and Shorrock had joined the group on the quarterdeck. He was starting to become impatient with talk of the impossibility of landing an army and he brightened at the sight of Sauzon.

'The third-rates can come close enough to bombard the shore and the boats will have only a few cables to row. An afternoon's work, at most.'

Albach took a few moments before responding; he still had to arrange his words before making a long speech in English.

'True, Mister Shorrock, but you are forgetting the land between here and Le Palais. Look how high it is and how it's cut through and through by those deep gullies. It would take an age to bring infantry across that ground, and guns may be entirely impossible. If I were defending the citadel against an attack from the west, I would contest every inch of ground and expect to wear my enemy down before he came to my real defences. Sauzon is tempting, but it's a dead end – a *cul-de-sac* as the French say – and I think that as soon as he was ashore your general would decide that he needed another landing in the east.'

Holbrooke nodded in agreement. He had a better understanding of land operations than his first lieutenant and could immediately see what Albach meant. Yet he could also see that Shorrock wasn't convinced. Without any experience to guide his opinions, the first lieutenant thought that soldiers made too much of the difficulties of moving large bodies of men on land.

***

Finch delivered the rough draft of his soundings before darkness closed off inshore operations. While *Argonaut* beat out into the Atlantic to find some sea-room for the night, Holbrooke convened another meeting of his officers.

They all looked tired, as well they might, most of them having been on deck since before dawn. The task of working the ship along the coast had fallen to Shorrock, while the sailing master was busy with his bearings and soundings. Albach had been a most eager helper, identifying points on the land from memory and offering a soldier's perspective on the feasibility of landings and siege.

'It's a good start, now I want your opinions on where we should concentrate our surveys. I've been given a free hand by the commodore, but the choice of a landing site is certainly not my decision. Mister Shorrock, would you start us off?'

'Well, sir. I'm still taken with Sauzon. I hear the gentleman's objections, but I find it hard to believe that the army can't find a way across the four or five miles to the citadel. It has good shelter and a good holding ground in the road. Ships-of-the-line can approach close enough to support a landing and the port appears big enough for the storeships to take the ground at half-tide. It seems in every way suitable for the main landing, or if not, then for a diversion or a secondary landing.'

Holbrooke glanced at Albach whose face betrayed nothing other than deep concentration. The Austrian started as though he had been asleep.

'Sauzon? On purely naval grounds I would agree with Mister Shorrock, but not when I think as a soldier. You heard my arguments against the place. Now, even as a diversion, I must dismiss it. The commander of the island's garrison will be delighted if the army lands there, he knows that it will take days for them to threaten the citadel. The battle for Belle Isle will be won or lost on the first day of the landing and any part of the force that is not available to defend against a French counter-attack is wasted. I would devote no more time to Sauzon.'

Holbrooke looked quickly at Shorrock to see how he was taking this dismissal of his opinion. He seemed entirely unmoved.

'Very well, what do you think of the coast to the east of Le Palais?'

'The landing will be more difficult and as I understand it your ships will have to lie off about two miles and so they won't be able to bombard the defenders. However, once ashore, the army can form up quickly on good ground and be ready to fight any counterattack in a very short space of time. It's better than Le Palais, but still I find the east coast most attractive – Port Locmaria and Port An-Dro – but I understand there is a problem with shelter for the landing.'

Holbrooke nodded.

'What do you think, Mister Fairview.'

Fairview pulled a long face.

'They're only little fishing harbours, sir, and you can see why they haven't been developed into greater ports. The whole shore is open to any wind south of sou'west; they can't be used above fifteen days in the month. With the wind so liable to back without warning at this time of the year, I fear that a landing, once started, could become fatally disrupted. Once that becomes a lee shore, the flatboats will find it impossible and there will be no more landing of supplies. The army could find itself half ashore and half on land. In a nor-westerly wind with fine weather it might be attempted, but not otherwise.'

Holbrooke stared absently at the master's chart. In a way, it didn't matter. He wasn't being called upon to advocate any particular landing site, but he still felt that he should have something to prioritise his efforts for the next week. A day at each place, including Le Palais and the citadel, might produce enough information for Keppel and General Hodgson to make their decision, but the poor commander of the landing force would be sadly short of detailed surveys and soundings. They were all looking at him.

'Well, gentlemen, I find that we must ignore the west of Le Palais and concentrate on the east of the island. We'll survey the north and east coasts two miles either side of Point Kerdonis until Saturday then we'll sail west for Sauzon and make a pretence of examining the area, and position ourselves to meet the squadron when it arrives.

***

CHAPTER SIXTEEN

High Command

Monday, Sixth of April 1761.
Argonaut, Eight Leagues West of Belle Isle.

The outlying frigates came into sight at noon, and then, one-by-one, the sails of the invasion force appeared, breaking the purity of the horizon until it was entirely obscured over a wide arc to the west. Holbrooke lost count, but it looked like over a hundred and twenty ships in all, between ships-of-the-line, frigates, sloops, bomb ketches, fire ships, transports and storeships. They were all moving slowly but purposefully before the light westerly airs, with barely a hint of the usual Atlantic swell. It was the sort of perfect spring weather that all sailors knew wouldn't last; it would be blown away with the next gale to come ripping in from the wild oceanic wastes.

Albach let out a low whistle. It was beyond anything he'd seen before, and it conveyed a sense of the British determination to bring the war onto French soil more than any mere words could do. He watched in wonder as the troop transports appeared behind the battle squadron.

'How many soldiers would each of those transports carry?'

'Oh, anything up to a company. They're of no standard design as you can see, in fact they're almost all chartered from the regular shipping companies – West Indiamen, east coast colliers and the like – and they'll go back when their work is over. The army likes to keep its men in tactical units even at sea, I'm sure you can imagine why. And a company can muster almost any number of men that the colonel sees fit – or that he can recruit – so it's quite a puzzle to use the available tonnage to its best advantage.'

Albach nodded. He'd never been involved in an amphibious operation, but he'd witnessed the deadly complexity of the withdrawal from the beach at Saint-Cast from a defender's perspective, over the sights of his battery of French guns. He could easily imagine how difficult it would be to organise the units immediately before the landing, and how many boats would have to be used just to bring the platoons, companies and battalions and all their equipment together before the assault. Of course, it would be completely hopeless to leave it until after the men had been put ashore. Just conceivably it could be done if the enemy granted the attacking force a week of grace before launching a counterattack, but no sane commander of a defence force would do that. If a seaborne assault was to be defeated, it had to be done at the high-water mark, otherwise it became a regular engagement between two field armies, a wholly different problem, and the defender's natural advantage would be lost.

'Of course it's a similar consideration for the supply ships. You'll be aware of the vast amount of ammunition that a field gun battery needs, and it must be delivered ashore at the right time and to the right units. The same goes for all the supplies. You soldiers may not like to hear it, but an attack on an enemy's coast is largely won or lost in the port of embarkation.'

Holbrooke grinned at Albach. They had been having a friendly rivalry – sea officer against land officer – ever since Albach had arrived in *Argonaut*, fresh from his flight across the Brittany countryside.

'Yes, I'm sure that's true,' Albach replied quietly out of the corner of his mouth, while keeping the approaching ships in his telescope's view, 'and yet I would prefer to be a fighting man rather than a storekeeper and transport manager.'

Chalmers barked a laugh. He missed nothing, not even words spoken low between a supernumerary and the captain.

'*Touché*. A hit, I believe.'

Holbrooke couldn't help smiling; it was good to see

everyone in high spirits before what he was sure would be a difficult period.

'Mister Fairview. You see the commodore's pennant flying in *Valiant?*'

'Aye, sir. The seventy-four in the vanguard of the squadron.'

'Then bring the ship under *Valiant's* lee, if you please. I don't expect Mister Keppel will heave to, not for my convenience, so have the longboat brought alongside and manned.'

***

Holbrooke hadn't invited Albach to join him and the Austrian hadn't asked to do so. It was all very well for his identity to be well known in a little frigate, but the general and his staff were soon to be put ashore on a dangerous mission, and it would be better if none of them had ever heard of this obscure Major in the Austrian artillery corps.

Keppel greeted Holbrooke as though they had known each other for years, rather than having only met once before, two weeks ago at Spithead. He seldom smiled and always wore a wig. If the rumour was true, he had neither teeth nor hair of his own, having lost both to scurvy during Anson's circumnavigation twenty years earlier. Perhaps he thought it was a fair exchange for the patronage of a man who would go on to become the First Lord of the Admiralty, and certainly Anson looked after his surviving officers from that epic voyage.

Holbrooke hadn't yet met the commander of the land forces. Major General Studholme Hodgson was a soldier of the old school. He'd fought under the Duke of Cumberland at Fontenoy in the last war, where he'd been an *aide-de-camp* to the old King's son, and again at Culloden during the Jacobite rising. In this present war he'd been a brigade commander during the abortive raid on Rochefort where he'd sat on the infamous council of war. Wolfe summed it up acidly by declaring that they had decided unanimously *'not to attack the place they were ordered to attack, and for reasons that no soldier will allow to be sufficient.'* Holbrooke knew all these things about Hodgson, as did anyone who followed the events of the French wars, and he knew that, like Keppel, the general had profited from the patronage of a powerful superior. He was prepared to be barely noticed by the general and was pleasantly astonished to find himself greeted warmly. The general interrupted before the introductions were properly completed.

'So this is the officer who has the latest intelligence on the landing's feasibility. I'm pleased to meet you, Captain Holbrooke.'

Keppel looked annoyed and broke in before Holbrooke could reply.

'Captain Holbrooke has been here for only a week, General, and he won't have had the opportunity to view the defences from the shore, but I hope he'll have something to say to us, at least.'

Holbrooke hesitated; had he stepped into a disagreement between two officers of high command? He'd noticed the word *feasibility* that the general had used. Did that indicate that he was less than wholly committed to this venture? Was he waiting to hear how strong the defences were? Holbrooke was aware that the mood of the war had changed, that Pitt daily expected a declaration from the Spanish. A combination of what remained of the French fleet and the pristine Spanish fleet would create a new and very real threat to the British Isles that would require its forces to be repatriated on a grand scale. Anson had already recalled most of the three-deckers – the first and second rate ships of the line – to fall back into the English Channel. Could the same logic apply to the twelve regiments of foot that had been sent on this expedition? He cleared his throat nervously.

'I have a report here, sir, and the results of what surveys we have been able to conduct...'

'I'll look at those later, Holbrooke. For now, we urgently need to know your opinions on the landing sites. I've already told General Hodgson that you have some experience of these matters.'

'You were captured at Saint-Cast while embarking the army were you not, and you were at Fort Niagara?'

The general looked genuinely interested, not merely mouthing pleasantries.

'I had that honour, sir, and I commanded a division of flatboats at Cherbourg.'

'Good, then you know the difficulties of these operations, and you may even speak in a language that I can understand. Pray proceed.'

Holbrooke unrolled a chart that he had brought with him. He'd annotated it with his observations, ignoring Fairview's objections at this wanton defacement of a good navigational chart. He was unsure who he should be addressing, so he took the safe route and looked first at Keppel and then at Hodgson.

'I looked briefly at the southern and western shores, sir. As I expected, they are rocky and barren and exposed, and there are only a few little coves where fishing boats are dragged ashore. There's no place suitable to land an army, in my view.'

Hodgson stared vacantly at the shoreline that Holbrooke had described, while Keppel looked away in frustration at this statement of what he considered to be the obvious.

'The French haven't bothered to fortify the southern side of the island at all. The northern side, however, is a different matter. Their engineers have been hard at work and every possible landing site has some sort of obstacle, and a battery at every headland to cover them. I regret that I could find no place that wasn't defended.'

Hodgson was frowning while Keppel looked impatient.

'The approach to the citadel at Le Palais is too shallow for heavy ships to get close enough for a bombardment and its guns cover an area that overlaps with the redoubt at Gros Rocher.'

He let that information sink in while he marshalled his

thoughts. It was important to give an impartial account of his observations; he knew very well that an opinion wouldn't be welcomed.

'This area between the Gros Rocher and Point Kerdonis is defended, of course, but at least our ships can get closer to the shore.'

'How about the eastern shore, Captain Holbrooke, I suppose that's defended also.'

Hodgson was getting impatient at the flow of bad news.

'It is sir. There are good landing places at Port An-Dro and Port Locmaria, here at the north and in the centre of that stretch of coast, but they're overlooked by batteries and the beach is strewn with abatis. It's also open to any wind from sou'-sou'west through to nor'east.'

'The very winds that we can expect at this time of year,' Keppel remarked.

The general jabbed his finger at the chart.

'Then how about to the west of Le Palais? This place Sauzon?'

'It's sheltered, it has a good anchorage, and the ships can get in close enough to support the landing. There are batteries here and here.'

Holbrooke pointed at the bold headland to the west of the harbour entrance and the lower point to the south.

'They're new, they weren't here a year ago.'

Hodgson looked thoughtfully at the chart. It was a strictly navigational aid, it showed the coastline and soundings, rocks and shoals, but it had little to say about features on the land. The high ground was only indicated if it could be used to fix a ship's position, otherwise the area between the coastlines was a featureless space. He snapped his fingers at an aide who stood attentively behind him.

'Bring the campaign map, would you?'

He stared again at the chart as a land map of Belle Isle was spread on the table beside him. It was better for his purposes in that it showed broadly how the land was folded and indented, where an army could march and deploy in battle and where it was constrained by the terrain.

'There are only two sensible ports on the island. Le Palais I think we can discount, what do you think Commodore?'

Keppel knew all about the citadel that guarded the island's main port and he'd already decided that it couldn't be successfully assaulted from the sea, nor could an army be landed under its walls until its guns were silenced.

'It's one of Vauban's works,' he said simply.

Hodgson nodded slowly in agreement.

'We'll have to lay siege to the place eventually, but it's not a place for a seaborne landing. Nevertheless, I'd like to have a look before we dismiss it. And then there's Sauzon. It's tempting but I'm concerned about all these ravines between there and Le Palais. I'm sure that the French have brought in reinforcements, and they'll meet us in the field if they possibly can, before they withdraw to the citadel.'

'You think Sauzon may be a trap, General? What does your confidential man say about it, Captain Holbrooke? Don't worry, General Hodgson knows that you have a particular person on board *Argonaut*.'

'Yes, your mysterious informant whom I cannot meet. Is he a qualified observer, does he understand the movement of armies on land?'

Keppel swept an arm towards Holbrooke, inviting him to respond.

'He's a soldier, sir, and he toured Belle Isle a year ago, before the French started their new defensive plan. His opinion matches yours, General. He fears that Sauzon is a trap that's been left temptingly open. It's likely that all these ravines have been shaped for defence and filled with abatis, whatever will hinder your army.'

Hodgson grunted.

'And that doesn't hold true in the east of the island?'

'Oh, the whole place is cut up by ravines, but to the east of Le Palais the land is mostly a fairly flat plateau. Good marching terrain, once you can get to the heights, he assures me.'

'Well, we didn't expect this would be easy,' Hodgson declared. 'Let's have a good look at the place tomorrow. Will this wind serve?'

'It will, General. The whole fleet can anchor in the Palais Road, out of range of the guns on the fortress, and we can inspect the coast at our leisure. I think, Mister Holbrooke, that I'll shift my flag into *Argonaut* for the day. You have a cutter, don't you? That may be useful if we need a closer look. You'll join me in the frigate General? If you have no more questions for Captain Holbrooke, we'll leave you in peace.'

***

Keppel and Holbrooke had the poop deck to themselves. The wind was refreshing, the sun was warm and the spectacle of the lovely green island to the east was entrancing.

'I'd hoped to keep the general away from your man, Captain Holbrooke, but I find that his information is too important. As far as I can tell there is nobody in the squadron or the army with more recent or more detailed knowledge on the defences of the island. Can you keep his name a secret at least?'

'His name, yes, that can be kept confidential, unless one of my officers inadvertently uses it, but it will be evident that he's neither British nor French, he has a strong accent.'

'I'll speak to the general, persuade him not to inquire too deeply. But are you telling me that his real name is known on board?'

'I regret so, sir. You see, I've sailed with him before, he was at Emden, and so was my sailing master and my bosun and coxswain. He spent some days on board my sloop *Kestrel*, and they knew him immediately. And then, he's not very discreet himself; he seems to view *Argonaut* as a safe haven.'

Keppel stared thoughtfully at the island.

'Well, a ship is no place to keep secrets, as we both

know.'

'Indeed sir. However, he knows that he'll never set foot in France again, not until this war is over, and even then he may not be safe. He doesn't seem concerned.'

Keppel gave Holbrooke an odd look.

'I've been told to leave the handling of our guest to you, Holbrooke. However, what you perhaps don't know is that I may use him again if I feel it absolutely necessary. That situation hasn't yet arisen, and I trust it won't, but if I ask him, will he go ashore again, for one more mission?'

Holbrooke stopped dead, then collected himself. Despite Admiral Forbes' warning, he had hoped that Albach was only with the expedition in an advisory role. Then a movement at the poop deck ladder caught his eye. A head appeared, followed by a body clad in plain black clothes hauling itself painfully up to the deck. He recognised him in an instant. It was Sawtree, the confidential adviser from the Admiralty.

***

CHAPTER SEVENTEEN

Reconnaissance

Tuesday, Seventh of April 1761.
Argonaut, at Sea, off Port Locmaria.

Holbrooke forced himself to stand still, to keep his hands from nervous fidgeting. He knew he shouldn't be ill at ease, but sharing his quarterdeck with the commanders of a vast naval squadron and a substantial army would test the self-confidence of any young man. And it wasn't just Keppel and Hodgson. The deck was crowded with the general's staff officers – brigadier-generals, colonels, majors and a lone army captain – all jostling for the best view of the passing shoreline and each asserting his God-given right to the few telescopes that were available. Sawtree was there also, keeping his distance from the staff but occasionally exchanging a word with Hodgson or Keppel. He watched in grim amusement as Fairview clung onto his own telescope in the face of a determined attempt by a senior personage's aide-de-camp to relieve him of it. Keppel's coxswain, his sole attendant, had of course brought the commodore's telescope and it had hardly left his eye since the eastern shore of the island came into view.

'I see what you mean, Holbrooke. They've been busy as bees since I was last down this way.'

The early morning sun shone full upon the coast revealing the awful extent of its defences. It was an iron-bound shore in any case, with only two breaks in the wall of rock. Ravines carved into the high plateau ran down to the sea at Port Locmaria and Port An-Dro, offering pocket-handkerchief sandy beaches where fishing boats could ride out the weather at anchor or be dragged ashore when a storm threatened.

'I inspected this coast pretty thoroughly, sir. You can see Port Locmaria from here and that little place Port D'Arzic, and soon you'll have a good view of Port An-Dro. In two months, with the onset of summer weather, they would both be more feasible, but as you can see they are wide open to any southerly or sou'westerly wind.'

Keppel looked up at his pennant flying bravely from the main t'gallant head, then over to the east where the sky was clear and bright except for a few clouds touching the faraway hills. He looked thoughtful and tapped the wood of the gunwale. He had that happy facility of being able to remember names, even after the briefest of introductions.

'Mister Fairview.'

'One moment, sir.'

Fairview straightened from the compass where he had been taking a bearing of Point Kerdonis, the northern extremity of this coast. He addressed Holbrooke rather than Keppel.

'Captain, sir. We're being set to the west somewhat. I'd like to come a point to starboard to clear the shallow patch off the point.'

Holbrooke was taken aback. Perhaps now he understood why Fairview, despite his seniority, his experience and his demonstrable competence, was still the master of a humble frigate. He knew of nobody else who would ignore a commodore in that way, not even to ensure the safety of the ship. He looked at the pennant and at the main tops'l and caught the quartermaster's encouraging nod.

'Will she take it, Mister Fairview?'

'Aye, sir. She'll just do it without wearing. Perhaps the mizzen will set a little by the lee, but it won't be for long. That'll give us five cables off the shallows.'

'Very well.'

Fairview did no more than nod at the quartermaster who gave the orders to the helm and to the sail trimmers. Fairview ignored the proceedings and turned to Keppel with his face set in an expression of dutiful obedience. If Keppel thought his behaviour lacked the deference that was due to his rank, he didn't show it. But Holbrooke could see the general's look of thunder; things were done differently in the army.

'What do you think of the weather, Mister Fairview?'

The sailing master swept his eyes around the whole of the horizon, lingering to the south and sou'west.

'The wind backed eight points in the night, sir. I don't see any sign of it backing any further, but it's possible. I'd say this southerly is set in for the day. I don't like that clear sky though; it could mean the wind will get up in the next few hours.'

Keppel didn't reply but looked again to the south, pursing his lips. He took a step closer to Hodgson, who was clearly wanting the commodore's attention.

'I'd dearly like to get straight at 'em, Commodore. We can take that little port out of hand and my men could be up on the plateau before ever the enemy could react.'

Holbrooke couldn't help overhearing and he instinctively looked astern at the great flotilla that was following in their wake. The general was right, and with the help of Keppel's signal book, the entire squadron could be ordered to heave to off this eastern coast and in an hour the grenadiers could be ashore. By noon Hodgson would have enough men on that high ground to snub his nose at anything the French could bring up to oppose them. And yet, one look at the waves beating on the rocks told him that it would be no easy task to put boats ashore.

Keppel nodded guardedly while all of the general's staff visible brightened. Holbrooke recognised the signs; he'd seen them before. An army was at its worst in the face of indecision. They all, from the brigadier-generals to the least private soldier, responded to the prospect of immediate action. It was a wonderful thing to see, but Holbrooke knew that it must be tempered by a sober assessment of the risks, and he knew how swiftly that confidence could be shattered.

'It's tempting, General, and a swift blow could bring this to a rapid conclusion. I'm just concerned about the weather.

Treacherous Moon

If it blows up any more the boats won't make it to the shore, and worse, your grenadiers and the others in the first wave may be stranded without any support.'

Holbrooke could see what was happening. Keppel knew that a landing today, in this weather, on this exposed shore, was foolhardy, but he also knew the recent history of combined operations on this coast. The recriminations after the failure at Rochefort were still reverberating through the navy and the army, and it was important that the sea officers shouldn't appear to be seeing dangers at every turn. The commodore was trying to manoeuvre the general into abandoning any thought of a rushed landing. He had to give the army credit; they were eager to get to grips with the enemy. He could see it in their faces, but it felt wrong to him and he hoped that the plan would be abandoned under the weight of evidence.

'I'll need six hours. If you think the weather will hold until noon, then for my part the army can go. It is, of course, a joint decision.'

There was a pause. Hodgson was waiting for Keppel to declare himself. Holbrooke could see Fairview out of the corner of his eye. The sailing master was shaking his head emphatically, being careful that neither of the senior officers could see him. Holbrooke felt obliged to speak; perhaps he could ease the commodore's task.

'If you please, sir.'

Keppel looked irritated at the interruption, but Holbrooke was committed and he pointed to the south, to windward.

'There's a squall coming. Perhaps it's nothing but it could be a change in the wind.'

They could feel it now. *Argonaut* leaned a little further to larboard and the sound of the wind in the rigging raised a quarter octave. There was no danger to the ship, they were already under easy sail to make a slow passage along the coast, but it was a timely gust that focussed the general's mind upon the dangers of the weather. The cool wind whipped across the deck and the commodore's pennant streamed boldly away towards the island.

Keppel shifted his stance to brace against the heeling deck. A colonel was taken by surprise and fell heavily against the binnacle from where he was brought to his feet by the expressionless quartermaster.

Keppel's face was like stone as he turned back towards Hodgson.

'I regret that I must formally state my opinion that the wind is too strong for a landing on this coast in this today, General.'

***

Holbrooke could sense how far this initial setback had affected the mood of the general's staff. They had all been eagerly studying the passing shore but when it became apparent that there would be no landing this day, they had started to break up into small groups, talking quietly and looking accusingly at the sea officers. Yet he could also see that the general himself looked relieved that the decision had been taken out of his hands by that fortuitous gust of wind. And the decision had been correct; that first gust had been merely the advance guard. In the following hours the wind backed into the sou'east and strengthened, making it evident to the dullest intellect that there could be no landing on the eastern shore.

They passed Port An-Dro with the general looking hungrily at the width of the inlet and the stretch of firm sand either side. It was so much broader than Port Locmaria, but it suffered from the same disadvantage of the weather, and they passed it in silence.

Argonaut stood up to the north to round Point Kerdonis then wore and started a run along the island's northern coast.

'You see how sheltered this coast is, unless the wind should back into the north.'

Keppel was attempting to be encouraging in spite of the glum faces all around.

Treacherous Moon

'It's the same all the way to Point Taillefer, past Le Palais, sir,' said Holbrooke, supporting his commodore, 'then the westerlies tend to swing around and bring a swell against that far nor'western coast.'

The general's staff had regained their cheerfulness at the sight of a shore with calmer seas. The talk was now all about the new defences. They could see the redoubt at Gros Rocher and could imagine the reach of the guns, and they could estimate how difficult it would be to surmount the obstacles on the beach.

'Are you satisfied, General?'

'Are you not going to look at Sauzon?'

Keppel looked faintly amused. It was always surprising at sea, when someone in authority didn't grasp the simplest dynamics of wind and current.

'I'd rather not take this frigate so far to leeward; we wouldn't be able to work our way back to the squadron until tomorrow,' he motioned to where *Oyster* followed happily on *Argonaut's* lee quarter. 'I plan to use the cutter to look into Sauzon.'

Hodgson looked doubtfully at the little craft and then at the size of his staff.

'I suppose I'll have to reduce the numbers in that case.'

'I'd recommend it, General. Apart from anything else, with the cutter drawing so little water, we can make a closer inspection, but that will expose us to the shore batteries. We wouldn't want all our eggs in one basket.'

Hodgson nodded to his chief of staff who went away to discuss who should transfer to the cutter. Sawtree intercepted him and it was clear that he was staking his claim to join the party.

'Mister Holbrooke. Please be good enough to hang out the signal for the fleet to anchor once we are abreast of the Palais Road.'

***

Keppel chose not to shift his flag. It was unnecessary and would only encourage the French batteries. In those sheltered waters *Oyster* came alongside *Argonaut* while the frigate was still underway.

'Captain Holbrooke, would you join us?'

Keppel turned on his heel after throwing out the invitation, and joined the general, who with his chief of staff was waiting to board the cutter.

Holbrooke handed over the frigate to Shorrock with instructions to anchor to seaward of the main group of ships, and he hastened across. He was surprised to see Albach scrambling across after him, sticking close to Sawtree who moved with great care, favouring his damaged spine.

Finch ordered the mainsail sheeted and *Oyster* reached away on the starboard tack to give Point Taillefer a wide berth. The cutter was fast with the wind on the beam and soon the Palais Road was left behind.

***

'Is this the quietest spot on this craft?' Sawtree asked, looking pointedly at the helmsman who was standing barely ten feet away.

'It is.'

Keppel's reply showed that he wasn't prepared to barter with this strange man from an office of the Admiralty that was barely officially recognised. Holbrooke could see that he immediately thought better of his treatment of Sawtree. Probably he was imagining a time when his expertise would become vital to the expedition's success.

'The cabin's too small for all of us and I regret that we can't do without a helmsman. Mister Finch, as you can see, has removed himself as far forward as his duties allow.'

'Very well, sir.'

Sawtree's manner suggested that he wasn't accustomed to accepting a commodore's word unchallenged.

'Now, gentlemen. This is the person that I told you about, and I'm prepared to introduce him in this smaller group, but I must impress upon you the necessity for discretion. Forgive me if I don't use names, but identification, as you can imagine, carries perils in this business…'

Hodgson held up his hand to stop Sawtree.

'I accept his anonymity, Mister Sawtree, but I find that I must at least establish his credentials. Pray interpose yourself if you find my questions going too far.'

Sawtree nodded reluctantly.

'Now, sir. You are a military man?'

Albach glanced sideways at Sawtree who bent his neck almost imperceptibly and winced at the pain that it gave him.

'I have that honour, sir.'

Hodgson looked surprised at Albach's accented English. Albach was clearly not a native of the British Isles, nor of France, then what?

'And I gather that a year ago you spent some time among the fortifications of this island.'

'I did, sir. I regret that I can't reveal the circumstances, but I viewed all the defences throughout the island as they stood at that time, and I have sufficient experience of fortifications to be able to assess their worth. I also viewed much of the ground, and again, I can offer a view as to its suitability for manoeuvre. However, I should point out that since the island became a point of interest, the defenders have addressed the weaknesses of all the possible landing sites, as you perhaps saw on the east coast.'

'Good, then you'll be able to help as we look at Sauzon. By the way, what's your opinion of a landing there?'

Albach was wearing the suit of plain clothes that he had worn to London. He felt uncomfortable without his familiar uniform, and he passed a finger between his stock and his neck. It was no tighter than the stock he had worn almost all of his life, it was just different.

'Sauzon is the only other large port on the island, sir, but it has no real fortifications and is in no way as well defended as Le Palais. If the weather is fair, if there's no swell from the north, then a landing would be simpler than anywhere in the south and it would be far easier to move the supplies ashore. That's not the problem, if I may say. The difficulty is how you move an army from there to the citadel.'

Hodson nodded. That was just the point that he had noted from a study of the maps, but it was useful to have it confirmed by someone who had trodden the ground.

'A year ago nothing had been done, but even then there was a plan to make the ravines that cover the western end of the island impassable.'

Hodgson stared hard at Albach, perhaps trying to guess at how this information had been obtained.

'Is that not true of the east? The maps show the whole of the island's plateau cut up deeply. Is there no plan to do the same there?'

'I agree, sir, that a map shows little difference between the west and the east. However, on the ground the problem becomes plain. In fact, once an army has gained the plateau in the east, there is little in the way of natural obstacles to prevent a march on Le Palais and the citadel. It would take an equal sized army to stop the invader, and there is no such army on the island.'

Hodgson looked thoughtful and exchanged a glance with Keppel. Evidently they had discussed this already.

'A trap then. The lack of established defences is perhaps a lure to put us ashore at a place where we can be of least danger. Nevertheless, I would like to see this place, Sauzon. Now, how close can we get in this craft?'

Keppel turned to Holbrooke. He could perfectly well have answered the question, but he wanted Holbrooke, the legal commander of both *Argonaut* and *Oyster*, to give his opinion.

'There's nowhere in the Sauzon Road that *Oyster* can't navigate, sir. The question is how much risk we take against the batteries. There are at least two covering the approaches. They probably only mount nine-pounders, but any artillery is dangerous for a cutter.'

He spanned the gunwale with his hand to show the

general how lightly *Oyster* had been built.

'None of these cutters were built for war; they are all taken up from the merchant service.'

Keppel smiled and broke in when Holbrooke had ended.

'Nevertheless, General, the cutter is fast and manoeuvrable. We can certainly get close enough to satisfy our needs.'

***

'How close should I venture, sir?'

Finch didn't look concerned. He had the carefree manner of a young man whose actions, reckless though they may be, were covered by the orders of a higher authority. No less than a commodore and a general in this case.

Holbrooke looked at the fast-approaching inlet wherein lay the little port of Sauzon.

'Nine pounders, is that right, Mister…?'

At the last moment he remembered not to use Albach's name and looked around guiltily to see who had noticed the near-slip.

'They were established for nine pounders when I was last here, sir, although they weren't mounted then. The French are short of larger guns, and I expect all of those will have gone to the citadel or to the redoubt.'

'In which case, Mister Finch, can you see those two batteries?'

The French were making no effort to conceal the little earthworks to the north and east of the inlet. The brown soil showed clearly and in case there was any doubt, the white of Bourbon France flew from a flag staff above each.

'Aye, sir.'

'Then come no closer than a mile. We should be safe even if they've mounted twelve-pounders.'

Finch gave an order to the helmsman and the cutter swung gently to larboard until the jib-boom was pointing straight up the inlet.

Holbrooke studied the advancing shore.

'It's almost as though they are inviting us in, don't you

think?'

Albach barked a short laugh.

'I'm sure they'll be delighted if we land here. By the time we've started the army moving they'll be ready to defend every fold in the ground between here and the citadel, and the army and militia of Brittany will be on the march to relieve them, if they can make the crossing.'

The general's chief of staff couldn't help but hear Albach's booming voice.

'You may be right, Mister whatever-your-name, but the French may be too clever for their own good. With the whole summer before us, it would be strange indeed if this army can't march half a dozen miles, however many battles we fight along the way.'

Holbrooke had noticed the suspicious looks that the general and his staff cast towards Albach. He supposed it was inevitable, when even the general hadn't been given enough information to allow him to form an opinion of the Austrian's trustworthiness. It would be a pity, though, if it led them to discard the only recent information to come from the island.

'They're firing, sir.'

Holbrooke could see that for himself. A puff of smoke hung over the southern battery for a few seconds before it was whipped away by the wind. A waterspout rose two cables on the larboard bow and very faintly they heard the boom of the gun.

'Nine-pounder,' said Albach with deep satisfaction.

Keppel nodded in agreement.

'Have you seen enough, General?'

Hodgson reluctantly lowered his telescope. Not for anything would he give the impression that he was concerned for his own personal safety, but the two commanders of the expedition were hurrying towards a well-emplaced enemy while they were protected by nothing more than the flimsy planking that was all that was afforded a commercially-built cutter.

'I've seen enough, thank you, Commodore.'

Keppel nodded towards Holbrooke.

'Bring her about, Mister Finch, and make haste to the flagship.'

***

Keppel had adopted Holbrooke as his temporary aide, if only even out the numbers when General Hodgson had his chief of staff in attendance. They stood together in a little group of four at the aft end of the cutter, hard against the taffrail. They were beating into the easterly wind now as Finch tried every trick he knew to bring the two great men back to the flagship without delay.

The general opened the discussion.

'Well, I've never seen a better prepared island. It appears that we'll have to fight our way ashore wherever we land, but land we must, of course.'

Keppel nodded cautiously. He was well aware of the importance of this moment. The words that they exchanged could be used to justify their action – or inaction – in the case of the expedition's failure.

'It appears to me,' the general continued, 'that we have a choice of landing in the east where we are subject to the vagaries of the weather, or in the northwest where we'll be committed to a long land campaign, perhaps. However, I must say that I'm not comfortable with relying on the word of this spy.'

Hodgson looked hard at Holbrooke, and Keppel followed his gaze. They'd both noticed the familiarity between the two men.

'Well, Captain Holbrooke. Is there anything you can say to reassure us? Within the bounds of confidentiality, of course.'

Holbrooke glanced forward where Sawtree and Albach were in conversation. He saw Sawtree look in his direction and he had the uncomfortable feeling that his thoughts were being penetrated. He cleared his throat nervously.

'I've known him on-and-off since 'fifty-seven, and I've

always called him a friend. He's not French, as I'm sure you can tell, and his circumstances lead me to understand why he would favour the British cause. Certainly he's valued at the Admiralty. I trust him, sir.'

Holbrooke ended abruptly. There was nothing more that he could say, not without straying across the boundaries that Sawtree had laid down.

'Then it will have to do. Now, General, the wind's backing still so if we move fast I can land you on the east coast in relative safety. Port An-Dro looks the most favourable. That would be my preference, but I can't answer for the weather more than a day ahead.'

The general showed no emotion. If he had hoped for the easy landing at Sauzon, the thought of struggling through prepared defences before he could reach the citadel probably swayed his own decision.

'Very well. Port An-Dro it is. Now perhaps we can encourage this cutter to move faster, for there's no time to lose.'

***

CHAPTER EIGHTEEN

Under Fire

Wednesday, Eighth of April 1761.
Argonaut, at Sea, off Port An-Dro, Belle Isle.

It was the size of the island that still surprised Holbrooke. The sea passage from the anchorage in Palais Road to Port An-Dro, weathering Kerdonis Point, was only five or six miles, depending on the draught and handiness of the ship. The assault could almost have been launched from the anchorage, but for the long pull against the wind. For it had indeed backed and was now blowing firmly from the east-nor'east, and with a fetch of only a few miles from Hoedic Island and the well-remembered Vilaine estuary, it threw up only a moderate sea.

'Will this last, Mister Fairview?'

The master sniffed the wind, as he always did, to the private delight of the youngsters who had a running competition for the best mimicry of this act, in the safety of their berth, of course.

'I can't really say, sir. If it backs any further it could end up as a regular nor'easter. It could stay like this for days, though.'

Argonaut was moving into position off Point Kerdonis. They'd had their orders before midnight and, probably because of his familiarity with the island, and certainly because of his shallow draught, Holbrooke had been given the task of closely engaging the battery that overlooked Port An-Dro. Further offshore in deeper water, *Prince of Orange* flying Keppel's pennant, Hervey's *Dragon* and Barrington's *Achilles* had formed a line to bring their heavier guns to bear. Two bomb ketches crept along astern of the line, but it was difficult to see what good they would do if they couldn't anchor. There were no other ships in sight yet, but Holbrooke could imagine that great invasion force weighing anchor now that the day had dawned. They'd need to stand up towards Hoedic Island before they could weather the point, but it would only take a couple of hours for them to reach their station off Port An-Dro.

'The flagship's signalling, sir.'

Shorrock was eagerly watching *Prince of Orange*, anticipating the order that would bring the frigate into action.

'Engage the enemy, sir!'

'Very well, Mister Shorrock. Starboard battery, I believe.'

'Loaded with ball, sir.'

Holbrooke had long known that his first lieutenant actually enjoyed this. He loved everything about an engagement: beating to quarters in the grey pre-dawn light, clearing for action, the deadly hush as they closed the enemy and then the first roar of the broadside. Further still, he relished the infernal din, the smoke, and the cries. Oftentimes Holbrooke had wondered if Shorrock would enjoy it so much if his ship was defeated, but he had the uncomfortable feeling that even then, he'd have thought it worthwhile.

'No closer than five cables, Mister Fairview.'

'Aye-aye sir. We should have five fathoms at five cables.'

Right on cue the leadsman sang out.

'And a half, ten.'

Fairview nodded. A mile off and ten fathoms, as he had expected.

'I can see the battery now, sir, just as the point slopes down towards the south. They're not flying a flag and they've made more of an effort of concealment, but you can see the colour of the new-hewn stone.'

Argonaut was moving in swiftly with the wind on her starboard quarter. Holbrooke looked over his shoulder to where the three ships-of-the-line were starting to follow him in. They couldn't safely approach closer than a mile, not on this lee shore, but *Dragon* had thirty-two pounders, far heavier metal than that battery could boast. Even *Prince of*

Orange and *Achilles* had twenty-four pounders. *Argonaut's* nine pounders were puny by comparison, but at half a mile he could be more certain of hitting the battery than the heavier guns could at a mile.

'By the mark, seven.'

'Wear ship if you please, Mister Fairview. You see the battery, show him our broadside.'

Albach had relieved Fairview of his telescope, a feat that not even a general had achieved the day before, and he was studying the battery closely. What was going through his mind, Holbrooke wondered? He was an artilleryman by profession, and he had commanded coastal batteries all over Brittany. Was he wishing he was there now, with those unknown gunners?

'Ah! They're firing!'

Albach's loud voice startled the quarterdeck. At this range the report of the guns could be clearly heard and the smoke lingered long enough to confirm the sound's origin. There was a sound like fine canvas ripping as four balls passed close overhead. Four spouts appeared on *Argonaut's* larboard side.

Holbrooke and Shorrock exchanged glances.

'Good practice for a first salvo,' Shorrock said with relish, 'we could reach them now.'

'Hold your fire, First Lieutenant.'

'Deep six!'

That was a new leadsman, more excitable than the first, and he had moved to the larboard chains to be clear of the broadside. He also had an illusion of greater safety being on the far side of the ship from the enemy guns, and that was important so that he could concentrate on the task of accurately reporting the soundings.

Another enemy broadside howled overhead and a severed mizzen shroud scattered pieces of tarred cordage over the quarterdeck. Holbrooke noticed Jackson directing a repair team. It was minor damage – the mizzen was supported by three shrouds and a backstay each side – and it would hardly be noticed when the frigate started receiving more hits. Nevertheless, it was as well to seize a span of cordage across the severed ends while things were still relatively quiet.

'By the mark, five.'

Holbrooke noticed that Dawson had settled the leadsman and was standing by him in case he should need to take over.

Argonaut was creeping over the ground under her tops'ls. The gun captains were tracking the battery over the simple sights of the guns, gesturing to the men wielding the massive hand spikes to shift the carriages slightly to the right as the frigate progressed along the coast. It was as though the collective breath of those on the quarterdeck was being held.

'What do you make of that range now, Mister Fairview.'

'Five cables I make it sir. And five fathoms of water,' he added with a look of satisfaction.

'You may commence firing, Mister Shorrock.'

Shorrock drew in a great breath.

'Starboard battery, fire!'

The broadside shook *Argonaut* like a rat in a terrier's jaws, and before the ship steadied the gun crews were hard at work worming and sponging and loading.

'Good for line but all a little low,' said Albach, the professional artilleryman. 'Five degrees higher I would say.'

Shorrock grinned. He'd already come to that conclusion but he was going to wait until the guns were reloaded to avoid confusion. At this stage in an engagement, he could still retain tight control and that was better than a free-for-all where each gun captain trained and elevated as he thought best. He waited until an arm was raised at every gun, then made a hand motion that set the captains tapping the quoins from side to side to withdraw them an inch or so. It was no good telling them to raise the elevation five degrees, there was no means of directly measuring it, but each gun's quoin was cut to a standard pattern and an inch should be about right.

Crash! A French ball ploughed into the bows, wreaking havoc among the complicated arrangements of cables and tackles that held the best bower anchor in its place. Jackson ran forward to inspect.

'Fire!'

That was better. The second salvo was a little more ragged, but of the twelve balls, three or four swept the embrasures and Holbrooke could see a cloud of dust, easily distinguished from the smoke, where hits had been scored on the masonry.

'The commodore's opened fire, sir.'

Fairview, as always, had eyes everywhere. Holbrooke turned to see the smoke hanging over the flagship and was in time to see *Dragon* and *Achilles* open fire.

'Well short,' said Albach.

He was right. The heavy guns had done no more than bring a minor landslide down the steep face of rock and dirt below the battery.

'Oh, oh! What I would give to be in *Dragon* now!'

Albach was in awe of a ship-of-the-line's fire power. Its ability to deliver thirty-odd thirty-two-pound balls far exceeded anything that field artillery could achieve, and it was a greater concentration of fire than any but the greatest of fortresses could boast.

Crash!

Argonaut staggered under another hit. This time the ball had struck the gunwale on the fo'c'sle, bring down two men in a shower of splinters and scattering the ragged remains of the protective hammocks far and wide.

'Twelve-pounders.'

Albach wasn't unmoved by the British dead, but it was in the nature of artillerymen the world over to stand unmoved under fire; it was their defining characteristic.

Argonaut kept up a brisk fire from the starboard battery. Holbrooke realised with a pang of guilt that he'd been indulging himself as a mere spectator when he should have been observing the wider situation. Shorrock was fighting the ship, Fairview was handling it and his other specialists were managing their particular responsibilities. He looked astern. While he had been engrossed in the action with the battery, the first of the transports had come around the point, each ship with two or four flatboats alongside. They were hard on the wind having tacked north and he could see that they would weather the point by at least two miles. They'd commence the landing as soon as they were in place, he was sure, because they couldn't back and fill for very long on this lee shore with no good anchorage.

'The heavy guns are reaching them now. Look, I think they're down to three guns and their fire is slackening.'

Albach couldn't take his eyes from the shore, and Fairview's motioning for his telescope to be returned elicited no response.

Holbrooke resisted the urge to look at the battery. He knew that he could rely upon Albach and Shorrock to keep him informed. He glanced at the flagship to see a signal run up the mast. He didn't need his clerk to tell him what it meant. The ships-of-the-line were shifting their aim from the battery to the enemy entrenchments that ran in an unbroken line across the top of the escarpment behind the beach. The early morning sun glinted off the French bayonets and picked out the few field pieces that punctuated the long line of turned earth and abatis. One or two were even firing, although what they hoped to achieve at that range wasn't evident. What was clear was that *Argonaut* would soon be unable to fire at the battery if he didn't start working his way north.

'Wear ship, Mister Fairview. Lay her on the larboard tack.'

They'd be slanting away from the battery but at least their broadside would still be able to reach it.

The noise was becoming overpowering. Three big ships just half a mile to windward were firing as fast as the gun crews could load, while *Argonaut's* own broadside joined in every three minutes. The occasional crash as a French twelve-pound ball hit the frigate contributed to the din.

'They're down to two guns now,' Albach shouted. 'Ah the magazine!'

Holbrooke swung around in time to see a large pall of smoke rising at the battery, followed by the sound of an explosion. It wasn't big enough to be the main magazine, which would certainly be at least fifty yards to the rear; it was probably the ready use store that was kept behind the guns. Well, that was the end of that!

'Mister Fairview. Belay wearing ship, bring us before the wind again!'

This was the time when he appreciated his officers. There was no fuss, little cursing, and between the master and the bosun and all the petty officers, they managed to get *Argonaut's* head to the south again.

'Mister Shorrock, the entrenchments.'

Shorrock grinned, his teeth showing white through the powder smoke as he turned to direct the guns. Holbrooke could imagine how the gunners in *Prince of Orange*, *Dragon* and *Achilles* would be raging at him as he crossed their field of fire, but he knew that his little guns fired from such close range would be more effective than the thirty-two and twenty-four pounders at over twice the range. In any case he would be through their line of fire in fifteen minutes.

Argonaut's guns were firing in a steady rhythm, and it was easy to see that they were having an effect on the entrenchments. However, it was not a serious problem for the defenders who would just keep throwing up more earth as a yard or so was beaten down. There was nothing like good soil to absorb the impact of a solid ball.

Back and forth *Argonaut* passed with only Fairview's skill and the leadsman's cries to keep them clear of danger, for after the destruction of the battery, never a ball came near them.

***

'There they go!'

Albach was almost hopping with excitement. From every transport a laden flatboat scudded away under the impetus of the oarsmen. Vast amounts of energy had been expended in organising them so that each boat held its own half company, and each pair of boats could move directly to their objective. The grenadier companies were distinguished by their tall hats as they led the assault.

Holbrooke could see Captain Barton of *Temeraire* standing in a boat in the centre, with a seaman with flags on poles to regulate the approach. He remembered when he had been a division commander at the Cherbourg landings, how it had been vital to arrange that the boats landed in their correct intervals and that no coxswain in his enthusiasm crossed lines with the adjacent company.

'Ah, they're in the surf.'

The coxswains were throwing out their grapnels to keep the stern perpendicular to the line of the beach and to afford a means of pulling off once the troops had been landed. It would be an embarrassing fiasco if the retreating tide left the heavy flatboats unable to be relaunched.

As each boat struck the sand, a pair of ramps was thrown from the bows so that the soldiers could at least start the campaign dry-shod. Holbrooke remembered designing and then testing those ramps up the Fareham creek back in 'fifty-seven. *Argonaut* was so close that he could make out the company commanders and the sergeants gesticulating to their men. Here and there a red-coated figure fell to the ground, but more – many more – came ashore and made it to the shelter under the escarpment. He saw them scrambling to climb up so that they could come to close quarters with the French, but to no avail.

'They need ladders! Do they not have any?'

Albach was right. The defenders had cleverly dug at the natural escarpment so that rather than being a slope, it was a vertical face or in some places it was even undercut. The attackers may have found shelter, but they couldn't move forward, not without the means to scale those little cliffs.

Barton was on the beach now. Evidently he could see the problem and he was holding back the flatboats, not letting them return for the next load. He was horribly exposed and the French field pieces saw their opportunity. All around him the sand was being flung up in fountains as the three and six-pound balls fell, but somehow he survived. Holbrooke felt powerless. He couldn't engage those guns, not with the British infantry only yards below them.

Here and there valiant bands tried to climb the scarp. Men stood on the shoulders of others. They thrust pikes into the soft earth to make steps, but every man whose head reached the top was sent back in bloody ruin, to lie on the sand as a testament to the futility of the attempt.

'Stand by your guns, Mister Shorrock. I fear we may be covering a retreat in a moment.'

Shorrock looked serious. He was among the crews now, impressing on the gun captains the absolute necessity of firing high, so as not to drop the shot among the retreating British infantry.

'They're running for the boats.'

Albach looked horrified. He knew the effect that a defeat had upon an army, and this was a very great defeat. Back they came, mostly in good order but here and there a straggler made his own way back to the boats. Some of the boats had already returned empty to the ships, before it was evident that they may be needed, and those that were left were horribly overcrowded. Fit men mingled with the wounded, and even many of the dead were brought back under that gleeful fire from the defenders. There was no sally by the French, they knew very well how savagely the British would turn upon them if they once left the safety of their abatis and their breastworks.

Shorrock was looking pleadingly at Holbrooke. He wanted to start firing, to cover the retreat, but there were too many men still close to the scarp. He watched as in small groups the last few ran down the beach.

'Now, Mister Shorrock. Commence firing.'

It was an ordinary broadside and well pointed, with every ball falling far beyond the fleeing soldiers, but to Holbrooke it sounded angry, as though the ship itself was determined to exact revenge for this disaster. Albach was plucking at Holbrooke's sleeve.

'Look over there, to the left.'

Almost hidden by an outcrop of rock, a pair of flatboats were still on the beach and apparently empty of soldiers.

'Good God, why are they still there?'

'Up, look up.'

Albach was almost mad with excitement for there, at the top of the scarp, he could see the tall mitres of British grenadiers.

***

CHAPTER NINETEEN

Brave Grenadiers

Wednesday, Eighth of April 1761.
Argonaut, at Sea, off Port An-Dro, Belle Isle.

It was a study in contrasting colours. The blue-grey of the sea stretched away from *Argonaut* to end in a white fringe of surf where the little yellow triangle of sand was wedged between the rocks. The dark grey of the of the miniature cliffs reached up twenty or thirty feet to be topped by the green and yellow of the spring growth of grass and the blooming gorse with the blue of a cloudless sky reaching into infinity. And in that region between yellow gorse and blue sky, Holbrooke could see the red and gold of the grenadiers' mitres, the flash of their bayonets and the puffs of smoke where muskets were being discharged.

'They should be withdrawing, what are they thinking of?'

'They're heavily engaged,' said Albach. 'It was a heroic effort to reach the top, but now they're unsupported and see, there are Frenchmen leaving the earthworks and starting up the hill.'

Shorrock was watching, eager to see how this drama would play out.

'Can't they run for the boats?'

'Not a hope! They're too closely engaged. They'll be easy targets as they scramble down the rocks. Look, over to the left. That must be the defenders' reserve being brought forward. They're trapped now.'

Holbrooke looked up at the commissioning pennant, then out to sea where the flatboats were hurrying back to the transports.

'We can discuss this later, gentlemen. Mister Fairview, bring us as close as you can to the grenadiers' flatboats, I believe we can close to two cables from the shore. Mister Shorrock, stand by with the starboard battery.'

He turned to Albach.

'I fancy they'll have to risk a withdrawal soon, or lay down their arms, what do you think?'

Albach hadn't taken his eyes from the top of the cliffs, but still all he could see was the top of the mitres, the bayonets and the puffs of smoke. He looked up at the mainmast that seemed to tower higher than ever above the deck.

'If I could see over the top it would help, sir.'

'You haven't been aloft yet, I gather?'

'No, sir, but I'm willing to try.'

Albach started towards the larboard main chains. He'd seen it done often enough and although the height and the flimsiness of the shrouds and ratlines appalled him, he was being driven by his urgent need to see the fate of the brave grenadiers.

'Wait. Dawson, lay aft here. Help the gentleman if you please, he will need to go to the main topmast head. Mind now, he's never been aloft before, you're to ensure he doesn't fall. You will need to carry the telescope.'

Holbrooke saw the two men start on their journey. It was hard to tell which of them looked the more concerned, the artilleryman who had never dreamed that he may need to climb the rigging or the coxswain who had been entrusted with his safety. But he had no leisure to watch them, not with his ship being manoeuvred just five cables off a lee shore while still under fire from field artillery.

***

Fairview was entirely engrossed in his task, ignoring everything but the navigation of the ship.

'I'll need to wear her, sir, there's no room to tack.'

Holbrooke had been expecting that. *Argonaut* had been standing out to sea on the larboard tack when Albach spotted the grenadiers. The wind was in the east-nor'east, and they would have to approach the scene of the drama on the starboard tack with the wind on the quarter. Surely it was folly to be running down onto an iron-bound shore. He

Treacherous Moon

glanced at Fairview, but the man had been transported onto a different level of existence. He was one with the wind and the waves. He was drawing conclusions from the leadsman's calls, from the wind on his cheek, and from the approaching shore that no ordinary man could possibly achieve. Holbrooke knew that he himself would never attain that level of seamanship and navigation, and if this job was to be done, then he would be wise to leave it in the sailing master's hands.

'Both batteries ready, sir.'

Shorrock's enthusiasm for a fight was noticeably absent and he couldn't keep his eyes off the shore, the horribly close rocks that he knew would soon be even closer.

Holbrooke looked aloft to see Albach being guided through the lubber's hole onto the main top. It wouldn't be high enough and after the briefest of pauses, Albach came back into sight, with Dawson carefully placing his hands and feet for the climb up the topmast shrouds.

Argonaut was starting to come off the wind. Holbrooke heard the orders for wearing, and it seemed to him that there was an edge to the bosun's voice.

Slowly, slowly, the frigate's head turned to starboard, towards the terrifying shore.

'Mister Jackson! We'll furl the main and fore courses as soon as we are on the starboard tack.'

Fairview's voice was steady, as though he was carrying out sail drills in the Channel, and it had the necessary effect on Jackson, who visibly took a grip of himself.

It was all happening without Holbrooke's intervention. He saw Shorrock send all the men from the guns so that the lower yards could be manned as well as the tacks and sheets. He could see how important it would be to take the way off the ship as soon as her bows were pointing at the land.

'Tops'ls, jib and mizzen, sir. That should do it.'

'Very well, Mister Fairview.'

Argonaut put her stern through the wind in the most elegant manner. It had only taken ten minutes from first sighting the lonely band of British soldiers on the cliff top to having the frigate move in the right direction to support them.

'Deck There!'

Dawson's voice came loud and clear from the main topmast head.

'We can see them easily now, sir.'

Holbrooke wondered why Albach wasn't reporting, but the next call was from the Austrian major, and the reason became clear. Albach's voice had been trained to be heard over the thunder of an artillery battery and in normal conversation he could cause pain to anyone within fifty yards. Now, however, his voice was thin and weak; muted, presumably, by the sheer terror of his lofty eminence.

'There are maybe sixty of them. It's a hot engagement and they're holding off the attackers for now. But there are two columns working towards them, perhaps two hundred men in each. Ah, they're starting to fall back towards the cliff path.'

Sixty men, that sounded about right. The two flatboats on the beach were of the smaller size that were usually allotted to the grenadiers, being nimbler for the difficult first assault. Holbrooke looked at them through his telescope. One of them had a lieutenant in command and the other what could be a master's mate or a midshipman. Their grapnels were laid out ready and each boat had a swivel gun in the bows with a seaman crouched behind it. The ramps were out, and four other seamen were holding them in place, ready for the anticipated rush, for even from that secluded cove they would have seen the general retreat of the main force. The oarsmen were ready with their blades in the water.

Holbrooke looked quickly over the stern to see that the longboat was still following obediently on its tether. He'd ordered a boat gun to be shipped and he could see its ugly, squat, black shape dominating the bows of the boat. In the stern, two barrels of water maintained the boat's trim.

Treacherous Moon

Albach's voice again, stronger this time.

'They're holding a line, but they can't last long. If they're coming it will be soon.'

Holbrooke snapped his fingers, coming to an instant decision.

'Mister Shorrock. Man the longboat, take a quarter gunner. You're to cover the withdrawal. And take a file of marines with their muskets, Mister Murray will join you. Send for the gunner, he can leave his magazine and take over from you.'

Oh the blessings of a well worked-up ship's company! Holbrooke needed to give no more orders and he could just watch as a man ran from each gun and the longboat was pulled alongside. A quarter gunner slung a tiny cask of powder over his shoulder on the lanyard that had been fitted just for that purpose, and before the leadsman was reporting five fathoms, the longboat was pulling fast towards the shore.

There was no time to wonder whether he was acting prudently. Most of those grenadiers were doomed to be killed or captured, and the remainder were probably not worth the risk to *Argonaut*. In fact, in a cold analysis of the risks, the two flatboats should have left them to their fate already. But Holbrooke knew how fragile the army's morale would be after this setback, and he knew how quickly the solidarity between the sea and land services would break down under the weight of recrimination. If a company of grenadiers were left behind by the navy, it would be seen by the army as a betrayal, and in the next assault the company commanders would be watching their backs to see whether they were being abandoned by the boats. Keppel had frigates aplenty, but Holbrooke guessed that after this morning's defeat, Hodgson would have less soldiers than he needed. He'd seen the red and yellow clad figures lying on the beach, and he'd seen the number of shattered bodies brought back by the boats. He must hazard his longboat, aye and his ship, if there were even half a dozen soldiers that could be saved.

'The enemy is among them. The left of the line has been overwhelmed. Ah, now the right is withdrawing.'

Albach must have forgotten his precarious nest so high above the deck for his voice was booming out in its normal manner.

Now the grenadiers could be seen from the deck as a pitifully small band spilled over the edge of the cliff and started scrambling down. He could see an officer rallying his men at each point where the path flattened out, sending a volley of fire into their pursuers. Yet the French outnumbered them ten to one, and for every puff of powder smoke from the grenadiers, there were a dozen from the top of the cliff. He saw that the flatboats had also come under fire, and the oarsmen were crouching low behind the gunwales, while their exposed fellows on the shore sought what shelter they could find behind the ramps.

'Master Gunner. You may start firing at the top of the cliff. You see your mark? Single shots and every gun is to be pointed by you.'

If the sailing master lived for the opportunity to handle his ship in such difficult waters, so close to the land, then the master gunner lived to be freed from the stygian underworld of the magazine and let loose to fire his own guns at the enemy. A navy that had seen too many calamities from ill-managed magazines had laid down that the gunner's place at quarters was down among his kegs of powder, but it always seemed a waste of a man who had spent a lifetime honing his gunnery skills.

Holbrooke turned his attention back to the scene in front of him. He counted around twenty grenadiers still scrambling down the cliff. As he watched, one of them spun around and pitched headfirst off the path and his body bounced twice off the rocks on its way to the beach, where it lay still. The longboat's crew were pulling like madmen, and he could see that Shorrock was aiming for the right flank of the two flatboats, so that he could fire slantwise across the beach, covering the path that any pursuers must take.

Bang! The first of *Argonaut's* guns spoke. Holbrooke didn't see the fall of shot, presumably it was too high, but that was just as well. Shot flying over the heads of the Frenchmen would focus their attention on their own survival while not endangering the grenadiers.

Bang! The second. The gunner was moving from gun to gun with a huge mallet, making careful adjustments to the quoins before he nodded to the gun captain to fire.

'Four and a half fathoms of water, sir. I'll bring her to, if you please.'

Holbrooke clenched his teeth. *Argonaut* drew three-and-half fathoms in her present state of loading. There was only six feet of water under her keel and he could see that there was two or three feet of swell running. There was no room for error, and he was acutely conscious that the wind and swell would be pushing the ship closer and closer to the shore. But the gunner had found his range now, and at each report from the nine-pounders, a puff of dust rose from the top of the cliffs. He could see that the pursuit was faltering; those Frenchmen already on the path were looking up to see whether it was safe to run back, while fewer of them exposed themselves on the lip.

'The guns are keeping them back,' shouted Albach, 'but they're forming up again in the dead ground. It looks like they're going to make a rush for the path. Oh, there's a field gun galloping up from the north.'

Now the grenadiers had won their way to the beach, and they were running for the boats. They could see that there was no advantage in making a stand, nor in trying to slow down the enemy; their safety was in the flatboats and nowhere else.

The master gunner was firing fast now that he'd found the right elevation, a gun every twenty seconds or so, and the depleted crews – they'd been robbed for boat's crew and sail trimmers and had only the bare minimum men left –

were hard pressed to load and run out before it was their gun's turn again. Holbrooke was conscious of Fairview handling the ship, and he heard the report after each cast of the lead. *By the deep, four*, was the last and his margin of safety was being eroded second by second. At least now that they were hove-to, the bows were pointing to seaward and it only wanted the foretopsail to be braced around and sheeted for the frigate to start moving away from the shore.

Holbrooke dismissed his concern for the ship. He could do no better than Fairview and his attention should be on the shore. The grenadiers were tumbling into the flatboats and as he looked he saw the ramps being thrown onto the sand while the brave seamen at the bows shoved the boat bodily astern and rolled over the gunwales. The coxswains were straining every muscle to haul on the grapnels. Ah, the first one was free from the sand, now the second. Twin puffs of smoke showed where the swivel guns had been fired, and then the boats swung slowly around so that their bows sought the open sea. He could imagine what the coxswains and the officers of the boats must be feeling as their unprotected backs were exposed to the fire from the shore.

There was a deeper sound as the longboat opened fire. Shorrock had ordered grape shot and the four pounder boat gun had been well pointed. The leading pursuers were caught as they reached the bottom of the cliff and a good half dozen fell to the hail of six-ounce balls.

The gunner had lowered his sights also and the nine-pound balls were raising spouts of sand all over the beach. The boats were all underway and it was high time that *Argonaut* found some sea room.

'Bring us out on the larboard tack, Mister Fairview.'

Crash!

A shower of splinters flew in all directions from the quarterdeck rail and a there was a dull thud as a six-pound ball embedded itself in the opposite gunwale. Fairview pulled out his handkerchief and wiped a trail of blood from the back of his hand, where a shard of oak had raked it.

'Warm work, sir.'

Holbrooke nodded distractedly. The flatboats and the longboat were out of range of the musketry from the shore and they were pulling fast towards *Argonaut*. However, Holbrooke had no intentions of waiting to pick them up, he was far more concerned to get his ship out of range of that field gun and into deep water.

'Master Gunner! You see the gun on the cliff? That's your mark, you may fire as you see fit.'

The gunner looked up from his task. He had been wholly engrossed in firing at the lower part of the cliff and had quite missed the fact that the frigate itself was under fire. He lifted his hat in acknowledgement and straightened himself.

'Broadsides!'

It would cost a further three minutes but the next thing that field gun would be aware of would be twelve nine-pound balls hurtling in his direction.

Crash!

A hit on the mainmast, but no six-pounder could bring down that solid spar.

Holbrooke could see that the gunner would only achieve one broadside and even that would have to be fired as the ship turned. He was unprepared for it when it came, and he staggered against the mizzen shrouds, thrown off balance by the force of the recoil.

He looked up to the cliff to see whether they had done any damage to the field gun but at that moment *Argonaut's* stern fell into the hollow in front of a swell and he felt a sickening thump, then another. They were touching ground! He looked askance at Fairview, but the master just smiled and pointed upwards. The topsails were all drawing and already the big courses were being loosened. The frigate was gathering way, and every few seconds gave them another foot of depth. He held his breath waiting for another touch, but it didn't come.

'Mark five,' called the leadsman.

They were safe and heading at last into deeper water. Holbrooke felt the tension run out of him and he held onto the gunwale to stop his knees shaking.

***

The gale came roaring in from the Brittany coast, as though the gods that watched over the French people were determined to heap further punishment upon the impudent invaders. The flatboats were caught before they had disembarked the soldiers and it was a choice of letting them brave the fury of the seas or risk damage alongside the transports. Keppel chose the latter. It was a good choice as the wind increased to a full storm and the loss of life would have been so great that the expedition must necessarily have been abandoned. The soldiers were saved, but the boats suffered so badly alongside the transports that fully half of them were rendered useless.

The storm lasted through the day, abated slightly in the night, but resumed with increased venom the next day. Only after their point had been firmly hammered home did the French gods desist, and a watchful calm descended over the waters around the island.

To the French defenders it must have appeared that the British had been defeated, that they would soon set sail for home, but they reckoned without the determination of Keppel and Hodgson.

***

CHAPTER TWENTY

An Urgent Need

Friday, Tenth of April 1761.
Valiant, at Anchor, Palais Road, Belle Isle.

'Pass the word for Mister Chalmers and the foreign gentleman. Pass the word for the chaplain…'

The call rang out along the deck even before the midshipman from the flagship had made his way back to his boat. It was a difficult passage because *Argonaut's* deck was crowded with carpenters lent from the ships that hadn't been so heavily engaged two days before. The damage to the gunwales was nothing; the carpenter made that kind of repair in his sleep, but the mainmast needed a fillet and it needed fishing to make it safe for the Bay of Biscay in spring, and no less than four warranted carpenters had gathered to lend a hand. A woodpecker's convocation, as Shorrock had dubbed it.

Holbrooke turned over the letter and studied it again as his servant fussed around him with clothes brush and sponge, making him ready to meet the commodore and, in all likelihood, the general. The text was short and to the point, and yet intriguing.

You are required to attend on board the flagship Valiant forthwith and you are to be accompanied by the Revd. Chalmers and the supernumerary officer who is carried in Argonaut.

The supernumerary officer was clearly Major Albach, there was nobody else on board the frigate that could be distinguished by so notable an omission of a name. Probably Keppel and Hodgson wanted to probe the major for more information about the island's defences after Thursday's debacle. But Chalmers? He'd noticed how Sawtree had gathered the chaplain into his confidence but had believed that to be merely a way of having someone in contact with Albach while Sawtree was in the flagship. Perhaps there was more to it.

And the note was short to the point of being rude. Surely after rescuing the grenadiers from Port An-Dro the commodore must think well of *Argonaut* and her captain. It didn't look like something that Keppel would have drafted; it was more in Sawtree's style. Holbrooke dallied with the idea of taking offence at being thus summoned, but it was a passing fancy. Sawtree may hold no naval rank, but he'd seen how Admiral Forbes had deferred to him, and after all, the note could have come from Keppel, in which case it would be dangerous to do anything other than comply with the demand.

Albach and Chalmers looked breathless when they arrived. They'd been in the foretop, to which height Albach had forced himself to climb at every stroke of the half-hour bell. He was determined to defeat the devils that pursued him whenever his feet touched the ratlines, and he was secretly proud that this last attempt had been made without Dawson's help. The foretop, not the maintop. For as well as the maintop being discouraged while the carpenters worked upon it, Albach still shuddered whenever he remembered the awful feeling at the main topmast head when the French six-pound ball struck the mast. He would attempt the mainmast again – he would – but only after he was able to climb to the foretop without his legs turning to gelatine.

'Ah gentlemen. We are bidden to the flagship. Pray make yourselves respectable, the boat will be ready in five minutes. Here, Mallett will help you, he's finished with me.'

Chalmers and Albach exchanged questioning glances, but it was too late, and the captain's servant was already offering water and towels and sending one of his mates for clean stockings. Holbrooke strode out of the door to give his instructions to Shorrock, who was on the deck keeping the peace between four self-willed carpenters.

***

Treacherous Moon

Holbrooke was ushered into the great cabin alone, to be met by an evidently embarrassed commodore.

'Thank you for coming, Captain Holbrooke. I know that it's usually bad policy to start with an apology, but you are owed one for the letter which went out under my name. It was thrust before me as I was trying to compose a letter to Mister Pitt, and to my shame I didn't read it. I hope you will forgive me.'

Holbrooke reddened and spluttered. He was still a small-town boy at heart, and he hadn't developed the ability to speak as an equal to these great men. He assumed that it came with a more prosperous breeding, but he knew many men from backgrounds as humble as his who had taken to it like a duck to water. Chalmers had it, perhaps he could take lessons…

'Well, you're here now,' Keppel continued, looking away to save Holbrooke's embarrassment, 'and you'll have guessed that Mister Sawtree is behind this meeting. I'll call him along with Mister Chalmers and your guest in a few minutes. The general will join us later. So, I have just a few minutes to give you the background. Please take a seat.'

Holbrooke had still not found a useful word to say and he was glad that Keppel was happy to talk without any encouragement.

'Thursday's attempt was wisely made, on the whole. If it had succeeded the general would be directing the siege of the citadel at this moment, but as it turned out it was a disaster. Yes, and I use that word advisedly. The army lost five hundred men, killed, wounded and taken by the enemy, and half of my flatboats were destroyed by the storm. You'll be aware from your own observations how susceptible an army is to discouragement, and the general's chief concern now is to bring his men back into order. That will take a week at least and then I'm hoping that Mister Pitt and Mister Anson will feel that they can release some reserves to replenish our force.'

'Then there will be another attempt, sir?'

Holbrooke bit his tongue. He'd been searching for something to add to the conversation, but what he'd said could be taken to mean that he'd already had enough of this expedition.

'Certainly there will be another attempt. We've tried a quick stroke to bring this to a rapid conclusion, now we have to plan a more measured attack. The soldiers think nothing of this in a siege, they call it a *coup-de-main*. They hope for success but they're philosophical at failure.'

Keppel stood and walked to the big stern windows from where he had a view of Le Palais and the citadel. The water was calm now that the gale had passed, and the sea and sky had that scrubbed-clean look that frequently followed hard weather.

'If they didn't know before, the French can be in no doubt now of our intentions. They still have strong squadrons at Brest and at Rochefort and although we have a greater strength at sea, if they can get out and concentrate on Belle Isle, they could do us great damage. Captain Buckle has thirteen of the line off Brest, but Rochefort is my concern, and I can spare no more ships than the few that are already there. And yet, it's not their fleet that concern me, not directly.'

He walked to a map of Europe that hung on the forward bulkhead.

'There is a purpose for me burdening you with all this, Holbrooke. The Duc d'Aiguillon is still in Brittany. He cannot ignore this peril on his doorstep and he'll guess that we must pause before a new assault, which will give him time to attempt to reinforce the garrison on the island. We know that Choiseul is collecting a huge force to send to Germany, to deal with Prince Ferdinand out of hand; some reports put it at twenty thousand men under Soubise and Broglie. Only a small proportion of that army would make Belle Isle impregnable; even more so than it seems already. Now, you'll know that I have a force already preventing any attempts to relieve the island, but it will only take another storm that pushes them off station, or the appearance of a French squadron, to make it possible for the French to cross to the island. I have some information on their ships, but the general has nothing on the Duc d'Aiguillon; he could be anywhere and his force is unknown. You can perhaps guess what's coming, can't you?'

Holbrooke inclined his head cautiously.

'The general will ask your friend to undertake one more landing. By the way, I still don't know his name, nor does the general, and I for one don't wish to. It will be an espionage mission, to discover what the French are doing and whether they contemplate an attempt to reinforce Belle Isle, and if so, in what force. Your guest is, of course, a free agent and he can't be compelled to land again in France. God knows it will be dangerous enough and he can expect no mercy if he's caught. That's where we need your help, to persuade him if he should appear reluctant.'

So that was it. His first inclination was to refuse. He knew what was being asked of his friend in a way that Keppel never could. He'd seen the strain on the Austrian's face when they met in that little cottage in Kermabec. He'd shared the anxiety of the flight across the marsh and the horrible danger in running across the sand to the longboat. It was unfair to ask anyone to do that again, and particularly unjust now that Albach was known as a spy. And yet, Britain was at war, and sacrifices had to be made. He had never balked before danger himself and he was certain that Albach wouldn't, if asked.

'I'll use what influence I have, sir. I assume the general knows the personal danger to my friend.'

'Yes, he knows, but he's also lost five hundred men already, and the danger to one man – a foreigner whose name he doesn't even know – won't lie heavily on his conscience. And of course, you'll be landing him, Holbrooke, and recovering him, I trust.'

***

Albach had been expecting it, that much was clear to Holbrooke. And not only Albach, but Chalmers too. It was evident that the two had become professionally close in the past few weeks and that while Holbrooke had been busy with his ship, the two of them had been speculating on whether Albach would be sent again into France. Vannes, that was the nexus, the place where information could be gathered, if information was to be had at all.

'Not Quimper?' the general asked, staring at the map.

'No, sir,' Albach replied.

There was a hint of assertiveness in his voice, as though his word would be final. Holbrooke noticed Sawtree nodding briefly in approval.

'Quimper is the headquarters for the militia, but d'Aiguillon has no use for them, not when he may have to meet a British army in the field. Regular regiments will come from Rennes or Angers, and they'll gather at Vannes and embark in the Morbihan Gulf, where they can't be disturbed.'

'How long will you need? I want to make another landing by…'

The general stopped in mid-sentence, realising that he almost gave valuable operational intelligence to a man who could be in French hands by this time tomorrow.

'…well, soon in any case.'

'I'm assuming that my contacts in Vannes have not been taken. It's quite possible, I never named one to another, unless they already knew each other, but any of them could have pieced together enough clues to know who I spoke to in each place. If I'm right, then I'll only need a day, depending on how far I have to travel after I've landed.'

All eyes turned towards Holbrooke. He was at least ready for this, having studied the charts with Fairview against just such a need, although he had cast it from his mind after it seemed that Albach wouldn't be set ashore again.

'I'll take *Oyster* in, disguised as one of those big coasting luggers. The moon's just approaching the first quarter and if this weather holds we'll be easily seen, so I won't go through the narrows until it's set, about two o'clock. They'll see me, of course, but with the help of the gentleman,' he indicated Albach, 'we can talk our way through. Once I'm in the gulf I'll be invisible among all the other luggers.'

Holbrooke didn't want any questions or comment; the truth was that it was an ill-formed plan and didn't bear scrutiny. It was only the certainty of confusion among the French that made it possible. It would be strange if the French had a firm grip on the Brittany coast, with Belle Isle under siege and army stores being run in small coasters from the shelter of one shore battery to another all the way from Brest and Rochefort to Vannes. He guessed that luggers came and went frequently, and it was too much to expect that each one of them would know what procedures would satisfy the batteries that commanded the entrance to the Gulf of Morbihan. Bluff and bravado would have to take the place of hard intelligence.

'How wide is the entrance?'

Hodgson just had to ask a question. It wasn't in his nature to remain quiet even when the discussion was on purely naval matters. Keppel darted him a glance of disapproval, but it passed him by.

'Half a mile, sir. Batteries on either side, and gunboats too, if they're needed.'

'And you know those waters? They look devilish difficult to me.'

'No, sir, but my sailing master does, and he'll come with me. It's a making tide and once I'm through the narrows I'll be at Vannes in four hours at most. If they're suspicious at the narrows, they'll hardly be able to stop me, and I'll anchor here, on the eastern side, which is largely uninhabited.'

'Good God! You intend to stay there during the day?'

Holbrooke shrugged; he was already starting to think and act like a Frenchman.

'I cannot get out again in daylight and in any case, if I

have to go in twice I double the risk of being caught.'

Holbrooke surprised himself with his assurance, but he remembered that he had more experience of this kind of operation than either the commodore or the general.

'Stealth won't answer, sir. I'll be bold and make it look as though I belong there. One more lugger will hardly be noticed but the same lugger coming and going – twice – runs a much greater risk of discovery.'

The general would have said more but Keppel broke in.

'Well gentlemen, I think we can leave the details to Captain Holbrooke, who seems familiar with this kind of thing. I think it best if they return to *Argonaut* now, and Mister Sawtree may wish to accompany them.'

***

The longboat was silent as it rowed back to the frigate. Dawson could tell that his captain wanted to think, and a single glance was enough to tell the oarsmen to mind their mouths.

Holbrooke was indeed thinking, and Dawson was at the top of his thoughts. *Oyster* had a perfectly competent commanding officer and coxswain but for tonight he wanted old friends around him, men who had stood beside him in difficult situations, and he had decided that nobody but Dawson would do to take *Oyster's* helm. He'd transfer Finch to *Argonaut*, the frigate would be short of officers if the worst should happen, and he'd take Fairview in the cutter. Chalmers spoke French almost like a native and he must come. At least Sawtree hadn't insisted on joining them.

***

Oyster spent the day alongside *Argonaut*, with both bosuns combining their expertise to turn the cutter rig into a lugger. Holbrooke gathered his principals together – Fairview and Dawson, Chalmers and Albach – and they pored over the only chart they had of the Gulf of Morbihan. Sawtree was there, like the ghost at the banquet.

'Can you get us to Vannes in the dark of the night, Mister Fairview?'

Treacherous Moon

The sailing master stroked his chin and a faraway look came into his eyes. There was something almost mystical about his approach to navigation, as though he was drawing on past memories to see the shallows, the islands, the rocks and the currents.

'Aye, sir, I can get you there and I know some nice out-of-the-way places to lie quietly through the day. It's not unlike Chichester Harbour, in a way. It's about the same size and with similar tides. There are more islands of course. Just imagine if a strange lugger anchored inside the sand spit at East Head, for example, or at the top of the Thorney Channel or in one of those creeks down from Dell Quay. Who'd know? Who'd care? Smugglers lie there quite happily and no notice is taken of them. I know places in the Morbihan, aye and in Chichester Harbour…'

They were all staring at him, most with an amused expression. Fairview? A smuggler? Yet it would explain much about his status with navy board and with Trinity House. He looked as though he'd been caught with his hand in the biscuit barrel and continued, somewhat subdued.

'…well, be that as it may, high water at Vannes is at 7 o'clock, so we can get right up close to put our guest ashore.'

Holbrooke looked from person to person. They were all mentally prepared and all looked composed, although Chalmers had that look in his eye that suggested he had something to say, and Holbrooke in a flash of intuition, guessed what it may be.

'He won't be going alone, sir,' Chalmers said. 'With your permission, I'll be going with him.'

Sawtree said nothing but looked straight ahead with the ghost of a satisfied smile.

***

CHAPTER TWENTY-ONE

Dark of the Night

Sunday, Twelfth of April 1761.
Armed Cutter Oyster, at Sea, Quiberon Bay.

Holbrooke gripped the taffrail and stared to the west as the sun dipped towards the high plateau that topped Belle Isle. The half-moon was at its apogee in the south and would soon start its own journey towards the western horizon, and Venus was already visible, following obediently a few hours behind the sun. Not a cloud disturbed the deep, deep blue of the sky, and the wind that had turned southerly after the gale carried the first real warmth of the year. It was a beautiful spring evening but still he shivered. It was like hearing an owl's hoot in a night-shrouded church yard, it was impossible to feel entirely at ease.

Holbrooke had spent hours with Fairview, poring over the charts and planning their course for the night. Wind and cloud, moon and tide, it was the old story for any night-time passage, but in this case he had to take account of what the enemy were likely to see and what they would deduce.

'They're still running stores up and down the coast, even with our squadrons off Brest and Rochefort and even with this great armada at Belle Isle. It's all in a day's work for them now; two full years of blockade of the Vilaine hasn't stopped them and if anything the great mass of men-of-war makes it easier to slip in and out unnoticed. They'll have delivered their loads to Brest and picked up whatever cargo is waiting for the south, then they'll run through the Raz, inside the Glenans and Groix and take the Teignouse passage in the dark of the night. The French keep a light on the northern side, it's still there, I saw it last night. Then a dash across Quiberon Bay for the narrows and they're home. There'll be a similar thing happening from Rochefort and the south, but it's the Teignouse Passage that concerns us tonight.'

Fairview had that strange look in his eye. It was clear that he enjoyed this kind of escapade; it gave him an opportunity to show off his skills and a release for all that pent up energy.

Holbrooke looked doubtfully at the chart. He knew all about the French coasting trade and how they crept from battery to battery, anchoring during the day and sailing only at night. He understood, in an intellectual sense, how it could be done but his mind still rebelled against the practical difficulties. But then, he was a King's officer and had never served in anything other than a man-of-war. He'd never had the opportunity to thoroughly know a coastline, not the way that a Frenchman would know the Brittany coast after years of fugitive passages in wartime, nor in the way that a smuggler would in peace or war. His was the fate of most sea officers, to spend only long enough in one place to know it superficially. He resisted the urge to quiz his sailing master once again.

'Then we'll weigh anchor an hour after sunset and steer for the Teignouse Passage.'

'Aye-aye sir. We should pass the light at about midnight. We'll be seen from the shore, certainly, what with that moon not setting until four bells in the middle, but it doesn't matter, they'll just take us for a French coaster. We can make a dash right across the bay and in this wind we should make the narrows about two o'clock. It will be quite dark by then and the tide will be on the make. I can follow the channel by the stars and soundings, I've done it often enough before, and we can be off Vannes before sunrise.'

That timing was important. Vannes was a thriving regional centre and no smuggler's lair. Its trade was somewhat stifled by the war but it was still a substantial place, and a small boat landing at night would be noticed. It was far better to have the cutter's gig rowed in at first light so that Albach could be put ashore in a respectable manner. Nobody would think it odd that a ship's master – for that would be Albach's disguise – was coming ashore at first light, and the gig could then row back down the channel to meet *Oyster* where she would be waiting.

'Mister Shorrock. I've agreed with the commodore that *Argonaut* will be detached from the squadron until this affair is over. Your orders are to remain at anchor until tomorrow sunset, then patrol between the Teignouse Channel and the Morbihan Narrows, you may use Mister Finch as a pilot. Keep a lookout for *Oyster* returning and render assistance as it seems fit. I can't give you any more specific instructions, just keep an eye out for us in case we're pursued.'

Shorrock looked concerned at the whole business and all he could manage was a flat acknowledgement of his orders.

Fairview and Shorrock; they had quite opposite views of this business. The sailing master saw only the navigational hazards and they were nothing to him, while the second in command – the fighting man – saw a completely different array of dangers, from shot and blade, from the wiles of the enemy and the treachery of friends. Perhaps Shorrock was right to be concerned, and looked at objectively it was a hugely risky undertaking. Yet Fairview's insouciance was infectious. Holbrooke felt the cold hand of fate creeping up his spine.

***

'Anchor's aweigh, sir.'

The cutter's bosun was a young man, a bosun's mate with an acting warrant, hoping for that vital recommendation that would propel him to the unimaginable heights of a real, warranted bosun. He had a wife and child in Portsmouth, and he longed for the security that came with the rank; he was desperately eager to please this post-captain who could write those vital words in his report. He was a literate man, he'd seen some of the reports that captains wrote, and in his mind he had already formulated the sentence:

Mister Tranter, the acting bosun, is particularly deserving of notice and is ready in all respects to become the bosun of a rated ship when a vacancy occurs.

Treacherous Moon

That was why he had slaved so hard to rig his cutter as a lugger and that was why he had volunteered to row the gig into Vannes, along with Matt Dawson. Sure it was dangerous, but his wife pressed him hard on the matter of his warrant whenever he got ashore, and she was so persuasive...

Holbrooke had sent almost all of the cutter's crew into *Argonaut*, leaving only a handful of men. A vessel of that size running up the French coast would have a crew of no more than eight and perhaps some passengers, any more would look odd, and with Holbrooke, Fairview, Dawson, Albach and Chalmers, that only left room for half a dozen. They were all carefully dressed to look like the crew of a French lugger, which wasn't difficult as seamen tended to dress alike wherever they came from. Just a smattering of red Monmouth caps completed the picture.

The cutter's big lugsail filled on the starboard tack and the little vessel reached away to the nor'east, bound for the Teignouse Passage and Quiberon Bay. Few people in the squadron marked their departure. There were no flags, no night signals; it was as though the great ships wouldn't abase themselves by taking notice of an oddly-rigged little armed cutter. And *Oyster* was different, her mission was one of those that sea officers didn't talk about, not in polite company, and Holbrooke wasn't at all sure that being associated with clandestine operations was good for his career.

***

'There's the light, sir. The French keep it burning for their coastal trade and it's useful to us as well, that's why nobody has interfered with it.'

Holbrooke couldn't see the beacon at first. Astern of the cutter, the ships in Palais Road and the lights of the town and citadel made a merry scene, but ahead all was blackness, with only a very few shore lights showing on the Quiberon peninsula.

'There, sir, just to larboard of the bows, the nearest light to our course. You're looking a little too far to the left, begging your pardon.'

Holbrooke shifted his telescope until the bowsprit – they had un-shipped the jib boom when they changed to a lug rig – just showed in the right of his field of view. Then he could see it, a dull orange pinpoint of light, lower than he had expected and only a hair's breadth displaced from their course.

'The tide's ebbing and setting us to starboard, sir, but I'll watch the bearing and come up a touch if needed. We're making about three knots, I would say. I'll start sounding when that light's about three miles distant, but there's no need to reduce sail; if we keep that beacon in sight we can sail straight through.'

'Very well, Mister Fairview.'

The deck of the cutter was crowded. None of the crew felt like sleeping, there was too much tension in the air, and all the officers were clustered around the binnacle.

'We'll be in the famous Quiberon Bay in an hour,' Fairview said aloud.

Nobody commented, they were all wrapped up in their own thoughts and they had fragmented into little groups. Holbrooke and Fairview stood close together, both deeply engaged in the navigation of this tricky passage. Albach and Chalmers, Dawson and Tranter stood together talking quietly, trying to imagine how it would be, rowing boldly into an enemy port in the light of a new day. The cutter's remaining crew were gathered around the mast, nervously fingering the unfamiliar halyards and sheets that came with the new rig. There were fewer of them than normal, but the lugsail needed less attention than the old gaff rig and the guns had been landed when the ports were boarded up, so the gun crews weren't needed. It was a drastically depleted crew and despite the assurances that it was only for appearances, they couldn't help but speculate whether it was to reduce the losses if the cutter was taken.

'By the mark, fifteen!'

Fairview straightened himself from where he'd been crouching over the binnacle.

'The light bears nor'-nor'east a half east, sir. The passage is about a mile wide here and we can come up to nor'east now and that'll be our heading for the narrows.'

Holbrooke nodded; there was nothing else to say and he had a mental picture of the chart. The seabed would be rising now as they moved into the passage, then it would drop away again as they reached across towards the narrows that led into Quiberon Bay. He guessed they were on time but didn't want to lose his night vision by bringing his pocket watch to the shaded binnacle light.

'Sail ho.'

The lookout's voice was little more than a loud whisper, but on this quiet night it easily carried back to the quarterdeck.

'Sail on the larboard bow. Looks like a lugger, sir, about a mile.'

Fairview gave it no more than a glance.

'It appears we are not the only ones to be running the Teignouse Passage tonight. That'll be a Frenchman coming down from the north. He must know this like the back of his hand, taking that cut through the rocks there.'

Holbrooke nodded again. He'd rehearsed in his mind all the things that could happen tonight and he was ready for this. There was nothing to fear; the newcomer would lead them through the passage and across the bay. It reinforced the idea that the lookouts at the batteries on the narrows would see nothing unusual in them coming through at night, and if there was a night signal, he could copy it.

'Dawson, you have the dark lanterns ready?'

'Yes, sir, they're both stowed under the hatch and ready to go. Blue glasses and red glasses, as you might need them.'

It had been a long shot, but he'd ordered those lanterns in case there should be a need to make a signal. He'd envisaged showing enough different lights to confuse the issue if they were challenged, but this was better, the unknown lugger would show them what the signal should be.

The lugger ahead turned off the wind when it was fairly in the passage and steadied on a course much the same as *Oyster's*. Fairview grinned and his teeth showed white in the darkness; it was further confirmation that his navigation was accurate. Soon the light was on the beam, then it moved steadily astern. The leadsman reported greater and greater depths as the cutter left the shallows behind and ran with the wind on the starboard quarter deeper and deeper into the pitch-black heart of the bay, following the dark shape of the French lugger.

***

They were soon across the bay and the next danger was the narrows with its batteries on either side that could blow the cutter out of the water with a single salvo. As they drew closer they were joined by two more coasters from the south, each running without lights and one of which didn't spot *Oyster* until it was almost aboard. Chalmers hurled a few coarse insults after it in his best French and received as good as he gave. It was like a confirmation of membership of some exclusive club; they were part of a group moving purposefully in a single direction, and Holbrooke's confidence grew as each vessel joined them. The lights on the batteries were as good as beacons to guide cautious mariners, and they found the approach channel easily without the use of the lead which would have drawn attention to them.

Far ahead they could see that the first lugger had lit a lantern.

'A signal, do you think, Mister Fairview?'

'No, sir. I believe it's just a deck lantern. They have no need for concealment now and they're just doing what they would normally do for shooting the narrows at night, in peacetime.'

'Then we'll do the same. Dawson, a white lantern in the bows if you please.'

Treacherous Moon

From the shore it would be impossible to say that *Oyster* was anything other than a middling sized French coasting lugger, one of four that had eluded the British cruisers and were steering for Vannes or perhaps one of the other little places in the gulf. They'd be on the lookout for anything as large as a brig, which could be a British man-of-war, or smaller than a lugger, which could be a cutting out party in longboats and yawls, but luggers must come and go every night. Nevertheless it felt odd, sailing as bold as brass so deep into French territory. Holbrooke had personally told every man of the crew what would happen to them if they uttered a word out loud when close to the shore or to French ships. Only he, Albach and Chalmers spoke French at all, and only Chalmers and Albach had any pretensions at sounding like a Frenchman.

Through the narrows and Fairview brought the cutter to starboard. Although the shore was mostly in deep darkness, it was a simple task to follow the channel's twists and turns that led to the western side of the gulf and up towards Vannes. The first lugger that they saw was bound that way and was still showing a light, helpfully guiding the way. Yet Holbrooke could see that Fairview needed none of these aids to his pilotage. He stood by the binnacle, occasionally taking a bearing, but otherwise appearing supremely confident of his way.

'This is the easy part, sir. It's deep water right up to these islands we're passing,' he motioned to either side of the cutter where the shadowy bulks slid past them, 'but we'll need to be more careful where the channel widens and becomes shallow. There used to be buoys all along there, but if they're still there it'll be a puzzle to see them tonight.'

Holbrooke looked astern to where the two coasters that had followed them in had disappeared into the night. Probably they'd anchored now that they were in safety, or perhaps they were bound to the eastern side of the gulf.

'Ah, he's coming to larboard.'

Holbrooke could see the lugger ahead of them swinging

out of the channel. Faintly over the dark waters he heard the sounds of an anchor being loosened from its ties and a windlass pawl being eased.

'There's a good anchorage just there,' Fairview said. 'I expect he doesn't fancy going any further until dawn.'

Holbrooke bit back an acid comment. If the locals thought it too dangerous to continue, why did Fairview think he could do it? But then, they didn't have to put a foreign agent ashore at first light, they weren't engaged in a life-or-death struggle to decide the fate of empires.

They were alone now, it appeared as though not another vessel was moving in all of the wide Gulf of Morbihan. They passed silently on, propelled by the fair wind and the following tide. Past islands and withies – he wondered what those simplest of channel markers, nothing more than straight tree branches thrust into the mud, were known as in France – and the occasional half-seen buoy, through another narrow passage where the channel turned again to starboard, then another where they followed to larboard.

'There's Vannes, right on the bow. We'll be in position in fifteen minutes, sir.'

The sky was lightening ahead, and the few lanterns of the town were almost lost in the pre-dawn glow. Suddenly the shape of the land started to become clear: hills and islands, inlets and villages came alive in the dim light of a new day.

'Bring the gig alongside Mister Tranter.'

Holbrooke had no intention of anchoring here. The tide was almost slack and the gig had only a mile to row; the cutter could lie here under sail quite happily until the gig returned. It was almost too easy, and Holbrooke had to shake himself to remember the dangers of their mission.

There was nothing more to say to Albach and Chalmers, it had all been said back in the comfort of *Argonaut's* great cabin. Tranter and Dawson would row back in the gig while Albach and Chalmers made their lonely way into the bosom of the beast. He watched them leave in the grey light and he paid no attention as Fairview kept the cutter backing and filling in the channel. Nobody disturbed them and the other coasters that had sailed into the gulf with them didn't appear. After what seemed like only a few minutes the gig came into sight, rowing unhurriedly. As soon as it had hooked on, Fairview got the cutter underway for a place he knew, a quiet anchorage out of the fairway between two small islands just off the little village of Arradon.

Too easy. Holbrooke wasn't a particularly superstitious man, not as sailors went, but the ease with which the operation had been conducted so far unsettled him and Dawson's breezy assurance that Chalmers and Albach had landed without any trouble and had last been seen disappearing up a street that led from the wharf, gave him scant comfort.

***

CHAPTER TWENTY-TWO

Pursuit

Monday, Thirteenth of April 1761.
Armed Cutter Oyster, at Anchor, Gulf of Morbihan.

Fairview was right about the anchorage. The cutter lay in two-and-a-half fathoms of water in a tiny run between the two islands, just a two-hundred-yard stretch of water at the bottom of the tide. They weren't concealed and they could be seen by the many craft that passed in the main channel to the north, but nobody gave them a second glance. Holbrooke had the whole day to study them and realise the truth of Fairview's assurances. Every possible kind of vessel passed them during that day. Fishing vessels of all shapes and sizes and about half a dozen coasters of the sort that the French called a *chasse-marée*. Lug rigs were the most usual, and he was glad that he'd made the change from the cutter's original gaff rig, but it appeared that the local custom was to step every spar that the owner could lay his hands upon and to hang a scrap of canvas from each extremity. Once he saw a French naval cutter making its leisurely way towards Vannes, but no telescope trained in his direction; they might as well have been invisible.

It was a strangely peaceful day. With a small crew and with no naval routine to be kept, there was nothing to do but wait for the evening when Albach and Chalmers would be taken off.

The afternoon brought a change in the weather. The southerly wind veered sharply into the west and a squall blew through, bringing a hard, cold rain for an hour. *Oyster's* bow swung to the wind at low water, and she bucked and surged against the steep little waves with her keel touching the muddy bottom at each plunge that she made. It was an uncomfortable hour, but then the flooding tide brought some order and her bows swung to the south. Then just as dramatically the wind backed through half the compass and settled in the northeast with low cloud and a fine drizzle, making the cutter snub to her anchor as the depth under her keel steadily increased.

'She doesn't much care for the wind against tide, does she, sir?'

Holbrooke had been watching yet another *chasse-marée* making its way upstream with the tide. It was larger than *Oyster* with two stubby pole masts, each with its dirty brown lugsail, and it sported a pole bowsprit of enormous length upon which was set a jib that could have graced a first rate ship of the line. The contrast with the French naval cutter that had passed earlier couldn't have been greater. The lugger was a utilitarian craft that had no pretensions for ocean voyages. Its spars, sails and rigging were simple and massive, and it was probably handled by a master and four or five crew. Fairview barely gave it a glance. Holbrooke was becoming more and more intrigued at his obvious familiarity with French trading vessels, and he'd once or twice shown an easy familiarity with the language that he hadn't previously admitted to.

'No, it's the short anchor cable that makes it worse, I believe. Less length to absorb the shock of each wave.'

Fairview nodded in agreement.

'This weather will be useful, if it doesn't change. There'll be no moon showing tonight and the wind and tide will carry us out in fine style.'

Holbrooke forbore to point out the perils of pilotage is such restricted waters in the dark of the night with a thick layer of cloud hiding the moon. It frankly appalled him, but he'd learned to trust his sailing master where inshore navigation was concerned. A certain delicacy had prevented him quizzing Fairview about his past, but the informality of their plain, seaman's clothing and the novelty of their situation had changed their relationship, at least for this day.

'I wonder, Master, how you come to know this place so well.'

There was a pause while Fairview pretended to an interest in the wooded island that lay on their larboard beam. The seconds passed and eventually Fairview turned back with an odd expression on his face, halfway to a smile but with a hint of wariness.

'I don't do well ashore,' he started, 'so when I'm not employed by His Majesty, I take whatever ship I can get, anything so long as it's a master's berth. Sometimes it's a timber ship running from Hull to Gothenburg, sometimes it's a West Indiaman, but when I can't get anything like that, I take whatever's on offer. For two years between the wars I had a little brig that traded between Falmouth and these places hereabouts. Now, you must understand, sir, that it's a keen business, fierce competition and tight profits. If it had been my own brig, I'd have been happy with what I had, but the syndicate was of a different mind, and they weren't satisfied with their eight percent. So, and this is between you and I, sir, there was a proportion of the cargo that wasn't unloaded in the normal way, not in a manner or place that attracted the attention of the revenue. Falmouth was usually the second port that I visited on the homebound run, the first being less formal and more out-of-the-way, if you understand me, and it was the same outbound. Now, this little anchorage here is handy to send a boat into Arradon over yonder and land a thing or two, and take a few extra bales or casks that bothered neither the customs officers at Vannes nor Falmouth.'

Holbrooke glanced sideways at Fairview. He had the look of a man who had confessed but was still unsure of absolution. Perhaps at this moment he was starting to regret his candour.

'That would explain your sudden fluency in French, Mister Fairview.'

'Aye, sir, and I regret keeping it quiet so long. I'm not fluent and nobody would take me for a Frenchman, but I know enough and can speak it plain enough to get by in the trade.'

Treacherous Moon

Holbrooke laughed quietly.

'Your secret's safe with me, nobody will ever hear it from my lips.'

Fairview glanced at him queerly, a look of incredulity.

'Oh, bless you, sir. Your officers all know it well enough and so in a discreet sort of way does Trinity House and the navy board. They would never employ me if it weren't for the shortage of masters in this war. They won't send me to a ship-of-the-line though, not unless her captain asks for me. I just hope that my service can be long enough so that I'll be superannuated in the end.'

'Mister Chalmers knows?' Holbrooke stared at the sailing master in frank astonishment. 'He's never said anything.'

'It's not the sort of thing that a man mentions, not unless he has malicious intent. But there, I've got that off my chest and I hope you won't think too badly of me, sir.'

Holbrooke clapped him on the shoulder and smiled broadly.

'Think worse of the Mister Fairview? If you can bring me safe into places like this, you're worth more than all the rubies in the east! Long, long may we sail together.'

Fairview's face relaxed into his own smile, as though a great burden had been taken from his shoulders. Holbrooke turned away, slightly embarrassed by the scene and caught Dawson watching them with a knowing look on his face. Did he know the master's secret? Did everyone in *Argonaut* know, except the frigate's captain?

***

'The wind's still dead foul for Vannes, sir.'

Fairview had cocked his head to the northeast, feeling the dry wind upon his cheek. The sun would be setting in an hour, but nothing could be seen of it behind the thick layer of cloud that lay over the Gulf of Morbihan.

'How far to the wharf from here, Mister Fairview?'

'Three miles, sir, but the flood will help, at least for the next hour and a half. The stand is very short here.'

Holbrooke had already thought of that. It was typical, this far from the open sea, for the period between the flood and the ebb to be brief, typically a half hour or so. He'd been considering whether to stay at anchor and send the gig the full three miles into Vannes, and the master's information settled the question.

'The gig can make it in forty-five minutes, and it'll have the ebb under it coming back, or at least the flood will have finished. I'll go in with Dawson and Tranter while you stay with the cutter, Mister Fairview. Burn a light as soon as it gets dark so that we can find you.'

Fairview made no comment. He'd come to the same conclusion as Holbrooke, but he had schooled himself in offering information but not ideas, unless it concerned the safety of his ship.

'Aye-aye sir. I'll lay out the killick from the stern while you're gone, so that our head will be cast to the south, and I'll bring the bower to short stay. That'll hold us until you're ready to get underway.'

Holbrooke smiled in the growing gloom; he hadn't thought of that. By the time he returned, there would be a strong ebb to match the nor'easterly wind, and there was little space to get the cutter's bows around once she was no longer anchored. Running aground on the falling tide would be disastrous, and it could be the ruination of the entire expedition.

'Thank you, Mister Fairview. We won't want to waste any time once the gig is back alongside.'

***

Tranter pushed the bows away and dropped back onto this thwart. The flooding tide and the brisk pull of the oars moved the gig quickly away from the cutter and in minutes it seemed remote and faraway, a separate entity, unconnected with the three men in the boat.

Holbrooke hadn't intended to go into Vannes on the gig and he couldn't say what had driven him to change his mind. The cutter was only a mile or so further away than it had been when Albach and Chalmers had been rowed in, and Dawson and Tranter could find their way easily enough. Perhaps it was the growing belief that things were running just too smoothly. He patted the pocket of his plain grey coat where his commission lay in a sealskin pouch. That was part of it, if Chalmers and Albach had been caught, his commission could at least save the chaplain, and it might even have some influence on Albach's fate. It would also protect Dawson and Tranter. But that wasn't the only reason. Somewhere deep inside him, hidden from conscious thought, lay the conviction that he should share in the dangers of his men. In the normal course of command such thoughts were unnecessary; a frigate's captain, along with the sailing master, quartermaster and steersman, were the most vulnerable men in action, far more so than the gun crews who had the protection of stout gunwales. And, he had to admit to himself, he was curious about how these things were conducted. It was all very well to speak of putting people ashore in an enemy's port, but was it really as easy as that? Did nobody ask questions?

They were well into the fairway now and the town of Arradon could be seen over the larboard quarter. They had considered landing Albach there because it was smaller and quieter than Vannes, but it was four miles from Vannes by road, and a foot traveller was always subject to questioning, much more so than a handful of men in a boat. Also, as Fairview had pointed out, the very busyness of Vanes was a protection. In Arradon, any boat coming into the harbour was likely to draw the men who squared their month's accounts by selling and buying uncustomed goods, and it would be hard to explain that no such thing was intended.

The light was fading fast as the gig swung to larboard into the approach channel. Dawson seemed to know the way well enough, and Holbrooke sat in silence, watching the buoys pass and steering in obedience to Dawson's jerks of his head. The steady rhythm of the gig was soporific and he had to fight to stay awake.

The wide channel twisted and turned, with all the mud banks covered by the still making tide. It was dark now, and Holbrooke was surprised when the wharfs of Vannes loomed into sight on the larboard bow. No challenge, and the few loafers seemed deeply uninterested by the little boat. He was unsure for a moment: should the gig go alongside or should he lie off until his friends appeared? He was just considering, when he saw two dark figures detach themselves from the shadows of a warehouse. They walked briskly towards the water while Dawson and Tranter, without any orders, pulled towards them. Tranter held onto an iron ring set into a piling while Albach and Chalmers dropped quickly into the boat. Holbrooke's swift glance confirmed that they were unhurt, although they had a hunted look about them.

'There's no time to lose,' Chalmers hissed breathlessly in English. 'Pursuit isn't far behind.'

***

Tranter pushed off and again took up his oar while Holbrooke motioned for Albach to sit in the bows to balance the boat. The tide was slack now but the wind helped, and the gig's bows swung quickly to starboard as the oars pulled hard for the centre of the channel.

'Did you succeed?' Holbrooke asked Chalmers as he held the tiller hard over to larboard.

'Succeed? Yes, I suppose we did. We found our man, or men, and we had our conversation. There's nothing in writing but the dispositions of d'Aiguillon's forces and much of the militia is in his head. But it didn't go as planned. There were too many people there, three of them, all militia and two of them left early. Although they all looked sincere and spoke sweetly, I don't doubt that one of them has betrayed us. As we left the house we saw a platoon marching in that direction. Luckily we ducked into an alley and it was already growing dark, but it was no normal military manoeuvre, there were two mounted men in plain clothes – good horses, not some farmyard hacks – both armed. It's

Treacherous Moon

certain that we are pursued.'

Albach was facing aft and by the light of a lantern on the wharf he saw a commotion as a group of figures poured out from a street.

'That's them! Oh, pull for all your worth.'

Holbrooke had an impression, no more, of a dark mass of figures spilling onto the wharf with two horsemen looming large over them. They paused an instant then one of them wheeled away, back into the town.

Dawson and Tranter needed no further urging and the oars fairly bent under the pull of their muscles. Albach took up one of the spare oars in the bow and Chalmers wriggled his way forward to take the other. Now the gig was moving fast through the still water. Holbrooke strained his eyes into the darkness ahead looking for the buoys, the withies and the twists and turns that he had tried to commit to memory on the way upstream.

Vannes was far behind now, entirely hidden in the night. How would they be pursued? It was impossible by land, Holbrooke thought. The Gulf of Morbihan was a mass of long inlets that reached far inland on all sides, and few of them were bridged except at their heads. Surely no horse could run faster than *Oyster* could sail to the narrows.

Holbrooke desperately tried to bring the chart into his mind, testing his optimistic hypothesis. Yes, there was a way. A horseman could take the westerly road out of Vannes, through Arradon and so to the left bank of the Auray river to a village called Baden at its mouth. Surely there must be a ferry there, or a boat that could be commandeered. Twelve miles perhaps to the river, a half hour to cross it, and then the battery was only a mile or so away. He must look closely at the chart when he reached the cutter, but one thing was now clear in his mind; a determined man on a horse, even at night, could make it in three hours.

'Pull, pull all,' Holbrooke urged as he realised their peril.

***

They came out into the fairway with the ebbing tide behind them. There was the cutter's light. Now he had a mark to steer for. Dawson and Tranter were still pulling well, and Albach was bearing up manfully, but Chalmers looked blown.

'One more effort, the cutter's half a mile away.'

Half a mile, perhaps ten minutes at their present rate of progress. Holbrooke pushed the tiller over and the gig swung into *Oyster's* channel as he opened the dark lantern that he'd kept beside him.

At first he could only see *Oyster's* light, a pinprick in the deep gloom that lay between the islands. Then, gradually, the shape of the cutter emerged. Closer they came, and now he could see Fairview moving across the lantern's light. Then he heard the click of the windlass pawls as the anchor was heaved in.

It wasn't elegant, and both the gig and the cutter would bear the scars of their coming alongside, but in a moment the five men were aboard *Oyster* with the gig lying astern on a painter.

'Bower anchor's aweigh, sir.'

'Very well, Mister Fairview. We have no time to lose. You may slip the killick and let's be underway. Make all speed possible for the narrows because I fear that we are pursued.'

Fairview needed no further orders.

'Hoist the lugs'l, hoist the jib.'

With his own knife he sawed through the thin cable that held the cutter's stern against the wind and tide, and with a jerk they were free, gathering pace as they rushed for the refuge of the open sea.

***

CHAPTER TWENTY-THREE

The Narrows

Monday, Thirteenth of April 1761.
Armed Cutter Oyster, at Sea, Gulf of Morbihan.

Holbrooke couldn't get the image out of his mind of that tall horseman hauling his steed's head around so purposefully. It was not the action of a man frozen by uncertainty; he knew exactly what he was about and Holbrooke was as certain as death what it was. It was a race for the narrows, horse against sail and each hampered by the moonless night. Did that rider know the road from Vannes that circled the gulf to the west? Holbrooke had to assume that he knew it well.

He took a quick look around at the islands speeding past on either side. It was useless; only Fairview could get them through these channels in the dark of the night, and it was better not to interfere.

'Where's the chart, Mister Fairview?'

The sailing master reached into the binnacle and pulled out the rolled chart. There was a shaded lantern that shed its light on the compass and Holbrooke reached for it.

'That's no use to me for half an hour, sir, not until we're past Port Blanc where the channel widens.'

Holbrooke's heart was racing. He moved to the taffrail to avoid destroying the master's night vision and pulled back the lantern's screen to let a shaft of light fall upon the chart. He beckoned for Albach and Chalmers to join him.

'If I'm correct at least one of your horsemen is galloping for the narrows as we speak. What do you know of this road?'

He traced his finger along the vague line that ran from Vannes, through Arradon and down to Baden. He knew better than to trust a road on a navigational chart; the draftsman may indeed have known of the existence of a road, or he may have merely guessed at it, but it was odds-on that he had no real knowledge of its course.

'There is a road and I have travelled it,' Albach replied thoughtfully. 'There's a militia post here at Baden that I visited twice. The chart isn't quite right because the road skirts around Arradon rather than passing through it, and when it approaches Baden there's a side road that runs down to a ferry landing at the point.'

'When do you think our horseman can make it to the ferry?'

Albach thought for a moment, remembering his own journey and thinking about the difficulties of a night ride.

'It's no great distance, ten miles perhaps, but the road isn't well kept. It's easy in daylight but at night he'll need two hours.'

Two hours! And forty-five minutes of that time had already sped by. Holbrooke looked again at the chart.

'This place here, Port Blanc, is there a battery?'

'No, sir. There are no batteries inside the gulf. He'll be making for the ferry, but he'll have to wake the ferryman, it closes at sunset.'

Holbrooke studied the chart again. It was difficult to see exactly where the ferry landings were, and how far the ferry would have to run between the two.

'It's a two-oared ferry and by my recollection it takes twenty minutes to cross to the western side of the narrows.'

'Does it run to the eastern side?'

'No, there's another ferry that crosses the narrows and that takes only ten minutes.'

'Then, gentlemen, we must assume that this horseman will alert at least the western battery before we arrive. That's some comfort because the master battery is on the eastern side, isn't that correct?'

'It is sir. There are only six-pounders on the western battery and all the gunboats are kept to the east. But as soon as he reaches the western battery they'll make the alarm signal. It's a single gun and a light. I fear that our passage will be contested.'

Holbrooke turned forward to see the shadowy shape of the sailing master, and beside him the reassuring form of Dawson, grasping the tiller. Everything else was in darkness.

'Every knot of speed that you can make, Mister Fairview.'

'Aye-aye sir. I'll need the lantern in fifteen minutes.'

Holbrooke looked at the passing shore. There were a surprising number of lights and on the larboard bow a little cluster showed where Port Blanc lay at the western side of the next set of narrows. Beyond that the channel opened into a wide lake. The cutter was making a good speed with the wind and tide at her stern, perhaps six or seven knots over the ground, but he was haunted by the thought of a well-mounted horseman eating up the miles from Vannes. He'd be ahead of them by now, perhaps approaching the ferry landing. Very soon he'd be shaking the ferryman awake, perhaps showing him a pistol to encourage him, and the poor man would be hurrying down to the landing with his oars over his shoulder. He had a sudden thought, a leap of hope.

'Can the ferry take a horse?'

Albach knew the answer and immediately knew it's significance.

'Yes. It's a flatbed boat, a large punt really, and it regularly carries horses and small carts.'

So that hope was dashed. The mile from the ferry landing to the battery would be eaten up by a determined horse and rider in just a few minutes.

***

Port Blanc passed in a blur of shadowy shapes and dim cottage lanterns. There was a ferry there but clearly the horseman hadn't turned off the road, and there was no good reason why he should, the ferry only ran to another island. Fairview had the lantern now, shining its narrow beam upon the compass, and it was easy to see why he needed it. The Port Blanc narrows were barely more than a cable wide and both sides had been visible, but then the channel opened out abruptly and the shores were lost in the darkness. Fairview was running on a compass bearing, aiming for the next choke point two miles away.

Tranter's shadowy shape loomed out of the blackness.

'We have four muskets sir, and the pistols that you gentlemen are carrying. There are half a dozen boarding pikes and two cutlasses. I've gathered them all by the mast, sir. The muskets are loaded and I've checked the priming and flints.'

'Very well Mister Tranter. They're not to be issued without my express orders.'

It was a good idea to bring all the firearms to one place, but it was hard to see what good they would do against nine and six pound guns in fixed batteries. It was tempting to use them to give the French gunners something to think about while they were laying their guns, but it would do more harm than good. He knew how difficult it was to find a mark at night. The gunners may see the cutter as a vague shape, but after the first discharge, the flash of the great guns would blind their crews and even at two or three cables *Oyster* would be almost invisible to them. The flashes of musketry would only give them an aiming mark.

Holbrooke saw a dark shape on the starboard bow. He called the chart to mind; it must be the island that marked the end of the lake and the start of the tangle of further islands and peninsulas that lay between them and the narrows. The ebbing tide was at its fastest now and it caused a small standing wave as it funnelled into the close channel. *Oyster* pitched heavily as it hit the wave and then it was through.

'A mile and a half to the narrows, sir.'

Fairview didn't even look at his captain, his whole concentration was on the passage ahead. He didn't once consult the chart but he cast occasional glances at the compass, conning the cutter by giving Dawson courses to steer.

Treacherous Moon

Three islands to starboard, Holbrooke remembered, and then they'd be in range of the guns.

Bang!

Holbrooke could sense everyone looking ahead but the flash of the gun was hidden by the islands.

Albach's fist pounded the gunwale.

'Six-pounder. Our man seems to have won the race.'

'He's won the race, but he still has to catch us and that won't be so easy.'

Holbrooke stared past the bows. A point of land was passing to larboard and now he thought that he could see the narrows, a lighter patch in the darkness.

Boom!

A heavier gun, an answering shot from the eastern battery perhaps, and the flash was visible this time, fine on the larboard bow. Fairview had performed a miracle of navigation and brought the cutter through the maze of channels and islands on a fast-ebbing tide in the dark of the night, and he'd done it without any loss of time, without even the slightest pause in their headlong flight.

Holbrooke looked up at the mainsail that stretched far above until it disappeared into the night.

'Can you wear her now, Mister Fairview? It may be inconvenient when we're in the narrows.'

The sailing master looked astern for the first time since he'd cut the anchor cable, then up at the sail. They'd been on the starboard tack the whole way down the gulf but with this nor'easterly they'd have to wear to pass through the narrows into the bay.

'We can haul in on the sheet and gybe her by force, sir. We may be sailing by the lee for a few minutes.'

'Very well, please do so.'

Tranter gathered his men. This was not a usual manoeuvre and in this wind and so short-handed, hauling in the mainsheet was a struggle. *Oyster* rolled heavily as the sheet came home.

Fairview judged the cutter's distance from the eastern

shore. Just enough room.

'Come a point to larboard, Dawson, then come back when she's gybed.'

Holbrooke felt the cutter swing to larboard, then the wind took charge and the loose-footed mainsail flapped awkwardly as it backed, followed by the jib. Then the yard – the lug as it now was – swung across and Dawson came back onto his course. Tranter let out the sheet and now there was nothing to do but run for the narrows.

'Get down behind the gunwales, everyone except Mister Fairview and Dawson.'

Holbrooke was still speaking calmly but he knew that in any moment they would be in range of the batteries. The cutter would be visible by now. Would they fire as soon as their guns would point, or would they wait until the cutter was squarely in the narrows? It was half tide and the ebb was at its fastest; *Oyster* would be through the narrows in a flash. The batteries would have time to fire two salvos as their prey ran fast into the bay, perhaps a third if they were well-trained. Holbrooke knew what he'd do if he were commanding either of those batteries. He'd wait until his target and the two batteries formed an equilateral triangle before firing his first salvo. If they delayed until the cutter was directly between them they'd be in danger of their shot falling on the opposite battery. They'd still have their two salvos but unless *Oyster* was crippled, there would be no third.

Crack!

Holbrooke caught the flash of a smaller gun on his larboard side and knew immediately what it was. A gunboat, probably more than one, was pulling out from the eastern shore. The signal of a gun from either battery must also be the signal for the gunboats to deploy. A three-pounder, he guessed, but it could still do serious damage to the cutter's frail timbers. He could see nothing in that direction and he dismissed it as irrelevant. They were almost at that magical point, the optimum time for the batteries to open fire. He looked forward; his small crew were all crouching behind the gunwales as he had ordered.

He could see them! His confusion lasted no more than a second and then he looked up to see that dreadful gibbous moon leering down on them through a gap in the cloud. A long second passed, and another, and then the world turned upside down. He saw the flash but he didn't hear the report of the guns through the tremendous sound of iron balls smashing into the cutter's hull. The little vessel staggered under the blows and a rain of splinters swept the deck. He heard a sound above and looked up to see the yard hanging at a dangerous angle. Their speed fell off with the reduction in sail area.

Bang!

That was the western battery adding to the damage, but they were through now, and Fairview, miraculously unhurt, was bringing the cutter to starboard to stay in the channel. He saw Tranter leap for the ratlines, swarming up to try to re-rig the luff downhaul that had parted. He shouted at him, but the bosun didn't hear.

This time he heard the loud boom of the eastern battery. Again *Oyster* staggered under the impact, and a fresh wave of splinters scythed across the deck.

'She's going,' shouted Fairview.

An unlucky shot – a nine-pound ball – had smashed through the shrouds and into the mast. A sloop or a frigate might have survived that blow, but a little cutter, with its standing rigging reduced to make it look like a lugger, had no hope. The mast wavered, there was a cry from Tranter, and then it was gone, falling over the starboard side carrying the helpless bosun down with it.

'Axes, axes. Cut away the mast.'

Fairview grabbed the tiller while Dawson ran for an axe. He and one of the cutter's crew slashed at the shrouds, the forestay and the remaining backstay, desperate to get rid of the useless assemblage of timber, canvas and cordage that was trailing on their quarter. All the time the blessed ebb tide and the nor'east wind were carrying them further and further out into Quiberon Bay. The clouds covered the moon again. A single shot split the night, from the western battery apparently, and all was black.

Holbrooke felt the deck surge forward under his feet as the mast floated free. The cutter was utterly unmanageable now, but at least wind and tide were carrying it towards safety.

Crack! Crack!

The cutter shuddered to a blow at its transom. Holbrooke had actually forgotten the gunboats. He looked astern but could see nothing. They couldn't be far away.

'Helm's not answering, sir. I think the rudder's been shot away.'

Dawson swung the tiller lightly from side to side. There was no resistance. The cutter was nothing more than a floating wreck with a tiny crew and a handful of firearms. In a few minutes the gunboats would be alongside. He'd fight, of course, but if they were handled with any resolution, the result was foretold. He may be able to beat off the first attempt at boarding, but then they'd just lay off and in twenty minutes, long before he could expect any help, the cutter would either founder or they'd all be dead. Yet it had to be attempted, while there was any hope at all. If he surrendered he could be sure that he and his crew would be treated decently, but not Albach; he'd be regarded – quite correctly – as a spy. If he was lucky he'd be shot, otherwise it would be the hangman's noose in some dank cell where no friendly face would witness his end. A deadly calm gripped him and he caught the Austrian's eye.

'Be so kind as to issue the arms.'

***

The tide and the wind were pulling *Oyster* rapidly down the channel. Perhaps they'd strike one of the rocks that guarded the narrows and put an end to Holbrooke's problems. Fairview destroyed that hope; he calmly took a back bearing on the light at the western side of the narrows.

Treacherous Moon

'Right in the centre of the channel, sir, we must be making a good three knots over the ground, what with the wind and the tide. We'll be in deep water in ten minutes. Ah, there's the moon again. Another hour and it would have set.'

Both men looked astern. There, shockingly close, lay the two gunboats. They were about the size of *Argonaut's* longboat but they had no sails, just a bank of long sweeps and that wicked-looking gun in the bows. *Oyster* must be perfectly visible in the moon's treacherous light. If the clouds could only have covered it for another half an hour...

Crack!

A shot landed alongside the cutter sending a spray of salt water over the quarterdeck. Soon they'd be so close that they couldn't possibly miss.

All hands were looking aft at the approaching menace. Nobody was looking to seaward. Then the sound of a gun boomed from ahead and they heard a shot pass somewhere above where the mast should have been.

'It's *Argonaut*,' shouted Dawson, the first to recognise the ship that was silhouetted by the silvery glow of the setting moon. Holbrooke took one look then turned back to the gunboats in time to see the single waterspout subsiding into the water far beyond them. Of course, Shorrock would aim high to avoid hitting the cutter, but there could be no doubt of the outcome if they persisted in their pursuit of the fleeing enemy. There wasn't a moment's hesitation from the Frenchmen; in that single shot they had seen the hopelessness of their cause. As though activated by a single mind, both gunboats backed their oars to starboard, their bows swung around and they turned for home, disappointed and frustrated of their prize.

***

CHAPTER TWENTY-FOUR

A Sordid Business

Tuesday, Fourteenth of April 1761.
Valiant, at Anchor, Palais Road, Belle Isle.

It wasn't a full council of war, just a meeting between the two principals and a few of their staff officers. General Hodgson was seconded by General Crauford and a pair of brigadiers who weren't introduced. Commodore Keppel had only Adam Duncan, his flag captain, and his saturnine secretary. Sawtree was there, of course, and Holbrooke and Chalmers took their places beside him, somewhat displaced from the great people. Albach hadn't been invited and he would have resisted if asked.

There was a new map on the bulkhead, showing the entire north-western part of France, from the Seine to the Gironde. It was dotted with towns and cities and criss-crossed by the main roads that connected them. Belle Isle was strangely skewed so that it looked as though the island's long axis ran from north to south. The Gulf of Morbihan appeared as a wide, featureless lake dotted with only a few islands; it looked like a place where ships could manoeuvre in safety without any fear of rocks and shoals, tides and wind. Holbrooke shuddered when he remembered the reality.

Keppel opened the meeting. The intelligence had been gathered by an agent of the Admiralty and his insertion and extraction were entirely naval affairs. Keppel wanted there to be no doubt as to who owned this vital information.

'Good morning General, Gentlemen…'

Keppel nodded his acknowledgement of the soldiers gathered around the table. They stared back blankly, reserving their judgement. They'd received intelligence reports before, and they were prepared to be disappointed by what they were to hear.

Treacherous Moon

'…The operation was a success, I'm pleased to say. Our agent returned four hours ago and Mister Sawtree has produced a preliminary report. If you would be so kind, sir.'

Keppel said nothing about the near destruction of the cutter, the loss of the keen young acting bosun and the horrors of that midnight pursuit and the fight in the narrows. It wasn't the army's business and set against their tally of dead, wounded and captured at Port An-Dro, the navy's losses in the Morbihan had been trivial.

Sawtree stood and bowed stiffly to Keppel and the generals, evidently his injured back still troubled him. He picked up a single sheet of paper and pulled a short pointer from his pocket.

'My agent met his contacts in Vannes, as planned. You'll forgive me if I don't elaborate on their positions, and how they came by the information, but I may have cause to use them again and I wouldn't want their identities to be known.'

Sawtree fixed each of the soldiers with his eye. Holbrooke knew that he was being at best disingenuous; if any of those men had survived the treachery of one or two of their number, they were already hunted fugitives, or they had been taken. In either case, they were hopelessly compromised and of no further use to the Admiralty's intelligence operations. It was just Sawtree's way of emphasising the need for secrecy.

'First, and perhaps of greatest importance, the Duc d'Aiguillon arrived at Vannes three days ago having galloped from Rennes at the first word that we had arrived off Belle Isle. His headquarters staff have been following as best they can and are arriving in the town day by day. He's taken summary command of the militia and he's sent out orders for all the Brittany regiments and companies – foot, horse and artillery – to muster at Vannes.'

Craufurd looked at Hodgson and raised an eyebrow. It was an eloquent way of expressing his disinterest in the movement of militia units. They were good enough for garrison work and manning batteries, but only the regular French line regiments could hope to stand against Hodgson's infantry. No militia unit could influence the course of events on Belle Isle. Sawtree noticed the exchange of glances and correctly interpreted its meaning.

'The militia may not concern you, General, but remember that they can take the place of line regiments who will then be available to the Duke for operations against our forces. Perhaps you'll be interested in the other information that my agent has brought.'

He paused for a few seconds. It was a most effective gesture, establishing his authority and demanding that his audience attend to what he was about to say.

'You'll be aware that Brittany is chafing at the navy's impressment of its men and its demands on the region's food production. In consequence, there *had* been a proposal to recall thirty battalions from Germany to maintain order and to guard the coast, but that was resisted by the army who need those battalions to gain a position in Hanover before peace breaks out. However, your arrival off Belle Isle has changed the thinking at Versailles and now at least twenty-two line battalions are on the march for Brittany as well as eight squadrons of horse. The whole of Soubise's order of battle has been affected, and Broglie's too. The Normandy troops are marching for Brittany, those of Picardy are dropping back to Normandy and the Flanders units are withdrawing to Picardy. That's what will hurt Soubise, when he has to release his own fighting regiments from Westphalia to secure Flanders.'

Hodgson held up his hand to interrupt.

'It begs the question why Belle Isle was left with such a small army when it was so clearly vulnerable.'

'Ah, there's been a flurry of questions in Versailles, and they have echoed all the way to Brittany where my agent heard them. Why couldn't d'Aiguillon reinforce Sainte-Croix in Belle Isle while the sea was open? The answer appears to be that Soubise's army has taken most of the men that had been allotted to coastal defence. The militia has been used to fill the gaps, but you will be aware that they are only activated for stated periods of time, and they must be released for the harvest, or France will starve. The French army has a manning problem, gentlemen, and it has given us this opportunity to act.'

Sawtree could see that he had the soldiers' attention now.

'The line units are all ordered to Vannes initially, with the intention of sending some of them across to the island and distributing the remainder along the coast, in case our real objective is not Belle Isle. The first units have already arrived in the Morbihan region, and it's expected that the majority of them will be in place by the twenty-fifth of April. That's the Duke's planning assumption, at least.'

Sawtree stopped at that and waited for comment. It was General Crauford who spoke first.

'Can we rely upon this information?'

Sawtree looked pained by the question, as though his personal honour was being questioned.

'The information comes from an agent who has served us for a number of years. General Hodgson has spoken to him and he's well known to Captain Holbrooke and Reverend Chalmers. For some years he has had free access to French military plans, both those of the army and of the militia. I regret that I cannot be more precise about his situation, and I am certain that you will understand why.'

The soldiers each turned towards Holbrooke and Chalmers. It was clear that none of them relished being involved in the sordid business of intelligence gathering, much less being in the same room as three men who had been so intimately engaged in it. They were good enough fighting men, but they liked to see their enemy, to stand square before the volleys of musket fire and decide the matter at the point of the bayonet. This talk of *agents* and *contacts* and *sources*, of subterfuge and spying, was not at all to their liking.

Holbrooke wondered for an instant whether he should say anything but a minute shake of Sawtree's head, observed by nobody but himself, told him that he should hold his peace. He had wondered why he and Chalmers had been summoned to the meeting. Neither of them had anything useful to contribute, at least nothing that could be said in such a public forum, and although they'd washed and dressed carefully, the last few days' fatigue and mental strain must show clearly on their faces. They were strangely at odds with the clean and rested soldiers at the table. But of course they were just part of the show, the only participants in this murky business whose faces could see the light of day. They were the visible confirmation that desperate measures had been taken to secure the intelligence, lending it an authenticity that words alone couldn't convey.

Keppel spoke, rather hastily to Holbrooke's mind, as though he was trying to shift the discussion away from the dangerous territory of the operation's methods and means. It was certain that the commodore already knew the answer to his question.

'And the French navy, what of them, Mister Sawtree?'

'My agent has less access to the navy, sir, but what he has discovered is that the Brest and Rochefort squadrons are being readied for sea. The Duke has demanded that a sufficient force be sent to clear the way so that his men can be carried across to reinforce the island. The information, such as it is, suggests that they will look for a suitable weather window – an easterly wind, I believe…'

Keppel nodded in agreement.

'… an easterly wind to blow our blockading ships off station and allow their own ships to get out to sea, any time from the twenty-fifth. That will be the earliest that the crews can be found and the ships prepared, and it matches the date that the army will be ready.'

Another silence as the soldiers digested the information. Hodgson spoke next, posing the question that was in everyone's mind.

'Can you maintain your position if the French get to sea, Commodore?'

Keppel almost squirmed in discomfort. He'd already discussed this with the general, but now he was being forced to bring it out into the open. It was the vital question for the navy. He could fight a French squadron of equal size or perhaps a little greater – and a combination of the Brest and Rochefort squadrons would be at least equal to his own – but that would put a large proportion of the home-waters navy in peril. He'd spent hours with Pitt and Anson, discussing just this subject. It was the spectre of Spain's joining the war that exercised their minds and stalked the corridors of Whitehall. Britain just could not afford to lose its navy's fighting power at this critical moment. Both he and Hodgson had written to Pitt, each demanding reinforcements, but even if Pitt agreed – and he'd have to take ships and battalions away from other projected operations – they could barely be here for the twenty-fifth.

'If the French can evade Captain Buckle's squadron and come out in force before your army is ashore, then, as you are already aware General, I shall recommend that we withdraw.'

Holbrooke kept an impassive face but he was truly shocked. He could vaguely glimpse the strategic issues that forced Keppel's hand, but still, the argument must appear weak and contemptuous to these soldiers.

'Then we have until the twenty-fifth, gentlemen. May I suggest, Commodore, that we reconvene this afternoon to review the situation?'

***

The soldiers filed out of the cabin but Sawtree indicated that Holbrooke and Chalmers should stay. Keppel looked irritated, he surely had a hundred matters that demanded his attention and he had assumed that Sawtree had now reported all the intelligence that Albach had discovered.

'There's one more matter, sir. It's an entirely naval issue which is why I waited for the general and his staff to leave.'

Keppel's secretary glanced meaningfully at the clock that hung from the forward bulkhead. Holbrooke had noticed it already, who wouldn't have? Clocks weren't at all common at sea for the simple reasons that a pendulum couldn't beat a regular rhythm in a pitching and rolling ship, and springs were affected by changes in heat and humidity. Presumably it was stowed when *Valiant* was underway and only set going in sheltered anchorages, but there it was, its loud tick and tock an ever-present sound.

Sawtree caught the glance but ignored it. There was more than a hint of the intelligence officer's arrogance in his dealings with senior officers, as though the usual hierarchy of the service didn't apply to him. Holbrooke and Chalmers knew already what he was going to say, but it was still uncomfortable watching Sawtree's handling of the commodore.

'It concerns those ships in the Vilaine. You'll be aware that there are only two left there now…'

'Yes, I know that very well and they're being watched.'

Keppel was also watching the time and he evidently didn't appreciate Sawtree's manner. Sawtree continued regardless.

'…*Robuste* and *Entendu*, a seventy-four and a forty. They're in poor condition but their hulls are sound and a few months at Brest will see them fit for the line of battle again. My agent discovered, almost as an aside, the name of the officer who brought out all the others. He is Charles-Henri-Louis d'Arsac, and he glories in the title of Chevalier de Ternay. His honorific means little, of course, he's just the normal sort of minor nobility that the French navy is burdened with, except that in his case he appears to have real ability. He was a lieutenant de vaisseau, stuck in the promotion system and unlikely to make the jump to captain in this war, that is until he brought out *Dragon* and *Brillant* in January. King Louis himself insisted upon his promotion and it appears that he's been posted into *Robuste*. He's flush with his success and he's brought out all the other ships,

Treacherous Moon

two-by-two, except this last pair and one that was wrecked in the estuary. His partner in these gallant exploits is Jean-Charles, the Comte d'Hector.'

Keppel was fidgeting with a pile of papers before him and the ticking of the clock set the tone for what was becoming a strained conversation. None of this deterred Sawtree in the least.

'It appears that blockading the Vilaine is more difficult than it seems at first sight, at least to a landsman like me. Every one of those ships, with the exception of a frigate, has made its escape to Brest or Rochefort…'

Keppel looked up sharply at this barely concealed criticism of the naval service.

'…and it is to be hoped that these last two can be prevented from joining their fellows. They will be ready by the end of May, with only half their guns and just enough stores for a week at sea, in order to reduce their draught so that they might cross the bar. It's reported that de Ternay and his friend will make the attempt at a spring tide, as they did for the others. They both need extensive work. Rochefort is short of resources at the moment, yet to make Brest they must pass your squadron and Hawke's, I cannot say which they will choose.'

Sawtree gazed abstractedly out of the window as the clock measured the passing seconds and minutes.

'Is that the full sum of the intelligence, Mister Sawtree, nothing else, no specific date?'

'Little do I know of the tides, sir, but I'm told that the springs happen every fortnight, so that should narrow the options.'

Sawtree's voice was heavy with sarcasm. The meeting was over, to Holbrooke's relief. It was uncomfortable being associated with someone as acerbic as Sawtree, and he could only hope that Keppel wouldn't forever link him with the man from the secret service.

***

Chris Durbin

CHAPTER TWENTY-FIVE

A Feint

Wednesday, Twenty-Second of April 1761.
Argonaut, at Sea, off Saint-Foy, Belle Isle.

The sound of gunfire filled the still morning air. *Argonaut* was, for the time being, a mere spectator to this renewed attempt to put the army ashore on Belle Isle, and Holbrooke was enjoying the novelty of it. His decks were crowded with marines, two hundred and fifty of them organised into two companies, and they made a colourful spectacle as they sat or lay upon the planks or walked wherever there was space to take a step. He'd anticipated the problems in finding sufficient deck space to handle the sails and *Argonaut's* people had been at quarters, staking out their deck space, since before the marines came on board at the very first lightening of the sky. Jackson had sent enough men into the tops to carry out any reasonable sail handling tasks, knowing that there was little chance of the topmen reacting swiftly if they were on deck. Holbrooke knew that he could have insisted that the marines stay in their flatboats alongside the frigate until they had landed, but he had sat on hard thwarts for whole days during Pitt's descents on the French north coast, and he knew how uncomfortable it was. The marines would fight all the harder if they were put ashore without cramped legs and sore backsides.

'That's a fine sound, Captain Holbrooke.'

Lieutenant Colonel McKenzie commanded the marine force and he'd embarked in *Argonaut* for the landing. His men hadn't been engaged in the earlier attempt and Holbrooke could see that he was putting a brave face on today's affair, because, as they both knew, the main landing would be made to the south of Locmaria, at a little place called Port D'Arzic. This landing at Saint-Foy was merely a feint to draw the French defenders' attention away from the south. There was another at Sauzon with the same objective. Nevertheless, to be effective, a feint must look as though it was a determined attempt, and McKenzie's five hundred marines would land with the rest of Brigadier Lambert's diversion force.

'It is, Colonel, it is. Those batteries are firing back though.'

Argonaut lay a mile out to sea, waiting for the moment when the French guns had been silenced and *Swiftsure* made the signal for the attack. There was a small battery to the west of Saint-Foy that was firing at the four great ships of the line that passed backwards and forwards before it, but it was only a matter of time before the huge preponderance of guns had its effect. Holbrooke's practiced eyes and ears had already noticed that the interval between the enemy's salvos had increased. Some of those thirty-two pounders from *Swiftsure* and *Hampton Court* must have found their mark. There would casualties among the French artillerymen as no doubt there were on the ships' gundecks.

Men were dying, and yet it was impossible to ignore the beauty of the day. The westerly wind had brought a clearing in the thick weather and merry white clouds jostled for position in the pure blue of the sky. The ships looked their best, each with a vast ensign at its stern and a long commissioning pennant at its main masthead. Even the dull transports had a splash of colour from the soldiers on their decks and in the flatboats alongside. The puffs of smoke from the guns only added to the gaiety of the scene. Before them lay the cliffs and rocky shores that bound this part of the island's coast, and above the cliffs a fringe of green and yellow where the fresh gorse grew in profusion. Beyond the hills that ranged above the cliffs and the gorse, the smoke of the bombardment at Port D'Arzic soared into the sky to be swept away on the lazy breeze.

McKenzie breathed deeply of the fine spring air. He'd borrowed a telescope and was keenly studying the features of the landing area.

'This part of the coast seems strangely undefended. One battery – just one – and I can't see any formed troops at all. They've stuffed every break in the rocks with abatis but they're not covered by entrenchments. No obstacle is of any value unless it's covered by fire… but excuse me sir, you know something about landing under fire, aye, and withdrawing a hard-pressed army.'

McKenzie took another look through his telescope to cover his embarrassment at lecturing Holbrooke about opposed landings. He had heard all about his exploits at Saint-Cast.

'I knew Treganoc, of course. He was a fine officer. Treganoc of Emden, that's how we remember him in the marines. Tell me, Captain Holbrooke, did he really march into Emden's front gate, alone, before the French had left by the rear, and while an Austrian detachment still held the walls?'

Holbrooke smiled at the memory.

'He did. He did that and much more. And he died trying to bring me off the beach at Saint-Cast, you know, it was the noblest action that I ever saw.'

McKenzie looked keenly at Holbrooke.

'Well, I hope that you'll honour me with the telling of the story when we have more leisure, Captain Holbrooke. I knew that he fell at Saint-Cast, but I've never heard the circumstances.'

Holbrooke suppressed a shiver. Whenever he remembered those horrific moments as the French bayonets sought his unprotected body, he felt a chill come over him. Without any conscious thought he felt in his pocket for the pistol ball that had been taken from his ribs by a French surgeon, a bitter reminder of his own life's fragility that he kept always about his person.

'Well, by the sound of that firing it won't be long now. I thank you for your hospitality and I'll get my men into the boats. I hope you won't see us again too soon, but as this is only a feint we may be back before dark.'

'In which case, Colonel McKenzie, if you should return so soon, would you bring me a sprig of that yellow gorse from the top of the cliff, as a remembrance of the day?'

***

'Preparatory flag from *Swiftsure*, sir.'

Holbrooke acknowledged the midshipman's report and looked over the side to where the marines were filing into the flatboats. There were four alongside the frigate, and their design had been improved since he had last had dealings with them. Improved, yes, and they carried a few more soldiers, but they still looked like nothing so much as the keels that carry coal out to the ships in the north-eastern ports. However today they had a more deadly purpose than shifting coal from ship to shore. Each of the boats could carry at least sixty marines, half a company, and the four boats that were allocated to *Argonaut* for the initial assault carried two hundred and fifty marines in total. McKenzie had five hundred under his command, but the other two companies were in the transports and would land in the second wave.

'Let me know when they're all in, Mister Carew.'

Holbrooke looked again at the shore. The little battery had been brutally silenced. It was impossible to tell whether the guns had all been destroyed, or the crews all killed or wounded, or whether they had been simply abandoned, but whatever the cause, they hadn't fired a shot for a quarter of an hour. The earth around the battery had been turned over by the thirty-two pounders, as though a giant plough had been at work, and the embrasures had an odd, lopsided appearance, like a row of scurvied teeth. There was still no sign of French troops on the cliffs or on the beaches.

'Boats are ready, sir.'

'Very well, Mister Carew. Now watch carefully for *Swiftsure's* next signal.'

Albach had come on deck now that the marines had left, and Chalmers was close behind. The two seemed inseparable, and Holbrooke had to remind himself that it was Chalmers' duty to stay close to the Austrian, ever since he had taken on the role of his handler. Sawtree had explained it in a quiet moment when they were alone. Apparently it was all too common for an agent, after release from years of tension, to blurt out secrets to anyone who would listen. It was policy to ensure that some trustworthy, intelligent person befriended him to give him an outlet for that confessional urge. Did Albach know that? Was he aware that he was being managed? It was quite likely; he was an intelligent man and he must have considered how his integration into a new, more open society would be handled. In any case, they both seemed happy with the arrangement. In fact, now that Holbrooke thought of it, the conversation with McKenzie was a good example of how things could have gone wrong. If Albach had been there it would have been very natural for him to mention that he knew Treganoc, that he'd been at Emden and that he'd saved Holbrooke at Saint-Cast after Treganoc fell. That would have been more than enough information for McKenzie to form a picture of this unknown gentlemen, and he'd have been certain to mention it to other marines, it being pertinent to their shared history. He was pleased that Chalmers had kept Albach below, although he'd thought it unnecessary at the time.

'That must be a strange experience, knowing that your landing is nothing but a ruse, and that you'll be back on board in a couple of hours, possibly leaving half your men behind.'

'Yes, I wondered at that. But, you know, Brigadier Lambert has orders to press home any advantage that he sees. If it looks as though he can relieve some of the pressure on Port D'Arzic, then I'm confident he'll do whatever he can. Whether it's an attack into the French flanks or merely a defensive action to soak up some of the enemy's force, my guess is that he'll try it. I wouldn't be too certain about seeing those marines again today.'

Albach didn't immediately reply as he was studying the

Treacherous Moon

shore himself.

'*Swiftsure's* signalling for the first wave, sir.'

Holbrooke waited. The marines were in the first wave, meaning they wouldn't have to wait to board the flatboats until they had gone inshore with their first loads and returned. However, they must let the grenadiers land first and then follow immediately behind them. He looked over the side at the eager faces and saw McKenzie looking up at him.

'The signal's been made; I'm watching for the grenadiers now.'

McKenzie raised his hat in salute.

'You know, that's not such a bad place to land,' he shouted back. 'If there are no defenders atop those cliffs, they can certainly be scaled, and then the land is quite reasonable for campaigning. Didn't General Wolfe do something similar at Quebec?'

Holbrooke was saved from the need to answer by the sight of the first six boats pushing off from the transports. He could see the tall mitres of the grenadiers, the company colours at the stern of the boats, and the flash of the bayonets that tipped the muskets, each held vertically between a soldier's knees. He leaned over the gunwale again.

'You may proceed, Colonel. *Argonaut* sends its best wishes.'

There was nothing else to say. He was aware of Shorrock giving orders behind him but he was too concerned with watching the flatboats pull away.

It was only the wave of sound behind him that told him what Shorrock had been doing. Every one of *Argonaut's* people were out on the yards, clinging to ratlines or lining the gunwales. They gave the marines a mighty cheer as they steered away into battle. These, after all, were their own shipmates.

***

'Bring her before the wind, Mister Fairview, and we'll have two leadsmen, I believe. Mister Shorrock, run out the larboard guns at full elevation, if you please.'

This was the second part of Holbrooke's orders. The third and fourth rates couldn't get close enough to the shore to cover the landing, they had to stand off so far that their shots would be as much danger to the attackers as to the defenders. *Argonaut* with her shallow draught could get much closer inshore and her nine pounders, fired from a range that would allow them to be sure of clearing their own men, could decimate entrenched infantry. There were none, as far as Holbrooke could see, but his guns would punch holes in those abatis and make it very much easier for the grenadiers and marines to advance off the shoreline.

He could leave Fairview to con the ship and pay attention to the soundings, and Shorrock to determine where the blows should be struck. He was free to watch the progress of the assault.

It was a well-managed affair, so far. Stanhope in *Swiftsure* had brought the transports as close as possible before launching the attack, and in only a few minutes the grenadiers' boats were running into whatever gaps between the rocks that they could find. There were little patches of sand here and there, some of them no wider than a boat, but they were sufficient.

'No fire from any defenders. In fact, I can see no sign of life at all now that the batteries have been destroyed. Now, if only they can scale those cliffs.'

Albach was watching eagerly and couldn't help himself from commenting upon every move. The grenadiers were all ashore, and without any delay the empty flatboats pulled back out into deep water leaving room for the boats carrying the marines. They almost clashed oars, such was McKenzie's eagerness to reach the shore, and in only a few minutes from leaving *Argonaut* they were spilling out onto the little pockets of sand.

'Ah, they've found a way up. There they go.'

Two thin threads of red were extending at a tremendous pace up the face of what appeared to be a sheer cliff.

Treacherous Moon

Holbrooke looked down at the marines waiting patiently to follow the grenadiers, and by the time he looked up again the first of the grenadiers were nearly at the top. He watched as the red dots reached the line of green and yellow then disappeared into the gorse.

Without the telescope it appeared like some sort of illusion. Half a dozen blocks of red were arranged at the bottom of the cliffs, in two divisions. From each division a single thread of red soared upwards to terminate at the green and yellow border between the cliff and the sky. The blocks were being replenished from fresh boatloads of men, but as fast as companies of marines and soldiers landed, the blocks were depleted as the soldiers took their turn at the path up the cliff.

'It really is too bad, you know. Just a half company could hold that cliff, but there's not a sign of opposition. It will be too late soon. When we have a full company at the top, nothing will stop us.'

It was interesting to hear Albach refer to the British army in that possessive way; it was a short journey indeed from reluctant ally of the French to enthusiastic supporter of British arms.

'Can you hear it now? Musket fire, coming from the cliff.'

Holbrooke cupped his ear to the shore. Yes, single shots rather than volleys. The French must have seen the grenadiers and marines, but random musketry wouldn't stop them. There was no break in the red thread and through the telescope it was clear that the attackers were spilling onto the top of the cliff in an unbroken stream. The gorse was trampled where the threads reached the top and now he could see that they were all moving forward. Then the French weren't forcing them back to the cliff edge, not yet.

'Captain, sir. *Swiftsure's* made the signal for all boats.'

What the devil could Stanhope mean? Holbrooke looked over at *Swiftsure* and saw its longboat pull away from the ship's side, then he saw a yawl, two yawls and a cutter, all heading for the shore and all full of sailors. Here and there he could see a musket barrel above the rows of oarsmen.

'Mister Shorrock. Man all the boats. Take as many men as you can, and issue all the muskets. Pistols and cutlasses when the muskets have run out, and a master's mate or midshipman to each boat.'

Holbrooke tried to think clearly in the whirl of the action. Should he send Shorrock to command *Argonaut's* boats?

'Captain, sir. One of *Swiftsure's* yawls is coming alongside. I believe there's a senior soldier on board.'

The midshipman looked wide-eyed at Holbrooke; he'd never seen anything like this before. Holbrooke looked over the side to see Brigadier Hamilton Lambert standing in the yawl's stern sheets. He cupped his hands around his mouth and shouted upwards.

'Captain Holbrooke. We may have the opportunity to turn this feint into a useful flank attack. Captain Stanhope finds that I may need a naval adviser and he hopes that you will join me immediately.'

Holbrooke froze in surprise. Desperate times need desperate measures and there was no good reason why he shouldn't comply with the order. The brigadier was looking expectant, demanding an immediate answer.

'Two minutes, sir.'

Holbrooke turned away. What did he need? Nothing really, only his sword which he was carrying and his pistols which were hanging beside the binnacle as they always were at quarters. His telescope! He remembered how frustrating it was on the occasions that he found himself engaged ashore without it. And he should have someone with him, in case of need. He couldn't take Murray, he was already with McKenzie's force of marines, and Chalmers must stay with Albach; their recent conversations proved how much the Austrian needed someone to talk to. A midshipman then.

'Mister Carew, take a cutlass and brace of pistols and join

Treacherous Moon

me. Mister Shorrock, you'll command until I return. Stay off Saint-Foy unless Captain Stanhope directs otherwise. I hope I won't be gone too long.'

Two minutes may not yet have passed but the brigadier was looking distinctly impatient as Holbrooke, without the normal ceremony of piping the side, dropped down into the yawl with Carew close behind.

'I'm told that you're familiar with the ways of us soldiers, Captain Holbrooke. I trust that you'll stay close to me. If you need to send a message back to *Swiftsure* then one of my aides will carry it. Ah, I see you have brought your own.'

Holbrooke carefully shifted his position so that he could see ahead. With the brigadier, three subalterns, himself and Carew, the boat was starting to look a little crowded. Still, it was a short row to the beach.

'You'll have seen that they've won the top of the cliff and they haven't been thrown back yet. Those grenadiers are from the Nineteenth of Foot, they won't be shifted now, not unless a whole battalion comes down on them, and as you can see McKenzie's marines are waiting to join them. I have high hopes, Captain Holbrooke, high hopes indeed. I've ordered the whole of my force to land and those sailors of yours will hold the landing site and follow up the cliff if needed. By God, I like your Captain Stanhope. One word and it was all done.'

Holbrooke looked around at the wide, calm sea. Every flatboat was on the water either returning from the shore or on the way out with a fresh load of soldiers, and the ships' boats were busily threading their way between them. So far only the grenadiers and marines had landed, but he could see that the musketeers of the line regiments were now racing towards the landing. Such a flood tide of fighting men; could anything stop them?

***

Chris Durbin

CHAPTER TWENTY-SIX

A Sprig of Gorse

Wednesday, Twenty-Second of April 1761.
Saint-Foy, Belle Isle.

They found a vacant gap between two rocks. It was too small for the flatboats, but the yawl just managed to squeeze in with the oars tossed. The brigadier leaped ashore without waiting to be helped by the crew and he was closely followed by his aides, each receiving a soaking up to the knee. Holbrooke waited for the yawl to steady before he stepped carefully ashore. He had never forgotten the advice he had been given about the importance of stepping ashore dry-shod. Wet boots and stockings were an inconvenience when one could readily dry them, but on a campaign it may not be possible for days on end. Lambert's urgency to take charge of the situation must have overcome his better judgement, but he was paying for it now, with boots full of water and sand. His feet would be rubbed raw before he'd gone half a mile.

The brigadier charged forward, making for the nearest path up the cliff, but Holbrooke paused for a moment. The scrap of beach below the cliff was jammed with soldiers, but there was a pattern. He could see the mitre headgear and the greenish-yellow coat facings that identified those at the base of the cliff as grenadiers of the Nineteenth of Foot. They were all waiting in disciplined ranks, taking their turn to make the climb in twos, for that was all that the path could accommodate. The marine companies were easy to see with their white facings and glazed black hats, and they were formed up as though on parade, waiting for the last of the grenadiers to make their climb. Behind him, the first musketeer companies were landing. A lieutenant from *Swiftsure,* whom Holbrooke vaguely recognised, was commanding the landing area. He was busy waving boats in and holding back the natural desire to rush onto the crowded beach, but he took the time to raise his hat to Holbrooke.

The hundreds of marines and soldiers were lined up in almost total silence, only the sergeants' voices cried out occasionally, and then mostly to silence the more exuberant men. There were a few musket shots from the cliff above, but nothing that suggested a general engagement, and with no enemy in sight the ships' guns had fallen silent. The scene was strangely familiar and it took a moment for Holbrooke to realise why. He'd once seen a military parade forming up at Horse Guards behind the Admiralty, and it had a similar sort of suppressed energy. There had been a large number of soldiers on that occasion, and they had been jammed into the small space, each company and regiment waiting for its turn to take its allotted place in the parade. Save the absence of a military band and accepting the different backdrop, it was a very similar spectacle. Another quick look told Holbrooke that he wasn't needed here.

'Follow me, Mister Carew.'

Holbrooke walked determinedly towards the path that Lambert had been heading for. The marines and soldiers naturally made a way when they saw him, perhaps wondering what a post-captain was doing in such a place. He recognised McKenzie's tall, martial figure and the marine colonel saw him at the same moment.

'Captain Holbrooke. I didn't expect to see you so soon, but I did remember my debt. I found a bush growing at the base of the cliff.'

He drew a sprig of gorse from his pocket and carefully threaded the stem through a buttonhole on Holbrooke's coat and patted it into place. It was a gentle gesture, almost tenderly performed, but Holbrooke felt no embarrassment as the marine stepped back to admire his arrangement.

McKenzie hesitated as an idea formed.

'May I follow you? If you're with the brigadier you'll be allowed up the path right away and I have a burning desire to be there before my marines.'

They reached the path just as Lambert started his ascent, followed by his aides. Access to the path was being controlled by a captain of the Nineteenth and an enormous sergeant-major, who mercilessly used his halberd's butt to maintain the integrity of the companies and platoons. The captain looked askance at Holbrooke, McKenzie and Carew, but a word from the brigadier, now some twenty feet above them, cleared the way. Probably he hadn't noticed McKenzie, or he didn't have time to make the distinction.

It was an easy climb for fit men, but even so Holbrooke could see why the French may have dismissed this as a possible route for attackers. Only infantry could make the climb; there was no chance of bringing up field guns until hoists could be rigged at the top of the cliff. Although the sergeant-major was allowing them up in pairs, the path was really only suitable for one in most places, but with two they could help each other up. At the very top the solid rock and loose stones gave way to a thin covering of soil, which the defenders had cut away at its base so that the final few yards were a genuine climb. Holbrooke heaved himself over the edge and fell flat on his face in the trampled gorse. He could see that the first grenadiers to make the climb had been faced with a significant obstacle, but their heavy boots and heavier bodies had worn away at the soil and trampled the bushes so that Holbrooke found it no more than an undignified scramble.

'Shocking, truly shocking.'

McKenzie's voice came in gasps as he pulled himself up behind Holbrooke.

'So much effort to fortify the island and they leave this path undefended. It must have been like this at Quebec. You can see that the gorse is reinforced by all these uprooted trees, but without a company of infantry to cover it, their time was wasted.'

Holbrooke had no time to listen to McKenzie. He still didn't really understand what part he could usefully play, but

Treacherous Moon

it certainly wasn't to be found loitering on the cliff edge. Behind him the last of the grenadiers were making the climb and far below he saw the marines' black hats bobbing up and down as they started up the path.

***

Holbrooke found himself on a plateau of undulating ground that extended as far as he could see. It was riven by small streams that had cut their way deep through the soil and into the rock, and between the ravines, the land was cultivated and divided into fields by drystone walls and wind-battered hedges that leaned to the east, as though making their obeisance. Small hamlets and isolated cottages were scattered across the ground. To the south he could see a pall of smoke where the main landing was still being contested and he could see the great second and third rates battering away at the French defences. The nearest stone wall was two hundred yards in front and that was where the grenadiers were gathering their force. As they ran forward from the cliff edge they were sent to join a line of men behind the wall, while over to the left and right he could see that smaller groups were guarding the flanks. He was puzzled for a moment by the musketry a hundred yards or so beyond the wall, until he saw a file of red coats break from their cover in a patch of gorse and move to the right. Skirmishers. The major who commanded that company of grenadiers knew his business; he was providing for a temporary defence to slow down any counterattack until a sufficient force had made the climb up the cliff.

He could hear McKenzie behind him, giving orders as the first marines hurried forward to join the grenadiers.

'Ah! Here they come!'

Lambert pointed to the front where four hundred yards away a column of white-coated soldiers appeared from one of the shallow ravines.

'There must be a road down there or a path at least. See, they were sent from Locmaria as soon as the commander there saw a landing on his left flank. What would you say,

Holbrooke, a half battalion?'

Holbrooke's telescope may have been an unwieldy thing to carry with an advancing army, but it was far superior to anything the brigadier had, and he could see Lambert hopping in impatience as he waited his turn while he scanned the advancing enemy.

'A strong half battalion, sir, perhaps three companies and they're all regular line infantry.'

He passed the telescope to the brigadier who said nothing while he studied the French advance. Time seemed to stand still, except for the steady stream of marines taking their places behind the wall. The grenadiers moved to the right and formed two lines while the marines took the left.

'Yes. Three companies and the battalion colours. You have a good eye, Holbrooke. Well, they'll see the situation and they'll attack quickly. They can't afford to wait until the entire brigade is before them, and they won't know that this isn't the army's main point of effort. Look, they're deploying into line, and here come our skirmishers.'

Holbrooke wanted his telescope, but the brigadier had balanced it on his aide's shoulder and it was evident that he wouldn't easily let it go. He was no longer watching the advancing French but was studying the ground two miles to the south where the main landing should be taking place. It was difficult to be certain, but it appeared that Crauford's force had not yet landed. Certainly they hadn't yet disturbed the long lines of Frenchmen that faced the landing site, and the continued naval bombardment suggested that the guns at Port D'Arzic were still in action.

'If we can stand against those fellows, I do believe we might lay claim to being the main attack.'

Lambert was still staring through the telescope and Holbrooke couldn't see his expression.

'That being the case, how would you signal to those ships that we have made a successful landing, Captain Holbrooke? Do you have some flags or suchlike?'

Holbrooke almost laughed; the idea was preposterous.

Had he been consulted during the planning he could have devised a signal, a shell from a mortar in a longboat, perhaps, but he had no such thing. But there was a way.

'Mister Carew can carry a message to Captain Stanhope who can signal the commodore.'

Holbrooke looked behind at the marines still pouring upwards. He could imagine how difficult it would be for Carew to make his way down against that surge of people rushing to the sound of the guns. He could shout all he liked about dispatches, but he would at best be ignored and at worst suspected of cowardice, of running away. And when he reached the foot of the cliffs he would have to find a boat. Once the French attack had been defeated, the delay would be intolerable. Carew would have to be pre-positioned.

'Mister Carew. Now, listen carefully. You're to make your way down the cliff immediately, don't let anyone stop you, you're carrying a message from the brigadier and from me. Speak to the lieutenant – I've forgotten his name but you know him – and commandeer a boat, the yawl if it's still there or any other ship's boat. Not a flatboat, they're too slow. Now, when you see me at the top of the cliff, waving my hat, you're to make best speed to *Swiftsure*. Tell Captain Stanhope, with the compliments of Brigadier Lambert and myself, that the landing has been a success and that this place is suitable for bringing the whole army ashore, that in our opinion the force at Port Locmaria, if it hasn't yet established itself ashore, should move north to this place. If you see Brigadier Lambert or any one of his aides waving his hat at you, then you are to assume the message has come from me. Now, repeat that, if you please.'

Carew was a bright lad. Holbrooke knew that, otherwise he wouldn't have trusted him with this message. He repeated the instructions, remembering the key points, and hurried away to the edge of the cliff. Holbrooke saw him push a marine aside and then he was gone.

***

The last of the skirmishers tumbled over the wall to take their places in the rear rank of the grenadiers. Over to the left and the right the flank guards fell back to fill the space between the ends of the wall and the cliff. The grenadiers and marines were all standing to receive the enemy, two ranks of levelled muskets with their wicked bayonets pointing at the advancing white line.

Holbrooke remembered another French attack, far away across the Atlantic and deep in the dense North American forests, at a place called La Belle Famille, a mile or so from the French-held Fort Niagara. The French had been in a hurry there also; they knew that the British force in front of them would be reinforced in minutes, and then there would be no chance at all. They hadn't had the leisure to form a proper line as they burst through the trees into the clearing, and it was a ragged attack by tired soldiers under poor leadership against a determined defence. This was not so different, except that here there were no Mohawk warriors to take the scalps of the dead and wounded.

A bugle sounded and a drum beat the *pas de charge*.

'Front rank take aim!'

The major of grenadiers was giving the order for the whole line, grenadiers and marines. The second rank was thinner than the front but every couple of seconds another pair of marines arrived to fill the gaps. All along the line he could see the sergeants using their halberds and pikes to correct the aim. After the first volley that would become impossible, but while they had the time it was wise to ensure that the muskets were at least all pointing towards the enemy.

The French line advanced at a walk over the rough field. It looked as though it had been recently planted. Turnips, perhaps, but under the weight of those boots there was little hope of a crop this year. A hundred yards. Now the drumbeat increased in speed, the march turned into a charge as the whole French line surged towards the wall.

'Front rank, give fire!'

Treacherous Moon

Crash! Two hundred muskets fired as one. For a moment Holbrooke could see nothing through the smoke, then the lazy west wind blew it back towards the cliff. The French were still coming on, and they were almost upon the wall. He could see the individual faces of the Frenchmen behind their bayonets, he could see their expressions of rage and determination as they charged forward.

'Rear rank, give fire!'

Crash! The second volley came only seconds after the first, but now the enemy was much closer and the grenadiers and marines were aiming at individuals rather than at an anonymous line. When the smoke dissipated Holbrooke could see the carnage that had been wrought. Perhaps half of the attacking force had fallen before the disciplined musketry and they lay still or writhed in agony on the brown field.

Yet still the survivors came on, forcing their way against the wall at the point of the bayonet. Holbrooke could see that the marines were bearing the brunt of this close quarters fighting. They'd had less time to organise themselves at the wall and their volleys had been consequently less deadly, allowing more of the French to reach them. He drew his two pistols and rushed to the left where he saw McKenzie rallying his men.

Most of the fury of the attack was blunted by the stone wall and the marines' muskets, but here and there a determined band of Frenchmen had won their way over the wall. Holbrooke ran forward to the nearest group in time to fire both pistols at a white-coated figure. He threw them aside and drew his sword, ready to add his weight to the defence. There were no Frenchmen close at hand, just a wounded man lying prostrate on the ground, and another who had thrown aside his musket. Holbrooke looked to the left and the right, but he could see only red coats. It seemed unbelievable, but in that short space of time, barely two minutes, the French attack had been beaten back. He could see little groups of white-coated men retreating over the turnip field. A few grenadiers and marines had climbed over the wall and had started a pursuit but they were called back by the major and the sergeants.

There was one comic scene where a grenadier, caught up in the excitement of the chase, had not heard the recall orders, or had chosen to ignore them. He ran forward alone, his unloaded musket and bayonet held before him in the charge. He was a hundred yards beyond the wall when he realised his peril. A small group of Frenchmen turned at bay, and it was lucky for the grenadier that they had all fired their own muskets and had not reloaded. For a breathless moment he paused, stared wildly to his left and right, then turned on his heel and fled for the wall to be met by his jeering friends.

Then it was over. The half battalion of Frenchmen were regrouping but it was clear that there would be no further attack. They were taking positions four hundred yards away.

'The Nineteenth and Marines will advance!'

A British drum started beating and the grenadiers and marines scrambled over the wall to form up in two large companies on the other side.

With a steady step the two lines marched forward. Every man now had a freshly-loaded musket and they left only a handful of their friends lying on the ground behind the wall. The Frenchmen stood firm. Now it was the British turn to charge. A bugle again, and a rapid tattoo on the drum and the lines surged forward. The French held their position, but uncertainly, and when the British lines reached a hundred paces they broke and ran.

Holbrooke jogged along behind the advancing British line, slanting across the ground to reach the brigadier, a question on his lips.

'Not yet, Captain, not yet. Let's see what's in that ravine in front of us.'

***

How much time had passed since he left the ship? It can't have been much more than half an hour but it seemed

Treacherous Moon

like he'd spent a whole day on the plateau.

The British line stopped at the top of the ravine. It was an impressive display of discipline and Holbrooke remembered how difficult it was to stop men who had started running, whether it was in pursuit or in retreat. The Frenchmen had withdrawn straight down the slope, and now they were climbing the far side, and slowing as they reached the top. Some were even turning to face their pursuers, making motions to construct a defence. The ravine continued far to the right and to the left, becoming shallower to the right where it cut inland, but still, it needed to be climbed, although it was no real obstacle to the grenadiers and marines.

Then Holbrooke saw a movement on the other side. The gorse was high at the lip of the ravine and it looked as though it was moving bodily to one side. Men were pushing it aside from behind and in an instant the reason become clear as the muzzle of a field piece thrust forward, then another and a third.

The general realised instantly what was happening.

'At 'em men!' he shouted. 'Grenadiers and marines, take those guns for me!'

The major of the Nineteenth of Foot and Colonel McKenzie pushed to the front. They exchanged glances and then with one accord they led their men in a wild charge.

Crack! Crack! Crack!

Holbrooke heard a whirring sound over his head. Grapeshot or cannister would have been deadly at that moment but they were firing solid shot. He saw a grenadier fall, cut through by a six-pound ball and the line of marines faltered as another ball sent up a plume of earth in front of them, but they charged onwards. Holbrooke saw the blue-coated French artillerymen fleeing before the onslaught, and the infantry close behind.

The brigadier stopped and looked with satisfaction at the rout that his men had caused.

'What do you see at Locmaria now, Captain?'

Holbrooke had been carrying the telescope on a sling over his shoulder. He had a good view across the fields to the south. A solid block of French infantry, presumably the reserve battalion, was still drawn up, waiting to see where Crauford's force would land, and the ships were still firing steadily at the shore defences.

'It looks like they haven't landed yet, sir.'

The brigadier looked behind to where the musketeer companies were now marching forward. Soon he'd have enough men to hold against that reserve battalion.

'Very well, then would you be so good as to send that message?'

Holbrooke turned and walked quickly – it wouldn't do for the soldiers to see a naval captain running away from a battle – back to the cliff edge. It was only four or five hundred yards but it took him ten minutes over that broken ground. He looked over the edge to see Carew gazing anxiously upwards. It was strangely quiet here, away from the sound of the guns, and he waved his hat and shouted for Carew to go, with all haste. He watched as the yawl pushed away and pulled lustily towards *Swiftsure*.

Stanhope's ship was close in, taking advantage of the light westerly wind, but it was evident that he was in sight of *Sandwich*, the great ninety-gun ship that was commanding at the Port D'Arzic landing site, and they were only some three miles apart. It didn't take fifteen minutes from Holbrooke's wave of his hat to the signal soaring up *Swiftsure's* mainmast. It was a pre-arranged signal to say that the landing force had established themselves ashore.

That was all that Crauford needed to know. After two hours of bombardment the French defences appeared unmoved, and he had started to wonder whether landing at Port D'Arzic was such a good idea. Holbrooke saw the flatboats leave the sides of the transports and he saw their bows swing firmly to the north. An hour's pulling brought them to the landing site and soon the companies and battalions were finding new routes up the cliff. By five

Treacherous Moon

o'clock the entire landing force from what was supposed to be the main attack had joined Lambert's brigade on the plateau.

Holbrooke had little more to do now and he watched as the whole body of men started moving towards the French positions at Locmaria. He could imagine what was happening over there. A pause to confirm the strength of the enemy, then a rapid withdrawal to the west, towards the citadel at Le Palais, before they were cut off by the advancing British army.

By sunset Crauford was in command of the whole western end of the island and the artillery officers were looking for the best places to land the guns, while the dragoons were chaffing to get their horses ashore. As the sun went down into the wide Atlantic, an enormous fire was seen in the direction of Le Palais, a signal certainly, and its meaning was clear even to those who weren't expecting it: the French were pulling all their forces back to defend the citadel. There would be no decisive action in the field, and Holbrooke knew from his conversations with Albach that the citadel couldn't be taken by a *coup de main*, so it would be a siege. Holbrooke was tired, more weary than he should be, and looking forward to dinner and a good night's sleep on his own ship. Just one of the advantages that the sea service had over their brothers on the land, he thought.

***

CHAPTER TWENTY-SEVEN

Reaction

Friday, Twenty-Fourth of April 1761.
Valiant, at Anchor, Palais Road, Belle Isle.

The pipes wailed and the white-gloved sideboys stood ready to help as Holbrooke stepped over the flagship's gunwale. He paused for a moment to catch his balance and held his hat to his chest to disguise the momentary hesitation. Then, recovered, he followed the flag captain down to the commodore's cabin. He'd felt that unsteadiness once or twice since he'd returned from the landings at Saint-Foy, and he'd noticed a difficulty in concentrating. His mind felt like a ship struggling to navigate through thick weather, groping from one clue to another. He was unable to recognise a pattern or hold to a single line of thought. Still, it would pass.

'Ah, Captain Holbrooke, thank you for coming so swiftly. I regret that our meeting will be brief, I have to go ashore to meet the general. He's naturally keen to plan the siege of the citadel and he wants to know how I can help with his supply problems. That was a fine piece of work at Saint-Foy, by the way, and I've commended your actions in my report to their Lordships. The general was just starting to consider abandoning the whole thing and withdrawing both Crauford and Lambert's forces. That could have been the end of the expedition, you know. It was a stroke of genius to send that midshipman with such a clear message. It's not quite a matter of marching now, but unless we're driven off by the weather, the Duc d'Aiguillon will never get his army across to the island. Of course, there's the matter of a siege to be completed, but General Hodgson has that well in hand. Sainte-Croix will hold on until honour is satisfied but he knows that short of a miracle we'll have this island by the summer. Oh, you look a little pale, please take a seat. A glass of water for Captain Holbrooke.'

Holbrooke sat gratefully. It was nothing, he assured the commodore, just a little weariness, a lack of sleep, he'd be perfectly fine in a moment.

Keppel still looked concerned.

'You need to be let blood, Holbrooke. I recommend you call for your surgeon the instant you're back in your ship.'

Holbrooke straightened his back and nodded agreement. He hated having his blood drawn and was secretly sceptical about its benefit, but he knew better than to argue with the commodore.

'Well, be that as it may. Much as I dislike being lectured by civil officers of the Admiralty, I have to concede that Sawtree made a good point about that seventy-four and the other one, the forty, in the Vilaine. With Spain threatening to join the war, we must concern ourselves with the strength of the French navy, which hasn't been something that has worried us for the past year. A combination of the Spanish fleet and the Brest and Rochefort squadrons could still change the course of the war.'

Keppel stopped dead and stared out of the windows at his vast squadron and fleet of transports. When he turned back to Holbrooke he looked embarrassed. He cleared his throat before he spoke.

'Now, what I didn't tell Sawtree is that I've had to withdraw Gambier's ships and send them to join Buckle's squadron off Brest. As we speak I don't have a single ship to watch the Vilaine.'

Holbrooke nodded guardedly. The weakness had passed and his mind felt clear and strong. He could imagine that Keppel had taken Albach's intelligence at face value and was gambling that the last two fugitive French ships wouldn't move until the end of May at the earliest. Still, it would look bad if they did make good their escape in the teeth of this vast invasion squadron gathered off the Brittany coast.

'You seem to have a talent for independent operations, Holbrooke. I'm going to detach *Argonaut* to watch over the

Vilaine. I can't afford another single ship, not with a hundred thousand or so Frenchmen gathering around Vannes and the Brest squadron apparently ready to sail. You heard that they'll wait for a spring tide, but I wouldn't put too much faith in that. One of them has a deeper draught than all the others that escaped and I'm not certain that it'll get over the bar even at the height of the springs, so I wouldn't be surprised if they've been dredging the channel and the bar, now that they're not being observed. If that's the case then they could come out at any time. Still, I'm sure you can draw your own conclusions. You have a free hand to station yourself as you see fit and your task is to bring word to me as soon as you see any signs of them stirring. They're supposed to have only half their guns, but even if that's true, you are not to risk an engagement unless the circumstances suggest that you can hold them up until my third rates can deal with them.'

***

It was a long row into the wind and Holbrooke sat comfortably in the stern sheets of the yawl with Dawson beside him, steering for *Argonaut*. Time to think before he was back in his cabin and deep into the endless round of reports and returns, questions and decisions, that bedevilled the captain of a King's ship. Never before had the weight of command seemed so heavy, never before had he so dreaded the knock on his cabin door heralding the next urgent decision that he must make.

He was being detached with the vaguest of orders. It was a compliment, he was sure, and proved that Keppel had a good opinion of him. He'd been recommended to the admiralty for his actions at the landing, too, and that always helped. In truth, there was little that he wanted from their Lordships at present. He had a frigate and while the war lasted he was unlikely to be left ashore. He didn't want to be moved to a ship-of-the-line, not yet. Privately he thought that he wasn't ready for it, that he had to grow into his rank of post-captain before he could step up to the additional responsibilities. In any case, he was far better positioned in a frigate to make valuable captures, and he was perfectly content with his officers and his petty officers, most of whom he'd have to leave behind if he left *Argonaut*.

All that was very satisfactory, but it was this next mission that worried him. He felt in his pocket where he had stowed his orders. He'd read them briefly while waiting for his boat to come alongside, and they held no surprises. Yet it was a difficult task with a high chance of failure. He could calculate the spring tides easily enough, but he knew very well that the French were nothing if not inventive, and this de Ternay sounded like a man eager for recognition, ready to try anything. If it was true that he'd been commissioned into *Robuste*, then he had an added incentive to get her across the bar and away to Brest or Rochefort for a refit. They'd met at sea, of course, when he'd failed to prevent the two sixty fours escaping into Brest back in January. He remembered the raised hat from the Frenchman's poop deck as the ship sped past to freedom. He and de Ternay could be said to be old opponents and Holbrooke was perfectly convinced that it wouldn't do to underestimate him.

A blockade, he knew, was a very uncertain thing, and Britain's naval history was littered with examples of squadrons – Dutch, Spanish and French, depending upon the opponent of the day – escaping onto the high seas despite the closest watch. Wind, tide, darkness, damage and sheer bad luck all played their parts in the long, long list of blockade failures. Well, it was up to him to make a success of this. He knew Quiberon Bay well by now, and he was familiar with the Vilaine estuary. It would take ceaseless vigilance and if de Ternay should cross the bar it would take a good dose of luck to find the commodore before the French were away to Brest or Rochefort. Nevertheless, if it was humanly possible then it must be done.

Why was the damned cabin swaying so? His ship was anchored in the lee of the island and he could perfectly well have installed a pendulum clock of his own, so sheltered was the Palais Road. He sat down to let the fit pass.

'You're not well, George.'

Chalmers' concerned face came closer to Holbrooke's as he examined the colour of his eyes.

'I'm no surgeon, of course, but Mister Collins is, and you need his attention.'

Without waiting for any comment, Chalmers stuck his head out of the cabin door and quietly asked Fairview to pass the word for the surgeon. By the time he was back at Holbrooke's side, his friend had recovered and looked as though nothing was wrong.

'It's just a passing weakness, David. It's been happening since I came back from the landing at St-Foy. I'm fine if I can sit for a moment.'

Chalmers gave him a quizzical look.

'You've been working very hard recently, George, it wouldn't be surprising if it's all catching up with you. Let's hear what Mister Collins has to say.'

'Well, he'd better say it quickly because I want to see my senior officers before dinner, to tell them what the future holds for us.'

Holbrooke could see that Chalmers was about to say something else, but a knock at the door heralded the surgeon. He examined Holbrooke's tongue, peered into his eyes and asked questions about his bowel movements. Holbrooke could sense it coming, the usual response from a surgeon when there were no visibly missing body parts and no obvious problem with the bowels.

'I'll just take a little of your blood, sir, and then I recommend some rest. No ardent spirits for a few days and you'll be on your feet again in no time. Now if you'll just remove your coat...'

'Mister Collins, I have no objection to giving you a few ounces of my blood,' he lied, 'but I have to speak to my officers first and then we'll be getting underway, so you can come back in the afternoon.'

Treacherous Moon

Collins put away the little knife that he had brought out of a case in his pocket. He looked disappointed, as though he'd been cheated of a treat, and he left quietly.

***

It was a small gathering, just Shorrock, Fairview, Chalmers, Finch and Albach. The Austrian seemed like part of the crew now, another officer but with unspecified duties, and Holbrooke valued his opinion, particularly where the French were concerned. Murray, the marine lieutenant, was still away with the landing force and the other warrant officers weren't concerned with *Argonaut's* mission; they would look after the fabric of the ship, and the weapons and the victuals, in the same way whether they did it at anchor off Le Palais or beating to and fro in Quiberon bay.

Holbrooke outlined his orders and watched his officers' faces. They'd evidently been looking forward to a quiet spell while the siege of the citadel ran its stately course.

'From memory, sir, there's a spring tide a week on Sunday, the third of May. If they're waiting for the end of May then it's the seventeenth and again on the first and fifteenth of June. I'll write them up for you once I've checked my workings.'

Holbrooke grinned at that. Fairview's memory was better than any almanac. He could bet on those dates and in fact it was an easy calculation, the tides followed the moon's phases, and the springs came with the full and new moons. A lunar month was twenty-nine days and a fraction of a day. That fractional day had to be considered every few months, but for present circumstances twenty-nine days was accurate enough.

'Just the two ships left, is that correct?'

Albach must have been thinking of something else for he started at the question.

'Yes, sir. They've been moved to anchor berths just inside the bar.'

'Then we should be prepared even before the end of May. How long until *Oyster* is ready, Mister Finch?'

'Mister Jackson's over there now, sir. He wheedled a spare frigate's topmast from one of the storeships and he's stepping it as we speak. His last report, this morning, was that he'd be running down the shrouds this afternoon and be finished tomorrow. Your sailmaker's over there too, and I should have a smart main, jib and staysail in a day or two. As we agreed, sir, the tops'l can wait for another day.'

'Well, there's no tearing hurry. We'll sail in the afternoon and look into the Vilaine before we decide how to proceed. Mister Finch, join me off Dumet Island as soon as you're seaworthy. Has your new bosun joined?'

'Yes, sir, thank you.'

Holbrooke had a sudden pang of regret. Tranter had been a promising young man who would have graced the ranks of warranted bosuns. The bosun's mate who had been plucked out of *Argonaut* would do a workmanlike job, no doubt, but it would be strange if he matched Tranter. Was he growing old? Did this sentimentality have a place in the makeup of a King's officer? And he was so tired, he just wanted the meeting to end and all these eager officers to be about their business. He didn't know how long he could maintain this pretence of energy and zeal.

'Very well. The wind's fair for the Vilaine, I believe, and if we weigh at four bells we can lie to in the bay overnight and look into the estuary at first light. So unless there are any questions, I thank you for your time, gentlemen.'

***

Holbrooke could hardly stand, and he so wanted to sleep. If he dispensed with dinner he could have two whole hours before he was needed again. Two hours of blissful unconsciousness and be damned to the doctor and his blood-letting. He staggered towards his cot and his servant helped him out of coat and loosened his stock. He was asleep before his head hit the pillow.

Asleep, yes, but like Hamlet's dark fears, he was tormented by dreams: visions of *Oyster's* bosun sinking slowly beneath the cold water of Quiberon Bay, of the ruin of the French line after they had suffered two brutal volleys from the grenadiers and marines. So much blood, so many broken bodies and grieving wives and mothers. He tossed and turned until his frightened servant called for Chalmers, who sat with him until Fairview reported that the anchor was up-and-down and the frigate was ready to sail.

***

CHAPTER TWENTY-EIGHT

Freedom Dash

Monday, First of June 1761.
Argonaut, at Sea, off Dumet Island, Quiberon Bay.

It had been a clear, cool night with a feeble northerly wind and the sky had been brilliant with twinkling stars. *Argonaut* kept her lonely vigil, stemming the flood and the ebb off Dumet Island. Then, as the middle watch drew to a close, great banks of fog had rolled in from the land, extinguishing the stars; now it lay thick over the Vilaine estuary.

'You think they may have come out; I gather.'

Chalmers was walking with Holbrooke on the quarterdeck and the other officers gave them all the space they needed. Over the past five weeks they'd become used to seeing the chaplain with their captain and they knew well enough why he had attached himself so firmly. They could all see that Holbrooke wasn't well. The strain of the past six months showed in every line of his face, in the way he stooped, in his frequent stumbles, and in his new-found introversion. He'd been on this station since January with only two short breaks, through all the weather that the winter could throw at them. He'd shouldered the responsibility for the clandestine operations alone, and he could speak of it to nobody but Chalmers and Albach. He'd known the chilling fear of the hunted man when he'd brought Albach out from a hostile shore and he'd stood with the marines and grenadiers at Saint-Foy. Then, for the last five weeks, while the great ships-of-the-line had spent much of their time at anchor, *Argonaut* had patrolled the Vilaine estuary, ceaselessly watching for the last two trapped French ships to emerge. Chalmers knew all this and when he'd tentatively suggested that Holbrooke apply to the commodore for leave of absence, to recruit his strength, he'd expected a strong reaction. Yet Holbrooke had taken it quietly, as though he could do nothing to shape the course of events, and for a moment looked like a little boy despite the undoubted ageing of his face.

'If they don't come out today then they'll have to wait another two weeks and with summer coming, the chance of thick weather grows less and less. The citadel must fall soon and then we'll have a regular naval presence at the island and it will be that much more difficult for them. Yes, I believe there's a good chance that they'll come, but whether we'll see them is another matter entirely.'

Chalmers glanced cautiously at Holbrooke. Six weeks ago he'd have been pacing the deck impatiently, plotting and scheming ways of defeating the weather, but now he just accepted it. There was a dispirited look in his eyes and a slackness in the jaw that had never been there before. A letter from the commodore had arrived yesterday; Holbrooke was to repair on board the flagship in two days' time. Chalmers and Collins had quietly discussed whether they could ask the physician of the fleet to examine Holbrooke. It was a difficult step to take and Holbrooke would surely resent it, but things couldn't go on like this. Shorrock had said nothing but it was quite clear that he had doubts about his captain's ability to carry out his orders, to find the enemy and report their presence before they could break out of the confines of the bay. It had become a matter greater than Holbrooke's health; it threatened *Argonaut's* very mission.

'It couldn't be worse for us. The top of a spring tide in the middle watch, fog in the morning and an easterly wind. Any landsman could get his ships out of the estuary today and be past the Cardinals before the fog clears, and this de Ternay is no landsman, far from it.'

Of all Holbrooke's signs of illness, it was this depression that most worried Chalmers. If Holbrooke had merely been physically weak, he could have had a chair beside the wheel and his devoted officers would have made sure that his every whim was satisfied, but this despair, this black humour, was so uncharacteristic that Chalmers feared for his sanity.

Yes, he would be bold and take the consequences. He'd speak to the surgeon on board the flagship and hope that he'd recommend that Holbrooke was sent home to recuperate. Shorrock was perfectly capable of commanding *Argonaut* in his captain's absence, even if there wasn't a spare post-captain in the squadron who could step in for a few months. Chalmers was working through the issues now and his mind was wholly taken up with plotting how he could best ensure that his captain had the rest that he so badly needed.

'Deck there! Right on the starboard beam, I can see a mast above the fog, it looks like *Oyster*.'

Holbrooke looked animated for a moment, and he called back to the lookout perched high up at the main t'gallant head.

'What's her heading?'

'Larboard tack, sir. She's heading right for us, maybe two miles.'

It must be quite light above the fog. Holbrooke looked at his watch. Yes it would be daylight even though he could barely see his own jib boom from the quarterdeck. *Oyster's* station in thick weather was deep in the Vilaine estuary where Finch could watch for any movement from the two French ships. If Finch was leaving that station now there must be a good reason. He probably hadn't seen *Argonaut* yet so he was steering for the centre of the frigate's patrol line.

'Bring her to, Mister Fairview.'

Chalmers stayed close to Holbrooke. He'd seen this before over the past weeks, a flash of animation when something interesting happened, then a depression deeper than before when it was over. He wondered whether his young friend's constitution could bear much more.

***

Treacherous Moon

Oyster rounded *Argonaut's* stern and lay hove to under her lee. Finch didn't wait for the backed staysail to catch the wind but leaned over the cutter's rail as soon as his voice would carry and made a funnel of his hands.

'They're out, sir. Two of them. They must have come out during the middle and they've anchored just outside the bar in barely four fathoms of water. They can't stay there long, not with the ebbing tide, they'll be aground in an hour from now.'

Holbrooke could rely upon Finch's knowledge of these waters; he'd taken his little cutter through every passage and into every bay. He knew the rocks and the shoals as well as the local fishermen did, and he could recite the soundings in his sleep; he probably did, in fact.

'Their yards are crossed, sails bent on?'

'I could only see their t'gallants, sir, above the fog, but they're bent on.'

Holbrooke thought for a moment. His orders were to find the commodore and report, but he thought he could do better than that. He could send *Oyster* to the Palais Road. Finch was articulate and confident; he could state the facts and tell Keppel that *Argonaut* would be shadowing the French.

'Away to the commodore, Mister Finch. Tell him what you saw and that I'll stay in contact with them if they attempt to leave the bay. I'll fire a gun every five minutes while the fog persists. With my compliments, tell him that in this wind I expect they won't attempt the Teignouse Passage, they'll round the Cardinals and make their offing. I can't tell whether they'll beat up towards Brest or run for Rochefort. With my compliments, mind. If he has no orders for *Oyster* you are seek me out and rejoin. Is that clear?'

It was always dangerous to thrust an opinion upon a senior officer, particularly when he would have the same facts and could make the same deduction. But Holbrooke knew only too well what a different perspective the commander at the scene had. Keppel's mind would be on stores and discipline and how best to support the army. If he was confronted with this new information, on a subject that wouldn't be at the forefront of his mind, he could be slow to make the right decisions.

Oyster's sails filled on the starboard tack and she reached away for the boat channel between Houat and Hoedic Islands. That was another reason for sending the cutter to carry the news. *Argonaut* couldn't possibly risk the boat channel on an ebbing tide; only Finch's deep knowledge of these waters and the cutter's shallow draught made it possible. Even then, it would be a tricky passage in this fog, but it would save two hours over the only really safe passage past the Cardinals. That two hours could make the difference between success or failure, between Anson's fleet growing by a captured seventy-four and a forty and the French fleet benefitting from the same.

'Lay her on the larboard tack, Mister Fairview, courses and fore staysail, we'll reach in towards the bar. Double up on the leadsmen if you please. And Mister Shorrock, beat to quarters and clear for action. My compliments to the purser, and breakfast is to be brought up to the men at their quarters.'

***

Argonaut reached slowly and cautiously towards the estuary. At first the lookout could see nothing, but as the leadsmen reported that the frigate was crossing the five fathom line the lookout's shout, oddly distorted by the fog, reached the quarterdeck.

'Sail ho! Two ships right on the bow, maybe three miles. They're letting their tops'ls and t'gallants fall, sir. I can't see their courses.'

'Damn!'

Shorrock punched his fist into his palm.

'If only we had caught them at anchor! We could have given them a broadside or two before they woke up.'

Holbrooke didn't comment. Would he have charged in if they were still at anchor? There was precious little room for manoeuvre with this falling tide and a seventy-four with only half its guns and stored for days, not months, drew hardly any more water than a frigate Even a single tier of twenty-four pounders was vastly superior to *Argonaut's* nine-pounders. It would be a desperate gamble indeed, and it would in all probability leave *Argonaut* too badly damaged to follow them when they tried to escape. No, that wasn't a frigate's job. The time may come for such measures, but not yet.

'Haul your wind, Mister Fairview. Keep a mile clear to windward and when they're abeam you may tack.'

'That'll take us close to a shallow patch, sir. May I wear now and take station on their windward bow?'

Holbrooke felt a flash of anger at being contradicted, but it faded quickly, before he committed himself to rating his sailing master on the quarterdeck. This fog on the water was nothing to the fog in his brain. It was his own fault, he should certainly have remembered that patch, *Le Mats*, it was called, and in peacetime it was buoyed, but now it was a dire hazard to navigation even for a frigate. Particularly for a frigate that was navigating only by soundings and dead reckoning. It would be an ignominious end to his command – to his career, probably – if the French gunboats were to find him high and dry when the fog lifted. And certainly they must wear ship, there was no sea-room to windward for tacking.

'Deck there! Fog's starting to lift, sir, I can see that little island off the starboard quarter.'

'That'll be Dumet, sir,' Fairview said as he reached for the speaking trumpet.

'What's the island's bearing, lookout?'

There was a pause as the lookout made his best estimate.

'Six points abaft the beam, sir. I can see land to windward as well.'

Fairview raised his hat to Holbrooke. He knew that most captains would have deeply resented being corrected on their own quarterdeck and he was trying to make amends.

'Then we have room to wear ship now, sir.'

'Very well, Mister Fairview, make it so. Mister Shorrock, once we are steady, fire a gun to leeward every five minutes, if you please.'

The fog was indeed lifting. First the island and the north shore came into sight and then, on the larboard quarter, the huge seventy-four appeared out of the fog with the forty looking almost as massive in the strange atmosphere, as though in some showman's conjuring trick. It was the light loading of course; it increased the freeboard, raising the ships' topsides far above their normal height. Holbrooke gave them an appraising eye. They were loaded even less than the two that he had encountered back in January. But that was as he had expected. French seventy-fours drew nearly a fathom more than their sixty-fours but they were constrained by the same tides and the same soundings over the bar. He guessed that they had only twenty-four pounders and twelves and provisions for a day or two. This de Ternay must be confident, but then he had a right to be after already bringing out four of the line in the teeth of a good proportion of the British navy.

Bang!

A nine-pounder fired forward. It had that flabby sound that came from an un-shotted cannon.

'Mister Shorrock. You may shot the guns in future; the sound will carry better.'

Shorrock opened his mouth as though he too was going to disagree with his captain, but he must have thought better of it for all he said was *aye-aye sir*, that most useful of naval expressions.

Holbrooke knew in an instant what Shorrock hadn't dared to say. Only yesterday the gunner had reported that he had only ten balls for each gun, and he'd asked that they replenish from the squadron. Shorrock's wish to engage immediately had been rebuffed, but he was correct in imagining that their guns may be needed in anger soon.

'Fire shotted and un-shotted alternately, Mister

Treacherous Moon

Shorrock.'

Shorrock smiled and looked relieved.

God, had he become so unapproachable? Holbrooke looked around at his officers for confirmation, and the truth was written in their faces. They were all walking on eggshells, afraid of incurring the wrath of this newly-unpredictable captain. He passed a hand across his brow. How he would love to lie down, to let all the cares of command drain away, but that was impossible of course, not in sight of the enemy. He thought of confessing his weakness and asking their forgiveness, but that also was impossible. Instead he took up his telescope and turned to study the enemy. He felt sure that his officers were exchanging looks behind his back, but he kept stolidly to his task.

***

Slowly, stealthily, the last of the fog lifted to reveal Quiberon Bay and the Vilaine Estuary in all the splendour of a late spring day. The hills of the Morbihan region showed clear and green and even the sea had taken on its summer hues. There was not a sail in sight, except the two fugitive Frenchmen. *Oyster* was long gone. By now Finch would be feeling his way through the boat channel and soon he'd be reaching away for the flagship, flying his dispatches flag to clear a way through the formalities of approaching the commodore.

Holbrooke had hardly taken his eye from his telescope since *Argonaut* had steadied on her course to shadow the two French ships. He wasn't in the slightest concerned that they would turn and set upon this lone British frigate, that would have been a most un-French thing to do. De Ternay had only one aim, which was to get those precious ships into a French naval base where they could be refitted and rejoin the navy's fighting strength. It was peaceful, in a way, like a yachting trip, except for the five-minute gun that never failed to catch Holbrooke by surprise.

'They're bearing away to pass close to Dumet, I see,' he

said. 'I think our first guess is correct, and they're making for the passage between the Cardinals and the Four, unless they take the passage inside the Four.'

Fairview was also watching them. He turned and studied the chart that he'd secreted behind the binnacle.

'They won't do that if they're making for Brest, sir.'

Holbrooke nodded. He privately thought that they would make for Rochefort, despite all the wishful thinking that said they must head for Brest, whatever the obstacles. It may not be the best place, either to refit or to join a squadron, but it had the huge advantage of being to leeward and it relieved the two ships of the need to pass by Belle Isle and Keppel's squadron. There was a small British squadron off Rochefort, of course, but there was a larger one off Brest. There were no easy options for a fugitive French seventy-four and de Ternay must know that he'd be lucky to reach safety without having to fight at some point, but he'd surely try to minimise the chances of meeting British ships-of-the-line in his weakened state.

'I do fancy, sir, that they're bearing further away than they need to for the Cardinals. Ah! They're wearing! Then they're going inside the Four shoal.'

Holbrooke felt the weight of the responsibility crushing him again. This Four channel was seven leagues from Palais Road where Keppel had anchored. Finch could just possibly be delivering his message now but it would take an hour for Keppel to weigh anchor, and by that time the French would be through the channel and running hard for Rochefort, with the lumbering, fully laden British a full eight leagues astern. Keppel wouldn't know that they were making for Rochefort, of course, but he'd deduce it as soon as he saw an empty sea to the sou'east of Belle Isle. What would he do then? If the north wind persisted, de Ternay would be running to the south of Isle de Ré and under the protection of shore batteries at dawn tomorrow. And all he could do was to follow tamely astern.

Bang!

Treacherous Moon

The five minute gun sounded like a mockery of all his efforts, and the familiar black thoughts came pouring back in defiance of the bright sunshine.

***

CHAPTER TWENTY-NINE

At All Costs

Monday, First of June 1761.
Argonaut, at Sea, the Four Shoal, Quiberon Bay.

'That's Croisic Road on our larboard bow,' Fairview said, pointing to the bay that lay on the southeast corner of the greater Quiberon Bay. '*Soleil-Royal* tried to anchor there before she ran aground on the Four shoal. It was coming on two years ago now, she was the French flagship, and she was separated from the fleet. A sad end and here we are mopping up the last French survivors from that night.'

This talk was irritating Holbrooke. *Argonaut* wouldn't be mopping up anybody, and short of a miracle it was highly likely that these two Frenchmen would be safely in Rochefort by this time tomorrow. Unlike the battle in November 'fifty-nine, there was no severe gale today, and no pitch-dark night to spread confusion among the enemy. They would sail happily inshore of the Four in this bright sunshine and mild northerly breeze, and there was never a British ship-of-the-line to stop them.

Shorrock joined the conversation. Were they colluding against him? Holbrooke frowned and turned away.

'Is it a clear passage inside the Four, Mister Fairview?'

'No, Mister Shorrock, it is not. They'll be there hardly an hour before the bottom of a spring tide and there's a three-fathom patch right in the middle, and another closer to the west. They'll have to choose between the three low-water channels but whichever they choose they'll have only five or six cables width. They'd never have tried it if the fog hadn't lifted, and even now they'll have to be right careful.'

Holbrooke was listening despite himself. Rocks, shoals, low water at a spring tide and five-cable channels, he was starting to be interested, but he just couldn't fight his way through the fog in his brain.

Treacherous Moon

The French ships were just abaft the larboard beam now and Fairview had been watching them wearing – a slow and lubberly process in his opinion – and now he lowered his telescope.

'Well, we couldn't expect any more, under the circumstances, not with them being short-handed and with no opportunity to practice their sail handling. Still, it could have been done better. I do believe the seventy-four is making for the furthest inshore passage and the other one for the middle passage. It will be a tight squeeze and no room for error, not a good place to lose a spar, but they're safe enough today. Would you like me to follow them or take one of the other two passages, sir?'

Holbrooke didn't answer immediately, he was watching the French ship and fighting his brain's sluggishness. Surely something could be done. Every fibre of his being rebelled against the idea of letting those two ships pass unhindered through the channel and into the open sea. Now Jackson was at his elbow; what the devil did the bosun want?

'Beg your pardon, sir, but I was just thinking how this looks like the Caicos Passage, back in 'fifty-seven, when you put that French forty-four aground, what was her name, sir do you remember?'

Holbrooke looked away, angry and ashamed at the way he was being manipulated. Jackson was one of his oldest friends and he deserved to be tolerated, but… and here was Chalmers, was he too joining in?

'*L'Outarde*, Mister Jackson. Bilged and wrecked as I remember.'

'Yes, that was it, thank you Mister Chalmers.'

A heavy silence fell, the only sounds were the wind in the rigging, the slap of the waves against the ship's side and the creaking of the rudder pintles, but they'd grown accustomed to that permanent music of the sea.

Chalmers could sense the internal battle as Holbrooke fought to think clearly. It was a crisis for his friend and he was by no means sure how it would end. He could see

Holbrooke's knuckles turning white as he gripped the quarterdeck rail. An age seemed to pass, but then he saw his friend's grip relax and a new determined set to his jaw. Holbrooke lifted his head and stared at the ships to leeward with an intensity that was almost hatred.

'Mister Fairview, make all sail and lay me alongside the forty-gun ship. Mister Shorrock, your broadsides are ready? You may load with chain shot, no more un-shotted guns, I think.'

Shorrock's smile lit up his face. This was the sort of order he understood, the order that a fighting man could obey.

'Aye-aye sir. Broadsides will be ready in five minutes.'

He strode towards the main deck, shouting orders at his guns crews while *Argonaut* bore away two points to intercept the fugitives.

***

Holbrooke studied the two ships afresh. De Ternay would be in the seventy-four of course, for that was his own command, his reward for saving so many ships from a slow death in the Vilaine estuary. Did the Frenchman recognise the frigate that had tried to pin them off the Glenan Isles back in January? And if he did, would that influence his actions? Holbrooke had been unsuccessful five months ago, but he'd made a damned good effort. A lucky shot could have disabled either of those ships leaving them easy prey for Gambier's squadron. If Albach's information was correct, de Ternay had been promoted on the strength of that escape, and he must know that he'd been fortunate not to end up a prisoner in Britain instead.

Fairview straightened from the binnacle where he'd been taking careful bearings of the enemy.

'They're separating, sir, clearly heading for the two inshore passages. We have perhaps a whole knot over them, sir. We'll be alongside of that forty-gunner while he's still in Croisic Road.'

'Very well, Mister Fairview.'

Treacherous Moon

Holbrooke stood by the quarterdeck rail; his mind clear for the first time in a month. He knew what must be done, and that certainty was sweeping away his of feeling of despair. He felt stronger in his mind, but still his legs were weak and he didn't dare stray too far from a solid support.

'Mister Shorrock! A moment of your time, if you please.'

As Shorrock came hurrying back from the fo'c'sle, Holbrooke swept up all his senior officers: Fairview, Jackson, Chalmers, and Albach who seemed to take it for granted that he was included. He looked them over. He still had that lurking feeling of gloom, the *Black Dog*, as Shorrock called it when others had been afflicted, and he still felt as though his limbs weren't really obeying their orders. But he knew he could do this, he could take his ship into action one more time, if it wasn't for too long.

'Those gentlemen have chosen to separate. Once they're committed to the passage of the Four, there'll be no turning back and they won't be able to support each other. I intend to make them pay for that mistake. I fear the seventy-four is a little ambitious for us but if the forty is armed only with twelve-pounders, as I suspect, then she's more our size. Now, Mister Fairview will act as though he's putting us alongside, to trade broadsides and perhaps to board.'

He looked around to see grinning faces. It was a disappointment to leave the seventy-four to continue her passage, but he knew it was the right decision. There would be a fog again tonight, almost certainly, and there was nothing that he could do to stay in contact with the enemy. In any case, the forty-gun ship would turn and engage *Argonaut* once they were clear of the land. This escape was for the benefit of the seventy-four, and the smaller ship was just a pawn to be sacrificed to the greater purpose.

'When I judge the time is right, Mister Fairview will bear up and cross her stern and Mister Shorrock will rake her with chain shot. You're to aim high of course…'

Shorrock bowed slightly, it was a joke, of course. Chain shot did little good against the hull of a ship, even the relatively soft target of the stern.

'…and then reload with ball to starboard. We'll pummel her so hard that she'll strike, founder or run aground. We can discount the seventy-four, she'll surely ignore her consort and run for Rochefort before Keppel's squadron arrives.'

Holbrooke glanced over to larboard. The Frenchmen were under all plain sail, probably they hadn't enough trained seamen to set their studding sails, even if they had them on board. Yet it was a noble sight with the new white canvas showing clearly against the fresh greens of this glorious transition from spring to summer.

The channel ahead looked innocent enough, but Holbrooke had studied the chart in the days before the weakness overtook him, and he could hazily remember the two minor shoals inside the greater Four shoal. De Ternay had gambled on an uncontested passage through these dangerous waters. Well, he'd be disappointed.

'Mister Jackson, your sail handlers are to be ready but not on show. The French captains must be persuaded that we're intending to fight broadside to broadside. Is everyone ready?'

He looked again at his officers and realised how lucky he was. If he'd had his marines he'd have attempted a boarding, such was their enthusiasm, but as Murray and his men were still engaged in the siege of the citadel, it really was too foolhardy.

Albach caught his attention.

'May I assist Mister Shorrock, sir? I have some experience with great guns.'

***

'You can see the breakers on the Four shoal now. God, it must have been terrifying at night and in that wind when Hawke chased the French into the bay. Three ships of the line were wrecked there.'

Shorrock had the leisure to look around now that his guns were loaded and ready. Fairview had noted the broken water, of course, but his attention was upon the shoals that couldn't be seen, the two patches inside the Four that could rip the bottom out of an unwary ship.

Holbrooke had also discounted the Four shoal; it was no danger in this weather when it advertised its presence so obviously.

'You're sure we have water over that nearest shoal inside the Four, Mister Fairview?'

'Aye, sir. We can pass right over it if we need to. Mister Finch sounded it a month ago. It has at least three fathoms at the bottom of springs, and there's no swell to speak of today. That forty would have to think twice, though and they'll never pass over the far inner shoal, and nor can we, not at this height of tide.'

Holbrooke said nothing. He would prefer not to sail over any shoals in his frigate, but at least he knew that he could do so if necessary.

They were slanting in towards the forty-gun ship and it was becoming clear that they'd be alongside before the Frenchman reached the narrowest part, between the Four channel and the three-fathom patch.

'Both batteries ready, sir. Larboard side loaded with ball, starboard with chain and bar shot.'

Shorrock was his usual cheerful self, but still Holbrooke was unable to match his mood. Today was a matter of endurance, to get this over with while his strength held.

'We'll be in range in a few minutes,' Shorrock added, watching the French ship closely.

Holbrooke heard the first shots, and the sound of chain shot whirring overhead. A shower of wood splinters, lengths of cordage and scraps of canvas bounced off the splinter nets. He was aware of Jackson leading a party aloft to knot and splice. The Frenchman had fired at long range and nothing important had been hit. He didn't need to tell Shorrock to hold his fire, and a glance at the gun deck, at the relaxed, eager gun crews, reassured him. Was he being too timid? His plan to haul his wind under the Frenchman's stern smacked of a tactic to preserve *Argonaut*, rather than one that would ensure the destruction of the enemy. Perhaps he could be bolder, but he was so tired.

'Mister Fairview. A change of plan. Range up alongside and we'll fight it out broadside to broadside.'

The quarterdeck of a frigate was no place to keep a secret and word of the plan ran like wildfire down the deck, and as it reached each crew, they cheered and those who had them waved their hats high.

***

Another broadside from the Frenchman. She had one deck of guns only, but they were twelve-pounders, and the heavy chain shot howled as it ripped into *Argonaut's* rigging. Still there was no serious damage. The Frenchman was a couple of cables away a few points forward of the beam.

'How far to the shoals, Mister Fairview?'

'A mile, sir. They're right in line with the Four.'

Holbrooke looked quickly over the starboard bow to see the lazy waves breaking on the shoal that had claimed so many ships.

'Can you bring her two points to starboard without wearing?'

The sailing master had been anticipating the question, clearly, and he came straight back with a firm response.

'I can sir.'

'Very well, pray do so. Stand by Mister Shorrock, you may fire when your whole battery bears.'

Fairview nodded at the quartermaster who gave the order to the steersman. *Argonaut's* bows moved slowly to starboard…

Crash!

Argonaut's broadside bellowed and an instant later Holbrooke saw a shower of debris as the nine-pound balls smashed into the Frenchman's hull, but the forty-gun ship barely flinched under the impact.

'You may slant in towards her now, Mister Fairview.'

Another broadside from the French ship. They were still

Treacherous Moon

firing chain shot, evidently intent on disabling their pursuer. There was no question of taking the British frigate as a prize today, not with a vast enemy squadron only seven leagues away. They couldn't know that Keppel had been alerted to their escape, but no sane Frenchman who was within an ace of gaining the open sea would take that chance. Flight, honourable escape, was all that was on their minds.

Crash!

Shorrock's second broadside was delivered at closer range and this time Holbrooke could see the damage that it wrought. Chain shot was all very well, but it didn't intimidate in the way that solid cast iron balls did and it couldn't penetrate even the flimsiest of gunwales.

Another French broadside.

Holbrooke heard a rending sound aloft and looked up to see that the fore tops'l yard had been shot through and the larboard arm was hanging from the slings.

'Bosun's on his way now, sir,' said Fairview. 'We'll pass just inside the three fathom shoal, sir.'

Holbrooke spared a quick glance over the side. The water was darker on the starboard side and he could just make out long tendrils of weed reaching up from the shallows. He thumped the rail in exasperation. They'd caught up with the French ship just too late. A few minutes earlier and they would have stood a chance of forcing him over onto the inner shoal, but they were moving into clear water now.

Shorrock was firing fast, unhindered by the Frenchman's chain shot. Holbrooke could feel *Argonaut's* speed dropping now that the fore tops'l wasn't drawing properly. The French ship was actually moving away from them now. Soon he would complete his escape.

'Mister Shorrock! The starboard battery!'

He was having to shout now and the effort cost him dear, he had to grip the railing hard to stay upright and he could feel that his knees had buckled. He was aware of Chalmers beside him. Shouldn't the chaplain be with the surgeon at quarters? Why was he on the quarterdeck, and Albach too?

'Bear up, Mister Fairview, shave her stern as close as you dare!'

Without the fore tops'l's leverage to keep the bows off, *Argonaut's* head turned swiftly to larboard. The starboard guns were manned now with their quoins out so that their muzzles pointed high towards where the enemy's vulnerable rigging would be. And all along the row of nine-pounders the gun captains' hands were raised.

'Fire when each gun bears, Mister Shorrock.'

There was no shock effect with chain and bar shot, and as the range to the French ship was increasing fast, it was better to fire early than wait until all the guns could bear.

Bang! Bang! Bang!

Shorrock's guns fired in quick succession as *Argonaut* sped across the Frenchman's stern. They were pointed well and from that angle they could rake along the whole length of the enemy's three masts. Holes appeared in sails, halyards and sheets and stays and braces cascaded towards the deck in their scores, but no spars fell. The Frenchman sailed on, moving further and further away and in that moment Holbrooke knew that he had failed. It would take hours to catch them again with his own wounded sails, and by that time they'd be far to the south and making for the safety of Rochefort. He grasped the rail and watched in despair, surprised that the world was spinning around him, faster and faster, and its pace matched the speed of the retreating French ship. The hard oak of the deck felt suddenly spongy and he knew that he was falling, but it was happening slowly, so gently, and he felt like he was watching himself from afar. It wasn't an unpleasant feeling and he was aware that Chalmers had wrapped his arms around his chest and that he and Albach were lowering him carefully. As he drifted into unconsciousness, he thought he heard a cheer, and through the cheer the huge sound of Shorrock's voice shouting something about the Frenchman's mizzen, and

Treacherous Moon

Keppel's squadron in sight, but he couldn't concentrate. He thought it may be a good thing but he wasn't sure, and then the greyness darkened and turned to black, and he knew no more.

***

Chris Durbin

CHAPTER THIRTY

At Peace

Thursday, Eleventh of June 1761.
Mulberry House, Wickham.

The first thing Holbrooke noticed was the curious sensation of waking in a bed with a real, flax-stuffed mattress and clean, cool sheets. He wasn't on board a ship, that much was certain, but his mind refused to imagine where he could be. He tried to piece together his memories. He'd engaged a French forty-gun ship; that much he could recall, and he had a vague recollection of disappointment, that it hadn't gone well. Ah, of course, he'd fallen to the deck! Then had his ship been captured? Had he been wounded? Was he a prisoner in France? He could feel no pain, but that, he knew, meant nothing. He could find no answers and his mind couldn't hold a train of thought for long, so he lay for a while with his eyes closed, afraid of what he might find if he opened them. His body was entirely relaxed and he felt mildly ashamed of his slothfulness.

The first hint came from a clock that chimed somewhere below him, three deep notes, and there was a familiar wheezing sound as the hammer was brought back between each stroke. He struggled to remember. He had a recollection of a clock like that, but it seemed that it belonged in a remote place and time, and he could find no connection with his current circumstances.

Intrigued, he cautiously opened one eye, but it was a struggle to keep it from closing of its own accord. He tried again. He was in a room with closed curtains that were vainly attempting to keep back the sun. It looked curiously like his own bedroom in Mulberry house, but his mind refused to believe it. In the diffused light the room appeared too big, there was too much space between the bed and the window and the ceiling towered way overhead, more like a

Treacherous Moon

cathedral than a bedroom. He turned his head and looked at the other side of the room where the shadows were deeper. Yet the essential features suggested that he was in Mulberry House. There was no denying it, he was in Wickham, however improbable it may be. In that case, it was afternoon because the sun had reached the front of the house. When he disengaged his ear from the pillow he could hear the sounds from the square, just the normal conversations and carts rattling over the cobbles, not the cacophony of a market day.

He was home, in Mulberry House at Wickham, and he was lying in his own bed chamber at the front of the house, immediately above the parlour. How long he had been there he couldn't say, but *Argonaut* would have taken three or four days at least to make Portsmouth and he felt as though he hadn't just recently arrived.

He heard the door open and kept his eyes closed and lay still. He couldn't have said why he did that, perhaps it was a desire to know what he was waking up to before he committed himself. He heard light footsteps and the curtains being partly drawn, then a hand – the cool soft back of a hand – was laid on his forehead. He opened his eyes to see Ann gazing down on him with a look of concern.

Good morning dear wife, was what he had intended to say, but it came out as an unintelligible croak and in any case he could say no more as Ann crushed herself against him.

***

'Well, it may surprise you to know that I've heard all about your last action against the French. Shall I start there?'

He'd been fed and washed and now they were waiting for the doctor to arrive from Fareham. Ann was satisfied that he was strong enough to hear an explanation of how he came to be lying in a bed in Wickham when his last memory was of a sea-fight inside the Four shoal off Quiberon Bay.

Holbrooke nodded and took another sip of water. It was inexpressibly delicious, but Ann gently restrained him from taking too much at a time.

'David and Major Albach told me all about your engagement with the French ship. I expect you can remember cutting across her stern, is that the right expression?'

Holbrooke smiled encouragingly. Speech was still difficult, and his neck hurt when he moved his head.

'They told me that you swooned before the most important event. The Frenchman's mast fell, it was the mizzen mast, the one at the back,' Ann smiled in triumph at her use of nautical language, 'and it took some of the next one – the mainmast – with it. At that point Mister Keppel's ships were sighted and before lunchtime they had captured the ship that you damaged and were in pursuit of the other, although as it turns out they didn't catch her. Wasn't that a dreadful, cowardly thing to do, for the larger ship to leave the smaller to be captured? David seemed to think it was justified by the circumstances, but I can't imagine a British ship acting like that. But David did make a point of saying that *Argonaut* was in sight when the French ship struck her colours. That's important for your share of the prize money, you know.'

Ann stopped and looked down on her husband, gauging whether he was strong enough for her to continue. She was torn between the desire to have him rest before the doctor arrived and her own joy at telling him about naval matters before anyone else could. Albach was in London and Chalmers was with William Holbrooke at his cottage, and she had this narrow window of opportunity to display her nautical knowledge to her husband.

'The commodore came on board and looked at the rigging and at your poor body lying feverish in your cabin and ordered Mister Shorrock to sail for home immediately. *Argonaut* arrived at Spithead four days later and David came directly to see me. We sent Billy Stiles for you in his coach and here you are, safe and sound. Major Albach is lodging with your father, when he's not in London. I offered him a room here, but he thought it not quite right until you were fit to agree. They're a bit cramped at the cottage with your father, David and the major all there, so I believe he'll move here if you make the offer. He was called to the Admiralty two days ago and he's expected to return this evening.'

'How long have I been here, what day is it?'

Holbrooke's speech hadn't fully recovered, and Ann had to puzzle for a moment to work out what he had said.

'Oh! I should have said that immediately. It's Thursday, the eleventh of June and you've been asleep for ten days. You were feverish until yesterday morning and the doctor was most concerned, but he came in the afternoon and pronounced that you were past the worst. Is that Billy now? He must have whipped those horses mercilessly to return so quickly.'

Ann looked down to see the coach had drawn up in front of the door and Billy Stiles was folding down the steps to allow the passenger to alight with dignity.

'He's brought the doctor. Oh, what a crowd of people are watching. They all think so much of you, and I've had so many people asking after your health.'

***

The doctor left satisfied, and Holbrooke spent the rest of the afternoon dozing in blissful lethargy. Albach and Chalmers arrived in the evening and Ann granted them a short session with the patient. Holbrooke was hungry for news from Belle Isle and the siege of the citadel.

'Was there any word at the Admiralty?'

'Precious little,' Albach replied. 'The siege is progressing to the general's satisfaction, which means slowly. The Brest and Rochefort blockades are keeping the French squadrons locked up tight and the commodore is keeping a close hold on Quiberon Bay and the Morbihan, so the citadel is unlikely to be relieved. The feeling is that the French commander has done all that honour demands in the defence of the walls, and a capitulation is expected at any day.'

'Then let us hope. But I do wonder at the value of the

island. We surely can't expect to keep it when peace comes, that would be too great a dishonour for the French to stomach. What do you think, David?'

'It's strange that you should mention it, because Admiral Forbes made a point of telling me his views. He thought that you would want to know.'

Chalmers paused for a moment. In the silence the clock's ticking sounded unnaturally loud.

'You're correct to wonder, and there is indeed no question of retaining Belle Isle when the war is over. Its value lies in the possibility of exchanging it for Minorca at the peace negotiations and its capture is all part of Pitt's plan to keep Spain out of the war. France is dangling Minorca like a carrot in front of the Spanish King. If Spain joins France in the war then Minorca will be theirs, but if King Carlos believes that France is likely to exchange Minorca for Belle Isle then his incentive to form a Bourbon family alliance is so much the weaker. It's just a bargaining chip, but an important one and if it succeeds in keeping Spain neutral then it may yet shorten the war by years. Certainly in the Admiralty it's seen as an important matter.'

Holbrooke tried to piece together what Chalmers had said. It made sense and in the devious reckoning of grand strategy – he had to concede – it was perhaps worth the lives and treasure that had been expended. Yet he couldn't get that image of *Oyster's* doomed bosun out of his head.

'Do you have any further commitment with their Lordships, Major Albach?'

'None, unless they should find further use for me, and I suspect I would decline if asked. It's all very well acting the intelligence officer when your name and face is unknown, but I have no wish to land in France again, not if I value my life.'

'Well, you would be most welcome here as long as you wish.'

Albach bowed. He was aware that he couldn't stay long in the cottage, not in decency, but Mulberry House had space aplenty, and Ann had already offered him a room before Holbrooke had recovered. It would have been sensible to accept the lady's offer, but Albach couldn't think of such a thing, not with the master of the house ill in bed.

'Then that's settled, here you will stay.'

'And yet, I am somewhat at a loss as to what will become of me. I can't go to any territories under the control of either the Empress or King Louis, which rather confines me to these islands. I find that I must carve out a new future here. I cannot act the leisured gentleman, not on the small pension that I can expect from the Admiralty, so I must find some new occupation. Mister Featherstone has already offered me a position in his corn merchant business, and do you know? I'm at half a mind to accept.'

'Ann's father? I had no idea that you were so well acquainted.'

'Oh, I met him back in March, before we sailed to Belle Isle, if you remember, and again soon after we brought you here. He's ailing, as you know, and he wants to spend more time with his grandson and his garden. He's looking to bring someone else into the business, and he knows that you are committed to the King's service until this war is over. Well, I'll think on it, unless you have any objections.'

'Please do, you would be doing me a favour. He expects me to take an interest but as long as this war persists the navy must be my first concern, and I see no immediate signs of it ending. Even then, I don't know whether the business would be for me.'

Holbrooke turned awkwardly in his bed and attempted to put his feet upon the floor but fell back exasperated.

'God, I'm weaker than I thought. How I wish that we could hear some news from Belle Isle. So much effort, so many lives, and still it isn't over.'

The sun was casting long shadows over the square as Polly came in bearing tea and toast on a tray. She turned to close the curtains, then stopped and stared out of the window.

'There's a real fuss going on in the square, sir. A coach has come up the Fareham road and everyone's gathered round. Can't you hear them cheering, sir?'

The door flew open and Ann ran in.

'It's victory. Belle Isle has fallen!'

Holbrooke could hear it now, the loud huzzahs from outside his window and then from the east, across the little Meon River, the bells of St. Nicholas' church rang out.

***

HISTORICAL EPILOGUE

At Sea

By 1761 the French navy was at its lowest ebb. It had lost a third of its ships in a doomed attempt to defend New France and its battle fleets had been ravaged at Lagos Bay and Quiberon Bay. It was unable to defend its sugar islands in the Caribbean, which were being picked off one-by one. The diversionary raid to the north of Britain in 1760 resulted in abject failure with the loss of three frigates, as well as two whole regiments that King Louis could ill afford. The capture of Belle Isle in June 1761, that ceded the command of the French Atlantic coast to the British Navy, was just the final humiliation. All that the French navy could do after that was to try to keep a fleet in being, protected in its main bases at Brest and Rochefort, in the hope that Spain would join the war and add its large, undamaged fleet to the cause.

Europe

Versailles now accepted that it was only by diverting its resources to the army in Germany that anything could be salvaged from this ruinous war. Assaulted by large and vigorous French armies, the allied forces could only hold the line in Westphalia. Meanwhile, in the east, King Frederick of Prussia had to go onto the defensive to avoid losing territory to the Austrians and Russians. All sides could sense the war ending and were desperate to hold their territory and to gain what they could as bargaining chips at the peace negotiations. Austria's avoidance of defeat on the continent could be counted as a win, but for France anything less than victory in Germany was a disaster. The invasion of Belle Isle forced King Louis to divert a significant part of his army to the Atlantic coast, thus depriving the Prince of Soubise, his commander in Germany, of the manpower that he needed to take Hanover.

North America

After some two hundred years of French colonisation of North America, the long dream of New France was over. French power in the continent was broken, leaving them only a few settlements in Louisiana and the far west. For the English-speaking people of the thirteen colonies and the Francophones of Quebec – now subjects of King George – it was a time to make plans for the future, and to decide what should be made of these vast new territories that had been opened up. Almost before the fighting had ended, the British colonists were agitating to expand to the west, across the Appalachians and into the territories that were owned by the Native Americans. They were becoming increasingly resentful of their imperial masters in England who took a more cautious approach. Few would have thought it in 1761, and even fewer would have said it openly, but the seeds of the American Revolution were sown at the capitulation of New France.

The Long War

With the sole exception of Minorca, France had nothing to bring to the table in the future peace negotiations and fought on in the hope of luring Spain into the conflict to turn the tide. Without Spain, and its undamaged fleet, France could not see a way to end the war before it lost the rest of its colonies, yet Spain couldn't afford to enter the war and was fearful of the consequences if it did. In 1761, diplomacy was more important to France than the strength of its army and navy, as it sought a way to enter peace negotiations with some sort of bargaining chips to regain its lost colonies.

***

FACT MEETS FICTION

Discovering historical connections is one of my greatest joys as a novelist, and I was delighted to find so many surrounding the British capture of Belle Isle in 1761. The measurement of the solar system, the survey of the Mason-Dixon Line, French support for the American War of Independence, and a truly inspirational French hero of the Seven Years War all emerged from my research for this book. If you want to know more, here are a few clues to start your own reading.

Escape from the Vilaine River

The Battle of Quiberon Bay was fought in November 1759, as told in the seventh book in the Carlisle & Holbrooke series, *Rocks and Shoals*. It was a resounding victory for Admiral Hawke's squadron, and it established British naval superiority for the remainder of the war. In an attempt to escape capture or destruction, a number of French ships sought refuge in the muddy and shallow Vilaine estuary, which empties into the eastern side of Quiberon Bay. They were still there in January 1761, but by the extraordinary efforts of a junior French sea officer, most of them escaped over the following six months.

I'm not sure of the order in which the French ships escaped from the Vilaine; the English historical record is ambiguous, and I haven't seen any French records. However, it appears that on the seventh of January 1761 Charles-Henri-Louis d'Arsac, Chevalier de Ternay, exploited a high spring tide and a dense fog to get away with two ships of the line and the frigates *Vestale* (34) and *Aigrette* (36). *Vestale* was captured the next day off the Penmarks by the British frigate *Unicorn* (28) while *Aigrette* narrowly escaped an encounter with *Seahorse* (20). *Unicorn,* under her first lieutenant – the captain died in the engagement with *Vestale* – came to *Seahorse's* rescue. De Ternay was rewarded with promotion to *Capitaine de Vaisseau* and given command of *Robuste* (74) which at that point was probably still trapped in the Vilaine.

Over the next few months de Ternay brought out four more ships of the line, leaving behind only *Inflexible* (64) to be eventually condemned and broken up. De Ternay's actions are some of the most inspiring events of the war and he would go on to command a successful raid on British Newfoundland. He enjoyed rapid promotion and in the following war, as a *chef d'escadre* – a rear admiral – he escorted the first French troops to America to assist the rebel colonists. He died on active duty and is buried in Holy Trinity Church, Newport, Rhode Island, close to where my wife and I were married in 1982.

I have assumed that it was *Brillant* (64) and *Dragon* (64) that escaped from the Vilaine in January 1761 and as I couldn't find a plausible date for *Robuste's* escape, I have incorporated it into Holbrooke's narrative in June 1761.

Transit of Venus

The Seven Years' War was fought during the period in European history that is known as the *Enlightenment*. One of the grand ideas of the enlightenment was that the pursuit of knowledge should be based upon reason and the evidence of the senses, rather than traditional doctrine. This nicely fitted in with the growing realisation that the contemporary techniques of ocean navigation were inadequate, and that a better understanding of astronomy was one way to improve the safety of ships at sea.

By the eighteenth century the size of the earth was quite accurately known, and the *relative* distances of the sun and all the major planets had been measured, but their *absolute* distances remained a mystery. In 1716 the English astronomer Edmund Halley worked out a means of measuring the distance from Earth to the Sun using a parallax method when Venus (the most convenient planet for the purpose) was observed to transit across the face of the Sun. This happened twice every hundred years or so and the next such event was scheduled for the sixth of June 1761. It was understood that the accuracy of the measurement would be principally determined by the length of the baseline between measurement points, and that no measurements could be taken if the sky was obscured by clouds. This led to a scramble to send observation parties to the far corners of the globe to extend the baseline and in the hope that a few of them would find clear skies to deliver usable results.

Despite straining every sinew to keep a fleet at sea that could master the French navy and deal with the looming Spanish threat, the British Admiralty released a frigate to take an observation party to Sumatra to achieve the greatest possible baseline of observations. This party was led by the astronomer Charles Mason and the surveyor Jeremiah Dixon in the frigate *Seahorse*. Unfortunately, *Seahorse* was badly damaged in an encounter with a French frigate that was escaping from the Vilaine River and had to return to Plymouth. By the time Mason and Dixon set out again they could reach no further than Cape Town in time to set up their equipment to observe the transit. In my narrative, Holbrooke met *Seahorse* in the Chops of the Channel after failing to prevent the escape of two French ships-of-the line, and accompanied her and *Unicorn* into Plymouth

Mason and Dixon are better known to history for surveying the boundary between Pennsylvania, Maryland, Delaware and West Virginia, part of which became the boundary between the southern slave states and northern free states, now known as the Mason-Dixon Line.

***

Chris Durbin

Capture of Belle Isle

Imagine during a war that an enemy force captured an island that lay between your two principal naval bases, only eight miles offshore, and held it with apparent ease for nearly two years, using it as a supply base for its domination of your vital coastline. That was the situation that France faced when a British army invaded Belle Isle in June 1761. It was a national humiliation and it cost France dear to regain it in the negotiations that ended the war.

The campaign against Belle Isle was largely as I have described it. With the exception of Holbrooke and his crew of the frigate *Argonaut,* the cutter *Oyster,* and the Admiralty intelligence officers, I have not needed to change any of the facts. The success at Belle Isle was the culmination of four years of trial and error in combined amphibious operations, and it created an operational doctrine (although that term wasn't used until much later) that has evolved into the way of amphibious warfare that we know today.

Lieutenant Colonel McKenzie commanded the marines at Belle Isle, and it was the first time that the marines – later to become the Royal Marines – operated at battalion strength in an opposed seaborne landing. The laurel wreath on their colours is believed to have been adopted in honour of their distinguished service at Belle Isle.

***

THE CARLISLE AND HOLBROOKE SERIES

Book 1: The Colonial Post-Captain

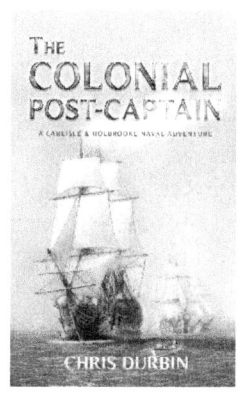

Captain Carlisle of His Britannic Majesty's frigate *Fury* hails from Virginia, a loyal colony of the British Crown. In 1756, as the clouds of war gather in Europe, *Fury* is ordered to Toulon to investigate a French naval and military build-up.

While battling the winter weather, Carlisle must also juggle with delicate diplomatic issues in this period of phoney war and contend with an increasingly belligerent French frigate.

And then there is the beautiful Chiara Angelini, pursued across the Mediterranean by a Tunisian corsair who appears determined to abduct her, yet strangely reluctant to shed blood.

Carlisle and his young master's mate, George Holbrooke, are witnesses to the inconclusive sea-battle that leads to the loss of Minorca. They engage in a thrilling and bloody encounter with the French frigate and a final confrontation with the enigmatic corsair.

Chris Durbin

Book 2: The Leeward Islands Squadron

In late 1756, as the British government collapses in the aftermath of the loss of Minorca and the country and navy are thrown into political chaos, a small force of ships is sent to the West Indies to reinforce the Leeward Islands Squadron.

Captain Edward Carlisle, a native of Virginia, and his first lieutenant George Holbrooke, are fresh from the Mediterranean and their capture of a powerful French man-of-war. Their new frigate *Medina* has orders to join a squadron commanded by a terminally ill commodore. Their mission: a near-suicidal assault on a strong Caribbean island fortress. Carlisle must confront the challenges of higher command as he leads the squadron back into battle to accomplish the Admiralty's orders.

Join Carlisle and Holbrooke as they attack shore fortifications, engage in ship-on-ship duels and deal with mutiny in the West Indies.

Book 3: The Jamaica Station

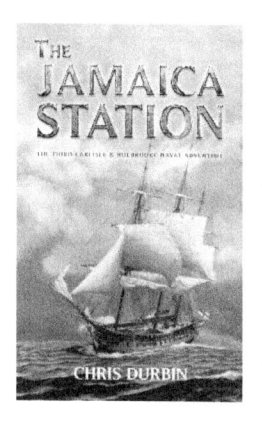

It is 1757, and the British navy is regrouping from a slow start to the seven years' war.

A Spanish colonial governor and his family are pursued through the Caribbean by a pair of mysterious ships from the Dutch island of St. Eustatius. The British frigate *Medina* rescues the governor from his hurricane-wrecked ship, leading Captain Edward Carlisle and his first lieutenant George Holbrooke into a web of intrigue and half-truths. Are the Dutchmen operating under a letter of marque or are they pirates, and why are they hunting the Spaniard? Only the diplomatic skills of Carlisle's aristocratic wife, Lady Chiara, can solve the puzzle.

When Carlisle is injured, the young Holbrooke must grow up quickly. Under his leadership, *Medina* takes part in a one-sided battle with the French that will influence a young Horatio Nelson to choose the navy as a career.

Chris Durbin

Book 4: Holbrooke's Tide

It is 1758, and the Seven Years War is at its height. The Duke of Cumberland's Hanoverian army has been pushed back to the River Elbe while the French are using the medieval fortified city of Emden to resupply their army and to anchor its left flank.

George Holbrooke has recently returned from the Jamaica Station in command of a sloop-of-war. He is under orders to survey and blockade the approaches to Emden in advance of the arrival of a British squadron. The French garrison and their Austrian allies are nervous. With their supply lines cut, they are in danger of being isolated when the French army is forced to retreat in the face of the new Prussian-led army that is gathering on the Elbe. Can the French be bluffed out of Emden? Is this Holbrooke's flood tide that will lead to his next promotion?

Holbrooke's Tide is the fourth of the Carlisle & Holbrooke naval adventures. The series follows the exploits of the two men through the Seven Years War and into the period of turbulent relations between Britain and her American colonies in the 1760s.

Book 5: The Cursed Fortress

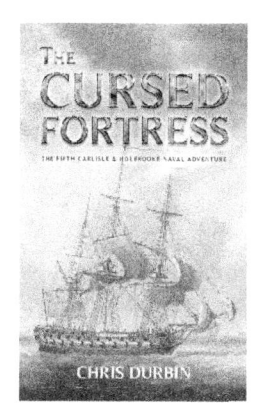

The French called it *La Forteresse Maudite*, the Cursed Fortress.

Louisbourg stood at the mouth of the Gulf of Saint Lawrence, massive and impregnable, a permanent provocation to the British colonies. It was Canada's first line of defence, guarding the approaches to Quebec, from where all New France lay open to invasion. It had to fall before a British fleet could be sent up the Saint Lawrence. Otherwise, there would be no resupply and no line of retreat; Canada would become the graveyard of George II's navy.

A failed attempt on Louisbourg in 1757 had only stiffened the government's resolve; the Cursed Fortress must fall in 1758.

Captain Carlisle's frigate joins the blockade of Louisbourg before winter's icy grip has eased. Battling fog, hail, rain, frost and snow, suffering scurvy and fevers, and with a constant worry about the wife he left behind in Virginia, Carlisle will face his greatest test of leadership and character yet.

The Cursed Fortress is the fifth of the Carlisle & Holbrooke naval adventures. The series follows the two men through the Seven Years War and into the period of turbulent relations between Britain and her American colonies in the 1760s.

Chris Durbin

Book 6: Perilous Shore

Amphibious warfare was in its infancy in the mid-eighteenth century, it was the poor relation of the great fleet actions that the navy so loved.

That all changed in 1758 when the British government demanded a campaign of raids on the French Channel ports. Command arrangements were hastily devised, and a whole new class of vessels was produced at breakneck speed: flatboats, the ancestors of the landing craft that put the allied forces ashore on D-Day.

Commander George Holbrooke's sloop *Kestrel* is in the thick of the action: scouting landing beaches, duelling with shore batteries and battling the French Navy.

In a twist of fate, Holbrooke finds himself unexpectedly committed to this new style of amphibious warfare as he is ordered to lead a division of flatboats onto the beaches of Normandy and Brittany. He meets his greatest test yet when a weary and beaten British army retreats from a second failed attempt at Saint Malo with the French close on their heels.

Perilous Shore is the sixth of the Carlisle & Holbrooke naval adventures. The series follows Holbrooke and his mentor, Captain Carlisle, through the Seven Years War and into the period of turbulent relations between Britain and her American colonies in the 1760s.

Book 7: Rocks and Shoals

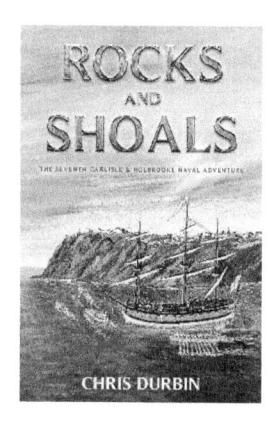

With the fall of Louisbourg in 1758 the French in North America were firmly on the back foot. Pitt's grand strategy for 1759 was to launch a three-pronged attack on Canada. One army would move north from Lake Champlain while another smaller force would strike across the wilderness to Lake Ontario and French-held Fort Niagara. A third, under Admiral Saunders and General Wolfe, would sail up the Saint Lawrence, where no battle fleet had ever been, and capture Quebec.

Captain Edward Carlisle sails ahead of the battle fleet to find a way through the legendary dangers of the Saint Lawrence River. An unknown sailing master assists him; James Cook has a talent for surveying and cartography and will achieve immortality in later years.

There are rocks and shoals aplenty before Carlisle and his frigate *Medina* are caught up in the near-fatal indecision of the summer when General Wolfe tastes the bitterness of early setbacks.

Rocks and Shoals is the seventh of the Carlisle & Holbrooke naval adventures. The series follows Carlisle and his protégé George Holbrooke, through the Seven Years War and into the period of turbulent relations between Britain and her American colonies in the 1760s.

Book 8: Niagara Squadron

Fort Niagara is the key to the American continent. Whoever owns that lonely outpost at the edge of civilisation controls the entire Great Lakes region.

Pitt's grand strategy for 1759 is to launch a three-pronged attack on Canada. One army would move north from Lake Champlain, a second would sail up the Saint Lawrence to capture Quebec, and a third force would strike across the wilderness to Lake Ontario and French-held Fort Niagara.

Commander George Holbrooke is seconded to command the six hundred boats to carry the army through the rivers and across Lake Ontario. That's the easy part; he also must deal with two powerful brigs that guarantee French naval superiority on the lake.

Holbrooke knows time is running out to be posted as captain before the war ends and promotions dry up; his rank is the stumbling block to his marriage to Ann, waiting for him in his hometown of Wickham Hampshire.

Niagara Squadron is the eighth Carlisle and Holbrooke novel. The series follows Carlisle and his protégé Holbrooke through the Seven Years War and into the period of turbulent relations between Britain and her American colonies in the 1760s.

Book 9: Ligurian Mission

It is the summer of 1760 and the British navy reigns supreme on the oceans of the world; only in the Mediterranean is its mastery still seriously challenged. Admiral Saunders is sent with a squadron of ships-of-the-line to remind those nations that are still neutral of the consequences of siding with the French.

Edward Carlisle's ship *Dartmouth* is sent to the Ligurian Sea. His mission: to carry the British envoy to the Kingdom of Sardinia back to its capital, Turin, then to investigate the ships being built in Genoa for the French.

He soon finds that the game of diplomacy is played for high stakes, and the countries bordering the Ligurian Sea are hotbeds of intrigue and treachery, where family loyalties count for little.

Carlisle must contend with the arrogance of the envoy, the Angelini family's duplicity and a vastly superior French seventy-four-gun ship whose captain is determined to bring the Genoa ships safely to Toulon.

Ligurian Mission is the ninth Carlisle and Holbrooke novel. The series follows Carlisle and his protégé Holbrooke through the Seven Years War and into the period of turbulent relations between Britain and her American colonies prior to their bid for independence.

Chris Durbin

Book 10: Nor'west by North

By late 1759 it is clear that France is losing the Seven Years War. In a desperate gamble, the French Atlantic and Mediterranean fleets combine to dominate the Channel and cover a landing in the south of England, but they are annihilated by Admiral Hawke at Quiberon Bay. Meanwhile, a diversionary landing is planned in the north of Britain, and it sails from Dunkirk before news of the disaster at Quiberon Bay can reach its commander. The ill-fated expedition sets out to circumnavigate Britain in an attempt to salvage something from the failed strategy.

George Holbrooke, newly promoted to post-captain and commanding the frigate *Argonaut*, joins a squadron sent to intercept the French expedition. The quest takes him to Sweden, the Faroes, the Western Isles of Scotland and then to Ireland and the Isle of Man. The final act is played out at a secluded anchorage in the Bristol Channel.

Nor'west by North is the tenth Carlisle and Holbrooke novel. The series follows Carlisle and his protégé Holbrooke through the Seven Years War and into the period of turbulent relations between Britain and her American colonies prior to their bid for independence.

Treacherous Moon

Book 11: Carlisle's Duty

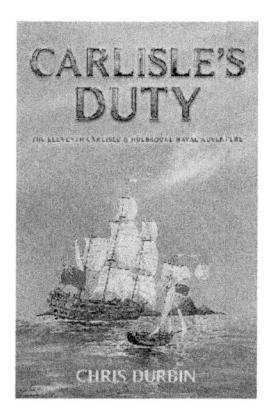

North America's French and Indian War may be over, but at the end of 1760 the wider Seven Years War is still raging in Europe and across the seas of the world. Nevertheless, the New England merchants are growing restless at the restrictions on their trade with the French islands, and one Rhode Island company is determined to defy the law and bring home a cargo of contraband molasses.

Edward Carlisle's ship Dartmouth is assigned to the Leeward Islands Squadron, tasked with blockading the remaining French Caribbean sugar islands. When he intercepts a New England ship suspected of trading with the enemy, he is left with a dilemma between his duty to his king and his loyalty to the colonies where he was born. What should be an open-and-shut case in the admiralty courts proves to be nothing of the sort.

Meanwhile, the French navy can still influence events, as Carlisle discovers when he is confronted by an enemy battle squadron with only a frigate to support him.

Carlisle's Duty is the eleventh Carlisle and Holbrooke novel. The series follows the two sea officers through the Seven Years War and into the period of turbulent relations between Britain and her American colonies prior to their bid for independence.

BIBLIOGRAPHY

The following is a selection of the many books that I consulted in researching the Carlisle & Holbrooke series:

Definitive Text

Sir Julian Corbett wrote the original, definitive text on the Seven Years War. Most later writers use his work as a steppingstone to launch their own.

Corbett, LLM., Sir Julian Stafford. *England in the Seven Years War – Vol. I: A Study in Combined Strategy*. Normandy Press. Kindle Edition.

Strategy and Naval Operations

Three very accessible modern books cover the strategic context and naval operations of the Seven Years War. Daniel Baugh addresses the whole war on land and sea, while Martin Robson concentrates on maritime activities. Jonathan Dull has produced a very readable account from the French perspective.

Baugh, Daniel. *The Global Seven Years War 1754-1763*. Pearson Education, 2011. Print.

Robson, Martin. *A History of the Royal Navy, The Seven Years War*. I.B. Taurus, 2016. Print.

Dull, Jonathan, R. *The French Navy and the Seven Years' War*. University of Nebraska Press, 2005. Print.

Sea Officers

For an interesting perspective on the life of sea officers of the mid-eighteenth century, I'd read Augustus Hervey's

Journal, with the cautionary note that while Hervey was by no means typical of the breed, he's very entertaining and devastatingly honest. For a more balanced view, I'd read British Naval Captains of the Seven Years War.

Erskine, David (editor). *Augustus Hervey's Journal, The Adventures Afloat and Ashore of a Naval Casanova*. Chatham Publishing, 2002. Print.

McLeod, A.B. *British Naval Captains of the Seven Years War, The View from the Quarterdeck*. The Boydell Press, 2012. Print.

Life at Sea

There are two excellent overviews of shipboard life and administration during the Seven Years War.

Rodger, N.A.M. *The Wooden World, An Anatomy of the Georgian Navy*. Fontana Press, 1986. Print.

Lavery, Brian. *Anson's Navy, Building a Fleet for Empire, 1744 to 1793*. Seaforth Publishing, 2021. Print.

Chris Durbin

THE AUTHOR

Chris Durbin grew up in the seaside town of Porthcawl in South Wales. His first experience of sailing was as a sea cadet in the treacherous tideway of the Bristol Channel, and at the age of sixteen, he spent a week in a tops'l schooner in the Southwest Approaches. He was a crew member on the Porthcawl lifeboat before joining the navy.

Chris spent twenty-four years as a warfare officer in the Royal Navy, serving in all classes of ships from aircraft carriers through destroyers and frigates to the smallest minesweepers. He took part in operational campaigns in the Falkland Islands, the Middle East and the Adriatic and he spent two years teaching tactics at a US Navy training centre in San Diego.

On his retirement from the Royal Navy, Chris joined a large American company and spent eighteen years in the aerospace, defence and security industry, including two years on the design team for the Queen Elizabeth class aircraft carriers.

Chris is a graduate of the Britannia Royal Naval College at *Dartmouth*, the British Army Command and Staff College, the United States Navy War College (where he gained a postgraduate diploma in national security decision-making) and Cambridge University (where he was awarded an MPhil in International Relations).

With a lifelong interest in naval history and a long-standing ambition to write historical fiction, Chris has completed the first ten novels in the Carlisle & Holbrooke series, which follow the fortunes of a colonial Virginian and a Hampshire man who both command ships of King George's navy during the middle years of the eighteenth century.

The series will follow its principal characters through the Seven Years War and into the period of turbulent relations between Britain and her American colonies in the 1760s. They'll negotiate some thought-provoking loyalty issues when British policy and colonial restlessness lead inexorably to the American Revolution.

Chris lives on the south coast of England, surrounded by hundreds of years of naval history. His three children are all busy growing their own families and careers while Chris and his wife (US Navy, retired) of forty years enjoy sailing their Cornish Shrimper 21 on the south coast.

Fun Fact:

Chris shares his garden with a tortoise named Aubrey. If you've read Patrick O'Brian's *HMS Surprise* or have seen the 2003 film *Master and Commander: The Far Side of the World*, you'll recognise the modest act of homage that Chris has paid to that great writer. Rest assured that Aubrey has not yet grown to the gigantic proportions of *Testudo Aubreii*, though at his last weigh in, he topped one kilogram!

Chris Durbin

FEEDBACK

If you've enjoyed *Treacherous Moon* please consider leaving a review on Amazon.

This is the twelfth of a series of books that will follow Carlisle and Holbrooke through the Seven Years War and into the 1760s when relations between Britain and her restless American colonies are tested to breaking point. Look out for the thirteenth in the Carlisle & Holbrooke series, coming soon.

You can follow my blog at:
www.chris-durbin.com.

Printed in Great Britain
by Amazon